BITTER REUNION

By

Deborah Barlow

This book is a work of fiction. Places, events, and situations in this story are purely fictional. Any resemblance to actual persons, living or dead, is coincidental.

© 2002 by Deborah Barlow. All rights reserved.

No part of this book may be reproduced, restored in a retrieval system, or transmitted by means, electronic, mechanical, photocopying, recording, or otherwise, without written consent from the author.

ISBN: 1-4033-1897-2

This book is printed on acid free paper.

1st Books - rev. 04/29/02

PROLOGUE

July 2

   Mile after endless lonely mile raced by as the boy slept fitfully in the back seat of the car. Evergreens gave way to sagebrush, sagebrush to cactus and daylight to black of night. The progression was much like the one that had so recently taken place within Joey Hamilton himself.

   Sometime just before midnight, he awoke. Slowly, wincing softly as contorted muscles rebelled, Joey uncurled himself and straightened to look out of the side window. What he saw in the midst of the blackness caused only the smallest spark of curiosity to flicker within his dull, lifeless eyes. The horizon was ablaze, dancing and undulating with an otherworldly light.

   It didn't cross Joey's mind to ask what the light was, because it didn't matter. Nothing mattered anymore. At first, Joey had still been able to feel, and the pain had been so deep and all-encompassing that he hadn't even been able to cry, but now he felt nothing. In removing himself from the pain, he'd removed himself from himself. There was no other way to survive.

   As he stared out the window, Joey seemed to see within the light a glimpse of the future, and he shuddered. The brilliance grew closer and brighter with each passing moment. He imagined they would drive into it, and it would swallow them like a fire-breathing dragon, destroying them and saving him from having to face that future. It was a good thought.

The boy's head began to nod. He knew he'd already been asleep for a long time, but for some reason, he was still so very tired. The light and the muted velvety sound of music from the dashboard radio surrounded him like a cocoon, lulling him back to sleep—but that was good, too. He needed to sleep. He wished he could sleep forever and never wake up. Or if he did wake up, maybe it would be yesterday again, and this nightmare would prove to have been just the dreaming kind. The sun would shine, Dad would sing "Happy Birthday" to him and they would play baseball in the park. This time everything would go the way it was supposed to.

"Oh, please," the boy whispered, taking one last drowsy look at the flaming mouth of the dragon, "let it be yesterday again."

Then his eyes closed, quenching the light…

CHAPTER 1

One Day Earlier.

　Friday, the First of July, began exactly the way a birthday should, full of hope and promise. Joey Hamilton awoke to the exhilarating realization that he was finally nine years old, a milestone he'd been anticipating since shortly after he had turned eight. That, in itself, made this day very special, but there was more. Today Joey would begin a new life. The thought brought a grin to his freckled face as Joey bounded out of bed and reached for the jeans lying in a heap on the floor by his closet door. A short search produced a rumpled red t-shirt from the space between his bed and the wall. Having been worn only three days in a row, Joey didn't think it looked too dirty. Besides, most of his clothes now resided in brown boxes neatly stacked beside the front door, and it was too much trouble to go looking for something else to wear. Elaine would never notice what he was wearing anyway.
　A gaping tear in the window shade above Joey's dresser revealed a brightly shining sun in a clear blue sky. His grin broadened at the sight. Humming as he dressed, Joey ran through his mind all the exciting things that would happen today, something he'd already done about a zillion times in the last twenty-four hours. Then suddenly, smack in the middle of the familiar script, out of nowhere, a new and unsettling thought jumped in. For the first time, it really hit him that he would never again sleep in his same old bed in his same old room.

Deborah Barlow

Not that it was such a great room, he thought, as he looked around. The furniture was all pretty old and those tattered curtains and bedspread were way too babyish for a kid his age. They had dinosaurs on them, but instead of being fierce and awesomely monstrous the way he was sure tyrannosaurus rex and brontosaurus had been, these frolicking prehistoric reptiles looked about as ferocious as teddy bears. Even worse, they were blue and pink and yellow with polka dots on them. It was pretty embarrassing for him and probably for the dinosaurs, too. When he had begged Elaine for something new, she'd said in that I'm-not-really-listening tone of voice, "When I get around to it." Joey knew by now what she really meant was, "Don't count on it." So he hadn't. Usually you couldn't even see most of the bedspread anyway. Dad used to ask if Joey'd been fighting the bad guys in his sleep. He said the bed looked like a battle zone every morning. Sheets, bedspread and pillow would be tangled together in utter chaos, spilling over the side of his bed and onto the floor. It might be run-down and dilapidated, but this one-hundred square feet of space had always been wholly his. Lighter shaded rectangles against the grubby walls marked the spots where he'd hung his posters and prized works of art from school. That spot by the window was where his Blazers poster had been, and there by the bookcase he'd had his autographed poster of the Oregon State Beavers. He was real proud of that one because it had every players' signature on it. His most prized poster had held the place of honor on the wall beside his bed where he could gaze at it and dream. He could still almost see it there—George Brett, his arm and bat stretched out as one, a split second after having made thunderous contact with the baseball. Under the picture of Brett were the words "Kansas City Royals" in bold blue letters. Joey enjoyed basketball and soccer, but baseball was his passion.

As Joey sat on the edge of the bed and tied his shoes, his mind wandered back in time to his very first t-ball practice when he was just six years old. He'd been so dumb, he didn't even know which direction to run the bases. Then Coach took charge and he knew everything would be fine.

"O.K., you guys," Coach had said. "We're here to learn how to play baseball and maybe to win a few games, but more important than that, we're here to have a good time. Do you think you can all do that?"

"Yes!" all the kids had yelled pretty much in unison.

And sure enough, Joey, at least, had a super time. In fact, it was way better than super. He ended up catching the baseball bug. Not only did he love it, but he was good at it, too. He supposed it didn't hurt any that Coach was also his dad and that he and Dad spent hours and hours tossing the ball to each other in the back yard.

The sun warm on his skin, the smell of freshly mowed grass in his nostrils, the rhythmic thud...thud of baseball meeting mitt resounding in his ears. Then Dad's voice, full of pride and encouragement, "Way to go, Joey! You're really getting the hang of this. Keep it up and you'll be the team's best catcher."

They were great, those backyard practices, the highlight of his week. It was just hanging out with Dad, being buddies, that made them so wonderful. His dad was the best dad in the whole world, which made Joey Hamilton the luckiest boy.

Elaine hated that Dad spent so much time with Joey, though. Joey would never forget the time he had overheard them arguing about it. He'd gotten up for a drink of water in the middle of the night. As he had approached the door to their bedroom, he'd heard Elaine's raised voice.

"You've always cared more about that kid than you care about me. If you aren't playing ball with him, you're coaching a dumb game. Maybe if you spent more time with me, I wouldn't be so depressed all the time. You never want to go dancing or partying anymore. You're just so boring, Todd!"

"Come on, Elaine," Dad had answered, sounding annoyed. "You know our problems are a lot more serious than that. You don't want to admit it, but you're an alcoholic."

Enraged, Elaine had interrupted, "That's just like you to turn everything around to make it my fault! A few little drinks and you accuse me of being an alcoholic. You're such a prude. Or maybe you're just jealous because I can still have fun and you've obviously forgotten how!"

"When are you going to admit it, Elaine? It's not just a few drinks anymore. You can't get through a day without drinking yourself into a stupor. I wish you could see yourself. It's pathetic. I mean it. Until you're willing to deal with your drinking, nothing else is going to help.

"Besides, Joey needs at least one parent that shows an interest in him. You're too wrapped up in yourself to even notice that he exists most of the time."

"That's unfair, Todd!" Elaine had screamed. "I just can't cope with it all. This little dump of a house, never enough money and all the responsibility of being a mother. It's just too much!"

"A mother? You call yourself a mother?" Dad had shouted back. "You won't even let your own son call you Mother. Why do you think you've earned the right to call yourself one? Elaine, you should never have had a child. You're still one yourself!"

That was when Joey had heard Elaine yell some words he hadn't understood at the time and then the sound of something crashing against the wall inside their bedroom. Elaine liked to throw things when she was mad, and she had definitely been mad. Joey had decided to go back to bed without getting a drink.

It had worried him to hear Dad and Elaine fighting about him again. What if Dad quit playing with him to make Elaine happy? It was confusing. Joey wanted Elaine to be happy, but he couldn't stand the idea of losing his dad's companionship. His mother was sick; he knew that. She had something called alcoholism that made her drink a lot of stuff that was bad for her and caused her to act strange and sometimes mean. He didn't understand how a disease could do that. Why couldn't Elaine just decide not to drink that awful stuff? Dad had tried to explain it to Joey, but it still didn't make a lot of sense to him.

Maybe if Dad did what she wanted and stopped paying attention to Joey, Elaine would finally be able to stop drinking and get better. It had made him feel guilty that he didn't care. He just wanted Dad to continue being his best friend.

Then, a few weeks ago, all of Joey's fears had been put to rest. It was a Saturday afternoon. Dad had suggested they go for a bike ride and then had grown suspiciously winded just as they reached the parking lot of the ice cream shop.

"Guess I'm not as young as I used to be," Dad had panted. "I think we're going to have to take a breather, Son.

"Well, will you look where we are," he'd gone on, acting all innocent. "I don't suppose you'd feel like getting an ice cream cone, would you?"

"Thanks, Dad!" Joey had yelled, already sprinting toward the door.

Once seated at the tiny two-person booth with a scoop of chocolate-raspberry for Joey and one of butterscotch-swirl for Dad, the atmosphere had suddenly turned serious.

"Listen, Joey, part of the reason I brought you here is that we need to have a little talk. I'm sure you know that things have gotten pretty bad between your mother and me, and there are going to be some changes. You need to know about them."

Joey's heart had begun to pound, and he'd been afraid he might throw up. *This is it*, he'd thought, panic-stricken. *Dad's going to tell me he can't do things with me anymore.*

Dad must have noticed Joey's apprehension, because he'd reached across the table and put his large hand over Joey's small one. "It's O.K. Please don't be afraid, Joey. These problems aren't your fault, and no matter what happens, I will always be there for you. Your mother and I, though, aren't going to be married much longer." He'd hesitated, looking suddenly very sad. "I've tried hard to be a good husband and to make our marriage work. I

Bitter Reunion

believe that marriage should be forever. I want you to know that. It isn't easy for me to admit that I just can't try anymore. I truly believe that the best thing for all of us right now would be for your mother and me to live apart."

"But Dad," Joey had interrupted, "are you going to leave me with Elaine? Oh, please don't leave me with her! I know she needs me to do chores and things for her, but please, please…" Joey's voice had begun to crack, and tears had threatened to spill onto his cheeks.

"No, no, Joey, I wouldn't do that!" Dad had hastily cut in. "I could never stand to leave you. If I couldn't take you with me, I would have stayed with your mother. You're only going to have to be with her for a couple of weeks until I can arrange for a proper place for us to live and find a sitter for you to be with while I'm at work."

The words had a magical effect on Joey. It had been as if a gigantic burden had been lifted from his shoulders. He'd wiped at his eyes and managed to take another bite of the ice cream now melting into a brown puddle resembling lumpy chocolate milk.

"Let me explain something to you," Dad had gone on. "Your mother isn't a bad person. There's a way in which I still love her and always will. It's just that she's…" he'd paused as he searched for the word, "weak. She was young when we got married, and she didn't really understand what marriage would be like. It can be a lot of work, and she wasn't ready for that. She wasn't grown up enough yet to handle it. I blame myself for not seeing that we were both too young to get married." Then Dad had smiled and said, "Our marriage wasn't all bad, though. One really wonderful thing came from it."

"What was that?"

"You. Do you remember the story of Joseph in the Old Testament?"

Joey had nodded, but he hadn't really been sure he did. He tended to get those Bible stories mixed up.

"Well, the reason I wanted to name you after Joseph was because he and his father, Jacob, loved each other very, very much. I knew right away that you and I were going to be like Joseph and Jacob. When I first saw you, all wrinkled and red faced, I thanked God for the miracle He had given me, and I still thank Him every day for you. Never forget that, Joseph Hamilton."

Joey had been embarrassed, but in a good way. He hadn't known what to say, so ice cream forgotten, he'd gotten out of his chair, walked over to Dad and flung his arms around his neck. He hadn't even cared who was looking. Then he'd said, "Come on, Dad, let's go home. I need to start packing."

His thoughts abruptly switching from the past to the present, Joey gave one last tug on a shoelace and reminded himself again that this was the day he'd been looking forward to since then. He'd wondered if it would really ever come, but it did. He was going to live with Dad!

Dad had arranged to pick him up on his birthday, probably knowing it was the best present Joey could get. Then they were going to go home—how good that sounded—eat pizza and open gifts, just the two of them. After that, maybe they would have some time to go to the park and break in the new baseball glove Joey was hoping to get for his birthday. He sure had dropped enough hints about how much he wanted it.

I just can't wait, Joey thought, dancing in happiness to his bedroom door and flinging it open. I wonder what time it is.

As if in answer to his silent question, Elaine's shrill voice startled him. "For Pete sake, Joey, the day's half gone! I didn't think you were ever going to come out of there."

Joey couldn't have been more surprised if he'd seen a cow grazing in the living room. How could he have slept in this late? He was always awake before Elaine, who slept till at least eleven every morning. But there she was, lounging in her favorite chair, a glass already in one hand and a cigarette in the other. Upon closer inspection, Joey was even more dumbfounded to see that Elaine didn't look all sick and tired and falling-apart like she usually did until a lot later in the day. Instead of the usual fuzzy pink robe, floppy slippers and scraggly hair, she was fully dressed, her hair was brushed and she even had on makeup. Her lipstick was a little smudgy, but not too bad. This was the way Elaine looked when she was getting ready to go out on one of her late-night dates.

"Wow, Elaine, you look really nice," Joey said. "How come you're all dressed up?" It occurred to him that maybe it was in honor of his birthday. Maybe there was even a birthday cake with nine candles hidden away somewhere.

Her answer quickly dashed that possibility. "There's no reason for me to hang around this town anymore, since you and your father are abandoning me. You know that guy I've been dating—Sam? He treats me really good, not like your father did, and he's rich, too."

And old and fat, Joey mentally supplied.

"As soon as Todd picks you up today, Sam and I are going to be leaving, too," Elaine went on. "We're going to move far away from here, and he's going to marry me. If the two of you can start a new life, why can't I?" It sounded more like an accusation than a question, and Elaine was glaring at him. "Well?" she said.

Her scrutiny put him on the spot. Joey felt his face getting hot, and he began to squirm inside. It was the same feeling that he got when the teacher called on him at school with a question that he didn't know the answer to.

"I, um, I guess so. I hope you'll be happy. Are you going to come back and see me sometimes?"

"We'll see. Now don't waste any more of my time. My favorite soap's coming on. You go and make sure all your things are packed and ready to go." She turned away from him to stare at the television.

I will not cry. I will not cry, Joey told himself. It's a wonderful day. I'm going to live with Dad. Dad loves me. It was a litany he'd been repeating often the last few weeks. Reminding himself of Dad's love was the only way he could overlook Elaine's indifference and neglect.

Joey headed for the kitchen to round up something for breakfast. He hoped there would still be some cereal in the cupboard. There probably wasn't any milk, but he could eat it plain. Halfway across the room, he glanced absentmindedly at the clock above the table and suddenly stopped in mid-stride. Two astonishing facts registered at the same time. Both hands of the clock pointed straight up, and the opening strains of the theme music for "To Live and Love" could be plainly heard

Bitter Reunion

rising from the television. Elaine watched that soap opera a lot and he knew that it came on at noon.

I just can't believe it, Joey thought. I have never, in my whole life, slept so late! I must have been really tired!

Just like on Christmas Eve, he'd been so excited and hyper last night, looking forward to this day, that he'd had a really hard time going to sleep. Counting sheep hadn't helped, so he had pulled some of his favorite books from one of the boxes by the front door. He'd first flipped to the Genesis 37 section of his *Children's Bible Storybook* which recounted the life of Joseph, his namesake. A few of the words were really long and hard for him to sound out, but Dad had read this one to him several times since their talk at the ice-cream store. Between the many colorful illustrations and the parts he could read himself, Joey was able to recount the entire story. And what a story it was, too!

Joseph's dad, Jacob, had loved Joseph so much that he had made him a "coat of many colors." Joey had giggled at the thought of his own dad at a sewing machine making him a coat. No way! But Dad had bought him that Little League jacket. It was sort of the same thing.

When Joseph's dad made him the coat, Joseph's brothers had been mad. And Joseph had enough brothers to make up a whole baseball team! Joey figured they must have lived in a lot bigger house than he did. Anyway, those wicked brothers, who reminded him of Cinderella's step-sisters, had sold Joseph as a slave! It was awful. Poor Jacob had thought his son was dead, and Joseph and he didn't see each other again until many, many years later.

Deborah Barlow

Of course, as Dad had explained to him, God used the bad things that happened to Joseph to do good things for his family and him. They probably would have all starved to death if Joseph hadn't been a ruler in Egypt. It had all been part of God's plan, and because Joseph trusted in God, everything turned out just the way it was supposed to. But still, Joey couldn't imagine how it would feel to be taken away from the father you loved. He thought maybe it was a good thing he didn't have any brothers.

When he'd finished the story of Joseph, he still hadn't been sleepy, so he'd read some of his *Encyclopedia Brown* book, too. He had no idea what time it was when he'd finally lost consciousness, but it must have been *really* late, and that's why he'd overslept so much this morning. It was an unexpected blessing. Now there was a lot less time to kill waiting for Dad, who had promised to pick him up no later than two o'clock this afternoon.

Two and a half hours later, though, Dad still hadn't shown up. By now, Joey was sitting on the top step in front of his house, absolutely sure that the very next car to come around the corner would be Dad's. But it wasn't. And neither was the next one or the next. A dozen or so cars later, Joey was starting to panic. What could have happened to Dad? He was always on time, unlike Elaine, who was never on time.

"Please, Jesus, don't let anything bad happen to my dad," Joey prayed.

He ran into the house to check the time. It was three-fifteen already. Anxiously returning to the sentry step, a big leaden ball of dread began to settle in the pit of his stomach. He knew for sure Dad would never be this late

Bitter Reunion

without calling unless something really terrible had happened to him.

"Joey!" Elaine was at the door. "Come to the phone. It's your father."

Just as relief began to well up inside of him, she dropped the bombshell. "He says he doesn't want you after all, anymore than he wants me. I guess Sam and I will have to take you with us."

Joey stared at her a moment before the words sunk in and began the insidious work of tearing his world apart. His mind reeling in denial and confusion, Joey raced for the phone.

"Dad... Dad, what's Elaine talking about? I know you aren't going to leave me here!" he yelled into the mouthpiece, holding the receiver to his ear.

There was silence and then Dad's voice, sounding strained and stern. "I'm sorry. I'm not coming."

"But wait, Dad...why are you..." He couldn't seem to say what he was thinking. There was a "click" on the other end of the line and then only the sound of his beating heart. Just like that, the birthday that had held such promise turned into a nightmare.

The rest of the day was a blur. It was as if he'd suddenly been changed from a boy into a puppet, Pinocchio in reverse. His mind didn't work anymore, but his body still went through the motions, controlled by an invisible string-pulling tyrant.

Eventually, without knowing how, Joey found himself in the back seat of Sam's car. By now, the pain had turned to a numbness which was almost as bad as the pain had been. He dully noticed the landscape speeding by outside his window and Elaine's arm draped around Sam's shoulders in front of him. A couple of minutes later, Elaine disengaged herself long enough to retrieve something from the brown paper sack which sat on the floor at her feet.

"Here," she said, twisting her body around to face him in the back seat. "Drink this." It was a small carton of milk like they had at the school cafeteria.

He shook his head.

"I mean it. I've put something in it to help you get some sleep. It's going to be a long trip, and you need to get some rest. Maybe you'll feel better when you wake up."

There was no use arguing. Without saying a word, Joey took the carton from her hand and drank its contents all down. Very soon he began to feel drowsy. Curling up in a ball in the corner of the seat, he let the blessed darkness of sleep overtake him.

CHAPTER 2

Just after one o'clock, the bell over the doorway of McLain's Sporting Goods jingled, and a tall man with tousled hair and anxious blue eyes strode hurriedly into the store while glancing at his watch with obvious impatience.

Across the room and behind the counter, Ned McLain looked up from the pages of a paperback murder mystery to register the arrival of a new customer. Immediately, his eyes lit up with recognition. Earmarking the book in such a way as to make a librarian groan, he shoved it under the counter and scooted his short, stooped body off of the high stool on which he'd been perched.

"Bet I can guess what you're here for, and you don't have to go far to find it," he said as the man approached. "I wanted to make sure nobody else would get it, so I took it off the shelf just yesterday."

With the flourish of a magician pulling a rabbit from a hat, the wizened old man removed a black object from a bag. He plopped it down on the counter top just as Todd Hamilton reached the cash register.

"Ah, the precious mitt," Hamilton said, smiling for the first time since entering the store. "How did you ever guess I'd be coming in for this?"

McLain chuckled. "That boy of yours has practically lived here ever since he caught sight of this thing, and he must have told me a thousand times that his birthday was July First. I figured I could count on you to get it for him. If you hadn't, guess I would've had to."

"You mean I could have saved myself a few dollars?"

"Hey, you don't fool me," McLain answered, putting the baseball mitt back into the sack. "I know that kid means the world to you."

Hamilton opened his wallet, removed two tattered twenties and a ten and handed them across the counter. "Yeah, he's a pretty special guy," Todd acknowledged, growing serious again. "Having to leave him with his mom has been killing me. It's just a good thing today is the last of it. Don't think either one of us could have hung on much longer. Joey tries to put a good face on it, but Elaine's parenting skills are nonexistent. I think Joey feels he has to take care of her, instead of the other way around."

McLain leaned conspiratorially over the counter and lowered his voice. "I don't mean to gossip or nothin'," he said, proceeding to do just that, "but I hear she's been partying big-time lately with some guy named Sam White. I just don't get it. She's got a great kid and you for a husband, and she goes and throws it all away. Nope, I don't get it at all."

"Neither do I, Ned," Todd responded, pocketing his change and looking at his watch again.

"And about Joey... I been worried about the kid. You know he's a sensitive boy, and she treats him worse than I treat Annie."

Annie was Ned's miniature schnauzer, and it was common knowledge that Ned treated Annie better than he did his wife, Cora. That aside, Ned's point was well-taken.

"Poor guy hangs out here for a little companionship. Breaks my heart sometimes. I-"

Todd could see McLain was just getting started on what could turn out to be a long

Bitter Reunion

conversation if Todd allowed it, and there wasn't time for one today.

"Ned, I really hate to, but I've got to get on the road. Promised Joey I'd be over to get him at two, and I don't want to be late today of all days."

"Hey, I hear ya. Go get him and tell him "happy birthday" for me. Got to admit, even though I'm glad he'll be with you from now on, I'm gonna miss seeing him in here. Bring him over every so often, would ya?"

"I'll do that," Todd replied over his shoulder, already heading for the door.

Once in his car, Todd took a deep breath and tried to release the stress that had been building since morning. He had planned this day for weeks, but so far nothing had gone exactly the way he'd envisioned it. For starters, his alarm hadn't gone off, so he'd been late for work.

Todd was the business manager of H & H Transport, a trucking company which had been originally founded by his grandfather. Since H & H was family owned, Todd felt compelled to prove to the employees, as well as to himself, that he had earned the title he now held within the company. Todd was punctual, conscientious and hard working, almost to a fault, and because of that, whisperings of nepotism were a thing of the past. With sole custody of a small boy, though, he knew he was going to have to make some changes—delegate more and feel less responsible for everything that transpired on the job. The last thing he wanted was to be a workaholic father. But he hadn't planned on starting his new personal policy this morning by being late to work. He'd already arranged to take the afternoon off in order to spend it with Joey. Joey's birthday and first day in a new home should be a pleasantly memorable experience, and Todd was going to enjoy making sure it was.

Then, wouldn't you know it, at the end of his workday, just as he was ready to step out of the door, one of his truck drivers, Abe Swanson, who was a habitual complainer, had barged into the office insisting that his paycheck was too small. Smoothing ruffled feathers was part of Todd's job description, probably his least favorite. Todd was a man of considerable patience, but some of his drivers could tax the patience of Job. By the time Abe had finally seen the logic in the fact that he wasn't going to get paid for hours he hadn't worked, Todd was running late again.

The way things are going today, I should just be glad Joey's mitt wasn't already sold to someone else, Todd thought, as he put on his blinker to make a left-hand turn. He smiled, remembering the day his son had dragged him to McLain's to take a look at "the most awesome baseball mitt you have ever seen in your life."

Indeed, it was a pretty good looking mitt, a supple black leather inscribed in electric blue with Willie Mays' name. And you'd have had to be deaf, dumb and blind not to have picked up on the hints Joey had been constantly dropping as to his burning desire to own the thing. Why, it was possible even Elaine had noticed.

Todd realized he was feeling distinctly more optimistic about the day's prognosis. If he picked Joey up before stopping at the video store, and if he wrapped Joey's presents later on, he could make up the lost time. It was still well before two o'clock.

Bitter Reunion

Less than five minutes later, Todd was walking up the sidewalk to the familiar ranch house where he had lived for nine years. The place was looking pretty unkept. Paint had begun to peel from the gray siding, and there were more than a few knee-high weeds littering the flower beds. He decided that he really should come over occasionally to mow the lawn or make some of the endless repairs that home ownership seemed to require. It was extremely unlikely that Elaine would make the effort.

As he started up the sidewalk, Todd suddenly realized that something was amiss. He'd have been willing to bet a year's income that his son would have been watching for him from the window or maybe the front steps. Joey, brimming with impatience and youthful anticipation, should have burst through the door by now. Todd knew it was irrational, but the house looked deserted, and it gave him a distinctly unsettled feeling. The feeling intensified when no one answered first the doorbell, and then his insistent knocking. He turned the knob and the door swung inward, creaking on it's hinges.

The boxes by the door were the first things Todd saw. There were two, stacked one on top of the other. "JOEYS STUF" was scrawled in childish letters on the side of the bottom box, and on top of the other rested a caseless black video tape. There was a note taped to it which, upon closer inspection, contained only two words. "Watch this."

The uneasiness that had begun earlier was now welling up and spreading out within him. He was beginning to entertain a very frightening and very unexpected possibility. What if Elaine had taken Joey and fled?

19

"Joey! Elaine! Are you here?" He tried to keep the fear out of his voice. Don't jump to conclusions, he cautioned himself. Maybe they went to the store, or maybe they're out back. There could be lots of explanations for their temporary absence. Besides, Elaine's car is still out front, so they couldn't have gone far. The logic behind this thought was reassuring, but for some reason, Todd's pulse continued to race, revealing the fact that he wasn't necessarily buying it.

Then there was this tape. The nearly illegible handwriting on the note was obviously Elaine's. Why would she leave him a note and a tape if she were still here or planning on returning?

"Where is everybody?" Todd yelled, as he began a quick search. A stray cat he unwittingly scared out of the back yard and a tiny colony of black ants on the kitchen counter were the only inhabitants on the premises. It didn't really look as if Elaine had left for good, though, either. Curiously, the only unusual thing Todd discovered was that the clocks were all off by a few hours. Everything else was in it's normal state of slovenly disarray. The furniture was all still here, Elaine's clothes were still in her closet and strewn around the house. There was even food, some of it fuzzy and green, in the refrigerator and a bottle of her favorite vodka on a cupboard shelf. Nothing was disturbed. In fact, it looked as if Elaine had made a new purchase. A video recorder Todd had never seen before was sitting on top of the television. Surely Elaine wouldn't leave a brand new VCR behind if she were to take off.

The recorder reminded Todd of the video tape, and he realized with surprise that he

Bitter Reunion

was holding it in his hand. He couldn't even remember picking it up. "Watch this," the note had said. Maybe that's what he should do. He felt sure that, one way or another, the tape would shed light on his confusion.

Todd popped the cassette into the gaping mouth of the machine and watched as it was sucked in. He pushed the play button, then pulled a tattered brown velour hassock to within a couple of feet of the television and took a seat. Expectancy and dread at what he was about to see battled for predominance. Dread was winning. He knew Elaine too well.

Static filled the screen momentarily and then was replaced by a hospital scene. Handsome doctors and gorgeous nurses were engaged in solemn conversation.

"She'll never make it without a kidney transplant," a distinguished looking older doctor was saying, his voice saturated with concern.

"But Cassandra refuses to be a donor. Someone has to convince her. Please try, Devon." The nurse in the implausibly short uniform with the implausibly blonde hair sounded as if she would cry but for the fact that tears tend to make mascara run.

"What the devil...it's a soap opera!" Todd wasn't sure whether to laugh or to cry in place of the dry-eyed nurse. He leaned forward and pushed the fast forward button. For several seconds, various members of the "Rich and Beautiful but Morally Bankrupt Elite" pantomimed at manic speed upon the screen while the soap opera continued. At last, there was a static break, followed by a radically different image. Returning the tape to normal speed, Todd came face to face with his recently divorced wife.

"Well, Todd, it's so good to see you," Elaine crooned, sarcasm dripping from every syllable. "How do you think I look on the screen? You used to say I could be a movie star."

She still looked good, despite years of abusing her body in just about every way. She could easily have been a nurse in that daytime TV hospital where staff member were apparently not allowed to be plain, to wear eyeglasses or to possess more than ten-percent body fat. A slinky black cocktail dress with a very low neckline accentuated all the right curves and brought out the gold highlights in her hair and the blue green of her eyes.

"Might as well get right to the point," she was saying. "You wouldn't be watching this right now if my plan hadn't worked. You've always underestimated me, Todd. You think I'm just a drunken tramp, but I can do most anything if I want to bad enough. Motivation, right Todd? I was motivated to put it to you but good, and it looks like I've succeeded. Little old dumb Elaine making a fool out of Mr. Perfect. I love it."

She tossed her head, a defiant glint in her eyes. Yes, it was obvious that she was loving every minute of it.

Perspiration dotted Todd's forehead.

"Get up. Call the police. Take action!" commanded his brain, but his eyes were glued to the set.

"It took me awhile to think of the perfect revenge. Oh, I knew that taking Joey from you would kill you, but even that wasn't enough for me. Guess what, Todd?" Elaine paused for dramatic effect. "I've managed to make him hate you in the process! So you'll appreciate how clever I really am, I'm going to tell you

Bitter Reunion

how I did it. Just let me get comfortable first."

She disappeared for a moment, then returned with a pack of cigarettes and a lighter. Retrieving a cigarette from the pack, she proceeded to light it and take a long drag, prolonging each movement and keeping Todd in suspense as long as possible.

"That's better," she said at length. "Now, where were we? Oh, yes. I have a friend, someone who would do just about anything for me. I convinced him that you're a wife and child abuser who is trying to take my only little boy away from me. A few crocodile tears, and he was putty in my hands." Elaine feigned a sorrowful expression. "He gave me this VCR and loaned me his video recorder. Wasn't that nice of him?

Now for the good part. I recorded a few soap operas and set all the clocks ahead by three and a half hours. Fooled Joey completely. I made the supreme sacrifice of getting up early myself to help convince Joey it was much later. You should have seen his expression when he saw that I was up before him!" Elaine laughed.

"So picture this. There was Joey, waiting and waiting. You got later and later, and I'm sure he began to think just maybe you weren't coming at all."

As Elaine must have hoped, Todd could almost see Joey, there in his mind's eye, and it broke his heart. Joey must have felt so betrayed! How could she have done this to a trusting nine-year-old boy? Elaine didn't even really want her son. Joey was nothing to her but a burden, a noose around her neck. That's why Todd had never considered that she might try to kidnap Joey. Neither had he suspected

23

she could be this cruel! He'd naively believed that Elaine still harbored some feelings of love for her son, some concern for his welfare. He should have realized that Elaine was capable of inflicting the ultimate revenge upon the man she hated so bitterly, even at her own, and Joey's, expense.

   Todd found himself clenching and unclenching his fists. It was probably fortunate for him that Elaine wasn't actually in this room, or his face could well have ended up on "America's Most Wanted". As it was, he had the almost uncontrollable urge to lunge at the television and shatter the image of her smug face into a million pieces.

   As if the woman on the screen could actually read his mind, Elaine went on, "Are you paying attention, Todd? This is the pais de resistance—bet you didn't know I knew French, did you? I was afraid that Joey might give you the benefit of a doubt and think you didn't show up because you couldn't. A car accident or something. Had to cover that base, so in the last couple of weeks, I've been tape-recording parts of those many little loving conversations we've had. My friend is an electronics wizard, and he managed to splice a few choice words together. To make a long story short, poor Joey got a call from you saying that you'd decided not to take him after all." She shook her head and tsk-tsked. "Very sad. Good thing yours truly agreed to take him."

   "Oh, by the way. You can have all this junk I'm leaving behind. I can afford to be generous. Did I mention that my new friend is rich?

   "I needed privacy for this final farewell, so I sent Joey outside to wait. I really should join him, now. My friend, who did such a fantastic job of making that phone call for you, will be here to pick us up any minute. Just one word of advise before I go." She paused for emphasis. "Don't bother to come looking for us, because you'll never find us." In mock sincerity, she added, "Have a great life, Todd, without Joey." Abruptly, the screen turned back to static.

Todd didn't even notice the sound of dead air as the video tape continued to play. His body doubled over and head in his hands, he struggled to get a grip on his emotions. In a few minutes, grief and despair turned to cold, hard anger. He welcomed the anger, because with it came the ability to think, to plan and to act. Todd Hamilton resolved to move heaven and earth if that's what it took to get his son back.

CHAPTER 3

TEN YEARS LATER
Saturday, May 6

William Erdman was an unassuming, introverted man. In the course of his fifty-eight years on earth, nothing unusually exciting or profound had ever happened to him. He'd never won anything. He'd never received any accolades, or reached any great heights of authority or power.

The components of William's life were few and simple. First, of course, was his job as a certified public accountant, which he found quite satisfying. Second, there was his cat, Mac. Aloof and independent, Mac relied on William only for food, water and shelter, which suited William perfectly. Last was an IBM personal computer, William's true soul mate and companion. The hours he spent with his PC were pure bliss. The blue-gray glow of a monitor thrilled him in much the same way as a candlelight dinner with a beautiful woman or court side seats for the Chicago Bulls might excite most other men.

William was a solitary person, but not a lonely one. He much preferred the company of animals and machines to that of humans, and he blamed his one brief foray into matrimony on overactive hormones. He was twenty-five when he'd married Arleen and had realized almost immediately that it was a mistake. It wasn't that Arleen was an unusually demanding woman. It was just that she was so pervasively there. In due time, Arleen grew bored with the pedantic pace of their married existence and

Bitter Reunion

divorced William in order to seek greener, not to mention more invigorating pastures. How fortunate it had been that she had walked out on him. William often wondered if he would have ever summoned up the courage and energy to risk the turmoil of leaving her.

All in all, William would have to say that he was happy with his life. Maybe to some it would be too mundane and predictable, but to him it was peaceful and undemanding, exactly the way he wanted it. He fully intended to live out his remaining years in the same fashion, staying in the background of the mainstream of life, avoiding undue recognition.

The morning of Saturday, May 7, began unusually early for William. By five-thirty, he was shaving, having already eaten a quick breakfast of juice and cereal. As he mowed swatches of pink across his lathered face, he contemplated with a mixture of dread and resignation the reason he wasn't still blissfully dead to the world.

Today he was embarking on a trip to visit his sister and brother-in-law. He did not relish the long drive to Cheyenne or what would transpire once he reached his destination. In fact, the only reason he was making the trip at all was to avoid the inevitability of Lois and Ralph coming to visit him instead. Lois had been pestering him for two years, writing letters and making phone calls trying to arrange a date for them to "drop in" on him. He knew what their idea of "dropping in" was. They would invade William's home indefinitely, robbing him of his privacy and demanding to be entertained. Lois would overwhelm him with her constant chatter. Ralph, who William considered slovenly and repulsive, would monopolize his favorite chair, turn the television up to an ear-splitting volume and litter the room with beer cans. By the time they finally decided to "drop out" and head for home, he would be a nervous wreck.

The whole idea was absolutely unthinkable. The problem was that William had used every excuse known to man to stall their visit, and Lois wasn't buying it anymore. She'd been very insistent when she called him two weeks ago.

"Listen here, Willy!" William couldn't help but listen. Even with the phone five inches from his ear, she came across loud and clear. "It's been four years since I've seen my baby brother. We're none of us getting any younger, you know. Now, I don't care if you are a little under the weather. What you need is your sister's good cooking and some TLC to get you back on your feet. Ralph and I just aren't taking 'no' for an answer. We'll be out a week from Saturday."

William's mind raced, trying to find a way out of this dilemma. Only one solution presented itself.

"You know, Lois," he'd said hesitantly, still weighing the merits of his new plan, "maybe what I need is to take a little vacation myself. Why don't I come see you, instead?" He cringed at the thought, but if he were the visitor instead of the host, at least he could determine the length of the visit, hopefully finding an excuse to make it a short one. Why, maybe he could even lodge at a motel each night instead of in their home. He would insist, on the grounds that their house was so small—thank goodness. The more he considered the plan, the better he felt about it. This would likely be the most painless way of getting Lois off his back for another four years.

"What was that?"

Lois was saying something that William had, in his musings, missed.

"I said, are you sure you feel up to it, Willy? I still think Ralph and I ought to come out. Save you having to do all that driving."

"No, no," William cut in. "I've just realized how much I need a change of routine, and I'll have no trouble getting away this time of year. I think this is just what the doctor ordered."

It was with great relief that William was finally able to hang up the phone a few minutes later. An arrival date was set and soon the whole wretched business would be behind him.

Now two weeks later and with departure eminent, William felt much as he imagined a condemned man facing the firing squad must feel. His stomach was definitely queasy. He took one last look in the bathroom mirror. The slight, bespeckled man with thinning gray hair who returned his gaze did indeed look as though he were on death row.

Moments later, suitcase in hand, William emerged into the misty morning, leaving his home, his fortress that kept the world at bay. Even the weather was dismal, reinforcing his mood. Typical of Oregon, a steady monotonous drizzle descended from the sky. He sprinted from the protective covering of his front porch to the blue Ford Taurus waiting at the curb. Hurriedly unlocking the trunk, he tossed the suitcase in, then fumbled to open the car door. Though he disliked getting wet, he hated the encumbrance of an umbrella even more.

Besides, only recent transplants from drier states ever bothered with umbrellas in Oregon.

Once gratefully settled behind the steering wheel, William heaved a sigh and contemplated the trip ahead. It was going to be a long and tiring drive traveling from his hometown of Albion, located sixty miles inland from the Oregon coast, through the states of Oregon, Idaho and Wyoming. It would be monotonous, too. Not a lot of interesting scenery, just miles and miles of sage brush and gray desolation once you left the lush green of Oregon's Willamette Valley behind. The alternatives were worse, though. There was no way he could go by plane. To say he had a phobia about flying was an understatement. Acute terror described his feelings better. Buses and trains were almost equally undesirable as a mode of transportation simply because they were filled with people. People who would have to sit near or next to him, and worse, who might want to talk to him. No, as tiring as driving twelve hundred miles might be, it was the only viable option.

"Enough stalling," William chided himself. "Let's get going." His hand was on the ignition key when a movement disturbed the deserted street. It was the paper boy pedaling toward his house. With a well-practiced flick of the wrist, the boy sent a newspaper sailing in an arch that landed just short of his porch steps. William silently berated himself and the kid; the boy for his careless aim and himself for not having thought to cancel the paper. Now if he didn't go fetch it, the stupid thing would lay there in the rain and become a mushy mess on his lawn. He guessed it was worth getting a little wetter himself to avoid the inevitable clean-up later. Another

Bitter Reunion

mad dash ensued. Finally, vowing to phone the *Albion Journal* at his first stop along the way, William pulled away from the curb.

. . . .

The coffee shop in the Blue Boar Inn of Boise, Idaho buzzed with activity the evening of May 6. Saturdays were always busy, but with a convention going on, it had been an exceptionally frantic day. Consequently, the mandate of "double duty" fell squarely on David Edwards' shoulders. Along with his usual bussing responsibilities, he found himself having to help the harried waitresses by filling water glasses, refilling coffee cups or fetching an occasional ketchup bottle. By eight-thirty in the evening, David had run the table-to-table marathon for four hours. Back and forth from the coffee shop to the various banquet rooms or to the kitchen, with orders coming at him from cooks, waitresses and customers, he'd barely had a moment to catch his breath. No problem, though. David preferred hard work. His motto was "the busier the better." Work kept his mind occupied, shoving away unpleasant thoughts and holding them at bay and it kept his body active, giving vent to pent up frustration and anger.

The dinner crowd in the coffee shop began clearing out, and the party of twenty-four in the banquet room finally left, making it a good time for a break. David got himself a cola and an order of french fries and took the end stool at the counter, an ideal vantage point from which to "people watch".

You could observe people from all walks of life in the coffee shop. Some wore designer labels, and some shopped at the Salvation

Army. There was the geriatric crowd, the children, the men and women coming in as families, as groups and sometimes alone. A party atmosphere dominated the room tonight. Darkened windows that made up three walls reflected a harmonious hustle and bustle, and the muffled sounds of laughter and friendly voices surrounded him. Though he'd never admit it, there wasn't one person in the restaurant that David wouldn't trade places with, given the chance. He liked to pick someone and imagine what it would be like to be that person. Tonight, there was a pretty good cross-section of subjects to choose from.

At the far corner booth sat a group of six teenagers, three boys and three girls. They looked about 19, David's age. He knew that if he were sitting at the table with them, at first glance he would appear to fit right in. Lean and muscular, with sandy blonde hair and blue eyes, he supposed he didn't look so different from the three all-American young jocks. Upon closer inspection, though, the differences would become apparent. They always did. The funny thing was that David didn't know exactly what the differences were—only that they existed.

He didn't want to be like them anyway, he told himself. They were obviously snobs. They were the type he resented, the rich and popular upper-crust. He could tell by their leather jackets and designer jeans, by their perfectly straight white teeth and by the girls' manicured nails and salon-styled hair. They were, of course, all having a wonderful time, laughing loudly at nothing. Pie and ice cream was all they'd ordered, just an excuse to sit and flirt, part of the dating ritual.

Bitter Reunion

David didn't date. It was only one of many things he didn't do that most teenagers did.

He didn't dwell long on the corner table. It made him too angry and defensive. His attention was drawn to a booth midway down one wall of wooden shuttered windows. A boisterous family of five was enjoying a late meal. Immediately, red flags began to wave. What a mess that one will be to clean up, David thought. A baby in a high chair was creating a typical baby disaster zone, cracker crumbs everywhere and food smeared on any surface she could reach. There was spilled milk in the high-chair tray and pieces of mangled beans and banana on the floor. Gross! The rest of the family, though, appeared to be having a great "bonding" experience. Mom, with sis on one side of the booth, and Dad, with the-chip-off-the-old-block on the other, were joking and laughing. No outbursts of sibling rivalry or parental reprimands, at least for the moment.

Why did everyone seem to be in such a blasted good mood tonight? Frowning, he took a mouthful of crushed ice and began to crunch on it.

Watching families, especially happy ones, fascinated David and made him uncomfortable at the same time. They were as foreign to him as those yuppie teenagers but more difficult to fathom. Even now the sight of Dad's arm draped protectively over his son's shoulder filled David with a strange mixture of longing and rage. He suspected there was something sinister behind that utopian facade of family togetherness. There had to be.

Moving on to less threatening territory, David's gaze zeroed in on the only solo customer in the coffee shop. Now this guy might be fun to fantasize about, David thought as he munched the last of his french fries. Talk about your stereotypical wimp. David was willing to bet he'd been named class nerd in high school about forty years ago. Herman, or Ernest, or whatever his name was, sat with his nose buried in a newspaper, sipping on a cup of coffee. There was a map laying beside a plate that contained a parsley sprig and some steak bones, the remnants of his supper. David wondered where good old Ernie was on his way to. Definitely not Disneyland. Maybe a convention for nuclear scientists. If he wasn't a scientist, he was probably a professor. David tried to envision Ernie, minus his three-piece suit and tie, bussing tables in a white apron. It was an amusing mental picture. Unfortunately, David really was supposed to be bussing tables. It was time to go back to work.

"Hey, David, shouldn't you be helping in the convention room to set up for tomorrow's breakfast?" someone demanded twenty minutes later.

David glanced up from the table he was clearing to see Alison Garvey, a short brunette waitress of about twenty-five, who always made it her business to mind everybody else's. Actually, he'd forgotten all about that breakfast. It irked him, though, to be bossed around, especially by Alison, who constantly rubbed him the wrong way. Maybe she was older than him, but she wasn't his mother, for Pete's sake.

"Yeah, Alison, I know," he lied, purposely slowing his pace and continuing, uninterrupted, with what he was doing. "I'll just be a few minutes. Don't bust a blood vessel."

Bitter Reunion

Alison gave him an exasperated look. "You don't have to be rude. I'm just reminding you, that's all. You better hurry, though. It's getting late." She flounced off in a huff.

There's always somebody on my case, David thought as he put a dirty dish and some silverware in the nearly full tub on his cart. A few swipes with the dishcloth and he was almost ready to move on. He reset the table with a clean, stiffly starched red napkin, a fork, a spoon and a knife, then topped off the salt and pepper shakers. Too bad he couldn't stall any longer. He'd just love to frustrate Alison some more.

Just as David was ready to move on, he noticed the discarded newspaper nestled in the corner of the burgundy Naugahyde seat of the booth. On impulse, he decided to check it out. It was one more clue into the real identity of Ernie, the nuclear scientist. Besides, Alison was looking his way, and he didn't want to give her the satisfaction of seeing him on his way to the convention room. Let her go ahead and bust that blood vessel.

David picked up and unfolded the paper. It opened to the human interest section which was captioned, PEOPLE. Below the caption, in grainy black and white, three faces stared out at him along with the words, "Local Businessman Honored."

Like opposite poles of a magnet, his eyes locked on the picture and widened in recognition.

Suddenly, David felt his heart racing. He was going to be sick.

It's just a joke, his mind screamed, trying to deny the validity of what he was seeing. This has to be some kind of joke!

He wanted to race out into the parking lot and see if Ernie might still be around, but his body was paralyzed. As if he were under water, everyone seemed to be moving in slow motion, and he couldn't get enough air. Then the room was spinning around him and getting strangely dark. Just as it occurred to David that he might be the one to burst a blood vessel, his knees buckled, and the *Albion Journal* fell to the floor.

Hanging onto consciousness by a thread, David collapsed into the booth and struggled to regain his equilibrium. For what seemed like ages, his heart continued to race and his hands shook like those of an old man.

"Are you O.K.?"

The words startled him. David looked up to discover with embarrassment that half the staff of the restaurant hovered over him with looks of concern on their faces. Alison was there, clucking over him like a mother hen, all ready to dial 911 and ship him off to the ER.

Finally, pulling himself together, David managed to convince everyone that he felt a little sick but could make it home on his own. Everyone but Alison, of course, who shot him a distinctly disapproving glare as, in a daze, he retrieved the newspaper from the floor, tucked it under his arm and walked shakily out of the restaurant.

Now, forty-five minutes later, he sat cross-legged in the middle of the bed, alone with his nemesis. An ordinary newspaper, but it could just as well have been a coiled cobra for the amount of dreaded apprehension it produced. David carefully uncreased the folds and forced himself to look once again at that picture. He stared, his mind reeling in disbelief.

There was no mistaking it. Beyond a doubt, the man in the photograph was the same man he had once called Dad. The features of the face were achingly familiar, and yet, altered by time and circumstances, they were also somehow alien. The man was seated at a table with an attractive blonde woman and a small boy. The caption beneath the picture read, "Todd Hamilton, Businessman of the Year, with his wife Gina and son Ben."

A naked bulb hanging from the ceiling cast a sickly pallor, enshrouding the small room in ghostly shadows. It was a fitting atmosphere for the darkness of David's soul. His eyes burned as they strained to read the small print of the accompanying article.

> Todd Hamilton, owner of *H & H Transport*, is the latest recipient of the "Albion Businessman of the Year" award. The award, given by his peers, is based not only on success in the realm of business, but also on consistently high standards of service within the community. Founded in 1939 by Lewis Hamilton, *H & H Transport* has grown from a small, four-truck enterprise, into the second largest trucking company in the state of Oregon. Hamilton says he has tried to retain the flavor of a small, family-owned business despite the demands such growth entails. Mayor Tom Calahan presented the award on Thursday evening at a banquet given in Hamilton's honor.

It was just a short piece, but David read it three times, his mind struggling to come to grips with the reality of it. For almost eleven years, he had studiously avoided thinking about Todd Hamilton at all. At night, though, David's daytime defenses melted away, and Hamilton became the demon that haunted his dreams. Maybe, just maybe, this was his chance to confront the demon head on.

Looks like you've made quite a name for yourself, Dad, David thought bitterly. It sure is easier to pour yourself into work when you don't have a kid around to get in the way. That must have been why you wanted to get rid of me.

His focus shifted to the woman and the child in the picture.

I guess now that you're rich and famous, you've made time to replace the family you threw away. You even managed to get a wife and son that look just like your first ones.

Uncannily, they really did. The little boy, especially, could have been Joey at about five years of age. The child gazed at his father with an expression of unabashed adoration. It made David want to vomit.

The sight of the boy had another, unexpected effect. David realized with horror that he was being transported into the past against his will. He found himself losing a fiercely fought battle for control, as a flood of memories burst through the dam that had held them at bay for so long. David gave in to them, and, for the first time, consciously allowed himself to remember his ninth birthday. The hurt…the betrayal…the death of everything good in his life. It hit him like a physical blow, knocking the air right out of him.

Suddenly, a rage unlike any he'd ever known consumed him. All of the anger that he had

Bitter Reunion

buried so deeply came spewing forth like hot lava.

"You lied to me!" he screamed, shattering the stillness. "You said you loved me!"

David scrambled from the bed, grabbed a rickety table with both hands, raised it above his head, and threw it with all his strength. It crashed against the wall and fell to the floor in a broken heap.

Curiously, the sight and sound of his own violence was soothing. The rage began to settle into a quieter, if no less lethal place. David slowly lowered himself into a sitting position on the floor, leaned against the wall, and relived the transformation of Joey Hamilton.

....

Las Vegas, Nevada, "the city of lights," turned out to be the destination of Sam and Elaine the day they and Joey left Albion, Oregon, behind them. It was ironic. In a place where quickie weddings were performed nearly every hour of the day, Sam never did marry Elaine. In fact, Sam didn't even stay in the picture for long. He rather quickly realized that getting involved with Elaine and her son had been a mistake of monumental proportions. Being a smart man, he knew when to cut his losses and run for his life.

Elaine was not without a man for long, though. After Sam, a succession of them were in and out of the small, dingy apartment she shared with Joey. They provided her with income and entertainment. Alcohol and drugs met all of her other needs. Joey, meanwhile, grew old beyond his years. He learned to fend for himself and to make himself scarce at appropriate times. He also became proficient at shutting out the lurid aspects of his life by escaping into another world that consisted of school, books, television, and his own vivid imagination. Though he played with other children at school, he never invited them to his home, so he had no close friends.

Life with Elaine came to an abrupt end about two years after the move to Vegas, when Joey came home from school one day to find her passed out on the couch. That, in itself, was not unusual. What was unusual was the fact that he couldn't wake her up, no matter how hard he tried. An hour later, when Hank Edwards arrived for his regularly scheduled "date," Joey was still sitting at Elaine's feet.

"The booze finally did her in," was all Hank had said. He stood silently beside Joey for several seconds. Then he broke the stillness. "Listen, kid, your mother's dead and you don't have a father. Well, I don't have a son. You come with me."

And just like that, Joey began yet another life, as David Edwards, the son of Hank Edwards.

Hank had insisted on changing Joey's name. "You're mine now, and I won't call you a name that was given to you by some other man," he'd stated adamantly. "You call me Pa, and you forget that you ever had any other family. I'm your only family from now on."

If things had been bad for Joey with Elaine, they were just as bad for David with Hank, but in a totally different way. Whereas Elaine had paid Joey little or no attention, Hank paid David too much attention. Hank had long lists of rules and regulations. Disapproval of David's behavior was dealt with swiftly and

Bitter Reunion

harshly. Beatings with a belt, or a stick, or even a fist became all too commonplace. David bore them with stoic tolerance, believing that he was somehow unworthy, deserving of punishment. Never once did he shed a tear. He had long since forgotten how to cry.

Hank did not love David. His motivation for wanting the boy was complex. In Hank's mind, a son was not a person, but a possession. More than any other thing, sons were the measure of a man's virility. He had learned that lesson from his own father, who had raised five sons. That women were worthless and that violence was the means by which to gain power were two other basic premises in the standards of morality that the old man had left as a legacy. Hank's father, strangely enough, had been a preacher, but the only gospel he knew or lived was anything but "Good News;" it was all "hell, fire and damnation." His concept of God was that of an omnipotent, cruel taskmaster, quick to judgement and retribution. "Spare the rod, spoil the child," was an admonition that the elder Edwards took to heart with zeal. Hank learned all about the ten commandments and the harsh consequences of sin, but he was never taught anything about forgiveness or about love.

The biggest disappointment of Hank's life had been in not having a son. It was, for him, a personal defeat. He had married three times. Only one of those marriages had lasted long enough to produce a child, probably because few women could tolerate the kinds of brutality that Hank subjected them to. Disappointingly, the child of his second marriage had turned out to be a girl. Hank had no use for a daughter. The marriage had ended when his wife had learned she could have no more children. At the age of forty-one and unmarried, Hank had resigned himself to the idea that he'd never have a son, that all-important symbol of continuity and manhood, to mold into his own image.

Then Elaine had died. He had seen her death almost instantly for what it was, the opportunity of a lifetime. He could acquire a son without having to be involved with a woman to do it. The fact that the child wasn't biologically his was something Hank dismissed from his mind. He would make the boy his by right of ownership. He took David without a moment's hesitation, not even caring that it meant packing up and leaving Las Vegas in the middle of the night. He was an old hand at eluding the police, but he wasn't too worried about being considered a kidnapper. From what Elaine had told him, there wasn't any next of kin who even knew to come looking for the boy.

In the next seven years, Hank and David moved frequently from place to place. David's school attendance was sporadic at best. Just as he was getting used to a new school and beginning to fit in, it would be time to leave again. Fortunately, David was a bright boy and an avid reader. He managed to lag behind his grade level only slightly.

Hank's career necessitated the constant change of venue. Simply put, Hank was a grifter, a con man. Separating people from their hard earned money was his special gift. He had a forceful, charismatic personality and a total lack of conscience, qualities that were tailor-made for his craft. Sometimes, his modus operandi was to romance women, steal their hearts and make off with their money. More often, though, the elderly were his targets. They were so unsuspecting and naive

Bitter Reunion

that they were no challenge at all. It was harder to steal candy from a baby.

At first, David was a real asset to Hank in his work. People tended to trust a man with a child. As the boy grew older, though, he began to rebel at having to join in on the con. It was a blow to Hank, that his son did not enthusiastically embrace a life of lying, cheating and stealing. Although punishment and threats could force compliance, David's less than enthusiastic approach to the job was more of a hindrance than a help. When David was sixteen, Hank reluctantly agreed to release him from the work he dreaded on the condition that David would drop out of school for good, get a paying job, and hand over half of each paycheck. David agreed. And the following three years were the best he had known since the day he'd left Albion.

. . . .

David sat on the cold hardwood floor, struggling to sort out the blurred details of his past. Only vague impressions of events, places and people emerged from the dense fog that seemed to surround them. One thing he remembered very clearly, though. The day Elaine died and Hank came to his rescue would be forever etched on his mind. How amazed David had been to think someone might actually want him. He would never be able to repay the debt he owed Hank for that. Sure, maybe Hank was a devious man, sometimes even cruel. David didn't always understand or like what he did. But Hank had willingly given David a home.

Todd Hamilton, on the other hand, had pretended to really care about his son, but it had all been just an act. Now, that was real cruelty. From the very beginning, he had set up Joey, the innocent child that David had once been, for a fall. And what a long, hard fall it had been.

David's thoughts now began to move in a new direction, his mind drawing conclusions he'd never quite put together before. Hamilton had tried to ruin Joey's life. David wasn't going to let him. He would turn the tables on Hamilton. He didn't know how, but there must be a way.

Seething anger from within created a need. The need, nebulous and unfocused at first, grew quickly into an obsession, and the obsession suddenly acquired a name.

Revenge.

CHAPTER 4

"David! What happened here? What's going on?" The gruff voice startled David. He had been so immersed in thought that he hadn't even heard Hank's arrival. It was as if Hank had materialized from thin air, a frightening apparition with no substance. Adding to the impression was the aura of intimidation and threat that Hank exuded.

At five foot eight, Hank stood a good six inches shorter than David. He had a slight build, dark thinning hair and masculinely craggy features that women found attractive. It was hard to say exactly what it was about him that was out of the ordinary. But Hank had a presence. A menacing presence. One knew instinctively that this was a man to be reckoned with. Maybe it was his eyes. Cold and hard, they lacked some spark of life that came from within. Or maybe it was simply that Hank was fearless.

Hank had faced many dangerous situations, without so much as breaking into a sweat. He'd had a knife pulled on him twice. There was even the time a jealous husband had held a gun to Hank's head. Cool as a cucumber, Hank had managed somehow to wrestle the gun away from the man. The poor husband was begging for mercy himself before Hank was done with him. Hank did not seem to know what it was to fear. He simply inspired it in others.

"I said, what's going on?" Hank repeated from the open doorway.

David quickly hid the newspaper behind his back but not before Hank had caught a glimpse of it.

"Nothing."

"Don't try to con a con-man. I asked you a question, boy, and I want a straight answer."

Glancing quickly around, as if looking for a place to hide, David slowly rose to his feet. "I, uh, just broke a table. I'll fix it."

"What's that behind your back? And don't even try telling me it's nothing. Hand it over."

David did as he was told.

"It's a newspaper," Hank stated, with a question in his voice. "You broke a table with a newspaper? That would have been quite a sight to see. We talking some newfangled karate blow? Or might there be another explanation for your wanting to hide this from me?"

"It's not even a local paper," Hank said, as he began to scan the page. Now he was really curious.

"You know I'll find out anyway. You might as well make this easy on both of us."

"It's my real father," David blurted out. "There in the picture at the bottom."

If Hank was surprised, he didn't show it. As David stood waiting for a reaction, Hank leaned his shoulder against the door jamb, silently read the article and then studied the picture that had opened the floodgates of David's rage.

It was something other than the picture that piqued Hank's interest, though, and caused him to continue to stare blankly at the page while he considered the possibilities. It seemed David's biological father was the owner of the second largest trucking company in a state that was heavily dependent on trucking to haul the timber which was its largest natural resource. Hank could almost smell the money. Lots and lots of money that could belong to him if he could just figure out the right way to go about getting it.

This Hamilton was assuredly much too smart to fall for one of Hank's run-of-the-mill con jobs. The man hadn't built up what was no doubt a multi-million dollar business by being an idiot. No, Hank was going to have to use a different approach entirely. Then, suddenly, he knew exactly what needed to be done. It was perfect. Absolutely perfect. And this one time David might even enjoy helping him.

"So, David, while we're on the subject," he said, finally looking up to meet David's challenging glare, "why didn't you ever tell me you came from a rich family?"

"He wasn't rich back then," David answered sullenly. "Besides, you never asked."

"Don't back-talk me, son! And don't you forget that I'm your real father!"

Hank seldom ever struck him anymore, and David was now bigger and stronger than Hank, but the older man still effortlessly commanded submission by virtue of the fear instilled throughout years of conditioning.

"I'm sorry, Pa. It's just that we never talked too much about my…about him," he muttered, gesturing toward the paper.

"You're right. Maybe it's time to start. How do you feel about the man after all he did to you?"

"I hate him," David said simply. "I wish he was dead."

"We could arrange that." Hank let the words hang there while he gaged David's reaction to them. At least the boy wasn't protesting immediately.

"What do you mean by that?"

"Think about it, David." Hank adopted his most persuasive tone of voice, the one he reserved for convincing little old ladies they needed to buy funeral insurance from him. "This is a rich man we're talking about. A man who dumped you like a heap of trash. With my help, you can make him pay for what he did."

"How?"

"The boy in the picture. We kidnap him and demand ransom. Enough for you and me to live on for a good long time. Once the old man pays up, if you want, we can kill him. Pow!" Hank made a gun with his forefinger. "Goodbye Todd Hamilton. Hello, lifestyles of the rich and famous."

"Are you serious, Pa? Kidnapping and killing? We've never done anything like that before. Why now?"

"Higher stakes call for more drastic methods." Hank considered. "We can draw the line at killing. That part's up to you. But if it was me, I'd want to do it. Yes, I surely would."

"What if we got caught? And besides, what makes you think he would pay ransom for his kid? He doesn't have a history of wanting his sons all that much."

Though it had always suited his purposes to let David believe otherwise, Hank knew Todd Hamilton had not abandoned Joey. Among the many secrets Elaine had divulged before her death had been the one about how she had duped her former husband by snatching the boy out from under his nose. Hank knew Hamilton would pay any amount of money before he would lose a second son.

"I think he'll pay. He's a big man now. He doesn't want to lose his only heir. And he's got a pretty wife he may want to keep happy. She could probably convince him to get her precious baby boy back." Hank caught the

Bitter Reunion

skeptical look on David's face and read his mind. "Not all mothers are like Elaine. Most of them seem to have some maternal instincts."

"Do you really think we could get away with it?"

Hank could see he was getting through to David. It surprised him. He'd expected more resistance. He'd always thought the kid was too soft, but maybe he'd underestimated him.

He'd hooked the big fish now. Time to reel it in.

"If he doesn't go for the ransom, we can always cut and run. What have we got to lose by trying?"

"What about our freedom, maybe our lives?" David countered, for argument's sake.

"Trust me. I won't let anything happen to you. We'll be careful. We'll have everything planned out to the last detail. Nothing will go wrong."

"O.K. Let's do it," David said.

The fish landed in the net.

. . . .

It took a little over a month for Hank and David to finalize preparations to once again pull up stakes and move on. This time, however, their destination wasn't being decided by the toss of a coin. They were heading to a specific place for a specific reason.

Albion, Oregon. David could barely remember the town. He seemed to recall that it hadn't been a big city, though. Not like Las Vegas. Or Omaha, or Houston, or Chicago, or any of the other countless big cities in which he'd lived. It probably wasn't a very small town, either. If he had to guess, he'd say somewhere between thirty and fifty thousand people.

Green. That was the color that came to mind when he thought of Albion. Lots of green. Green grass, green trees, green hills gently rolling into the distance. And rain on his face and stomping his feet in puddles to make the water splash. He also had hazy memories of the ocean and saw himself running barefoot in warm sand, daring icy salt water to reach out and grab his toes.

Sure enough, the map Hank had produced validated his impressions. Albion was smack in the middle of the Willamette Valley, a heavily forested area due to the fact that, as in most of the Pacific Northwest, the climate is mild and rainfall is abundant. Albion was also about 60 miles from the Pacific Ocean. The names of Newport and Lincoln City, two of the coastal towns on the map, even seemed vaguely familiar to David.

Funny that in all of their traveling all over the country, they were now the closest they had ever been to David's home town—only about five hundred miles. And then there was the newspaper and the way it just happened to be left where David had found it. It had to be fate. Fate was giving him a chance to start again, to finally put the past behind him. In the last month, he had come to realize that the only way he could do that was to eliminate Todd Hamilton completely. He avoided thinking in terms of killing; it would be, instead, a just retribution, an evening of the scales. As long as Hamilton was alive, David would always be a victim, a prisoner shackled by the bands of hatred. With Hamilton gone, David could finally break free. This was the real beauty

Bitter Reunion

of Hank's plan. Getting rid of Hamilton. The rest was just icing on the cake.

As far as David could see, there were only two good things about Hank's occupation. You got to see a lot of different cities, and you learned how to pack up and move in no time flat. Hank never rented a U-Haul. If their stuff wouldn't fit in the car, it got left behind. Consequently, David had never accumulated much of anything.

As he threw the last of his meager possessions together, David thought about the plan. Hank had decided it would be best if he and David stayed away from each other in Albion. They would live in separate places and meet only as necessary. The job of actually kidnapping the boy and collecting the ransom was David's. Hank was to be the backup, the unseen player. David was smart enough to realize what Hank was doing. He was putting all the risk on David, so if anything went wrong and David was caught, Hank could cut his losses and run. David had no illusions about Hank's motives, but he didn't care. It was all or nothing for David anyway. The need for revenge now far outweighed any concern for his own safety.

Laying the groundwork in Albion was Hank's job, and he had already been there for over three weeks setting things up, finding a place for both of them to stay, and fine-tuning the details of the plan. Three days ago, he had called to say that everything was ready. David could come.

David had worked his last shift at the restaurant today. It had been strange to walk out the door, knowing he wouldn't be back. Originally, he had planned to leave for Oregon tomorrow morning, bright and early. But now that there was nothing tying him here, he found he couldn't wait any longer to get under way. The thought of spending even one more night in this depressing place was unbearable. The road to Albion was beckoning, and nothing could keep him from answering its insistent call.

   A navy blue sweatshirt seemed to be the last thing left in the closet. It landed atop the messy pile of clothes already crammed into a battered old brown suitcase. David dropped the lid, snapped it shut and took a quick look around. The neatly made bed, corners tucked in military-style, stood in contrast to the broken remains of the table which still lay on the floor, a dent in the wall marking the place where it had hit. The otherwise barren space exuded all the warmth and personality of a motel room. But then, it always had, just like every other room in every other place David had lived with Hank. None of them had ever felt like home. He picked up the suitcase with one hand, snatched the car keys from the dresser top with the other, and left the house.

   Outside, the sky was a vast expanse of pure, endless blue, without a hint of a cloud in sight. It was the kind of day that was made for taking a long, long drive. David felt light, almost buoyant, a distinctly unfamiliar feeling. Setting the suitcase down beside the red 1993 Camero he had proudly purchased seven months earlier, he opened the door. Then he hefted the unwieldy suitcase onto the back seat, upsetting a resident honeybee that had been trapped inside the car. David shooed it out, while thinking that it was a good thing Hank wasn't around. The incident had reminded

Bitter Reunion

him of the one and only time he had ever seen Hank afraid.

It had happened not long after David had become Hank's son. Hank had been driving in the summer, with the windows down. David couldn't remember where they had been going or why, but a bee had flown into the window on the driver's side, landing forcefully against the dashboard. The stunned insect had instantly recovered enough to begin buzzing angrily around the front seat. David hadn't particularly liked bees, but he'd been aghast at Hank's reaction. The man was really freaking out! It was a miracle they hadn't had a wreck, because Hank had totally lost control of the car in his frantic endeavor to avoid the bee. He'd swerved wildly off the road and braked to a screeching halt. Then, flinging his door wide open, Hank had jumped out of the car and refused to get back in until David had gotten the bee out.

Hank's display of abject terror was so out of character and out of proportion to the threat involved, that David had been completely stunned. "It's just a bee, Pa," he had said in his confusion.

"I'm allergic to bee stings." Hank seldom condescended to explain his actions to David, but this time he had. He was allergic, not in the way that David was allergic to strawberries, but in a way that could kill him. Once, he had nearly died from a bee sting. Now, he kept a hypodermic needle and some medicine with him most of the time, just in case. They hadn't been in the car that day, though. From then on, David noticed that Hank always drove with the windows all the way up. Thank goodness for air conditioning.

David settled himself behind the steering wheel, then retrieved his sunglasses from the glove compartment and put them on. With one last look at the shabby duplex that symbolized the past from which he was escaping, he put the Camero into reverse and backed out of the driveway.

Ten minutes later, David hit Interstate 84 on the outskirts of Boise and headed west. It was exhilarating, the freeway beneath his wheels, the wide open expanse of Idaho stretching out endlessly before him. He'd never been away from Hank for this long, and though a complicated mixture of loyalty and fear kept him from entertaining ideas of leaving Hank, he was temporarily heady with the freedom of being completely on his own. David stepped hard on the gas pedal and rolled his window all the way down, letting a warm rush of air hit him in the face.

"Goodbye, Boise! Goodbye, Alison! Don't miss me too much," he shouted, laughing. Then, doing his best imitation of a true country-western twang, he began to sing a loud rendition of a famous Willy Nelson song.

Ah, yes. It felt good to be on the road again.

CHAPTER 5

Wednesday, June 21

"Hey, mommy, look what I found!"

Five-year-old Ben Hamilton or Beej, as his family often called him, came bursting excitedly into the kitchen, where his mother, Gina, was putting away the last of the dishes from the dishwasher. Breathless, he halted at Gina's side and started digging something out of his pocket.

"He was sitting on the deck all by himself. I think he's lost."

"Whatcha got there, bud?" Gina asked, as she bent to see what Ben was now clutching in his small fist. Something was protruding from between two chubby, less than clean fingers. It was brown, wiggly, and decidedly mangled. "Ah, a worm. Glad to make your acquaintance, Mr. Worm." At least it wasn't a spider, slug or snail this time.

She couldn't keep a hint of amusement from her voice, as she said, "Worms don't really like it in the house, Beej. They belong outside. If you go put him out in the grass, he'll be much happier."

"But, Mom, I think he likes me," Ben said, looking suddenly crestfallen. "Why can't I keep him?"

"His family might be worried about him," Gina quickly improvised. "Maybe they're looking all over for him. You'd better go put him back. How do you think I would feel if somebody took you away where I couldn't find you?"

"Not so good, huh?" Ben said.

"You better believe it. Now, hurry and put him back. Then go wash your hands and put on your shoes and we'll go for a walk."

"Hooray!" Ben shouted, as he bounded out of sight.

A peaceful quiet descended upon the kitchen at Ben's departure, and Gina Hamilton stopped a moment to drink it in and to gaze with satisfaction at her domestic domain.

She loved this room. It had recently been completely transformed from a small, dowdy space boasting 1940's plain off-white cabinets, cracked gray-flecked Formica counter tops and 1970's avocado colored appliances, into a cook's paradise, a bright and cheerful place in which to create all those delectable gourmet concoctions which Ben invariable refused to eat.

Having the kitchen lavishly remodeled had been Todd and Gina's one large concession to the fact that they were now wealthy. Gina still couldn't quite relate to that word—wealthy. Rich was just as bad. But they were. It had been about a year and a half now since Todd's dad had succumbed to a massive heart attack and his mother had died only a year earlier in an automobile accident. Todd was left with sole ownership of H & H Transport and a fairly large inheritance was split between him and his sister, Suzanne, who lived back east with her husband and four children. Once the shock of Dad's death had worn off, Gina and Todd had begun to contend with the fact of their newfound financial status. In the last several years, due to hard work, a spotless reputation and some lucky breaks, H & H had grown by leaps and bounds. And now Todd was the sole owner and CEO of a multi-million dollar company.

Bitter Reunion

Previously, as business manager of the company, Todd had made a more than adequate income but because they had both preferred that Gina stay home to be a full-time mother, they had remained comfortably middle-class. How did you adjust the mental image of yourself from middle-class to filthy rich overnight, Gina had wondered. As it turned out, neither one of them had wanted to. They quickly discovered how uncomfortable they felt hobnobbing with the elitists of their community. They were out of their element. Like children dressed up in grown-up's clothing, they were playacting and looking silly in the process.

Gina quickly learned that money could alienate friends and steal one's sense of motivation. Having too much threatened to change them in some intrinsic way, causing them to lose touch with the day-to-day struggles and joys of the average person.

And then there was the matter of material possessions. They didn't want Ben growing up pampered and spoiled by being given too much too soon without having to earn it.

While Gina faced temptation every day to let herself splurge needlessly on this or that, from the mundane to the outrageous, she had never been tempted to abandon this old house in favor of a new one. She enjoyed touring fancy showplaces, some of them so gorgeous they took your breath away, but they were just that—showplaces. They weren't home.

This is home, Gina thought, as she walked from the kitchen, through the dining room and living room, then up the stairs to the master bedroom to change into her walking shoes. Built in 1938, and situated on the very edge of the town's historic district, Gina had fallen in love with the quaint charm of this cape cod from the moment she had first laid eyes on it. Todd had been harder to convince. All he had seen was its then shabby, neglected condition. He seemed to have no capacity for visualizing potential. The price had been right, and Gina had been persistent; so now, seven years later, evidence of their blood, sweat and tears could be seen everywhere. They had risked life and limb, not to mention sanity, to do most of the renovating of the house themselves, and the results were gratifying.

What emerged from the ashes of that sad and forlorn fixer-upper they had bought was a lovely house, uniquely their own. Even as they'd transformed the house, they had also been in the process of building memories in it that would last a lifetime. They had loved, laughed and cried here. This house was, to Gina, a symbol of the permanence and stability of her little family. She would be perfectly content to live out the rest of her days right here.

"You ready to go, Mom?" Ben called up from the bottom of the stairs. "I've been waiting and waiting and waiting!"

"Hold onto your horses. I'm coming," Gina replied, stuffing a few crumpled dollar bills into her jeans pocket. Then descending the stairs at much too fast a pace for someone of the advanced old age of thirty-four, she arrived breathless beside her son.

"Just one more minute. Let me get a sack of bread crumbs, so we can feed the ducks."

"Can we take Smokey with us?" asked Ben, as Gina once more retreated to the kitchen. He was referring to the shaggy little mutt that he'd received as his first birthday present,

Bitter Reunion

who was now staring hopefully at the door, stubby tail vibrating furiously in anticipation.

Smokey had been billed as a pure-bred Cocker Spaniel when Todd had bought him. Since he'd had no papers, they'd gotten him for a steal, only fifty dollars, compared to two hundred for papered dogs. It soon became apparent, though, that if Smokey was really one-hundred percent Cocker, he was probably the strangest looking one of the breed. His curly black and gray hair grew and grew, to the point that he looked far more like a filthy purebred mop. When even his eyes disappeared behind a veil of hair, Gina had taken him to a groomer. She returned with a dog that in no way resembled the one she had gone in with, but still didn't fit the bill as a Cocker Spaniel. Ben had cried, sure that mommy had switched dogs on him, and it hadn't been easy to persuade him that this was what Smokey looked like underneath all that hair.

Smokey may not have been what they thought they were getting, but what they got was the best. He was all the things that a dog should be; loyal, gentle, protective, playful and adoring. None of them would trade him now for any other dog in the world.

"Sorry, hon. Can't take him today. I thought we would stop and see Aunt Kellie and have some frozen yogurt before we come home, and Smokey can't go inside the shop," Gina answered, entering the room. "Here I am, and I think we're all ready now. Let's blow this joint!"

Gina and Ben emerged into a day that was nothing short of picture perfect. Gina sometimes got sick of Oregon rain, but she had to appreciate that it made a day like this one possible. When the sun was shining in Oregon, there was no more beautiful place on the face of the earth. June was sometimes still quite cool and wet, but it was unseasonably warm today, and the profusion of colorful flowers along with the deep green of grass and trees created a palate of beauty only God could have painted. It was impossible to take it in without feeling your spirits soar.

"If you're going to go darting off, stay close enough so I can see you."

"O.K., Mom," Ben called over his shoulder, already half a block ahead of Gina.

Gina watched him contentedly as he jumped, skipped and ran, occasionally stooping to inspect some item of interest. She thanked the Lord once again for blessing her with a wonderful family.

It was indeed a miracle that Gina and Todd had managed to end up together. The odds were against it. They had met at a Bible study group, but both were in the throes of grief, at the time. Gina was recovering from the untimely death of Brad, her first husband, from cancer, and Todd was still dealing with the loss of his son, Joey. In addition, Todd had taken an instant dislike to her. Much later, she discovered that for the first time in her life, a man had been repulsed by her looks. Her shoulder-length blonde hair, blue-green eyes and slim build had reminded Todd of his first wife, Elaine, whom he loathed. God must have wanted them together, though. Eventually, Todd realized that, looks being only skin deep, Gina was really nothing like Elaine. Once that barrier was broken, Todd and Gina began to open up to and take comfort from one another. There was such release in knowing that they weren't completely alone in their

Bitter Reunion

feelings of loss. Someone else could actually empathize. The rest, as they say, was history.

Gina would have never guessed that she could be this happy. Oh, what a marvelous God, to grant the deepest desires of her heart! Pushing everything from her mind except her son and the perfection of the day, she raced to catch up with Ben.

"You ready for that frozen yogurt, now?" Gina asked Ben an hour later as they left the park, having made absolutely sure that not one duck had gone hungry.

"Yes!" was his enthusiastic reply. But he was holding Gina's hand now, and his steps were sluggish. Gina hoped she wouldn't end up lugging him the last few blocks home. Maybe the yogurt would revive him.

To stroll through this part of Albion was, in some respects, like going back in time a hundred years. The historic district was well known for it's large variety of architectural styles. Queen Anne Victorian with lacy gingerbread trim, Craftsman Bungalow, French Second Empire topped by Mansard roofs, stately Italianate, Rural Vernacular and stick. They were all there in lovingly restored abundance, rubbing shoulders with one another. Historic home tours were held twice a year in Albion, attracting people from all over the state.

Complimenting the historic district and next door to it was Old Town Albion with its conglomeration of small specialty stores, the majority of which dealt in antiques. Many of the buildings in Old Town were constructed in the late 1800's to early 1900's and had stood the test of time. The rest had been remodeled to look older than they really were. Sometimes, it was hard to tell the difference.

At the end of the block stood one such edifice. No one would have guessed that Ellie's Edibles had been a relatively modern sporting goods store as recently as eight years ago.

There were only two customers sitting at one of the dozen or so round wrought iron tables that dotted the room. Ellie's Edibles was a deli that only incidentally sold frozen yogurt, but it had the look and feel of an old fashioned ice cream parlor. A player piano was plunking out rag-time tunes as Gina and Ben walked across the polished black and white checkered floor.

"Well, if it isn't my favorite nephew! Come here, kiddo. Belly up to the bar and give Auntie Kellie a great big kiss."

Ben, having miraculously regained his vitality, hurtled toward Kellie, Gina's eighteen-year-old sister, who beckoned to him from behind the counter.

A sixteen-year age difference was only the beginning of the differences between Gina and Kellie. Kellie was actually the taller of the two by at least two inches and had inherited her soft brown eyes and reddish-tinted brown hair from their father. Her boisterous, sometimes quirky sense of humor, and her enthusiasm for sports, especially tennis, were also traits that Gina had never possessed. Gina had been labeled "academic," Kellie, "social." Gina liked things to be orderly, while Kellie preferred a "lived-in" look. Despite these differences, however, they were very close. The things they did share were the important things. Love for the Lord, their families, each other. And a lot of other, less basic things, like nearly all kinds of music and sentimental movies.

Bitter Reunion

"Can you take a break and have some frozen yogurt with us?" Gina asked, joining her son and sister at the counter.

"Sure," Kellie replied. "It's been pretty slow this afternoon. I'll just go ask Carol to cover for me."

Soon they were all seated near the window enjoying the afternoon sunlight that spilled in upon them.

"So, how do you like your new summer job? This should be a pretty fun place to work," Gina commented.

Kellie considered before answering. "Let me just say this. It's a heck of a lot better than baby-sitting Mrs. Thompson's four little monsters like I did last summer. Pays better money, too." She put her spoon down and leaned forward, "I figured it out. If I live at home, I should have enough money saved up by the time school starts to pay for the whole year. That is, barring any other financial setbacks."

Gina couldn't help adding, "Like that teeny-weeny little speeding ticket you got last month?"

"Hey, I learned my lesson. That won't be happening again. My friends are calling me Granny Kellie, I drive so slow." She picked up her spoon again and took a bite.

"There's no reason you shouldn't be able to live on campus, if you really want to," Gina said, turning serious. "You know Todd and I would like to help you foot the bill. What good is money if you can't use it to make the ones you love happy? Campus life is important, hon, and you're going to get tired of that 25 mile commute."

"Yea, I know, but…well, you know how Mom and Dad feel about you guys giving us handouts."

"Not that again." Gina sounded frustrated. "Beej, would you please tell your aunt that a gift is not a handout."

Ben, surprised to hear his name in the middle of a grown-up conversation, looked up. "Huh? What's a handsnout?"

Kellie and Gina both laughed, causing Ben to look even more confused.

"O.K., O.K., I give in, for now," said Gina, "but this matter is not yet resolved. I think I'm going to have a little talk with Mom and Dad. You know how stubborn I can be. It may take some time, but I'll wear 'em down. Either that, or I'll drive 'em crazy trying."

"However it turns out, Sis, thanks for the offer," Kellie said sincerely. "I really appreciate it."

"What are sisters for, anyway," Gina answered. "Speaking of which and changing the subject…I need my little sister to help me decide on a good vacation spot for this time of year. I was thinking of Disneyland or Disney World, but they'd be so hot and crowded in July."

Now there was a word or two that once again diverted Ben's attention away from his bowl, which was nearly empty, anyway. "Are we going to go to Disneyland, Mommy? I really want to see Mickey Mouse. And Brian went there and he says it's lots and lots of fun! They got trains and boats and Toon Town and stuff. I saw some of it on T.V."

"Yes, we will definitely go there someday, honey. I'm just not sure we want to go in the summer. You have to wait in really long lines in the summertime, and you hate really long lines."

"Like at the grocery store?" Ben asked skeptically.

Bitter Reunion

"Worse," Kellie joined in.

"We better not go in the summer," Ben decided.

"Here, Ben." Gina put a couple of quarters in his pocket. "You go and wash your sticky face and your sticky hands. Then you can put a quarter in the piano."

Gina took a sip of her iced tea and waited till Ben was gone before continuing. "I don't know if you've ever noticed, but Todd gets depressed every summer around the anniversary of the day he lost Joey. Sometimes it lasts for a few weeks, sometimes longer. He's been really moody lately, and I think that's the reason. Maybe it would help if we went away for awhile this month. The distraction might keep his mind off other things. Do you think it's a good idea?"

"Oh, gosh, Gina," Kellie said, looking stricken, and ignoring the question, "how sad! It must be awful not to know where your own son is or if you'll ever get to see him again. Joey would be around my age, wouldn't he?"

"Pretty close. Let's see, he was taken away on his birthday, July 1st. That means he would have been twenty in a couple of weeks, so he'd be a little over a year older than you are. If he's still alive." Gina sighed. "Time is supposed to heal all wounds, but I think that in some ways this one just gets worse. With each passing year, it's that much more time apart if Joey is out there somewhere. And if he's dead, which Todd doesn't believe is true, then it's that much more time living with the unknown."

By rights, Kellie's break was over, but she knew that unless a new customer came in, she could stay where she was. Right now, she hoped nobody was hungry. "Why would you think Joey might be dead? Didn't you tell me he was just taken by his mother out of spite?"

Gina's hand flew to her mouth, as she realized what she'd let slip. "Oh, I didn't mean to say that! I've never gone into the whole story with you, Kels. Todd's really uncomfortable talking about it, and I'm not so sure he'd want.."

"Come on, Gina, you know I won't breathe a word. We're sisters! We never hide anything from each other."

Gina glanced over at the player piano and saw Ben insert his quarter in the coin slot. He settled himself on the bench and waited for the music to begin. After a moment in which she seemed to debate with herself, she spoke. "O.K. I guess you're old enough to keep a confidence. Just remember that the subject's really painful for Todd, and it's best not to bring it up around him."

Kellie nodded, an encouragement to go on.

Gina spoke in a low voice as she recounted the story of Todd's search for his son. "Todd was obsessed with finding Joey at first," she said. "He went to the police, but they weren't very helpful. They said it was a domestic dispute since there was no court appointed custody arrangement, and they wouldn't get involved. So then he hired a private detective and spent hours and hours of his own time trying to get leads on Joey's whereabouts. See, it wasn't just that Todd loved Joey and wanted him back. It was also about Todd being afraid for Joey's safety. He didn't think Elaine would be a fit mother. Evidently, she was an alcoholic, pretty far gone. So he was frantic to find Joey. But nothing happened for the longest time. It was about two and a half years after the kidnapping that the detective

Bitter Reunion

finally got a lead. He tracked down the man Elaine had run off with, a guy named Sam White. Todd spoke personally to this Sam and found out that Elaine and Joey were supposedly in Las Vegas, Nevada. At least, that's where they were when Sam had seen them last. Imagine how elated Todd was! It was the hottest lead he'd had." Gina paused to take another sip of tea, and Kellie noticed the hand holding the glass was trembling. "It turned out to be a disaster," Gina continued. "What they discovered in Las Vegas was that Elaine was dead and Joey was gone."

"What happened?" Kellie gasped.

"It appeared that Elaine died because of her lifestyle—too much alcohol and drugs. But nobody knows what happened to Joey. There were records indicating he'd attended a nearby grade school up until the time of his mother's death. But Joey wasn't around when a lady in a neighboring apartment discovered Elaine's body, and no one saw him after that."

"You're kidding." Kellie knew it sounded lame, but what else was there to say?

"It was a dead end," Gina went on, as if Kellie hadn't interrupted. "Todd still employs the private detective, but there hasn't been a single new lead since then that has turned up anything."

"Poor Todd," Kellie said, feeling terrible for him and for Gina, and especially for that little boy, whatever might have become of him.

"He was completely devastated, Kellie. But thank goodness, his church and family rallied around him. They made him see that there was only one way Todd would ever find any peace of mind. He had to let go and trust Joey to the Lord, completely. I think he's able to do that most of the time now, but he still has his struggles with it. He's going through one of them right now." Gina looked at Ben standing beside the player piano, mesmerized, watching the keys move of their own accord, and she wondered if she would be able to handle losing her son as well as Todd had. She doubted it.

"Thanks for telling me," Kellie said, as she reached across the table and squeezed her sister's hand. "Mom and Dad know, don't they?"

"Yes. You can let them know I told you. It wasn't that we were trying to hide anything from you, but you were just a kid." Gina tried to lighten the mood as she said, "I suppose now that you're eighteen, it's time to let you in on some of our grown-up secrets. Welcome to the real world."

"Next time, make them happy secrets, would you please?" Kellie glanced at her watch, and reluctantly rose from her chair. "If I don't get back to work, I'll be fired my very first week. I'll be praying for Todd, though, Gina, and I'll be thinking of a good vacation spot, too. I'll let you know what I come up with tonight. You do still want me to baby-sit the rugrat, don't you?"

"Sure do. See you around seven-thirty," Gina replied, as she, too, abandoned the table and went to claim her child.

CHAPTER 6

There it was. Albion. The sign overhead announced the end of one journey and the beginning of another. David exited the freeway and gradually slowed to a stop at the intersection.

So this is home, sweet home, he thought derisively, as he glanced around. Pretty unimpressive. It was obviously the industrial part of town. Massive structures of concrete and steel belched out angry gray clouds of steam, filling the air with a pungent odor. David wrinkled his nose. What a fitting welcome.

He parked at the first convenience store he saw, strolled in and purchased a map of Albion. Then he returned to the car to study it. His watch indicated that it was two-seventeen in the afternoon. Remembering it was still set on Mountain time, he moved it back an hour. As anxious as he'd been to get here, David had made the drive in two days, rather than one, sleeping overnight in his car at a rest area somewhere in the vast arid nothingness of Eastern Oregon. He'd wanted to arrive well rested and with plenty of daylight left in which to explore this town. There was no way he'd be able to sleep before he had satisfied the irresistible urge to see with his own eyes the house in which Todd Hamilton lived. Who knows, maybe he'd even catch sight of Hamilton himself. The thought made his heart pound and his mouth feel as if it were full of cotton balls. You've got to be careful, cautioned a voice from within. Don't get in such a big hurry. This is too important to blow by getting impatient.

Forcing himself to concentrate on the task at hand, David retrieved a rumpled piece of scratch paper from the glove compartment where he'd stashed it yesterday. It had the address of his temporary home scribbled on it. 1359 Sherman Street SW.

"It's perfect," Hank had told him, referring to the small house he had rented for David. "Took some time to find, but it was worth the effort. You'll see what I mean when you get here."

In less than five minutes, the address had been located on the map and the directions to it committed to memory.

David pulled out of the parking lot, took a right and headed slowly south. A disorienting deja vu struck within half a mile. He had entered "Everycity, USA" where there existed an assortment of fast food restaurants and chain stores that were clones of those found in virtually every town in which David had lived. McDonalds, Wendys, Taco Bell, Burger King...they seemed to all be present and accounted for.

Once past the commercial district, David turned east into a residential section of town, and the scenery changed dramatically for the better. Rows of stately, well-maintained houses surrounded by impeccably manicured lawns sat just beyond the shady, tree-lined streets. An occasional bicycle or skateboard left carelessly in a yard provided just the right touch of domesticity to the otherwise lifeless picture of tranquility. How would it be, David wondered, to live in such a place? This wasn't the Albion he'd conjured up in his foggy memories. He wouldn't be at all surprised to find out that Hamilton lived in one of these houses, though.

Gradually, grand elegance gave way to mediocrity and then to seediness. David was nearing his destination. He found himself driving down a pot-holed street that eventually petered out to nothing more than a narrow, badly rutted dirt road. Most houses here hadn't seen a coat of paint in well over a decade and could be better described as shacks. Dogs slept lazily on porches piled high with cast-off household debris that spilled out into yards consisting mostly of dandelions and crabgrass. The whole area was permeated with a sense of hopeless despair.

1355 seemed to be the last forlorn house before the road dead-ended in a tangled mass of blackberry bushes and moss covered trees. Upon closer inspection, however, David discovered a cleared spot in the undergrowth that was evidently a makeshift driveway. The house that the driveway led up to was set well back from the road. It was totally secluded, sheltered as it was amidst the overgrown profusion of vegetation gone wild. A little bit of back-woods country smack in the middle of town. Hank was right. It was absolutely perfect.

The house itself was nondescript. In some ways, it outclassed its neighbors. The white paint looked to be only a few years old. None of the windows were broken, and the roof seemed to be in fairly good repair. It sure wasn't anything fancy, though. David parked the car in the lean-to carport, stretched his legs, and walked around to the back. It was a pretty day, he noted. Must have brought the Idaho sunshine with him. He searched for and found a large rock beside the trunk of a towering spruce. Underneath was the house key that Hank said would be there. David opened the side door by the carport and stepped into the kitchen. It was small and old, but clean. He quickly toured the rest of the house. Two bedrooms, one bathroom, and a living room. The house was meagerly furnished, but, like the kitchen, it was clean, though it had a stale, unlived-in smell. Opening a few windows ought to remedy that. Yes, this would be quite adequate to use as a hideout for a couple of weeks.

David brought in his suitcase and used the bathroom. Afterwards, returning to the kitchen, he searched the cupboards. He hadn't eaten since breakfast, and he suddenly realized how hungry he was. The cupboards, however, proved to be barer than Old Mother Hubbard's. He was going to have to get some groceries. First things first, though. He'd grab a bite to eat somewhere and then…it sent a shiver down his spine…then he would do it. He would begin the process of hunting down his prey. Impatience was nipping at his heels, urging him to get on with it. Fortunately, the first step was simple. He could do it now.

David went into the living room and reached for the dog-eared telephone book that was lying on the end table next to the phone. Please don't let the number be unlisted, he thought, as he searched through the H's. Hamel..Hamer..Hamill. There it was! His finger stopped beside the name. Hamilton, Todd and Gina. The address was right there for all the world to see. 1221 7th Ave. SW. And a phone number.

David picked up the telephone's receiver, relieved to hear a dial tone. On impulse, he dialed the number. It rang three, four times, and then the answering machine message abruptly came on. "You've reached the Hamilton residence. Please leave your name, number and message. We will return your call as soon as possible."

For some reason, it took him completely by surprise, blind-siding him. *The voice.* The last time he'd heard it had also been over the telephone. It had brought pain then. It brought pain now. With a quick movement of his hand, David swept the entire telephone off the table. It crashed loudly to the floor, the receiver landing face up, where it continued to hum, unheeded. Then, he stomped from the room, slamming the front door behind him.

Ellie's Edibles, the sign proclaimed in flowery Victorian script. In smaller letters, underneath, were the words, "A Delicatessen." Driving in the general direction of Seventh Avenue while looking for a place to eat, David had stumbled upon an area of town that was tugging insistently at the ragged edges of his memory. It was nothing at all like the shopping mecca he'd driven through earlier. Every storefront was completely unique—one of a kind. He knew he had been here before. As he walked toward the deli, he tried to put the pieces of the puzzle into place.

Across the street was the bicycle shop where he'd gone with his dad. David remembered that day well. He must have been about five, and full of clumsy rambunctiousness. He'd accidentally bumped into one of a dozen or so big bikes all lined up beside each other. It had fallen sideways creating a domino effect. Bike after bike fell until the whole row was on the floor. He had cried, mortified, but Dad and the store owner had been understanding. They had set about picking up the bikes, laughing and joking about it until he'd been laughing, too. And then he'd seen it. A bike that was just his size. It was red and shiny and had a big horn on the handlebars. The fact that it also had training wheels was icing on the cake. Two weeks later, that bike had been sitting under the Christmas tree. The training wheels hadn't lasted long, but the bicycle had lasted till he left Albion. David wondered what had happened to it and to all his other childhood treasures. He supposed they'd been sold for a pittance at a yard sale or hauled to the Salvation Army. No one would have valued them as he had.

Scanning the block, he also thought he recognized the book store, an antique store and a bakery. It was eerie, this strolling-down-memory-lane business. He didn't like it one bit. It hurt. Everything lately seemed to hurt. He reminded himself that he was here to make the hurting stop. Soon.

Along with the hurt, David was experiencing confusion. There was a puzzle piece that just didn't fit. There should be a sporting goods store right here somewhere. He was pretty sure of it. Shaking his head as if to clear it, David walked into Ellie's.

It wasn't exactly rush-hour for the deli at three twenty-five in the afternoon. The two women behind the counter were working hard at looking busy.

"What can I get for you?" asked the younger, prettier one, a brunette identified by her name-tag as Kellie.

He placed his order and watched as she began to build a turkey sandwich with the works.

"Nice day, isn't it?" Kellie glanced up. David couldn't help but notice she had a beautiful smile. One slightly crooked front tooth just added to its charm. "Do you live

Bitter Reunion

around here? I don't think I've seen you before."

As if she really cares, thought David. Aloud, he said, "I'm from California. Just got here today." Recalling the college he'd seen as he drove into town, he ad-libbed, "I'll be attending college here in the fall."

"Hey, that's great," Kellie answered, increasing the wattage of that brilliant smile. "You going to the community college or Oregon Christian near Fairview?"

"Community college," David mumbled, starting to feel uncomfortable. He'd never much liked lying, even when Hank had forced him into it. It was too easy to get tripped up.

"Oh. I'm going to be going to Oregon Christian, but we'll probably run into each other once in awhile. It's a pretty small town, and if you like turkey sandwiches, we make the best ones around. You come back, and we'll even give you our VIP treatment."

This girl was adding to David's overall confusion. He was used to females coming on to him and he knew just how to brush them off. Kellie wasn't flirting, though. She seemed genuinely interested in him and exuded a non-threatening friendliness David had not encountered in those of the opposite sex.

"Well, I don't think I'll be able to eat out much," David said, as he paid for the sandwich, a bag of chips, and a diet Pepsi.

"Yeah, I know what you mean. Struggling college students, right? We'll probably be living on Ramen noodles and coffee." Her eyes met his. They were a soft brown and held a twinkle of merriment in their depths.

Suddenly and surprisingly, David was hesitant to leave this spot. "I used to live here, a long time ago," he volunteered, surprising himself again. "Didn't there used to be a sporting goods store somewhere on this block?"

"This is it. No, really, it is," she insisted, registering his skeptical expression. "It used to be McLain's."

McLain's! That was it! David had loved that store with its row of baseball bats and gloves.

"Old man McLain sold out about six or seven years ago, and they remodeled the building. You'd never know it was the same place, would you?"

"It's amazing," David agreed. He wanted to ask her some more questions, but the other woman behind the counter was pointedly staring at him. Something about her reminded him of Alison. Maybe it was the pinched way she held her lips together. He strained to read the name-tag. Carol. Carol probably wasn't going to be giving him VIP treatment anytime soon.

"Well, thanks Kellie," David said as he picked up his tray of food and prepared to take it to a table.

"How did you know…oh, the name-tag. I forget I have it on sometimes. Do I get to know your name, so we're even?" Kellie asked.

"David," he said, before remembering to lie.

"Glad to meet you, David."

"Same here," David said.

He took the food to a small table and ate slowly. Several people meandered in off the street forming a line at the counter and filling some of the other tables. Loneliness and depression pressed in heavily around him. Gone was the feeling of exultation and freedom he'd felt upon leaving Boise. The small exchange with Kellie had only served to illuminate how alone he was. The thought of seeing Hank helped some, but not much. Hank wasn't going to want a lot of contact with David here in Albion. Maybe when the work here was done, he could start a normal life somewhere. David felt a little better, thinking about the job at hand. He was letting himself get distracted too easily. Going off on tangents. Letting old memories get to him. Enough of all that. It was time for action.

David polished off the rest of his sandwich, feeling the familiar urgency return in full force. It was with relief that he pushed open the heavy door and emerged into the sunlight of the afternoon.

"Boy, am I glad he's gone," Carol whispered conspiratorially as she slathered mayonnaise on half of a french roll and watched David's retreating back in triplicate through the mullioned window. "That guy gave me the creeps."

"Did he really?" Kellie glanced at Carol and noticed how tired she looked. A single mother of two, Carol led a difficult life. The premature gray in her short, frizzy black hair and the lines in her thin face were evidence of that. Today the dark circles under her eyes seemed more pronounced than usual.

"I thought he was nice. Kinda shy, but nice. There was something different about him. But he wasn't creepy, for goodness sake."

"You were just blinded by his drop-dead good looks," Carol continued, bagging the to-go order that was to be picked up imminently.

"No way. I would never be swayed by a pretty face. Besides, I didn't even notice that he was absolutely the best looking male I've ever seen that wasn't on a movie screen," Kellie replied, sounding exaggeratedly offended.

"Kellie, girl, you are hopeless," Carol laughed. "You only see the best in everybody. Shoot, I'll bet you're even polite to telephone solicitors."

"Well, they have to make a living, too," Kellie said, smiling broadly.

The tinkling of a bell announced three new customers at the door, and David was quickly forgotten.

David sat in his car, parked under the shading canopy of a towering maple, and peered at the house across the street. The modest gray cottage with white trim and midnight-blue shutters surprised him in its simplicity. There were two small windows jutting out from a steeply slanted roof, and a compact front yard that was home to a profusion of marigolds, bright red geraniums and tiny white alyssum. Lazy wisteria wrapped itself around a lamppost in the corner where sidewalk and driveway met, its glossy leaves occasionally spilling over with delicate purple flowers that hung like graceful clusters of grapes swaying softly in the breeze. 'Comfortable' and 'cozy' were words that came to mind. He'd been expecting something more grandiose, like the mini-mansions he'd seen earlier in the day. It made him wonder if Hamilton was really as rich as Hank seemed to think he was.

It was late afternoon. He'd been sitting here for at least half an hour, and so far, he'd seen nothing of interest. There was no way to tell whether or not anyone was home short of sneaking a peek in a window, and David wasn't stupid enough to chance anything like that. Eventually, though, somebody had to either come or go, and David had all day with

Bitter Reunion

absolutely nothing more important on his agenda than watching this house.

An old man with a shock of unruly white hair pedaled by on a bike. He labored under the double burden of a bulging backpack and a front bicycle basket full of groceries. Passing within inches of David's open window, he smiled, revealing several missing teeth. Then he held up his right hand, finger to forehead, in a brief salute before wobbling on down the road. David slouched lower in the seat.

It was a lazy afternoon, warm with the barest hint of a breeze rustling the leaves on the trees. The muted sounds of a driveway basketball game in progress floated on the air around him. It mixed with the aroma of early summer flowers and someone's backyard barbecue, a soothing potpourri. David closed his eyes and let the peacefulness of the moment wash over him.

As if advancing slowly from a great distance, a discordant note forced its way through the perimeters of David's consciousness. A car door slamming. With a start, David scrambled to attention and realized a car had pulled into the driveway of the Hamilton home. He'd been half asleep and almost missed it! There was now a man standing beside the driver's door of a forest-green Pontiac Grand Am. His back was to David. Resisting the temptation to stick his head out the window for a better view, David strained to see better. The man turned toward him, and for only an instant, David could swear their eyes met. Then the man completed the turn, shattering the illusion.

He looked a little older but otherwise the same. He still carried himself with confidence as he walked to the door and disappeared inside the house. A tall, well built man in a gray business suit—most would have found him attractive, but David found him loathsome. It was Hamilton alright. A monster passing for a human being. Some other poor, unfortunate kid's father, maybe, but not his. And soon, thanks to him, Hamilton wouldn't be anybody's father. Not ever again.

   David had seen what he came to see. Pain, anger, humiliation, hurt, outrage. All these emotions and more fused into a steely cold resolve, a rock solid assurance of what he must do. What he would do. David pulled onto Seventh Avenue and drove, eyes straight ahead, not looking back.

CHAPTER 7

Gina looked up from the book she'd been reading and momentarily allowed her eyes to feast upon the sight of them, the two men in her life. Ben looked just like a miniature carbon-copy of his father. They were lying on the floor, side by side, watching the Lion King. For some reason, Todd couldn't watch television sitting in a chair, like a normal person. Looked like Ben was carrying on the tradition of being a floor lounger. Both were on their stomach, chin cupped in hands and elbows resting on the oatmeal colored Berber carpet of the family room. Even Smokey was joining the act. His immodest position flat on his back and spread eagle, however, did not mimic that of the other two. Smokey's eyes were closed, and a paw twitched now and then as if he dreamed of chasing cats through tall grass.

Ben must have already seen this movie at least thirty times, but he never got tired of it. He could quote whole sections of the script verbatim and frequently did while acting the part of Simba or Timon or Pumba or all three at once.

Ben was extremely imaginative, maybe because he had no siblings to play with. Not that Gina and Todd hadn't wanted to provide him with one. Two years after Ben's birth, Gina had undergone a hysterectomy, ending their chances of having another child. Though sometimes this made Gina sad, all she had to do was look at Ben and Todd to realize she had no cause for sorrow. She had blessings enough for ten lifetimes. To demand more would be just plain greedy.

The doorbell rang. Gina set the newspaper down, and went to answer it.

"It's me," Kellie said as she burst through the door bringing the cool evening breeze with her. "I know I'm a little early, but I came straight over after work. I'm beat. Do you have anything good to eat?"

She walked to the kitchen and began to rummage through the refrigerator. Gina followed. Kellie didn't look tired to her. She looked, as always, full of life. She was wearing a baggy oversized sage-green sweatshirt and denim shorts that showed off long, lean, lightly browned legs. Bulky ribbed socks and Birkenstocks completed the look that was uniquely Pacific Northwest.

"Yuck, does somebody in this household actually eat this stuff? Don't tell me you managed to make Ben believe it'll make him strong, like Popeye." She pointed accusingly at a container. "I think feeding spinach to kids could be considered child abuse. And come to think of it, feeding it to adults could be considered adult abuse. As soon as I eat, I'm reporting you to somebody."

"Don't they ever feed you at the deli?"

"Didn't have time to eat. It got pretty busy after Brandon came on at four-thirty. In fact, I probably would have stayed to help out a couple more hours if I hadn't promised to baby-sit for you. Thanks for the excuse. On second thought, maybe I won't report you." Kellie grabbed a jar of raspberry jam and headed for the cupboard to get the peanut butter. Her culinary tastes were simple.

"So, how's Todd?" Kellie asked, turning serious.

"Pretty quiet again tonight. Maybe it'll help getting together with the K-Group.

Sometimes I don't know what we'd do without them." 'K-Group', "K" standing for Koinonea, the Greek word for fellowship, was the term used when referring to the four couples Todd and Gina met with twice a month for Bible study and mutual Christian support. "They're better than a marriage counselor and a psychiatrist put together and a heck of a lot cheaper."

"Did you realize that sometimes when you say K-Group fast, it comes out sounding like 'kegger'?" Kellie asked. "For a minute there, I thought you and Todd were going out drinking all night." It was hard for Kellie to stay totally serious for long. She scooped peanut butter from the jar with her index finger and stuck it in her mouth.

"Bmm ma mway. Aboum vacagum."

"What? And you accused me of slurring my words! Try repeating that…this time without the peanut butter. I swear, Mom and Dad must have given up on teaching table manners after they raised me."

Kellie gulped, then started over. "I said, by the way. About vacation. I thought about it, like I said I would, and my personal preference would be New England."

"Oh, I already brought the subject up with Todd over dinner. He can't get away for a vacation right now, so we decided to go to the coast for a couple of days next week. Hopefully, that will be enough to help."

"Why is it that I knew I'd find you here?" Todd asked, coming into the kitchen with his small shadow hot on his heels and Smokey bringing up the rear. He gave his sister-in-law an affectionate hug.

"Food and Kellie. The two words sort of go together, don't they?" he kidded. "Like love and marriage, horse and carriage. You can't have one without the other," Todd sang the words.

"Very funny!" Kellie punched him playfully on the arm. "Gotta fuel this tennis-playing machine, you know."

"Kellie!" Ben ran out from behind his dad and tackled her around the legs, while Smokey made his bid for attention with one short yap, tail wagging. "Do you want to play Candyland or Old Maid?"

Kellie set down the loaf of bread she was holding and swooped Ben up into a tight hug. "It doesn't matter to me. I can beat the socks off you at either one, kiddo."

"Huh uh."

"Uh huh."

"O.K. you two. No fighting now," Todd laughed as he looked at his watch. "We'd better take off." Then to his son, "You be sure to mind Aunt Kellie, Ben, and go to bed right when she tells you. No whining."

"O.K. Daddy," Ben replied. He was pulling Kellie by the hand, Mom and Dad already half forgotten. Todd looked at Gina and shook his head. "Gee honey, it's too bad that leaving Ben with a sitter is so traumatic for him."

"I know. Do you suppose we should chase after them to say good-bye or just quietly sneak off into the night?"

"Why interrupt their fun? Let's just go."

Todd and Gina walked the three blocks to the home of Sid and Kathy Simon whose turn it was to host the meeting. Sid and Kathy were Todd and Gina's closest friends. They had an eight year old daughter, Jaimie, and a son, Kevin, who was Ben's age. Many golden moments had been spent with the Simons. Trips to the

Bitter Reunion

beach, picnics in the park, playing Uno with the kids, or Pinochle without them. Their friendship was invaluable.

Mark and Carolyn Matthews were already there when Todd and Gina arrived. Moments later, Pete and Juanita Chambers joined the group, bringing with them the news that the fifth couple, John and Annemarie Nesbaum, wouldn't be coming tonight.

As usual, the first half hour was full of catching up with each others lives, laughing and joking and celebrating being together again. Usually the next twenty minutes or so were devoted to prayer and the remaining time was spent on some sort of Bible study. Flexibility was a given, though, and sometimes the group never made it beyond prayer time. No one had a problem with scrapping the study time entirely if sharing the burdens of the week took longer than usual, or if one of them needed extra time and help grappling with a problem. They provided each other with one of life's most basic needs—a listening ear. Encouragement and sound advise were by-products.

Nita and Pete were responsible for many a missed study. The two of them credited the K-Group with the fact that they were still married. Both having come to the Lord within the past five years, they struggled constantly to erase the ingrained patterns of the old, destructive habits they'd spent a lifetime building. Financial problems and the challenges of parenting three small children made them even more needful of the group's support.

The term "opposites attract" certainly did not apply to Nita and Pete who were cut from the same cloth. They were both loud, boisterous extroverts with unvarnished manners and still occasionally salty language. In physical looks they were bookends. Both were short with rounded bodies and rounded features, like the Pillsbury Doughboy, and both wore glasses. As if to provide Pete with a unique characteristic of his own, his hair was bright red and being prematurely pushed back by an ever expanding forehead. One day soon, his receding hairline would transcend to baldness.

The group was now seated in a circle around the living room sharing their prayer needs. Pete was saying, "So, I found out yesterday I made that promotion to foreman. I want to thank you guys for prayin' for me. I kept tellin' myself that if I didn't get it, it would be O.K., that the Lord had something else in mind for me, like you said, Mark. But I gotta admit, I'm glad the Lord was wanting me to have this job."

"We're so excited!" Nita joined in, almost bouncing off her chair. "We can start paying off some of those bills, if only Pete doesn't go deciding he has to have a new motorcycle or something." The way Pete spent money was a subject the group had heard a lot about.

"Nita's right. You could pray that I won't blow the money," Pete said. It was a sign of his growing maturity that he was willing even to admit his weakness. There had been a time when he had denied, rationalized and fought it. "Not to brag or nothin', but we've been tithing for almost a year now. The Bible is really right when it says God will bless you for it. Things have been going a lot better for us."

"That's because you're putting God first and trusting Him with your finances," Kathy said.

Bitter Reunion

"It's not always an easy thing to do, but it's the only way to truly experience all God wants to give you."

"Yeah, we're puttin' our money where our mouth is," Pete said. "And it feels pretty good."

Mark and Carolyn were next in the circle to share. Diminutive of size and with delicate features, Carolyn emitted a false aura of fragility. Those who knew her well knew that she was really a rock instead of the Dresden doll she resembled. They all, at one time or another, had benefitted from her unflagging energy and solid common sense. Mark was the comedian of the bunch, specializing in practical jokes and bad puns. The two of them had three teenagers, twin girls and a boy. That, in itself, was grist for the prayer mill. As they shared their concerns about the boy that seventeen year old Melody was dating, Gina glanced at Todd sitting quietly on the folding chair at her side. She hoped he'd be able to open up about how he was feeling. It would help. He'd barely said a word since they got here, and she knew he was preoccupied with something. It had to be Joey.

It wasn't long before she found out she was wrong. It wasn't Joey at all. Todd's turn was next, and he began by saying, "I've been debating whether or not to say anything about this. I haven't even discussed it with Gina, yet." His eyes met Gina's in a look of apology. "But I'd like you to be praying for me about it." He shifted on the chair and paused, searching for the best way to say it. Absentmindedly, he combed the fingers of his right hand through his sandy hair, a lock of which fell into his eyes. He brushed it aside.

"I've gotten two threatening letters recently. They're probably nothing but a little harassment," he hastened to add, "but I'd feel better just knowing you were praying about it."

It wasn't at all what Gina had expected Todd to say. She was speechless as someone expressed outrage and someone else asked who the letters were from and what they were about.

"I don't know who they're from. They're anonymous," Todd answered. "As far as what they're about, well, the word "homophobe" crops up in them every so often. I guess I made the mistake of not being politically correct."

It had begun three weeks earlier in Todd's office at H & H. His secretary had buzzed to inform him that a Mr. Howard Sneed wished to talk to Todd about a charity event. Todd had agreed to see him, and Sneed was ushered into the office.

He was a compact man of about thirty-five, dressed conservatively in an expensive looking gray suit, shiny black Oxfords and a red silk tie. He had a firm, no-nonsense handshake and a direct stare from steely blue eyes.

Once he was seated, he got right to the point.

"It's good to meet you, Mr. Hamilton. I'm Howard Sneed, chairman of the fund-raising committee for ARA which stands for Aids Research and Awareness. Thank you for sparing me a few minutes of your time." He went on to briefly describe the five-hundred-dollar-a-plate banquet that was to be held in Portland to raise money for AIDS research and ended with a plea for Todd's active participation in the form of money.

"I'm sure I can count on your support, Mr. Hamilton. You are well-known for your generosity in donating to worthy causes, and today there isn't a more urgent concern than the spread of AIDS."

"Do you mind if I ask you a few questions, Mr. Sneed?" Todd asked, leaning forward on his chair.

"Of course not."

"If I should donate my money to ARA, what will it be used for, specifically?"

"Research into finding a cure for AIDS."

"Until a cure is found," Todd persisted, "or if, as in the case of cancer and the common cold, a cure isn't found for decades or never, despite all your research…what then?"

"What do you mean?"

"I mean, what is ARA doing to prevent the spread of AIDS in the eventuality that prevention is the best weapon?"

"Well, we've already had breakthroughs in terms of prolonging life and we feel sure that a cure is on the way, but of course, we also fund education in AIDS prevention," Sneed said, beginning to sound slightly annoyed with Todd's questions.

"And the message of this education in prevention is…what?" Todd continued.

"Why, condom use and spreading awareness of the danger in sharing needles. I'm sure you've seen some of our commercials to that effect on television."

"Yes, I've seen them," Todd said. "And no, I'm sorry, but I don't think I'm interested in contributing to your cause."

Anger registered plainly on Sneed's face. He clearly didn't like to be turned away empty-handed. "I don't understand," he said. "Don't you want to see AIDS wiped out? Do you realize how many people are dying from it every day?"

"Don't get me wrong, Mr. Sneed. I would love to see AIDS eradicated. But we seem to have a fundamental disagreement when it comes to methods." Todd went on, "Have you ever considered the fact that if every person were monogamous, limiting themselves to one sexual partner for life, this disease could virtually disappear in a relatively short period of time? You should keep looking for that cure, but I think you should also be advocating abstinence outside of marriage and faithfulness within it. Until you begin doing that, I'll confine my contributions to helping find cures for deadly diseases which aren't preventable."

Todd hadn't expected Howard Sneed to agree with him, but he was surprised at the vehemence of the man's reaction. He swiftly rose from his chair, and, palms on the desk that separated them, leaned toward Todd. Their faces only inches apart, Todd could smell the fragrance of Sneed's aftershave and see the evidence that he'd nicked himself shaving this morning.

"I know what this is really all about," Sneed hissed. "You're homophobic, aren't you?"

"You're out of line to even ask me that question," Todd said, straining to keep any hint of anger out of his voice. "But since you've asked, I'll tell you." He casually opened a desk drawer and withdrew a rather large, black book. Then he stood to meet the challenging glare focused upon him.

"I'm not afraid of homosexuals and I don't hate them, so depending on how you define homophobia, I don't think I suffer from it.

And I'd never persecute anyone or refuse to hire them because of their sexual preference. But that doesn't mean I approve of the practice of homosexuality. Far from it. Most cases of AIDS are transmitted by male homosexuals. That should be reason enough to conclude that a homosexual lifestyle isn't healthy. And I fail to see how any person familiar with the rudimentary concepts of biology could believe that homosexuality isn't unnatural."

"But, Mr. Hamilton!" Sneed was all but shouting in an effort to interrupt.

"Let me finish," Todd said firmly. "You're the one that forced the issue."

Resigned, at least for the moment, Sneed sat back down in the chair.

"I only mention these reasons because the most important one I have for not condoning homosexuality probably won't mean anything to you." Todd set the book down on the desk. The words "Holy Bible" seemed to jump off the cover. "I'm a Christian."

"I wouldn't have taken you for a religious fanatic," Sneed mumbled.

Ignoring him, Todd continued, "I believe this book is God's word, given to us for our good. It's really that simple for me. The Bible says God created woman for man. That's the way it should be, sexually speaking. Not man for man, or woman for woman. You can call homosexuality an 'alternate lifestyle' all you want, but I still call it perversion. If you call black, white long enough, some people will buy it, but that doesn't mean that the color of black has changed, only that the terminology has."

Todd continued over Sneed's obvious outrage. "The Bible also calls homosexuality a sin, and

God warns us against sin because it destroys us. In lots of different ways."

"Frankly, I'm surprised that a man of your intelligence is so narrow-minded and judgmental," Sneed finally managed to interject.

"Unfortunately, that's the way most of us who take God's word seriously are viewed," Todd responded, in a curiously calm manner. "But you're wrong. I judge myself by the same standards and that makes me a sinner, too." For the first time, he sensed he had Sneed's full attention. "Oh, I'm not a homosexual, but the sin I commit is no less serious in the eyes of God."

"What are you saying, then? I don't get it," Sneed said.

"Listen, the Bible tells us what sin is and that we're all guilty of it. But it doesn't stop there. It also tells us of the remedy for sin which God Himself provided out of His love for us. He sent His only Son, Jesus Christ, to die in order to pay the price for our sin."

Howard Sneed was looking skeptical again. Todd hurried on before he could object. "But there are conditions. We can't receive Christ's gift unless we admit to our sin and repent of it. When we do, God helps us to overcome the power of sin in our lives. Condoning homosexuality doesn't do the homosexual any favors. It just keeps him from seeking out the forgiveness and help he really needs from the only one powerful and loving enough to give it."

"Are you finished?" Sneed asked abruptly, standing again. "I didn't come here for a sermon, and since you haven't enough compassion to donate any money, I might as well be on my way." He turned his back on the Bible and on Todd and headed for the door.

"True compassion encompasses the needs of the soul, Mr. Sneed," Todd said softly. "Not just the body." The sound of the door slamming was Howard Sneed's answer.

Silence covered the room like a lead blanket when Todd finished recounting the meeting with Mr. Sneed. Carolyn was the first one to break it. "It's so hard for them to consider having to give up their lifestyle," she said and shook her head sadly. Everyone knew that Carolyn's sister, whom she loved dearly, was a lesbian. "And it's so hard for us to walk the fine line between unconditional love and standing firm in our convictions."

Todd cleared his throat before he continued. "About a week after that meeting, I got my first letter. Well, really just a note. It was typewritten and postmarked out of Portland. About all it said was 'You made a big mistake. You'll pay for being a homophobe.' Words to that effect." He wasn't about to tell them exactly what the letter had said.

"I threw it away. Then I got another one last week. It was pretty much the same. I called Howard Sneed, and without accusing him of sending them, I made it pretty clear that the notes must be a result of our meeting. He adamantly denied any involvement and hung up on me."

For the first time since the announcement of the existence of the letters, Gina spoke. "Todd, I wish you had told me about this. It's scary. I think we should call the police and let them know about it." Several in the group nodded agreement.

"I thought of that," Todd said, "but you all know I don't have much faith in the police, after what happened with Joey. I'd be surprised if they'd be able to do anything about the letters until an actual crime was committed. Besides, I'd like to keep a low-profile on this. I don't want to see the media get wind of it. They'll escalate it into a 'hate' issue, and who knows which side will end up sounding like the bad guy. Besides, I have a feeling it's nothing but a scare tactic, and soon the nut sending these notes will get bored and that will be the end of it. It's been over a week since I got the last one."

"Geez, I just can't believe it! This world is full of sicko's!" Pete was hopping mad and his face matched his flaming red hair to prove it. He loved everyone in this room, and the fact that someone was threatening one of them was unthinkable. "I wish I knew the stupid shi… I mean the scum that was doing this. I'd like to get my hands on him."

"Violence isn't the answer, Pete," Sid said. "It's the problem. Let's all take this situation to the Lord." Sid bowed his head, and the rest followed suit. Then, one by one, they prayed.

Later, after returning home and saying good-bye to Kellie, Todd and Gina lay beside each other in bed, their hands intertwined.

"Todd, are you sure there isn't anything to be afraid of? It's unnerving to think that someone out there hates you enough to send you those letters." Gina said quietly.

"Honey, maybe it wouldn't hurt to be extra observant and careful for a little while, but I don't want you to worry. I really think the letters are just a scare tactic. There's bound to be opposition when we stand up for our beliefs, especially on an issue as volatile as this one. We'll just have to trust God to protect us."

"You're a good man, Todd Hamilton," Gina replied. "And a wise one, too."

They kissed, and Gina snuggled closer to him and closed her eyes. It wasn't long before her deep, even breathing wordlessly proclaimed that she was asleep. But Todd lay awake, the luxury of sleep elusive. Phrases kept playing themselves back in his mind. "Homophobes deserve to die. You'll regret the day you were born. Watch your back, gay-basher." He tried not to recall the crude profanity that had punctuated the letters, but they too kept coming back, refusing to leave him alone.

If only he were half as confident as he had sounded to Gina and their friends. But he knew from experience that bad things happened to those that loved the Lord, just as they did to everyone else. Why couldn't he have just gone along with Howard Sneed? Would it really have hurt him to donate some money to AIDS research? Was voicing his opinion worth the risk of putting his family in jeopardy?

"Oh, Lord," he whispered in the dark, "I don't know if I could stand it if anything were to happen to Gina or Ben. I really don't." Then, as they did every night of his life, his thoughts turned to Joey. "Please be with him, God, wherever he is."

CHAPTER 8

It was late by the time David pulled back into the driveway of the small house on Sherman Street. Night was stealthily creeping into the landscape, turning it into a shadowy oasis in muted shades of gray. The overgrown branch of a lilac tree reached out and swept across the windshield as he turned into the partially cleared space that passed for a yard. Hank's car, a white Ford Tempo, was already parked under the roof of the carport.

"Well, it's about time you showed up," Hank said, as David stepped into the living room, struggling to juggle three brown sacks of groceries while maneuvering around the door. The glow of a cigarette punctuated the spot where Hank sat in the gathering darkness. "Been out partying or something?"

"Hi, Pa," David said in greeting, glad to see him. "I had to get some food and stuff. There wasn't anything in the kitchen."

Hank continued to sit and smoke silently while David put away the groceries and then returned to join him. "It's dark in here," David said. He switched on a lamp and sat on the couch next to it, across from Hank.

David allowed the silence to reign until Hank spoke. "I've had a productive three weeks," he said without preamble. He rubbed out the remaining embers of his cigarette on the flat surface of the end table before elaborating. "I think things are pretty well set up for the job, and I've brought you a care package that you'll be needing to complete it." He gestured to a box placed unobtrusively on the floor by his feet.

"First, though, I'll fill you in on what I've been doing."

"I'm renting a ritzy place on the other side of town, and got myself a membership at the country club. You know the routine."

David did. It was the usual way Hank got acquainted with wealthy women in the cat-and-mouse con games he played.

"I managed to get in thick with this broad who somehow knows everything about everyone in Albion. Her name is…get this…Belinda Montgomery. Even sounds rich, doesn't it?" Hank smiled slyly. "I've learned some very interesting things from Belinda."

"About Hamilton?"

"About Hamilton. First, he's every bit as rich as I suspected. According to Belinda, he has tons of money, but you'd never know it."

David remembered wondering why Hamilton lived in such a modest house.

"In Belinda's circle, Hamilton is considered eccentric because he doesn't flaunt his wealth," Hank went on. "That is not, by the way, a problem we're going to have when we're rich. I think flaunting is going to come real easy for me. What's money for if you can't have a little fun with it?

"In fact, Belinda says Hamilton loves to give his money away. Seems like every charity in the country has taken him for a bundle. Except one," he said with sudden relish. "He flat-out refused to give a dime to some AIDS outfit that hit him up a few weeks ago. Can you believe it? Of all the organizations to hold out on! The red-ribbon crowd wouldn't like it a bit. Good thing he doesn't live in Hollywood." Hank chuckled.

David was having trouble figuring out why Hank was sounding so excited about Hamilton not contributing to an AIDS organization. Other than the fact that Hank hated homosexuals, calling them fags and queers, it didn't have much to do with why they were here.

"Anyway, it gave me this great idea. Twice in the last couple of weeks, I made a little trip up to Portland where the organization is based. I found a library there and used their typewriter to write some pretty graphic threat letters to Hamilton all about how he was going to pay for being a homophobe. Then I mailed them to him from there."

The light was beginning to dawn. It really was a stroke of luck, David realized, that Hank had stumbled onto the perfect way to divert suspicion away from them for what they were planning to do. After the kidnapping, the police would naturally suspect the letter writer, who they would conclude was a member of some fanatic fringe of the homosexual community. No wonder Hank was fairly beside himself with glee.

"What do you think?" Hank asked.

"I think you're a genius."

"Absolutely right. Got any beer in the kitchen?" Hank asked, changing the subject momentarily.

"Not cold," David answered.

"I don't care. I'll drink it anyway. It's stuffy in here. Open a window and get me a can of beer."

When David returned from the kitchen, Hank was bending over the box that he had earlier called his care package.

"Come over here and let me show you what I brought," he said, beckoning to David. He picked up the box, set it on the end table and removed its lid. Then, he took the can David

Bitter Reunion

offered him, popped the top and chugged thirstily. Wiping his mouth with the back of his hand, he put down the can and reached into the box. As he took out the contents, he spread them out on the couch. A coil of white rope, some rags, a bottle of pills, another small bottle, a bulging envelope and...a gun. Shiny, black and lethal, looking out of place against the rust and gold floral print of the couch. Like a lion in a pet store. David couldn't take his eyes off it. He reached over and picked it up.

"She's a beauty, isn't she?" Hank said with something like reverence.

"She sure is."

David had seen this gun before, but he had never held it in his hands. Hank had three guns. This one, a Colt 45, was the gun he had wrestled from the grip of a man who had tried to kill him.

"This one's dead accurate," Hank said, smiling at the pun. "It shouldn't take more than one shot." Hank had spent hours out in the Idaho desert teaching David how to shoot a pistol, and David, always a quick learner, had become a master sharpshooter, even by Hank's standards. "It's already loaded, by the way, and I didn't bring extra ammunition. Won't be needing it.

"I guess you can figure out what to do with the gun. As for the rest of this stuff, you probably know what to do with it, too. The rope's for tying up the kid if you need to. Those are sleeping pills to keep him quiet and out of trouble while we're holding him for ransom."

Hank picked up the other bottle. "This is chloroform. Wasn't easy to get, believe me. When you snatch the kid, just hold a rag soaked with it against his nose and he'll be out like a light. He won't be yelling or screaming and getting attention. There isn't much of it, so don't waste it." He put the chloroform back in the box and handed David the ordinary white envelope. David lifted the flap, which wasn't glued down. Inside was a thick bundle of green bills. "That ought to get you through till the job is done," Hank said. "Any questions?"

"When do you want me to kidnap the kid?" David asked.

"Anytime. But I'm warning you. Don't act impulsively. Watch and wait till the right moment. It could take days, even weeks, but we have plenty of time so don't rush it. Try to get the kid by himself or when the mother's distracted. I don't, and I repeat, don't, want you to get caught in the act of kidnapping him. That would be the end of everything."

"I won't let that happen," David said defensively.

"One more question. Once I've got him, I'm supposed to bring him here, right?"

"Right. Then call me. Here's my number." Hank reached into a shirt pocket and extracted a piece of paper with a phone number on it and gave it to David. "Call me from here only when necessary. It's better to call from a pay phone."

"O.K. I think I have everything straight." David inhaled a deep breath. He was on the brink. It felt like standing on the edge of a rocky cliff just before plunging into the inky water far, far below. Exhilarating and liberating, but frightening.

"Good. I'll be waiting to hear from you." Hank raised his right arm and rested it upon David's shoulders in the closest thing to a

Bitter Reunion

hug David had ever known him to give. Then he surprised David even more by saying, "I'm proud of you, Son. If this job is successful, and I'm sure it will be, I want you to have that gun. My gift to you." Then, before David had a chance to respond, Hank withdrew his arm and walked briskly to the door. "Good luck," he said and was gone.

David returned all the items to the box except the gun. Suddenly exhausted, he fell back onto the couch and laid his head against the cushion, gun in his lap. He was drained, too tired to lift his body from this spot. His mind wandered, fragmented thoughts languidly entering and exiting without conscious effort. He wouldn't let Hank down. No matter what, he wouldn't let him down. Hank cared about him. He was the only one that ever had. David stroked the pistol in his lap lovingly, as if it were a favorite cat. The gun was smooth and silky. It felt like power. He could see himself raising it. He was pointing it at Todd Hamilton's heart. His finger was slowly tightening. And then, inexplicably, the image changed. For the briefest instant, he saw a brilliant smile and a pair of sparkling brown eyes. The girl from the deli. Suddenly sleep descended like a huge black vulture, snatching her away and leaving nothing but darkness in her place.

CHAPTER 9

Friday, June 23

From his vantage point a block and a half away and around the corner, David peered through a pair of binoculars that still had a price tag hanging from it. This job was proving to be harder and, paradoxically, more tedious than he had anticipated.

There weren't that many hiding places or ways to disguise what he was doing. This was a residential area, and David couldn't stay in one place for too long a period of time for fear of attracting attention. Nothing was guaranteed to arouse suspicion quite like a guy with a pair of binoculars raised to his face. There probably weren't that many bird watchers in this part of town.

His bright red car didn't making the job any easier, either. It was so glaringly noticeable. This was only the second day on the watch, and already David half expected a policeman to pull up beside him at any moment. It was probably just paranoia, but it seemed as though every person that strolled by, enjoying another beautiful June day, looked at him in a peculiar way.

Adding frustration to uneasiness was the fact that he hadn't come even close to having an opportunity to snatch the kid. Most of his time had been spent doing exactly what he was doing now, watching the house. There was only one word for it. Boring. For David, whose need for retaliation grew more intense with every passing moment, this waiting was tantamount to slow, excruciating torture.

Bitter Reunion

There had only been two small reprieves from the mind-numbing boredom, and both had occurred yesterday. The first was in the morning, as he was reconnoitering on foot, and it had uncovered yet another problem. David had discovered that the Hamilton back yard was a veritable fortress, enclosed within the walls of a six-foot high cedar fence. Crouched low in the cover of weeds and undergrowth that fringed the alley behind the house, he had peeked through an oversized knothole and had been surprised to see his prey for the first time. David's pulse had raced at the unexpected sight of the child standing only a few feet beyond the barrier that separated them. It had been frustrating beyond words to be so close to him without being able to do anything about it.

And then he'd seen her. A floppy straw hat had covered her head, shading her face as she dragged a hose around, watering the rhododendrons, azaleas and shrubs bordering the yard. Despite the hat, dowdy work clothes and floppy thongs, David could see Hamilton had done well for himself. She was very pretty, in a quiet, understated way. He'd realized that she bore a resemblance to the fuzzy image he retained in his mind of Elaine, but Elaine had been flamboyant and brash. Gina was softer and somehow younger looking, though surely she was at least as old as Elaine had been when she died. She was too good for Hamilton, that much was clear. David had searched his memory for her name, and it had come to him. Gina.

For about an hour he had watched them, hoping Gina would go back inside the house, but wondering what he would do if she did. He'd come prepared. A rag and the bottle of chloroform were stuffed deep in his jeans pocket. He'd been able to see the gate to the fence across the yard, though, and his heart had sunk. Even from where he was, the latch that locked it from the inside had been visible. Could he possibly scale the fence, get to the boy before he yelled, and carry him out through the gate before she came back? He'd thought it doubtful.

Ben was cute as the picture had indicated. The picture, however, hadn't even begun to convey the spirited animation of the real live boy. He seemed to be in perpetual motion as he swung high in the air, hung from his knees, built something indistinguishable inside a yellow-edged sandbox and rolled squealing with laughter in the grass with a small but feisty mutt.

David wondered if he had ever been that carefree. If so, it had been in another lifetime.

By the time mother and son had joined hands and gone back inside the house, sharp pains had begun to shoot up David's cramped legs and he'd barely been able to straighten up. He'd also known as he'd walked slowly back to his car that kidnapping Ben was going to be a lot tougher than he'd thought. It had only taken a few minutes to see that Gina was much less like Elaine in her mothering instincts than she was in her physical appearance.

Elaine had been known to actually lock him out of the house when she didn't want to be bothered. She had seldom been aware of where her son was or what he was doing. But the way Gina had chatted with her son, touched him and looked at him, you could tell that she wasn't one to leave him unattended for long.

Bitter Reunion

The second incident had reinforced that conclusion. At one point in the afternoon, the garage door had risen, and a burgundy Ford Windstar had emerged from within the yawning black hole it created. Following the van from what he hoped was a safe distance, David had ended up at the grocery store where he had spent another futile hour. Tracking Gina and Ben, with their burdensome shopping cart, had been easy. Catching them apart was not. Never once did Gina allow Ben to wander far from her side. The only thing David ended up having to show for his efforts was two bags of groceries full of great things to snack on while wasting hours of time staring at an empty-looking house. After following the pair back to the safety of their homey little refuge, a despondent David had given up for the day. He had stopped to purchase the binoculars on his way home.

As he reflected on yesterday's discoveries and defeats, David tried not to despair. After all, this was only day two in what could be a long, arduous wait. He'd get a break eventually, if he could just be patient.

It was mid morning when, through the lens of the miniature binoculars, the familiar Windstar once again appeared. David felt a surge of optimism. The engine of the bright red Camero roared to life as he turned his key in the ignition.

....

The phones weren't exactly ringing off the hook at the Crisis Pregnancy Center. Gina debated whether that was a good sign or a bad one. It could mean there weren't that many women out there who found themselves unhappily pregnant. That was the best case scenario. Unfortunately, it could also mean abortion clinics were going to be extra busy because no one was looking for an alternative.

Every Friday, Gina and Kathy dropped their children off at the Matthew's to be watched by one or both of the twins while they volunteered their services at the center. It was their small way of joining in on the battle to save lives.

Ironically, at a time in history when organizations lobbied vigorously and loudly for animal rights and the government drafted laws to protect endangered species and their offspring, laws were also drafted that made unborn human babies expendable, of no comparative value.

But what was even more incomprehensible in Gina's mind was that any woman could actually chose to destroy the miracle of life that was forming within her. The protectiveness she'd felt for Ben had begun long before his birth. She'd never been so careful about what she ate and drank and the activities she engaged in as when she was pregnant. It had bordered on paranoia. The moment her son had been born healthy and whole was one of the most victorious and wondrous of her life.

Gina's abhorrence for abortion was so strong that it was sometimes hard for her to feel compassion for the scared and confused women, often mere girls themselves, who were considering it as an option. But compassion was the key to gaining their trust and helping them conquer their fear. It had to be genuine. That's why Gina prayed for God's compassion to flow through her whenever she answered the pregnancy hotline.

Bitter Reunion

The center was located in an old house on the outskirts of downtown. It's furnishings were homey, in keeping with the setting and the need for an intimate atmosphere in which to work with troubled women. There was always plenty to do at the center besides answering the phone. The local, church-supported organization had only one full time paid employee, Charlene Monroe, whose job it was to organize and utilize volunteer help. Charlene was a pro at her job. No one could foster a willingness to help in others quite like she did. Maybe it was because at sixty-three with graying hair that she wore in a loose bun on the top of her head and wire-rim glasses that tended to slide down on her nose, she looked and acted like every person's idea of a grandmother, which in fact she was five times over. Her ample lap seemed custom-made to hold a child. She wore a constant smile and had an infectious enthusiasm for life in general and the center in particular.

At the moment, Charlene was in her office, a room that had once been a bedroom and was located directly off the large front room. It's door was wide open, and Gina occasionally heard snatches of Charlene's side of an animated telephone conversation. It sounded as though she was speaking to someone who was hoping for a chance to adopt an infant. Words like *frustration, wait, patience, and keep trying* kept coming up. Gina's heart went out to the person on the other end of the line. She could only imagine how heartbreaking it must be to want a child so badly and not be able to have one. That's what kept Todd and her from adding their own names to the list of those waiting to adopt. They at least had one child, and they didn't want to keep someone else from knowing the joy they knew.

"Has Todd gotten any more of those awful letters?" Kathy asked, looking up from a pile of correspondence she was sorting.

"No, thank goodness. I'm beginning to think there won't be any more."

"I sure hope not. Sometimes I can't understand what this country has come to. Gina, do you ever wish you had been born about fifty years earlier?" Kathy posed the question seriously. "I mean, America used to uphold the family and lift up Biblical morality as a standard. Now it seems as if everything has been turned upside down, and those things are ridiculed, if not condemned. It's getting harder all the time. I feel as if I have to monitor everything, especially where the kids are concerned. Movies, television, what Jaimie's being taught in school and told by her friends. The list goes on and on. I just get so tired of being a morally outraged drill sergeant."

Gina had to smile at the idea of Kathy as a drill sergeant. She was nothing if not feminine, and Gina had seldom heard her raise her voice.

"I know what you mean. I…" Gina began, when the ring of the telephone on her desk interrupted her in mid-sentence. She let it ring once more as she silently prayed.

"Crisis Pregnancy Center. This is Gina."

"Hi." The voice was hesitant, but mature. "My name is Sylvia. I feel a little foolish about calling."

"Please don't," Gina said. "You've made the right decision to call. It never hurts to talk things over, and I would really like to help if I can."

Bitter Reunion

"Well, O.K. I don't know where to start."

"Wherever you like. Just tell me why you needed someone to talk to."

"I found out last week that I'm pregnant," the voice said, matter-of-factly. "I'm forty-one years old. My youngest child will be graduating from high school in two years. I just can't face starting over again at my age."

"Sylvia, I can't say that I know how you feel, because I don't," Gina began. "I do know women who have been in your situation, though. My own mother is one of them. My sister was born when I was sixteen and Mom was thirty-nine. She struggled with the idea of raising another child, too. I can give you her name and phone number. She would be more than happy to share her experiences with you. One thing I can tell you. She has never regretted having given birth to my sister."

"But what if I decide not to? Have my baby, that is. Can you recommend someone to do an abortion?"

"I'll be straight with you. Our job is to provide alternatives to abortion, partly because we're pro-life, but also because abortion damages the women who undergo it. And not just physically. It can, and most often does, leave lasting emotional scars. You said you have other children?"

"Yes, three," Sylvia said quietly. "One is married herself and thinking about starting a family."

"Well, Sylvia, what if the circumstances had been such that you had chosen to abort one of them. They wouldn't be here now living the lives that you allowed them to enjoy. And you would have never had the chance to know and to love them."

"I know. I've thought about that."

"Someday," Gina continued, sensing that she was making progress with Sylvia, "if you have this child, it will be just as inconceivable for you to imagine life without him."

"It's not that simple," Sylvia interrupted, and now she was sounding near tears, a small quiver in her voice. She hesitated, then reluctantly continued. "I'm a married woman. My husband had a vasectomy years ago. This isn't his baby that I'm carrying."

For a moment there was silence on the line as Gina tried to absorb the new twist in the conversation.

"That raises some questions," she said gently. "Do you want to save your marriage?"

"Oh, yes," came the heartfelt reply. "The affair was a big mistake. I realize it now. I was just thinking I could have an abortion, and Larry would never have to know about it."

"You realize, don't you, what a huge deception that would be. It would be bound to undermine your relationship. No matter what you do about the pregnancy, you need to tell your husband. I can give you the name of a good marriage counselor who can advise you on how to break the news and help you repair your marriage afterwards."

"Even if Larry doesn't leave me, he would never raise another man's child," Sylvia said, forlornly. "How could I ask him to? Every time he looked at the baby it would be like a slap in the face." Sylvia began to softly sob.

"Then, please, for the baby's sake, consider adoption. We aren't interested in seeing children brought into the world only to be unloved or abused, and there's no reason that should ever happen. You'd be amazed how long the list is of couples who are desperate to adopt. I know it would be very hard for you and your husband to go through the nine months of your pregnancy. But it's a sacrifice that would mean life for the child and untold joy for some couple who has never held a baby of their own in their arms." Gina spoke with the conviction of one who believed what she was saying with all her heart. "And you would know you did all you could for your child. Don't add one more layer of guilt to the load you're already carrying."

"You're right. I know you're right," Sylvia said, between sniffles. "I just don't know if I'm strong enough to go through with it. What will my children think…my friends? I've made such a mess of everything!"

"Sylvia, you can't undo what's already done, but you can keep from making it worse. You can turn it around. Believe me, something good can come from all of this, and we're here to help you see that it does. Would you come in and let us talk with you some more? Please."

Gina breathed an inaudible sigh of relief when Sylvia agreed and set a time to come in on Monday. Now if only she followed through. So many of them never did. Satan, working overtime. But if she made it in, Charlene would talk to her, and Charlene had more ammunition against Satan than anyone Gina knew.

The rest of the afternoon went by without incident. At three-thirty, two other recruits showed up for duty, and ten minutes later Gina and Kathy pulled up to the curb in front of Carolyn's house. It was one of the twins who met them at the door. Even though Gina could usually tell which identical twin was which, today it was impossible to know who it was standing in front of her. The girl had a cordless phone to her ear, a greenish-brown mud pack on her face and half of her hair rolled up in pink spongy curlers, making her look like a lopsided alien from outer space. Gesturing toward the side of the house, she said, "Melissa's in the back with them." Then, "No, I'm not talking to you, Shawn. Had to answer the door." She waved at them absentmindedly and shut the door in their faces.

Out back, giddy bedlam reigned. Along with Jaimie, Ben and Kevin, there seemed to be three or four extra children. They were running around in a game of armed tag, their moving bodies impossible to count. Melissa sat in a lawn chair reading a magazine and sipping on a tall glass of lemonade, seemingly impervious to the chaos around her. "I gave them squirt guns," she said to Gina and Kathy as they paid her. "I hope you don't mind."

"No, that's fine," said Gina, enjoying the sight of the children at play.

They were having such a good time. Their squeals of laughter transformed an ordinary afternoon into something poignantly magical.

With a sudden pang, Gina thought of Sylvia and the decision she was about to make. Focusing on Ben, who had noticed her arrival and broken away from the pack, she wondered what her life would have been like without him. To think that with one choice she could have caused him to never be born, irrevocably altering the course of so many lives forever—it was frightening to even imagine.

Moments later, the women began to load the children into the minivan. From his slightly soggy condition, it appeared that Kevin had taken more than his fair share of hits from watery weapons.

Bitter Reunion

"Hold up, everybody! You better unload those guns," Gina said.

She watched as water was drained from the last of the plastic toys, and then herded their owners into the sliding side door of the van. Kathy made sure the children were buckled in, as Gina walked around to the driver's side. Just as she slammed her door, a bright red car pulled around the corner, but she had turned toward Kathy and didn't see it.

CHAPTER 10

Saturday, June 24

He never thought he'd see the day, but David was getting sick of his car. It was starting to feel like a prison, the confines of which was causing claustrophobia to set in. Littering the front seat were empty wrappers, pop cans, magazines and newspapers, and he'd eaten so many Twinkies and Slim Jims that he was sick of them, too. In fact, he was sick of this whole tedious waiting game. There had to be a better way to carry off a kidnapping. There just had to be.

The trouble was, he was out of his element here. He had no idea what he was doing, and there wasn't anyplace to go for classes to learn how to do it right. Kidnapping 101. That's what he needed. If something didn't break today, he was going to call Hank. Maybe the two of them could come up with another way to get to the kid, by working together.

David wondered how Hank was spending his time. He hadn't contacted David since the other night, and David had been hesitant to call him unless there was an emergency. Well, Hank would probably be mad, but David really needed to talk to him. He hated to admit it, but he couldn't stand this much longer. He was used to being too active to reflect on his past. He liked it that way. With all this time on his hands, it was getting hard to keep the demons at bay. Too many memories crept into the front seat of the Camero with him, and with each one, his anger grew hotter and harder to control.

Bitter Reunion

Strangely enough, it was the best memories that were the worst. Like the time Joey and his dad had traveled to Seattle to take in a Mariner's game. He hadn't thought of that day for years, but for some reason, it had popped into his mind today. David remembered how they had browsed the farmer's market downtown and then toured the waterfront and the site of the 1962 World's Fair. He could almost see the Space Needle again, through the eyes of the eight-year-old child that he had been. Rising skyward till it seemed to touch the clouds, it had looked like something from another world, and he had been mesmerized by it. But even it had been totally eclipsed when later in the day they had arrived at the King Dome and seen professional baseball at its best. He could no longer remember what team the Mariners had played against, but he would never forget how he had felt, sitting high in the stadium, on top of the world. He was like a balloon being filled with so much wonder, excitement and happiness that he thought he would burst. It had been the highlight of Joey's short life. A big part of the reason was that he had shared it with his dad.

It should have been a good memory. It had been until that day in July when all of the happy times he had ever spent with his father were rendered null and void. It was worse than if they had never happened at all, because they'd ended so abruptly and finally. And because they'd been built on a lie.

Now the memories haunted him, and he knew that if he had to sit around like this much longer, they would push him into doing something stupid, but sitting seemed to be all he could do. That and driving.

Deborah Barlow

Yesterday, he'd tailed the van and watched as Gina picked up a woman and two kids, then dropped off all the kids at another house. He'd been hopeful when a slight, fragile-looking teenager he assumed was the baby-sitter had eventually emerged from the house, followed by about half a dozen kids of assorted gender and size, one of which was Ben. But short of snatching the boy out from under all their noses, there hadn't been a chance of getting to him. Maybe he should have tried it. He was beginning to think it would turn out to have been his best shot. At least the girl had been young, and half of the time she'd been so intent on her magazine she probably wouldn't have noticed if her lawn chair were on fire.

After that, he'd followed Gina seemingly all over town. Dropping off the dark haired woman and her kids, another stop at another grocery store, and then the library, a variety store and a dry cleaners. The whole time, the boy was practically glued to her side. It was so frustrating! It was worrisome, too. If Gina was an observant person at all, she was sure to eventually notice that the same red Camero coincidentally turned up at all the same places she went. If she hadn't noticed already.

Today was the first he'd seen anything of Hamilton himself, except for brief stints from the Grand Am to the house. He'd been outside most of the afternoon. First, he washed his car. Then he mowed and trimmed the yard and applied fertilizer to it. He was a different man in shorts, an old tee-shirt and tennis shoes, a baseball cap on his head. This was the good-old-boy look David remembered from

Bitter Reunion

the past. It made Hamilton appear deceptively harmless.

David was being forced to witness touching moments of marital and family bliss. Gina had come out once, bearing a glass of something cold for her oh-so-wonderful, strong and handsome husband. She and Hamilton had hugged and kissed like high school sweethearts right there in the front yard for all the world to see. And earlier, when Ben was helping his father wash the car, any observer would have sworn in a court of law that Hamilton should get the Father of the Year award. "Wake up!" he wanted to shout to Gina and Ben. "It's nothing but an act. I know, I've been there."

It was sure a good thing David had chosen not to bring the gun with him in the car. He didn't know if he would have been able to control the burning desire to drive slowly by and simply shoot Hamilton point blank, see his blood flow and know it was over. Oh, how he wanted it! It would be so easy, but he'd be letting Hank down and David couldn't do that. He just had to find a way to get the kid! He was beginning to entertain the idea of taking the boy from Gina at gunpoint. It might be risky, but it also might be the only way.

At four-thirty in the afternoon, Hamilton went back into the house. An hour and a half later, when no one had reemerged, David decided to leave and take the rest of the day off. You could only handle so much inactivity before you went stark raving mad. Maybe he'd even treat himself to a decent meal at a sit-down restaurant before returning home to a solitary evening of television. His mood improved slightly at the thought of something to eat that didn't come in a bag at a drive-up window and taste of grease.

Pulling into the street, David drove half a block and stopped at the intersection. That's when he saw the burgundy van back out of the Hamilton driveway. He was tempted to keep on going in his own direction. But then, at the last second, he changed his mind. Why not see where they were headed? It probably wouldn't take long, and the restaurant would wait.

The Concert in the Park was held in Albion every Saturday evening for three months during the summer. In the beginning, fourteen years ago, the concert had attracted sparse crowds and performances were usually put on by small-time talent from within the state of Oregon. That was no longer the case. These days, performers with recognizable names and on the fringes of real success came to Albion from such places as Nashville and Hollywood. On a given night, the audience had been known to soar to over five thousand in number.

On Saturday, June 24, the head liners were a group that had been popular in the 70's, but could still draw crowds on the basis of nostalgia alone. The concert didn't start till seven o'clock in the evening, but people started to arrive as early as six. Seating was on a first come, first served basis and consisted of blankets and lawn chairs set up on the grassy knoll that sloped down toward a large bandstand. By six-thirty, little could be seen of the lush green grass that covered the five-acre section of Lonsbury Park where the concert was held. It was obscured by a solid mass of chairs, bodies and blankets.

The outdoor setting was one out of a storybook. Tall Victorian lampposts dotted the park, adorned with hanging baskets of fuchsias

Bitter Reunion

or blue and white lobelia, pansies of various colors and red ivy geranium.

Behind the quaint covered stage, the Willamette River flowed by tranquilly, providing a backdrop of unparalleled panoramic beauty, and lush green Maple and Oak trees lent their majesty and their shade to the concert-goers.

A food court was situated at the end of the park opposite the stage. Folks could bring their own picnic or choose to spend their money at one of twelve or so concession stands offering a variety of traditional and ethnic foods. Some, if not many, people came to the concerts more for the food and carnival atmosphere than for the music.

Fifteen minutes before show time, Ben sat at his mother's feet on a burnt-orange and red Mexican blanket devouring a naked hot dog on a bun. Music bored him, but he had a coloring book and crayons handy for later on. For now, he was content to munch his food and listen to Mom, Dad, Grandma and Grandpa talk.

Two sets of conversations were going on at the same time, and he had to divide his attention between them. Grandpa and Dad's was the most interesting. It seemed to be all about where and how to catch the biggest fish. Mom and Grandma were talking about Kellie and college, and they were arguing just a little. Ben didn't like that part.

"Gina, you had to pay your entire way through college when you were Kellie's age. It made you appreciate it more and it built your character," Lila Reynolds, Gina's mother was saying. "It would be good for Kellie, too."

"We just want to help her a little, Mom," Gina retorted. "Not pay her whole way." Sitting side by side in matching lawn chairs, mother and daughter looked enough alike to be immediately recognized as family. It was also obvious that they shared a stubborn streak. At the moment, both exhibited a firm set of the chin and a firm tone of voice.

"College is a lot more expensive these days. Besides, we want to do it, Mom. God has blessed Todd and me, and we just want to share those blessings. Please don't keep us from doing that."

Gina could tell that her mother was weakening, when Lila said, "Well, let me discuss it with your father. You know how he hates charity."

Gina also knew that both of Walt's daughters were the apples of his eye, and he wouldn't allow pride to stand in the way of Kellie's happiness. The battle was over halfway won.

"O.K. Just talk it over with Daddy and pray about it. Then you can let me know. Of course, if the answer is no, I'll have to badger you some more. So save us both some trouble and make the answer yes."

Lila chuckled, all tension between the women gone. "Gina, sweetheart, life wouldn't be challenging without you and Kellie to badger me."

"By the way, where is Kellie? I thought she was coming to the concert tonight. She mentioned wanting to hear some songs from the dark ages, back when I was young."

"She'll be just a little late," Lila said. "She's coming from work. She should be getting here anytime now. I hope she can find us in this crowd."

There was indeed a large crowd on this Saturday night. It was the first concert of the summer and the evening was perfect for being outside. The recent spell of dry, hot

Bitter Reunion

weather was unusual for the month of June, and everyone was taking full advantage of it. Jackets would be needed as the night wore on, but there wasn't an umbrella or raincoat in sight.

At 7:03, the audience hushed as four men took the stage. Seconds later, music began to fill the air. Todd moved his chair closer to Gina's and took her hand in his. Not wanting to be left out of things, Ben climbed upon his father's lap. For a moment, all the restless, fidgety energy within his small body quieted, and he enjoyed the comfort of being at one with his parents, wrapped in the warmth of their love.

Kellie could hear the opening strains of music, too, though they were not as clear seven blocks from the park where she'd finally managed to find a place to park her car. She could have walked from the deli. It wasn't that much farther away. She covered the distance quickly, jogging most of the way, but slowed her pace when she neared the entrance to the park. Winding, weaving and stumbling her way through the mob toward the general vicinity where her family was supposed to be was like maneuvering through an Army obstacle course. She stopped for a moment to get her bearings. Scanning the undulating sea of bodies, her gaze randomly fell upon two men standing near a large oak tree on the edge of the crowd, and she realized with surprise that one of them looked like the guy she met at the deli the other day.

David. That was his name. He was engaged in a heated conversation with an older man. The wild way he was gesturing and the intense expression on his face told Kellie that he was upset about something. She wondered idly what that something was.

The older man seemed familiar, too. She had seen him somewhere before, she thought as she watched him toss a cigarette stub on the ground and rub it out with his shoe. He had the kind of face you didn't forget. Chilling, that's what his face was. He reminded Kellie of Jack Nicholson, who she thought was the best bad-guy actor around simply because he looked the part. Shrugging off an involuntary shudder, she turned her gaze and her mind back to the task at hand, which was to find her family. She stepped gingerly to avoid treading on a fuzzy bright blue blanket or the people sitting on it and forged on.

When David had first arrived at the park, he had been encouraged by the crowds and the resulting melee. It would have been easy for a kid to get separated from the adults in that kind of atmosphere. Unfortunately, Ben's parents had seemed to realize that, too. One of them was always holding his hand as they meandered through the food court. Then they were setting up green-webbed chairs and spreading out a blanket. From that point on, they hadn't budged. David had sat on the grass, the seat of his pants getting damp from its moisture and watched them from a distance. At least here he hadn't had to worry about being inconspicuous. The crowd around him was the best possible camouflage.

Two older people had soon joined the Hamiltons. David had guessed them to be Gina's parents based on the older woman's resemblance to Gina. The man was tall and slightly overweight with graying dark hair and aviator glasses. He seemed like the demonstrative type, all the time patting or hugging. It had been hard to sit there, lost and lonely in the crowd and watch the five of them obviously having such a good time. Especially Hamilton, who was so smug in his deception. He'd wanted to wipe the contented smile off of the man's face.

After some time, hunger pangs had driven David to head for the concession stands. Unless sitting on the grass constituted a sit-down meal, he was going to miss his chance for one tonight.

That was when he'd seen them.

At first, he hadn't been sure it was really Hank. He looked out of place in the pastoral setting of the park among the garden variety of people who enjoyed such common pleasures as an evening of music. There had been a woman beside him on the blanket though, leaning seductively into him and whispering in his ear. No doubt the famous and wealthy Belinda was the one who'd been able to persuade Hank to attend.

The woman must have been at least fifty-five, but she could have been much older. Rich women could stave off the ravages of age. Her silvery blonde hair was worn chin length in a wavy, cardboard-stiff bouffant fresh from the beauty salon. Around her eyes and cheeks, the skin was tight in a manner that blatantly suggested she'd had a face lift, and she wore too much bright, garish makeup to be attractive. Heavy gold hoops hung from her ears, her neck and her wrists, and nearly every finger sported a gem large enough to do damage in battle. A baggy hot pink jumpsuit tried without success to conceal the bulges of her plump body. She definitely wasn't the type

Hank went for, but he had endured far worse for the sake of money.

Since David had been wanting to speak to Hank anyway, he'd decided that there was no time like the present to do it, so he had headed straight for them. He'd been about ten feet away when Hank had spotted him. Hank had recoiled, surprise and anger registering on his face, but it had been too late to turn back.

"What are you doing here?" Hank had demanded when David reached them. He had shrugged the woman off of him and risen to his feet. "I'll be back," he'd said to her. Then, without another word, he'd grabbed David by the arm and practically drug him to the section of the park where they now stood.

"That was stupid!" Hank was reiterating for about the tenth time, or so it seemed to David. There were veins standing out in Hank's neck. "I didn't want us to be seen together, especially not by Belinda. You're going to screw everything up if you aren't careful. I should have known better than to think you could handle your end of the job."

David felt humiliated, angry and defensive all at the same time. "O.K. So, maybe I shouldn't have come up to you in public, but I had to talk to you. Besides, I'm doing all the work while you're out playing around with some blonde floozy. Have you even been wondering how things were going with me?"

"So, is this the gratitude I get for all I've done for you? Whining and accusations." Hank looked as though he wanted to strike David. "You think this is fun for me, hanging out with that fat cow? She's helping to fund this little project and providing inside information about Hamilton that she doesn't even know she's giving out. If you weren't such a sniveling complainer, you might appreciate what I'm doing."

David hung his head. Maybe Hank was right. "I'm sorry, Pa." How many times had he said those words to Hank? Probably thousands. "It's just…I'm afraid I'm going to get caught. I need some help. My car is too recognizable, and the Hamiltons never let their kid out of their sight."

"It's only been a few days," Hank said as he pulled a cigarette out of the pack in his shirt pocket. It was the second one since their conversation had begun. "Don't chicken out on me yet. There's no reason you shouldn't be able to do this, David. I'm going to be very disappointed in you if I end up having to do it myself. You're a man, now. Prove it."

Hank was staring directly into David's eyes, challenging him. Suddenly, David saw himself as a failure, just as he knew Hank did.

"You're right, Pa. I know I can do it. Don't worry. I guess I just haven't been trying hard enough."

"Then you'd better try harder. It's the least you can do for me." Hank turned his back on David in a gesture of dismissal. He walked a couple of steps back toward the crowd, then turned his head to glance once more at David. "I'm warning you. Don't screw this up. No son of mine is a loser. Do you understand?"

It was with a heavy heart that David headed back to the concession stands. He'd kind of lost his appetite, but he thought maybe he should eat something anyway. It could be a long night. He stood in the middle of the sidewalk that marked the edge of the park and tried to decide which stand looked the most promising. He didn't want french fries or a hamburger, that was for sure. Maybe something light. But nothing looked good. Even the smell of food made him slightly nauseous. Maybe he was coming down with something. That's all he needed—to have to take a couple of days off while he puked his guts out because of the flu. No way. He'd tough it out. David decided on the booth selling Taiwanese vegetables and entered the line behind its counter.

As he stood there, he surveyed the people milling around him. They all looked happy. He was sure the whole world was happy but him. A moment later he revised that opinion. The woman he was standing behind was the one possible exception. She must have still been in her twenties and had probably been attractive at one time, but world-weariness had eroded her looks, dulled the sheen in her hair, and erased the sparkle in her eyes.

"Charlie, get OVER here," she screeched, summoning one of the three young children that appeared to be hers.

Charlie ignored her and continued to wander ever farther away. The two other children began to wage all-out war on each other, yelling and slapping and crying. The harried woman turned her back on them all. She paid for a plate of vegetables.

"Amanda, quit that hollering and take this!" She handed a paper cup to the oldest child, a girl with glasses too big for her face. Then, balancing the steaming Styrofoam plate in one hand and two colorful dripping sno-cones in the other, she stepped aside and made room for David at the counter.

As he prepared to step forward, another child almost ran into David as he darted by, not paying attention to where he was going. David's eyes followed the boy and suddenly he

Bitter Reunion

felt his heart surge within his chest. It was Ben! For just an instant, David was too stunned to react. Then, recovering, he looked quickly around. There was no sign of Gina or Todd or the older couple. Luck was on his side. The boy was on his own.

He couldn't waste a moment in hesitation. The boy was disappearing. David left the line and walked hurriedly after him. Sliding his hand into his pocket, he felt the reassuring hardness of the chloroform bottle. Without breaking stride, he removed it, unscrewed its cap, soaked the rag from his other pocket, and slipped it back.

It was obvious that Ben was heading for the ice cream stand, but he wasn't going to make it there. David was closing in, reckless now in his need to have the boy in his grasp. Just a few feet still separated them. In a moment, he would sweep the child off the ground from behind, covering his mouth with the rag, and duck into the bushes just off to his right. Then he would carry Ben to his car. It would look as if he were carrying a sleeping child, worn out from the festivities, if anyone should happen to see him. It was perfect.

Two more strides, slower now. His hand was reaching out. He could almost feel the soft fabric of Ben's red jacket. The child was so close, so tantalizingly close.

"Hey, David!"

In shock, he spun around, the momentum nearly tripping him, his mind in turmoil. Who could possibly be calling his name?

"Hi. Remember me? We met the other day at Ellie's Edibles. You know, Kellie from the deli?" The girl smiled lopsidedly at the rhyme.

David stared without responding, trying to grasp it. She was standing now beside Ben, having been somewhere nearby. It was Kellie, the cashier from the delicatessen. He just couldn't believe it! The only person in the whole town who knew his name besides Hank and she happened to materialize right here, right now. He cursed silently but vehemently as he hastily stuffed the incriminating rag back into his pocket.

The girl was staring at him now with a curious expression on her face. Belatedly, it occurred to David that he needed to appear normal. He searched frantically for something to say.

"Oh, yeah, I remember you now," he stammered. "I didn't recognize you at first with your hair down. I think it was tied back when you were at the deli." It amazed him that he remembered that at a time like this.

Ben had turned around and was now staring at David, too. "My name's Ben, short for Benjamin, which means son of the right hand. That means I'm really special," he said matter-of-factly and stuck out his own right hand like a real gentleman.

Taken off guard by a sudden realization, the words left David's mouth before he could stop them. "Benjamin, Joseph's younger brother."

Ben's face lit up, as he said excitedly, "You know that story, too? It's my favorite!"

"Uh, well, I used to read it when I was little." David was getting more uncomfortable by the second. He shouldn't be here, and he was saying way too much, but he didn't know how to gracefully get away.

Kellie was resting her hand on Ben's shoulder. "Let me introduce you two," she said. "David, this is my nephew, Ben Hamilton.

Bitter Reunion

Ben, this is a new friend, David...," the sentence dangled.

"Ross," David supplied. At least he wasn't going to tell her his real last name.

This was an unbelievable coincidence. The girl was Ben's aunt! Which meant she was Gina's sister. What were the odds of this happening? And then it struck him. Maybe there was a way he could use this to his advantage. He needed to think it through, but maybe he could get to Ben through Kellie. That was it! He could work from the inside, instead of the outside. For the second time this evening hope surged up within him. This could be the break he'd been waiting for.

"And your last name is...," he directed at Kellie.

"Reynolds. As in Rudolph the Reynolds Reindeer." She giggled. "When I was a little girl that's what I thought the song said. I was very disappointed when I found out otherwise."

David smiled. Smiling was easy to do around this girl. "It looks like you guys were headed for ice cream. Do you care if I join you? I really haven't met that many people in Albion, and I'm getting a little tired of my own company."

"That would be great, right Beej?"

Ben nodded solemnly, and reached out and took David's hand. This was easier than David had thought it would be. Maybe he'd learned something from Hank after all.

"The more the merrier," Kellie continued, as the trio made their way to the ice cream stand. "So you didn't come here with that guy you were talking to earlier?"

Her offhand comment stopped him momentarily in his tracks.

"I saw you when I first got here as I was looking for my family."

"Oh, that was just a guy I ran into that my father used to know. From when we lived here years ago," David said, stumbling on the words. It sounded like a lie to his own ears, but Kellie didn't seem to notice.

David insisted on paying for their ice cream cones despite protests from Kellie. Then they found a clear spot of grass nearby and sat down to eat.

David found it hard to take his eyes off Kellie as she sat cross-legged on the ground, uninhibitedly licking the dripping edges of her cone. Her loose hair cascaded past her shoulders in a luxurious mass of dark brown waves and curls, unruly tendrils framing her face. She was pretty and she was nice, a rare combination. He was lucky to be here. Hank was stuck with horrible Belinda for the evening. David nearly laughed out loud thinking about it.

They talked for awhile. David tried to ask all the questions so he wouldn't have to answer any. Conversation was a field full of land mines, one of which could explode at any moment. How he wished that he had Hank's gift of improvisation—the term Hank used for lying. He was doing his best and trying to mentally note the lies he was telling so he could remember them later on. That was the hard part. He needed a piece of paper to jot them all down.

Now and then Ben interjected observations, opinions and sage bits of preschool wisdom. Like the fact that his friend Tyler could hold his breath till he turned blue or that he wanted to be a cowboy in the rodeo someday so he could ride the bucking broncos. David

Bitter Reunion

hadn't been around children much, and he found Ben to be enormously entertaining.

"So what are you going to major in?" Kellie asked after telling of her desire to become an elementary school teacher.

"I'm not sure yet. I'm just going to take some basic courses to start with. I'm thinking of journalism. I really love to write."

He didn't know much about college courses, and he sure as heck couldn't tell her about his desire to find a class on the fine art of kidnapping. He stifled the urge to smile at the thought and casually changed the subject. "What do you do in your spare time around here?" he asked.

"Well, the usual, I guess. Movies and stuff. I played tennis in high school and still get together with my friends at the court. Do you like sports?"

"I do!" Ben piped up. "Basketball and baseball and soccer and…what's that one with the little white thing called a bird that you hit over the net?"

"Badminton," Kellie supplied. "And it's a birdie."

"Yeah, and that one, but I don't know why they call it a birdie 'cause it doesn't look like one, and I don't like bowling 'cause the ball is too heavy. They should have some that kids like me can lift," Ben went on, the brow beneath his red Blazers baseball cap furrowing slightly at the confusions and inequities of life.

"I've played a little bit of most sports and like pretty much all of them," David said when Ben finally ran out of steam. "I didn't ever play team sports, because I changed schools too often." That, at least, was true.

"If you live in Oregon, you have to be a basketball fan. The Blazers have their ups and downs. O.K., so maybe more downs than ups, but I'm still a loyal fan."

"You ought to play tennis with us sometime," she said, changing the subject back to the sport she obviously enjoyed most.

"I'd like that," David said, and realized that he really would.

The sun was beginning to melt into the horizon leaving an orange and salmon stain in the sky. The air was turning cool. Enveloping the night were the soft and tender strains of a love song, the melody familiar to David's ears. He couldn't remember when he had ever felt so at peace. If it weren't for the depth of his need for revenge, he could almost have forgotten why he was here.

Kellie, too, was enjoying the moment. Just wait, she thought, until she told Carol who she'd run into tonight. She'd have a fit! But David wasn't weird at all, and Kellie had liked getting to know him better. He seemed nice and was easy to talk to. She could tell Ben liked him, too. Besides, the guy must be lonely in a town where he didn't know anybody. Kellie had lived here all her life. She could help him get acquainted, she thought, while at the same time convincing herself that his good looks had nothing to do with her wanting to see him again. She wasn't *that* shallow. It was just the Christ-like thing to do. So why did a little voice in the back of her mind mutter, "Yeah, right. Who do you think you're kidding?"

It was getting late, Kellie suddenly realized. The concert must be nearly over, and her family would be wondering why they were gone so long.

"I hate to say this, David, but Ben and I should be getting back. We're here with his parents and mine, and they're probably getting worried about us. Hey, would you like to come and meet them?"

"I'd better not," David said hastily, looking at his watch. "It's a lot later than I thought it was. I should leave before the concert ends, since my car is blocking some others. Besides, it's been a long day, and I'm really beat. Thanks, though."

Kellie stood and brushed off the seat of her pants. Then she pulled Ben to his feet. He was a lead weight, a dead giveaway that he was tired.

"One more thing. Would you like to go to my church? It has a great college group. We have lots of fun; I think you'd really enjoy it." Before David could answer, Kellie gave him the name and address of her church and its meeting times. "I hope you'll come."

With that, they parted, going their separate ways.

CHAPTER 11

Sunday, June 25

There were only three Reynolds in the book, David found out Sunday morning at eight o'clock, and he dialed the right one the first time. For a change, everything seemed to be going his way.

"Hi, Kellie, this is David Ross. I hope I'm not calling too early," David said after Kellie's father had put her on the line.

"Hi, David. Heck no. We're all getting ready for church. What's up?"

"Well, you know how you said I should come to your church? I'd kind of like to. It's been a long time since I went to church. Anyway, what I was calling about…are you going to go with your family?"

"I was planning to. Why?"

"It's nice that your whole family goes to the same church. Does that include Ben and his family, too?"

"No," Kellie said, sounding slightly confused. David couldn't blame her. There was something he needed to find out, and he was having a tough time doing it without sounding like a complete idiot. "My sister's family belongs to a different church. Well, I'll amend that. All Christians are members of the same church in the literal sense. But they attend church in a different building."

That was what David had wanted to know. Now he could proceed without being afraid of meeting up with Hamilton.

"Would it be too forward of me to ask if I could take you to church and then for pizza afterwards?"

Bitter Reunion

Kellie barely paused at all before she answered, "That would be great, David. Let me give you my address and explain how to get here."

David wrote down her directions and arranged to pick her up. He was in a state of semi-shock as he hung up the phone. He realized now that he had been holding his breath, and his palms were sweaty. Did every guy react that way to asking a girl out? He doubted it. Most had a lot more practice than he did. But she'd said yes! That was the truly amazing part.

It was stupid, he knew, to be so excited about having a girl agree to go to church with him. It wasn't exactly a date or anything. It was just part of a bigger plan that happened to involve the need to get to know Kellie better. All the same, he was humming ten minutes later when he stepped into the shower.

Kellie lived two miles outside of town in a house that sat on three acres of wooded land. David found himself knocking nervously on her front door, then momentarily forgetting his mission as she stood in front of him looking great in a gauzy red summer-print dress. David, now suddenly self-conscious, wondered if he looked O.K. for church. He didn't even own a tie, but at least he was wearing his only pair of Dockers and his newest knit shirt.

He couldn't remember ever having been so nervous. It was crucial that he make a good impression.

Kellie invited him in and introduced him to her parents, whom he felt he already knew from having watched them at the park. Her father, Walt, gave him a firm, hearty handshake and acted as though they were old friends. Lila, her mother, was more reserved, but also friendly. Falling back on what he had learned years ago as the young apprentice of a gifted con artist, David was polite and courteous and soon seemed to have won over Kellie's parents. Fortunately, Walt and Lila didn't have time to ask him many questions, so he didn't have to invent too many lies. All in all, the meeting seemed to go pretty well.

As they exited the house, David noticed that Kellie was carrying a Bible. He didn't own one of those either. He hadn't believed in God for a very long time, and it was going to take every ounce of acting ability he possessed to hide that fact. If going to church is what it took to get closer to Kellie, he would go to church. But he wouldn't like it.

"Nice car, David," Kellie said, once they were seated and on the road. "Did you see mine back at the house? It's an eye sore, but it has character. I'm kind of attached to it, actually. It's a 'Charlie Brown and the puny little Christmas tree' kind of thing. I always feel sorry for the underdog. By the way, I noticed the Idaho license plates. Didn't you say you were from California?"

David cursed his stupidity. Hank had gotten Oregon plates for him to switch to as soon as the kidnapping was accomplished, but in the mean time, the Idaho plates were conspicuous. Besides, he now remembered he'd told her he was from California. That was the trouble with lies. One always seemed to lead to another.

"I didn't live in California long enough to get the license changed," he said. "We moved around a lot. My Dad kept getting transferred with his company."

Bitter Reunion

Trying to avoid further conversation, he turned on the radio, and they listened to soft rock the rest of the way to church.

An hour and fifteen minutes later, David sat in a sea-green padded pew beside Kellie and tried to sing the words projected on a screen at the front of the sanctuary. He'd be glad when this horrendous morning was over. He'd already had to endure Sunday school. Even though everyone had been nice, it had been hard to listen to all that garbage about God's love. Now he would have to sit here in the prism of light streaming through a stained glass window and hear more of the same. He could have told them all a thing or two.

He'd believed in God and in Jesus, once. In that other life, as Joey, but he'd found out that Christianity was for naive children and charlatans. Hank had pulled off many a con under the guise of a man of God. And Hamilton, the worst liar and hypocrite of them all, had been the one who had taken young Joey to church, read to him out of the Bible and prayed with him. Only a naive fool would believe that God, if there was a God, really cared about him. There was too much evidence in the world to the contrary.

Kellie obviously believed it, though. Conviction rang out in every word as she sang, and he could see it in the rapt attention she paid to the sermon. He felt sorry for her. Someday she would find out the truth, and it would hurt. He wondered about Mr. and Mrs. Reynolds sitting in a pew three rows ahead of him. Did they really believe this stuff, or were they, like Hamilton, just using religion to cover some hidden agenda? He would probably never know.

For about half an hour, which was about half an hour too long, the preacher talked about the importance of forgiveness. David had to hand it to the guy. He really knew how to pour it on. He quoted scripture and told anecdotes, and, if David hadn't known better, he could almost have been sucked in himself.

"If you have a grudge against someone, you need to forgive them," Pastor Smith summed up when his sermon had nearly run its course. "Until you do, the peace you seek will elude you."

David almost laughed out loud. "Sure, Dad, it's O.K. I don't blame you for ruining my life. I forgive you for pretending you loved me and then walking out on me on my birthday. No problem!"

There were some things that were beyond forgiveness. Fortunately, he had a better solution.

Just as David's endurance had almost totally run out, church was over, and he and Kellie were on their way to the pizza parlor she had recommended. Once there, they discovered a mutual liking for pepperoni, mushrooms and olives, which they proceeded to order.

Over amicable conversation, they waited to be served at a cozy table for two, their secluded island amidst a sea of people. Forty minutes later, a lanky auburn-haired waitress with freckles, small myopic eyes behind thick-lensed glasses and a harried expression arrived at their table and placed their order in front of them.

"Whew!" she said, shoving the heavy glasses back up her nose with one hand and straightening a wrinkled, pizza-stained green apron with the other. "Yours finally came up. I'm really sorry about the wait. It's been

Bitter Reunion

crazy around here today." She bent closer to David, her glasses falling down again in the process, and lowered her voice. "Plus, I think they lost your order. If I hadn'ta checked up on it, you'da probably been here all day."

"Thanks, but it doesn't seem like it's been that long," David said to her, smiling across the table at Kellie. "I guess good company makes the time fly."

The waitress reluctantly straightened and took a step back, but her eyes never left David's face.

"Well, if you need anything at all, just let me know," she said, a touch of wistfulness sneaking into the routine offer. Once again, she pushed up the pesky spectacles, then seemed to remember where she was and turned to go.

"Was it just my imagination, or did she seem a tiny bit anxious to please?" Kellie chuckled, once the girl was out of hearing distance.

"Pretty good pizza," David said, ignoring the obviously rhetorical question. "I have a pizza recipe that's better, though. The sauce is incredible."

"You like to cook?" Kellie asked, sounding surprised.

"Um, yeah, sometimes." David felt his face grow warm. "Not a very macho hobby, is it?"

"Hey, I think it's great. When you think about it, most famous chefs are men aren't they? And besides, my brother-in-law, Todd, likes to cook too, and he's definitely no wimp."

"Sounds as if you like him," David replied, suddenly looking down at his plate. His face was even warmer now, but no longer from embarrassment. Hamilton's name had come out of the blue, giving David no time to control his reaction.

"What's not to like? He's great. Couldn't have asked for a better brother-in-law if I'd ordered him myself. My sister's lucky."

Careful, don't get into this, David cautioned himself. Let it go, or you'll blow your cool. He took a deep breath, looked back up at Kellie, forced himself to smile and changed the subject. Soon they were back on safe conversational ground.

David would have never believed it could be so easy to talk to a girl. They had always made him feel embarrassed and tongue-tied or else angry. Come to think of it, he had never before known a female, including his own mother, that he had enjoyed being with.

Kellie seemed to sense he was uncomfortable talking about himself, so she steered clear of that topic. He was grateful. It meant he didn't have to be quite so on guard. They talked about movies, sports and other aimless, trivial subjects. With some reluctance, David reminded himself that this date with Kellie was just the means to an end. There was work to be done.

"Your nephew sure is a cute little guy," he said.

"He took a liking to you, too. You should have heard him go on about you to his mom and dad."

"I'd really like to see him again. Maybe we could take him to a movie or something. Do you think he'd like that?"

"I've got an even better idea," Kellie said. "Todd and Gina…that's his parents…are going to the coast for a couple of days. They leave tomorrow, and Ben will be staying with us. Why don't you come on over for a visit?"

He couldn't believe his luck! She was playing right into his hands. "Yes, sure, that would be great," he said, trying not to sound quite as excited as he felt. He had to be cool. It wouldn't do to scare her off now. So far, things were working out even better than he had hoped.

When the last of the pizza was polished off, David's euphoric mood remained. He hated to see the afternoon end, but they'd already lingered so long over their meal that the lunch crowd had disappeared, leaving them alone to draw pointed stares from a waitress who probably wished they would get up and go. Before he could think of a way to prolong their time together, Kellie made it unnecessary.

"Do you own a pair of tennis shoes?"

"Well, sure," David replied, looking down at his feet. He'd forgotten that he was wearing loafers. He only wore them on special occasions. The rest of the time he lived in sneakers.

"You do know that the best thing to do while wearing tennis shoes is to play tennis, don't you? How about it? Would you like to take me on? My sister gave me a membership to the Country Club for my birthday last year, and I have a guest pass you can use. I've got an extra racquet for you, too. The club has awesome tennis courts."

"Sounds like fun, but I'm not exactly dressed for tennis," David said.

"True. Why don't we stop by your apartment so you can change, and then you can take me home so I can change, too."

Oh boy, David thought, what had he told her about where he lived? Something about an apartment, evidently. No way was she going to find out where he was staying. "I have a better idea. There are a few things I need to take care of at home. Why don't I drop you off and then meet you at the club later. How about four o'clock?"

"Sounds good to me," she said.

"And if you let me win, I might even tell you the secret ingredient in my pizza sauce."

When he arrived, she was waiting for him at the entrance to the Country Club, looking relaxed in navy blue knit shorts and a white tee-shirt that said "West Albion Tennis Team" in red letters across the outline of a gold tennis racquet. Something about the easy way she moved suggested that this type of attire, rather than the formality of this morning's dress, was what Kellie was most comfortable and at home in. To David, it didn't matter what she wore. Everything looked great on her.

"Come on," she said, taking him by the hand and pulling him through the door. "Let me show you around, and then let's hit those courts."

It was impossible for David to answer, since he hadn't registered one word she'd said. All he could think about was the way her hand felt in his, warm and soft and intimate in a way he'd never experienced before. He hoped she'd never let go.

. . . .

"Come on, Thomas, let's go back to the bar and get a drink. It's so hot, I'll never make it to the last hole anyway. Sweetie? We can come out later, when it cools off."

Belinda looked hot, alright, Hank thought. Beads of perspiration on her forehead were turning to rivulets running down her face, and there were big wet stains forming at her armpits. Even her hair was wilting. She's repulsive, thought Hank, not for the first time. Maybe a good stiff bourbon would help him put up with her awhile longer. Golf really wasn't his thing anyway. Drinking was much more to his liking.

Belinda and Hank, using the alias of Thomas Kellog, boarded a golf cart and headed away from the sixth hole. They traversed expanses of velvety green punctuated at intervals by the crystal blue of cool ponds and the soft tan of treacherous sand traps. Providing a purple border in the distance were some of the many majestic mountains of the Willamette Valley. And above their heads, feathery wisps of white danced in a cobalt sky.

But any beauty the day might hold was lost on Hank and Belinda. He did not appreciate nature, only luxury and the things money could buy. And she was far too busy focusing on her own discomfort on one hand, and Thomas, the man she was currently trying to get her hooks in, on the other, to notice her surroundings.

"I think I sunburned my arms," she complained, inspecting the faint blush of pink that appeared on her skin. "These stupid sun block lotions never seem to work on me."

Hank didn't reply. They were passing the tennis courts, and he had slowed the cart. Then the cart stopped entirely and he jumped out of it.

"What are you doing?" Belinda protested. "Why are we stopping here?"

Hank was gesturing for her to go on without him. "I just saw someone I know, and I need to talk to him. I'll join you later at the bar. I won't be too long."

He sounded agitated, and Belinda knew better than to argue when he was upset. She moved over into his place and took off, leaving him walking toward the courts.

It was impossible, but true. The closer he got to the far right court the more sure Hank was that the young man sailing a lime-green ball over the net was indeed David. *His* David. It was like a dream in which you see someone you know, but the setting is all wrong and they are doing something totally incongruous and out of character. David was with a girl about his own age, and he was laughing. Then, with a shock of recognition, Hank saw the girl's face and surprise turned to something else entirely. He knew that girl. She was Hamilton's sister-in-law, Kellie Reynolds. Hank had seen her before right here at the Country Club with the rest of the Hamilton clan.

Hank was furious. From behind a tall hedge of arborvitae that served as a retaining wall, he watched them play. The girl was very good, but David managed to hold his own. Hank had never seen a tennis racquet in David's hand and hadn't had any idea that he even knew the game. Seeing David like this, in a whole new light, unleashed some primal urge within Hank to lash out and punish him, just as he had when the boy was a child. He'd never thought of David as having his own life with his own needs, desires, and interests apart from Hank. He saw David's obvious enjoyment of the girl's company as a betrayal, as well as colossally stupid. How could David, at a time like this, risk everything this way? It was a sign that the weakness he had tried to break in David was still there.

Bitter Reunion

Kellie was walking over to David's side of the court now. She stood beside him and said something that Hank couldn't hear. Then she was putting her hand on David's, showing him the correct way to hold the racquet or to swing it. Or some such excuse to touch him. Hank knew if he watched much longer he wouldn't be able to control the fury that threatened to boil over and cause him to do something he might later regret. He turned and walked away without having been seen.

. . . .

Later that evening, David stood in the country club parking lot and waved to Kellie as she drove off. Crossing the pavement to his own car, he thought about how it had felt to be with her. Even though the secret pizza sauce ingredient was still his alone, he didn't think he had ever had such a good time in his life.

Baseball was the only sport that David didn't enjoy. For some reason, he couldn't bear to play or even watch it. He loved almost every other sport, though, and he was good at most of them, too. The trouble was, he had rarely gotten to participate in them. P.E. and a rare impromptu game of basketball or football after school had been about the extent of his involvement.

Boy, had it ever felt great to be out on that tennis court! He'd started to get the hang of the game, and it was more fun and challenging than he would have guessed. Especially with Kellie for an opponent. He had a heck of a time returning her serves, and when she smashed the ball at the net, there was nothing he could do but watch it soar by.

He felt pretty good though. By the end of their match, he'd managed to actually win a few points. If only he had the chance to play more often, he knew he could eventually beat her.

But he wouldn't get that chance, and the thought made him sad. He'd never met anyone like Kellie. He wouldn't have enjoyed himself half as much if it hadn't been for her. She knew how to make him laugh, and when she looked at him with those incredible brown eyes of hers, it made him forget all the ugliness in his life. He could almost pretend he was just a guy having a great time with a girl he liked.

It was all so confusing! Why couldn't he have met her some other time and place when this whole business with Hamilton was over? As it was, there was no future in their relationship. A few more days and he would never see her again. It was an unsettling thought that cast a shadow on his euphoric mood. Seconds later, his heart sank even further when he saw Hank leaning up against the Camero.

"So you're alone. Where's your friend?" Hank said, keeping his voice low.

"You saw us, huh?"

"Yes!" Hank hissed. "Now, where is she? She's not going to show up here any moment, is she? I don't want her to see us together."

"Too late." David regretted having said it the moment the words were out of his mouth. Hank looked as if he'd been struck. "Go ahead and get in the car. She's already gone."

"What do you mean, too late? Are you trying to tell me that she's already seen us together?" Hank wasn't about to be sidetracked, and the volume of his voice was raising as his anger gained momentum. "And what the devil are you doing with her anyway? How could you be so dumb? I taught you better."

As both men slid into the front seat of the car, David tried to think of a way to mollify Hank. He had to admit it had probably been a mistake to have come to the club to play tennis with Kellie. It had been totally unnecessary, not part of the plan. He'd done it just because he wanted to. Who'd have guessed that Hank would have been here, too? Albion was starting to seem like a very small town.

"O.K. She happened to see us together when we were talking at the park last night. No big deal, Pa. She didn't think anything of it. I told her you were an old friend of the family, and that was the end of it."

"No big deal?" Hank demanded, slapping his flat palm against the dashboard for emphasis. "It's a very big deal! I'm sure you know who she is, and whether she remembered it at the time or not, she has seen me before, with Belinda here at the club."

"So what? I'm the one who's taking all the risk here. I'm the one that's going to kidnap the kid and kill his old man."

"And now Kellie Reynolds can tie us together, David. Don't you get it? This whole thing could blow up in our faces because of her! You don't have a police record. Tracing you won't be easy with nothing to go on but a description. But I'm another story. I've been around. My mug shot and fingerprints are on record. Let me tell you something, boy. I was in prison once for only a short time, but it was long enough to last a lifetime. Do you know how long we could be put away for what we're going to do?"

David was scared. What if Hank called off the whole plan? He couldn't turn back now. It would be like trying to keep a diver from reaching the water once his feet had left the board. The momentum of his obsessive need had no choice but to reach its destination. Nothing could get in the way of that. Nothing.

"You don't understand," David said, panic coloring his voice. "Getting to know Kellie started out as an accident, but then I realized how I could use her to get to Ben. You should understand. You're the pro at using women, and I'm just following your example."

Hank didn't look exactly flattered by David's compliment, but at least he wasn't yelling at the moment. "Besides," David went on quickly, "it's working." He proceeded to tell Hank of his invitation to the Reynold's and how he planned to proceed from there.

Hank was quiet for so long that David was beginning to think his arguments had been in vain. Finally, Hank broke the silence.

"I'm giving you a chance to make this work. Three days. That's all you have to get the boy, or I pull the plug. And be very careful about what you say to that girl. Every word could come back to haunt you. I want that money, David. Hamilton owes it to me for raising you, and you know he owes it to you. But I don't want it at the price of my freedom. Remember that."

David breathed an inaudible sigh of relief as Hank got out of the car to return to the club. He wasn't aware that Hank, in the dark confines of his twisted mind, had come up with a plan of his own, one he hadn't shared with

Bitter Reunion

David. It concerned Kellie and how to eliminate her as a potential threat.

All David knew was that he'd gotten a reprieve, and he wasn't going to throw it away. No more distractions, he vowed for the last time.

The streets were quiet in Albion on a Sunday night after nine o'clock. David had stopped for a bite to eat before heading for home, and now it was late. It wasn't yet dark enough to disguise the house as he slowly cruised the streets, though. After all these years, he recognized it immediately. It was the house where Joey Hamilton had lived. He hadn't even been aware he was near it, until suddenly it was there, looming in the gathering dusk like some ghost from the past.

In an action that was pure reflex, David's foot hit the brake the moment he saw it. He pulled his car off the road, got out of it, and walked haltingly to the sidewalk in front of the house. Numbness filled his heart and mind as he stared at the steps where a small boy had once sat waiting for his father to pick him up. His actions belied the absence of emotion, but he was only vaguely aware of the things he did before getting back into his car and driving the rest of the way home.

CHAPTER 12

Monday, June 26

"I betcha grandma will let me help her make chocolate chip cookies," Ben said, as he sat at the breakfast table dawdling over his third Mickey Mouse shaped pancake. "I'm a really good cook. She says the cookies are always better when I help make them."

Gina, who was already clearing the table around him and marveling at the amount of sticky syrup that had escaped his plate, said, "I wouldn't be surprised. Just don't eat them all at once. Remember last time Grandma let you eat all that junk food? You got a bad tummy ache."

"Yeah, Grandma spoils me. But she can't help it, though. That's what Grandmas are for. And also, she's crazy about me."

"You are so right," Todd said, tousling Ben's hair. He, too, was lingering at the table, drinking a cup of coffee and reading the morning paper. "And she isn't the only one. You're a pretty popular kid around these parts. I think your mom and I are going to miss you just a little while we're gone."

He glanced at his watch. It was early morning, but he couldn't wait to get away. It had been an especially stressful month, and a break was definitely in order. First there had been the letters, which fortunately had stopped coming. Then, on Friday, he'd had to fire a truck driver. Even though Calvin Manning had it coming and then some, Todd had regretted having to do it. He only let someone go as a last resort, but he would not tolerate a driver who had been caught drinking on the job. Innocent people's lives were on the line.

He had tried to soften the blow as much as possible, but even so, he had managed to make an enemy out of Calvin. There had been an ugly scene, with Calvin first tearfully pleading and then progressing to the ranting stage in which he shouted obscenities and threats. Todd supposed it was understandable, in a way. The man had to support a wife and six children. He was in a world of hurt, and he blamed Todd for putting him there. It was easier than blaming himself. Todd just hoped that once Calvin calmed down a little, he would see that Todd had no choice.

Todd took his responsibilities as a business owner seriously. He'd never been able to limit his involvement to a nine-to-five, punch-the-clock day. The business was like a living organism that needed to be nourished to survive. It was the employees, the men and women who depended on their jobs to feed their children and pay their bills. He saw his job as being more about them than about hauling wood products from one place to another. When one of them had personal problems, it impacted them all, but most of all Todd, because he was the boss. The burden was heavy sometimes.

It was going to be a blessing to leave the office behind, even if only for three days. Todd scanned the articles in the newspaper as he made his way toward the section that included tide tables for the coast.

Maybe he and Gina would get a chance to do some crabbing, and slack tide would be the best time to go. During the hour just before or after high tide or low tide was when the crab moved around. The rest of the time they tended to stay nestled in sand on the ocean floor. There was a place in Waldport that rented out boats, bait and crab traps and even cooked the crab after you caught it. He and Gina could buy some cocktail sauce and eat the delectable seafood right out of the shell back in their hotel room. It was a messy undertaking, but the crab always seemed to taste just a little better that way. Todd made a mental note to pack a nut cracker, or in this case, a shell cracker.

"What's this?" he muttered to himself, a short article on page two having caught his eye. It was an account of a vandalism that had occurred the previous night. What made it interesting to Todd was that the address given was of a house he had once owned. The current owners had come home from a late-night party to discover the damage. Evidence indicated that someone had picked up stones from a rock garden in the yard and thrown them with considerable force, breaking all the windows and pock-marking the aluminum siding. The owners claimed to have no idea who would have done such a thing or why.

It's sad, Todd thought, that people don't seem to even need a reason any more for their acts of destruction and violence. He folded the paper and set it on the table, no longer interested in tide tables. The article had upset him, because it had made him think of his old home, and that inevitably led to thoughts of Joey. They were always there, in the back of his mind, ready to ambush him at the slightest provocation.

On top of everything else that had been happening lately, it was nearly the anniversary of the day his first son had disappeared. Once, Todd had thought time would erase the pain he felt over Joey's loss, but

Bitter Reunion

he now knew it would always be there to some degree.

Thank God for Gina and Ben. They had brought love and joy back into his life and made it possible to for him to go on. He watched Gina as she stood at the kitchen sink and gently wiped syrup from Ben's face and realized for the hundredth time what a Godsend she was. She had an inner beauty that showed clear through to the outside. Oh, she was pretty physically, too, but Todd knew better than to place value on the outer beauty of a woman. He had made that mistake once, and it had cost him dearly.

In his mind's eye he could still see a young and vibrant Elaine, rooting for him in her skimpy cheerleader's outfit, her long golden hair bouncing and sparkling in the sunlight, a come-hither look in her smokey blue-green eyes and a vivacious smile on her flawless face. At seventeen, he hadn't been able to see beyond her stunning physical attributes, and he had thought what he felt for her was love. Elaine had been one of the most popular girls in high school, and she could have gone with any guy she'd wanted to, but she had chosen to lavish her attention on Todd. He'd been so flattered, felt so special, and all of his friends had been jealous.

When he was nineteen, after two years of going steady, Todd had proposed to Elaine. He had been to college for a year and she had just graduated from high school. Intellectually, he had known he should wait. They were so young, and a part of him had reservations about Elaine. She was flighty, self-centered and fickle, but when she chose to pour on the charm, he could and did overlook all her faults.

Then, too, there was the fact that he'd wanted to take her to bed. Their physical relationship had heated up to the point that Todd's self control had been nearly used up, and Elaine's overt willingness to accommodate him sexually had been an unbearable temptation. As a Christian, the only solution he had seen to the problem was to marry her. Unfortunately, he had ignored the Bible's and his parent's admonitions about being unequally yoked. He had known Elaine wasn't a Christian, but he had thought he could lead her to the Lord once they were married. How hopelessly naive he had been, and how blind. He had never once asked the Lord if it was His will that he marry Elaine. He had probably been afraid of the answer.

The only good thing that had come from his decision to take Elaine as his wife had been Joey. And then Joey was gone because of Elaine, leaving nothing salvageable from the ashes of a marriage that should have never been. Todd had vowed to remain single for the rest of his life, partly as a penance for the horrible mistake he had made, and partly because he would never risk making the same mistake again. And then he had met Gina.

The first time he had seen her was at a Bible study group meeting that his parents had pressured him into attending. She had been seated demurely on a gray metal folding chair, and he had disliked her immediately, irrationally and intensely. She had reminded him so much of Elaine. But over time, a wondrously miraculous thing happened. With the Lord's help, Todd had been able to let go of his hatred for Elaine and then he'd been able to see Gina differently. When he thought back to that time, he marveled that the revulsion he had initially felt for her had turned to love. Not attraction, or infatuation, but love. It was because of who she was on the inside, where the true beauty had been. Now, when he looked at Gina, she didn't seem to look anything like Elaine at all. They were as different as night and day.

Todd put down his coffee cup and walked over to his wife and son. Leaning in close enough to smell the fresh scent of her hair, he whispered in his wife's ear. "Hey there, good lookin', I suddenly have this intense desire to get you alone in a hotel room, with or without an ocean view." Tenderly, he cupped her face in his hands and kissed her.

"Me, too," Ben said, tugging on Todd's sleeve and forming his lips in an exaggerated pucker. "I need a kiss, too."

Todd and Gina both laughed and took turns obliging him.

"Now, let's go get our bags packed so we can get you and Smokey out to Grandma and Grandpa's," Todd said. "Your mother and I have some important business to attend to on the coast."

The first thing they did on the coast was to go to lunch at Tidal Raves, where they ate fresh seafood and watched the Pacific ocean through a wall of windows. Then they checked into the Gleneagle Inn, unpacked and headed for the beach.

It was a rugged beach, as are many along the Oregon coastline. Beyond the vast stretch of velvety sand, black outcroppings of jagged rock loomed. A stiff breeze prevailed this Monday afternoon, but the sun shone brightly, making the wind a welcome guest. Kite flyers dotted the sand, filling the sky above with a riotous array of color.

No matter how stressed he was, a day or two away at the coast always succeeded in providing Todd with a measure of peace. It worked far better than any tranquilizer. The soothing ebb and flow of the tide or the sight of giant waves crashing against the rocks, salty sea air on your face, the sound of the surf and the plaintive cry of sea gulls. It was a different world here, one totally removed from the hustle and bustle of daily life. It was as if God had created this particular spot expressly for the purpose of showing off his creative power and majesty. To look out across the endless expanse of rolling, surging water never failed to impress upon Todd his comparative insignificance. There was no choice but to stand in awe of the One who had caused it to be.

Todd and Gina walked hand in hand across the warm sand until they reached a rocky promontory where the footing was more treacherous. Nestled in the rocks were countless tidal pools, teeming with anemone, sea stars, hermit crabs and other interesting small creatures of the sea. Todd stooped to inspect one such pool, as Gina continued exploring on her own.

"Over here, Todd! Look at the sea lions!"

Todd caught up with her and followed the direction of her gaze. Even though the sea lion population had grown to the point where they were now a pest, wreaking havoc upon the fishermen who competed with them, and even though you could now see dozens of sea lions basking on various piers within throwing distance of land, it was still fun to watch them out in the open sea. As Todd's eyes

Bitter Reunion

scanned the ocean, a sleek dark head momentarily popped above the surface of the water. In the near distance, the cumbersome football-shaped body of another sea lion inched its laborious way up the side of a gigantic rock in an effort to join several comrades already draped across the top. It always amazed Todd that sea lions could climb such steep slopes without the aid of arms or legs. He imagined himself trying to climb that rock handcuffed with a pillowcase tied around his waist. It was highly unlikely he'd do as well as the sea lion, who had just flopped down near the crest. After a few moments in the sun, the animal changed in color from a dark to a lighter, mottled brown, making it much harder for Todd to see him. Unless you looked closely, it would be easy to miss the fact that there were any sea lions on the rock at all.

Todd and Gina searched for a rock of their own. Most were covered with barnacles and mussels, making them uncomfortable perching places for humans. Eventually, though, they found a relatively smooth surface on which to sit, and from there they quietly observed all the beauty that nature had to offer.

Todd felt as though he didn't care if he ever left this rock. This moment was a priceless treasure to be cherished for as long as possible. Peace washed over him, filling his mind and his soul.

After some time, Gina broke the companionable silence. "Did you see Kellie's face today when she was telling about that guy she just met? It positively lit up. If you ask me, I think she really likes him."

"If you say so. I didn't notice anything different about her, but then I'm a man and you're always telling me that men are hopelessly obtuse about those kind of things."

"How true," Gina teased. "Seriously, though, I know I sound like an overprotective big sister, but I hope Kellie takes her time to get to know him before getting too involved. She's got a level head on her shoulders, but you know how hormones can affect one's judgement."

"Hey, woman, just what do you mean by that crack? Are you trying to say I'm going to use bad judgement when we get back to the hotel?" Todd asked playfully.

Gina elbowed him in the ribs as a response. "Well, I just want to see Kellie end up as happy as I am some day, with a wonderful, though hopelessly obtuse husband."

"Just because she happens to like some guy doesn't mean she's about to marry him," Todd said. "She's had lots of boyfriends before and will no doubt have lots more before she gets married. Besides, she's said a million times that she wants to complete college first."

"I guess you're right. It's just this funny feeling I have." A small frown creased her brow.

"Listen, honey, you're worried about nothing. Kellie's a big girl and much wiser than I was at her age. She's not going to make the same kind of mistakes that I did, either. Just trust her. Besides, you're not to waste one more second of this trip worrying about anything."

"Aye, aye, sir. Your wish is my command!"

"In that case, this is going to be a great three days," Todd said, a wicked grin on his face.

Neither of them noticed that there were clouds forming on the horizon.

Bitter Reunion

....

At almost exactly the same time as Gina and Todd were discussing Kellie, Kellie herself was thinking about David and the effect he had on her.

Monday was Kellie's day off so she was at home doing yard work, straining, sweating and engaging in intense introspection. She was weeding flower beds as her father mowed the lawn. Beside her, Ben wielded a shovel in his endeavor to dig a hole all the way to China. Smokey lent his four paws to the project, furiously flipping dirt behind him and creating a small mountain at Kellie's feet. The roar of the lawn mower drowned out all other sound and made conversation impossible. As she knelt and tugged at a particularly stubborn dandelion, she allowed her mind to follow whichever path it chose.

It chose the path of David Ross.

She was attracted to him in a way that was different from all the other guys she had gone out with and she wasn't sure why. Maybe it was just because she hadn't known him long, even though in some unfathomable way, she felt she had. Most of her dates had been with guys she had known for years. There had been no mystery to them, no process of discovery. But she honestly thought it was more than that. And *yes*, more than the fact that he was great to look at.

She sensed he was vulnerable. He seemed like a lost little boy sometimes, and it made her want to reach out to him. She hoped he would eventually be able to open up to her, but for now, he was definitely holding back. He had a reserve that went deeper than politeness.

One thing was certain. David needed the Lord. When she knew him a little better and felt that he trusted her, she would talk to him about Jesus. IF she got to know him better. After today, she wasn't too sure when she would see him again.

David had called this morning, found out that Ben was already there and asked if he could come over. He'd had lunch with them and stayed till around three-thirty in the afternoon. Although he had seemed to have a good time, he was more subdued than he had been yesterday. It was as though he had something else on his mind. Kellie wondered if that something had to do with his impending trip back to California. David had told her that he would be gone for several days because of loose ends he had to tie up there. He hadn't said anything about calling her when he got back, though, and Kellie had felt an unexpected stab of disappointment. Of course, that didn't mean he wasn't going to call, she reminded herself. She was pretty sure he liked her as much as she liked him.

If nothing else, he had really hit it off with Ben. Kellie had almost felt like a third wheel at times, but that was one of the things she liked the best about David. He seemed to be so good with children.

"Kellie! Noelle's here!" Lila was standing at the back door calling to her, and Kellie realized that her dad had finished mowing. She had indeed been deep in thought.

"Coming, Mom!"

Shoot, thought Kellie, I didn't know it was getting so late. She straightened up with some difficulty and wiped the sweat from her brow with the back of one gloved hand. Then she left Ben to his hole, noting that he still had

Bitter Reunion

a ways to go before he popped up in a rice paddy and surprised an unsuspecting Chinese farmer.

Noelle Garrison, Kellie's best friend for the last six years, had shown up on schedule to practice a musical special with Kellie that they were to perform at church next Sunday. She also planned to stay for awhile and keep Kellie company while Kellie babysat Ben. Lila and Walt were soon to leave for their regular Monday evening potluck and bridge party.

After greeting Noelle, Kellie retreated to the bathroom for a quick shower. By the time she returned, her mother and father had left and Noelle was playing Old Maid with Ben.

"I won again!" an exultant Ben crowed, as Noelle sat holding one lonely card.

"When are you ever going to get the hang of that game?" Kellie asked her teasingly. "I keep trying to tell you that the object is to get RID of the Old Maid!"

"I forgot," Noelle said mournfully, shaking her head. "I never was much of a card player."

"I'll rescue you from the card shark then. Come help me fix sandwiches."

Kellie, Noelle and Ben ate a small supper of grilled cheese sandwiches, grapes and potato chips. Then, for half an hour, around continuous interruptions from Ben, the girls struggled to practice their duet to the accompaniment of a cassette tape. Finally, in frustration, Kellie turned off the recorder.

"What's gotten into you tonight, Beej? You're bouncing off the walls, and I didn't even feed you anything with sugar in it. Why don't you and Smokey play something in your bedroom? Grandma got you some new coloring books and crayons. Check the toy box. I think she picked up some toys at a garage sale, too."

Much to Kellie's surprise, Ben didn't argue with her. "O.K. Come on, Smokey."

The dog picked up his ears at the sound of his name and followed Ben, tail wagging enthusiastically. Kellie started the tape again.

· · · · · · · · · ·

Ben stepped inside the room that his grandma and grandpa had designated as his when he was staying with them and waited for Smokey to enter after him. Then he shut the door firmly and ran to the large window against the far wall. Pulling back white gauzy curtains, he peered intently through the glass. Nothing was out of the ordinary. The dogwood tree five yards from his widow stood alone. David wasn't there yet. Ben let the curtains fall back in place and headed for his toy box.

· · · · · · · · · ·

"So what's the story? Who's the hunk that came to church with you yesterday?" Now that they were alone, Noelle couldn't contain her curiosity any longer. If Kellie wasn't going to volunteer the information, Noelle was going to have to worm it out of her.

Kellie and Noelle had practiced enough for one night and were now sprawled across the furniture listening to a CD and sipping colas. It was time for girl talk.

They were soul sisters, but as different as night and day in looks. Noelle's heart shaped face and upturned green eyes gave her the appearance of a mischievous pixie. Shoulder-length strawberry blonde hair worn stylishly shaggy and a lean body added to the illusion. Most people were surprised when they found out that she had a serious side to her.

"He's just this guy I met at the deli one day last week. Then we met again a few days later at the concert in the park and kind of hit it off. Really, it's no big deal. We're just friends."

"Did you ask him if he has any brothers for me?" Noelle asked.

"I thought you and Chad were still going together."

"Well, we are, but that guy is gorgeous!" Noelle let out a long low sigh. "What's his name?"

"David Ross. And come to think of it, I don't know if he has any brothers or sisters, or much of anything else about him, really. He doesn't talk about himself."

"Unbelievable!" Noelle said, a look of astonishment on her face. "A man that doesn't talk about himself? You better grab him, quick, Kel. I swear that all Chad talks about is himself. Sometimes I think he forgets I'm even around. I could probably sneak off, and he wouldn't know I was gone for an hour."

They both laughed and continued to talk and joke about the opposite sex, their jobs, college plans and anything else that crossed their minds.

At eight-forty, it was Ben's bedtime, so Kellie interrupted him in the midst of coloring Simba and Nala with his new neon crayons by asking him to brush his teeth and get into his pajamas. Then she ushered him to bed, listened to his prayers and tucked him in. As she was leaving the room, Ben asked her to shut the door, so she did. As soon as she was gone, Smokey hopped from the floor to the bed and settled down beside him.

It was quiet in Ben's room. He lay staring at the ceiling, where shadows were beginning to form, and tried to remember exactly what David had told him.

He was almost sure, no he WAS sure that David had said he would be waiting by the tree when Ben went to bed. Ben was supposed to go to the window where David could see him, and then David would come over and help him get out. Ben smiled to himself. They were going to surprise Kellie. It would be lots of fun. But David wasn't by the tree yet. He hoped he hadn't decided not to come.

David was cool. He was just like David in the Bible story who killed a great big giant with his sling shot. Kellie's boyfriend David could probably kill a giant, too, if he wanted to. He was big and strong. And he was nice too. Ben liked him a lot.

It was earlier in the day, when David had been visiting and Kellie had gone to talk on the telephone to Noelle, that David had asked to see Ben's bedroom. Ben was showing him his favorite teddy bear that he always brought with him to grandma's. And that's when David had asked Ben if he could keep a secret, because he wanted to surprise Kellie, and it would be ruined if Ben told.

"I'm good at secrets," Ben had assured him. "I never told Mommy what Daddy got her for Christmas. It was a ring and it had her red birthday stone in it. I almost told once, but then I remembered not to."

"Well, that's good," David had said, "because this is kind of like that, and you have to help me. O.K.?"

Bitter Reunion

Ben had felt so proud. David was treating him just like a grownup.

"I'm going to help you get out of your room tonight after you go to bed and then you can go with me to my car and we'll carry some pretty flowers and candy to the front door. We'll ring on the doorbell and Kellie will answer it. She'll be so surprised and happy to see us both standing there with presents for her!

"Is it Kellie's birthday?" Ben had asked.

"No, but it doesn't have to be a birthday to do something nice for somebody. Boys give girls presents sometimes just because they like them. And I like Kellie a lot."

"Yes, I know. I like Aunt Kellie a lot, too. She's really, really nice."

"Alright! Then how about it, buddy? You going to help me?"

Ben hadn't needed to think it over. It had sounded like a wonderful adventure to him.

He just couldn't lay still a moment longer. He was too hyper. For the fourth time, he went to the window and moved the curtains aside. And this time David was there beside the tree just like he had said he would be. In his excitement, Ben nearly called out David's name, but he caught himself just in time. Kellie would hear, and it would spoil the surprise. Then David would be mad. Ignoring a funny fluttery feeling in the pit of his stomach, Ben waved wildly.

CHAPTER 13

Hank picked up the phone on the third ring. It was late. He had just gotten home from Belinda's. So what could she possibly want now?

"Hello," he answered irritably.

"Hank, it's David. I did it! I have the boy here at the house now!"

Hank was suddenly alert, every muscle of his body standing at attention. "How did it go? Did you have any problems? Did anyone see you?"

"No. It went without a hitch. It was beautiful!" David said, his voice loud over the phone, almost giddy. "Nobody will suspect me, Hank, I swear."

David explained how he had enlisted Ben's help in his own kidnapping. Hank had to admit that it had been a good idea. It would seem as if the kid had disappeared into thin air. But this wasn't over yet. Things could still go wrong.

"I thought there might be a problem when I got Ben to the car," David went on, "you know, because he wasn't expecting me to take him away, and I didn't want to use the chloroform on him. But I told him I forgot the flowers and we'd have to go back to my house to get them. When I got him here, I gave him some hot chocolate with a sleeping pill in it. Then I let him watch a little TV while I hunted for those nonexistent flowers, and he conked right out. It was a piece of cake. I can't believe how gullible little kids are."

"Listen, David, don't do anything until I get over there. It might take me awhile. There's something I have to do before I come.

We'll talk about the ransom demand when I get there."

Hank slammed down the receiver and headed for the door. David had said that Kellie's parents weren't at home. This was his chance, and he didn't have a moment to lose.

....

After arranging to meet for a game of tennis the next evening, Noelle said goodbye to Kellie and left for home. It was still early for a night-owl like Kellie, so she decided to watch some TV before going to bed. She was reaching for the remote control when she heard it.

She didn't know what it was at first, the high-pitched sound that came from down the hall. As she walked toward it, though, she realized it was Smokey whining on the other side of Ben's closed door, wanting out. As much noise as the dog was making, it was a wonder he hadn't woken Ben.

In a few quick strides she reached the door, turned the knob quietly and pushed it open. Smokey came bounding out and jumped against her legs as she peered into the room. Immediately she noticed the wide open window, curtains billowing inward and raindrops falling on the sill. As she crossed the room to close the window, she happened to glance toward the bed.

Ben wasn't in it. By the blue glow of a night-light, Kellie could make out rumpled covers and a pillow which still bore the indentation where his head had been. His teddy bear lay discarded in the middle of the bed.

He must have gone to the bathroom, she thought, her mind refusing to draw a connection between the open window and his disappearance. A quick search, however, proved he wasn't in the bathroom or the kitchen, or any other room of the house. She called his name over and over again, but he didn't answer.

She raced back to the bedroom. In a panic now, she switched on the light, as if in its illumination she would suddenly see Ben safe and sound in his bed where he was supposed to be. But the room was the same as she'd left it, devoid of human life, looking somehow even emptier in the stark glare of the ceiling lamp. For a moment, Kellie's mind and body went numb, and then suddenly a cold chill broke through to her senses, reminding her of the open window. Turning back toward it, she noticed for the first time that the screen was unlatched at the bottom and hanging loose.

Her heart stopped and she gasped audibly. Ben must have gone through the window. He must be out there somewhere in the rain that was now invading the room, soaking the curtains and the carpet beneath the window. But why? What could possibly have made him leave the comfort of his warm bed to venture out into this dark and miserable night? Her mind searched frantically for answers but found none.

I've got to find him, Kellie thought, a small sob catching in her throat. He must be cold and wet and scared out of his wits. But first she had to find her shoes. Where had she taken them off? She couldn't think.

After what seemed an eternity but was only seconds, she saw them peeking out from under the sofa in the living room. She grabbed one battered Nike and jammed it on her foot.

Without taking time to tie it, she reached for the other one, and as she did, she prayed.

"Please, God, help me find him. Let him be O.K. Oh, please!"

Finally, both shoes in place, laces flopping, Kellie loped for the door. Just as she reached it, the shrill sound of a telephone ring pierced the stillness of the room and the chaos in her mind. She hesitated, debating whether to answer it. The desperate need to start searching for Ben pulled her toward the door—but what if the call was important? It might be about Ben. She raced back to the telephone and picked it up.

"Hello, is this Kellie Reynolds?" an unfamiliar, husky male voice inquired.

"Yes, it is." Kellie's own voice sounded shaky and unnatural to her ears.

"Listen, I work at the Chevron station on highway 23. I was driving home from work when I saw this little kid standing by the side of the road. I stopped my car and tried to find out what he was doing there all alone, but he was too upset to tell me. The kid was really crying his eyes out. Well, I hope you don't mind, but I brought him on home with me. I couldn't very well just leave him out there."

"Oh, thank you, sir. Thank you." Relief flooded Kellie from head to toe, leaving her limp. "Just tell me where he is now, and I'll come right over and get him."

Kellie wrote down the address and then the directions the man gave her.

"Tell Ben I'm on my way," she said before she hung up. Then she walked out into the night.

After so many days of dry weather, the darkened sky had finally opened, letting loose a torrential downpour. Great heavy drops of water furiously pelted Kellie's body like fire from a cosmic machine gun, and she was drenched by the time she got to the car at the end of the long circular driveway.

As Kellie turned out onto the highway in front of her house, she struggled to see. Windshield-wipers swished frantically, losing an intensely fought battle to keep up with the demands placed upon them. From behind a wall of water, the landscape in the illumination of her headlights was surreal and forbidding, evoking the atmosphere of a horror movie. Trees beside the road took on the appearance of frightening monsters, giants with outstretched arms waiting to grab the innocent and unsuspecting.

Kellie fought the temptation to break the speed limit. As anxious as she was to get to Ben, it wouldn't do to get in too big of a hurry. Driving was treacherous in this rain, and the roads she found herself traveling were dark and full of twists and turns.

It was a challenge just to make out road signs in an effort to follow the directions she had written down. Why couldn't the guy have lived in town or at least someplace she had been before? She hated driving unfamiliar country roads after dark, especially on a night like this.

Kellie brushed stray strands of dripping hair from her eyes and thought about Ben standing alone by the side of the road. How in the world did he end up there? It didn't seem likely that he was sleep-walking, but she couldn't think of any other explanation that made sense, either. Now that the initial relief of the phone call was over, it occurred to Kellie that she hadn't asked many questions of the man who had taken Ben home—not even

Bitter Reunion

what his name was. Oh well, it was enough just to know where Ben was and that he was safe. She could ask him all the questions she wanted when she got him home. Poor baby. She hoped he hadn't been too traumatized. The man had said he was really upset.

Thank God, a good Samaritan had come by. Kellie didn't want to think about what could have happened to Ben if the Lord hadn't been watching over him.

Suddenly there was the glare of headlights in Kellie's rear view mirror. She had been vaguely aware of a car behind her for the last mile or so, but she hadn't realized it had gotten so close. Talk about tailgating! This guy was really riding her bumper.

"Go around!" she said aloud, slowing to let the driver pass her. Instead, unbelievably, the lights loomed even brighter and closer, nearly blinding her and instantly turning her irritation to fear.

Adrenaline shot through her body as she floored the gas pedal and gripped the steering wheel tightly with both hands. Her decade-old Cavalier made a valiant effort and put some distance between the two cars. But only for a moment. Then the lights were back, the other car as close as it had been before.

What's he doing, Kellie wondered frantically. The guy must be drunk or crazy or both! He was going to get them killed! She watched the marker on her speedometer go steadily upward. The road ahead was eaten up faster and faster. Still, she couldn't seem to outrun those lights! Her heart in her throat, she wondered how much longer she could keep the car under control.

For the second time in one night, Kellie turned to God in the midst of her terror, uttering a plea for help. As she did, the blinding lights shifted, and she realized that the car was pulling beside her.

What happened next was sudden and totally unexpected. A deafening sound filled Kellie's head, and the window to her left exploded, sending pieces of glass flying toward her. At the same time, she felt an impact, and the steering wheel flew out of her hands. Then the night and all its unseen terrors rushed forward to meet her in its embrace, as the Cavalier careened wildly and shot off the side of the road. Like a toy car thrown from the hand of a petulant child, it tumbled end-over-end down a steep, grassy embankment and plowed into a screen of evergreen trees, where at last it rested, a tangled mass of twisted metal. A moment of expectant silence reigned before a thunderous explosion ripped it apart and set it ablaze.

Back at the road, Hank sat in his car and looked with satisfaction on the destruction he had created. In the time it took him to light a cigarette, he watched the rain and the fire compete for control. Then, before someone could come along and discover him there, he drove away.

CHAPTER 14

Walt and Lila returned home at ten-fifteen, to find all the lights on, the front door unlocked and no one home but Smokey. They both knew immediately that something must be wrong. It was far too late for Kellie to have gone anywhere with Ben, and even if she had, she would have left them a note so they wouldn't worry. The way they were doing now.

Because Kellie's car was gone, their first thought was that Ben had gotten sick or had an accident and Kellie had taken him to the hospital. A call to Albion General put that fear to rest. Neither Kellie nor Ben had been admitted there.

"Walt, what should we do now?" Lila asked, after Walt got off the phone with the last of Kellie's close friends. None of them but Noelle had seen her today, and Noelle claimed that everything had been normal when she'd left the house at around nine-fifteen. Ben had already been in bed and she was sure that Kellie hadn't intended to go anywhere.

"I'm looking for David Ross in the phone book, but he doesn't seem to be listed yet. Kellie's seen quite a bit of that young man in the last few days. Maybe he knows where she is," Walt replied, and Lila knew how concerned he was when his eyes met hers. He didn't want to scare her by admitting that he was afraid, but Lila had been married to this man for thirty-eight years. Communication between them went deeper than words. A touch, a look, a gesture—she knew how to read him, and what she was reading now was fear.

Walt picked up the phone once more and dialed directory assistance, only to learn that they didn't have a number for David, either.

They had reached a dead end. It was now ten-fifteen, and there was still no sign of Kellie and Ben.

"I...I think we should call the police." Walt had no choice but to say it. "I don't like this, Lila. Not one bit. Maybe we'd better call Todd, too."

Lila struggled to hold back tears as she nodded her head in agreement. "Yes. Call them."

Before Walt had a chance to reach for the phone, it rang, startling them both. He grabbed the receiver and in the moment before putting it to his ear, he dared to hope it would be Kellie calling to say that everything was fine. They had gone to a movie and she was sorry she'd forgotten to leave a note. But it wasn't Kellie's voice that he heard next.

It was a male voice, deep and menacing. "Listen to me carefully," it said, "because I'm only going to say this once. I have kidnapped your grandson. Tomorrow, I'm going to want to talk to his father to discuss how he can get him back."

Walt had been standing, but now he dropped heavily onto the gray tweed sofa beside him, as if his legs would no longer support the weight of his body. Shock threatened to drown out what the man was saying. He made a monumental effort to focus on the incomprehensible words coming from the disembodied voice of a monster.

"Ben is fine for now," it went on. "But I won't hesitate to kill him if I find out you have contacted the police. No one is to know about this call but Hamilton and his wife. Do you understand?"

Bitter Reunion

"Yes," Walt said, his voice barely audible. He cleared his throat and repeated it. "Yes. But Todd and Gina aren't in town right now."

"Well, Hamilton had better be at his home tomorrow afternoon. That's when I'm calling for our little chat." The voice paused, then spat out one more sentence. "Gay basher's don't deserve to have children!" The line went dead.

Somehow Walt managed to tell Lila what the man had said, though he could see that every word was cutting into her like a sharp and lethal knife. She moved to his side and sat clinging to him as if to a life preserver. He could feel her desperation almost as well as he could his own. Her entire body was trembling.

"He didn't say anything about Kellie?"

"No," he answered softly. And then he felt the tears on his cheeks and he knew he was crying.

Lila suddenly slipped from the sofa to the floor on her knees and pulled her husband down beside her.

"We can't handle this, Walt. We can't." And then she was directing her words to the Lord, as she simply asked Him to handle it for them.

"Yes, Lord," was all Walt could manage to say, but he knew God was aware of what was in his heart, and it gave him a small measure of comfort.

When at last he rose again to his feet, Walt felt strong enough to call Todd, but once again, the telephone rang before he had a chance to pick it up. This time he did not expect it to be his daughter.

....

After a drive that felt like an eternity in which their emotions were a horrible kaleidoscope of fear, anxiety and confusion, Todd and Gina arrived at the Albion General Hospital at twelve-fifty AM. They had both tried not to, but they couldn't help it; they feared the worst. Otherwise, why wouldn't Dad have told them the details of what had happened on the phone? All he would tell Todd was that something had happened to Kellie and Ben, and that they were to meet Walt and Lila at the hospital as soon as they could get there.

"It'll be O.K. I'll tell you the rest when you get here," was all Walt would say in response to Todd's frantic questions. And the way he'd said it didn't inspire confidence that he'd really meant it.

The only doors to the hospital that were open this time of the night were those to the emergency room, and Todd and Gina entered them soggy, disheveled and out of breath. Neither had taken much time to dress in their haste to get packed and get back to Albion, and neither cared about their appearance. Gina hadn't even bothered to comb her hair and her face plainly displayed the signs of her inner distress. It was pasty white, her eyes dark holes of anguish. She had aged ten years overnight.

Walt was waiting for them just inside the doors. He too looked haggard as he solemnly took his elder daughter in his arms and embraced her.

They pulled apart and Gina looked searchingly into his eyes.

"Let's join your mother, and then we can talk," Walt said and then led them away from the busy admissions area to a small, quiet waiting room that was deserted except for Lila. Gina could tell that her mother had been crying.

"We shouldn't be bothered here," Walt began solemnly. "I asked a nurse for a place where we could have some privacy." When they were all seated, Walt took Gina's hand and began recounting the events of the evening, pausing only after he had told of the kidnapper's telephone call.

Gina sat in stunned silence, but Todd's reaction was violent. He burst from his chair.

"I don't believe it! It can't be happening again! Isn't once in a lifetime enough?"

Lila rose and put her arm around Todd's waist. "You've got to have faith, Todd. We'll get Ben back. We will—with God's help."

"I'd like to believe that Lila. But I didn't get Joey back, did I?"

Todd shook his head mournfully, the steam of his rage having evaporated as quickly as it had come. He sat back down beside Gina. "I'm so sorry, honey. It's all my fault."

She looked at him in surprise.

"What do you mean?"

"Isn't it obvious? Someone is trying to get back at me for what I said. You remember the notes I got? If I had just kept my big mouth shut, none of this would be happening."

"What notes are you talking about?" Walt asked.

Todd explained to him about Howard Sneed, his attempt to get money from Todd for AIDS research, and the resulting confrontation.

The kidnapper's last cryptic statement suddenly made sense.

"You had every right to state your opinion, Todd, without fear of reprisal. You aren't to blame for any of this, and I don't want to ever hear you say that you are," Gina said when Todd had finished. "Whoever did this—he's the only one to blame,"

"Gina's right, Todd," Lila joined in. "There will always be people who disagree with us, but we have to be true to our beliefs. Those of us who work at the Crisis Pregnancy Center constantly face heated opposition. We can't worry about it, because if we did, we wouldn't be able to help anyone. I guess it's always a risk to take a stand, but how can we live with ourselves if we don't?"

Todd didn't reply, and he still looked so miserable that it was impossible to tell if Gina and Lila had gotten through to him.

In all of the explanations of the night something was being left unsaid, and suddenly Gina knew what it was. "Dad, you haven't mentioned a word about Kellie. Where is she? Why isn't she here? Tell me that the kidnapper didn't…"

Lila cut in. "Kellie had an accident. That's why we're here."

"Oh, no," Gina cried out, her hand flying to her mouth.

"It's O.K., sweetheart," Walt assured her. "Kellie is going to be fine. We can go in and see her in a few minutes. They're going to keep her overnight for observation, though. She's got a concussion, a lot of bad bruises and some cuts that had to be stitched up. But miraculously, she wasn't seriously hurt."

"What happened?" asked Gina. The revelations just went on and on, and each one was like a physical blow leaving her weaker than the last.

"It was a car accident. Kellie was thrown out, or she wouldn't be alive right now. The car exploded." Walt's voice shook. "She always wears her seat belt, but she was distracted and rushed. She forgot to put it on this time. Thank God."

Lila broke in, "We rushed right over when the hospital called to say she was here. She was disoriented and confused when we saw her, and she kept saying we had to go get Ben. He'd be wondering why she wasn't there yet. We couldn't understand what she was talking about because we assumed she knew Ben had been kidnapped. Once we were alone with her and Kellie finally became coherent enough to explain, we found out that she didn't. She was completely stunned when we told her." Lila went on to tell of Kellie's discovery that Ben was missing and the phone call that had sent her out after him.

"It was a set up. Someone tailed her, shot at her and ran her off the road…they tried to kill her." Lila said, the shock of it heavy in her voice. "We can check out the address that Kellie was given tomorrow if she can remember it, but I'm willing to bet it's a phoney one."

For the first time in several minutes, Todd joined the conversation. "I guess that proves whoever has Ben wouldn't balk at hurting or even killing a person."

He regretted having said it the moment the words were out of his mouth. He hadn't considered the impact they would have on Gina. Tears filled her eyes, and she looked as if she were on the verge of collapsing. He longed to protect her from the pain he knew she was feeling, but he felt powerless to do so. The sick, nightmarish deja vu that had him in its grip was too strong. He was locked within himself, unable to break free to reach out to her.

"I can only imagine how you must feel right now, Todd, but try not to despair," Walt said. "It sounded to me like the kidnapper is after money. If you give him what he wants, there's no reason to think he would harm Ben."

"I'll give him whatever he wants, however he wants it. We'll go entirely by his rules, but he won't see a dime unless I get Ben back safe. We have to count on his greed being stronger than his vindictiveness," Todd said bitterly. "And heaven help us all if anything happens to my son."

"That brings us to another question. What are we going to tell the police about what has happened tonight?" Walt asked. "They know, of course, about Kellie's accident, but I'm not sure what she told them about it. If they suspect she was run off the road, they'll be asking a lot more questions, and it will be hard to keep the kidnapping a secret."

"We have to," Todd said. "I'm not risking Ben's life by getting the police involved. Kellie will just have to lead them to believe that it was a drunk driver instead of a killer."

It was a somber party that quietly entered room 224 ten minutes later and gathered around Kellie's bed. Gina sat down in a chair beside her sister and gently stroked her still damp hair. Kellie looked so fragile lying there, a large bandage on her forehead, and bruises already beginning to show on her exposed arms.

Gina tried to shut her mind away from everything except the fact that Kellie was here, alive and safe, but there was no way to keep from thinking of Ben, even for a second. The longing for him was both physical and emotional. Her arms ached to hold him and every instinct told her that she should be doing something, anything to get him back. But there was nothing she could do. Helplessness threatened to drive her mad.

"My fault," Kellie mumbled from the bed, struggling against the groggy state that drugs and exhaustion had produced.

"No, honey," Gina said. Her eyes met Todd's. "Why does everyone insist on blaming themselves? I might as well blame myself for being at the coast instead of home with my child, and Mom and Dad can blame themselves for having gone out for the evening. Let's all just accept that it happened and none of us had any control over it. O.K.?"

Kellie managed a small nod of the head, which immediately produced a grimace. "Ow, my head aches."

The door opened and a middle aged nurse entered the room. She was tall and wiry with shocking red hair that had to have come from a bottle.

"So how are we doing, here?" she asked cheerily, clearly oblivious to the morose looks around her. She walked briskly to Kellie's side and took her blood pressure, all the while chatting on about the storm, her upcoming vacation, her grown son's new job as a male model and her inability to understand why he didn't yet have a wife. She switched from subject to subject without transition or bothering to take a breath. It was a distinctly manic bedside manner.

"I think we can let you get some sleep now, honey," she said, patting Kellie on the arm a tad too enthusiastically and causing her to flinch. She cast knowing glances at the others in the room. "Doctor will check on her first. Can't be too careful with concussions. And I think we should wrap up our little visit now.

Our girl needs her beauty sleep." She giggled as if she'd said something funny, and without further ado, exited the room.

"I don't know about you," Walt said, trying to lighten the mood with the barest hint of a grin, "but after that, I know I could use a rest."

He leaned over the bed and kissed his daughter. "Thank God, you're alright, Sweetheart," he whispered in her ear, completely serious again. "I love you. More than even I realized until now."

Lila followed suit, her kiss followed by a gentle, yet intense and prolonged embrace. Her daughter was safe here in her arms, and she felt as though she never wanted to let go of her again. It was with reluctance that she finally straightened back up and turned to lead the rest from the room.

"Mom," Kellie said. "Please, could we pray for Ben before you go?"

"Of course," Lila said.

She reached out for Gina's hand on her right and Todd's on her left. Forming a chain forged by blood and by the Spirit, they lifted their voices and opened their hearts to the Lord.

CHAPTER 15

Tuesday, June 27

David was up early Tuesday morning. He'd wanted to be sure to be awake before Ben, who was bound to be upset and confused when he awoke in a strange place. Besides, David hadn't been able to sleep much anyway. The excitement and thrill of having pulled off the kidnapping so easily had teamed up with anticipation of what was yet to come, producing a mind too full to rest. Things were starting to go his way, but the best was yet to come.

He could tell last night that Hank had been proud of him, too. Not that he'd said anything. That wasn't Hank's way. But something had changed between them. Hank had shown him a kind of respect, man to man. And before this was over, David was going to prove to Hank that he had earned that respect.

David opened the now well-stocked refrigerator and removed a carton of eggs. He cracked four of them into a clear glass bowl with one hand and began to beat them. If he'd stayed at the restaurant long enough, he probably could have worked his way into a cooking position. Due to necessity and an innate interest, he had learned a lot about the culinary arts. For most of his life, he'd had no one else to cook for him, and he enjoyed eating far too much to settle for the likes of hot dogs, sandwiches or macaroni and cheese from a box every day. At twelve, he'd been the only kid in his class that regularly watched cooking shows on TV, and by the age of fourteen, he knew his way around a kitchen almost as well as Julia Child. For many years now, Hank had given him free reign when it came to preparing meals for the two of them.

With only a small fraction of his mind on what he was doing, David added grated cheese, fresh sliced mushrooms and chopped green pepper to the eggs before pouring the mixture into a frying pan. The bulk of his attention was being paid to the radio announcer who was giving the latest local news. David listened his way through a warehouse fire, a threatened sanitation strike, the discovery of the body of an unidentified vagrant and the rescue of a dachshund from a gopher hole. Then a woman, enthusing about some clothing sale, tried to make it sound like getting ten percent off on selected items was more exciting by far than winning a million dollar lottery. Finally, music again. Not a word about a kidnapping or a missing child. Hamilton was playing it safe.

David reached across the kitchen counter and turned the knob of a radio that, like everything else in the house, looked to be at least thirty years old. Whoever owned this place sure wasn't tempting anyone to make off with any of the furnishings. You could find better stuff at a thrift store.

He guessed he wouldn't have much to do in the next few days except cook, eat and hang out with the kid. Hank wanted him to lay low and guard Ben until the ransom demands were met. The inactivity wasn't going to be easy, but David would just have to keep reminding himself that waiting was a necessary part of the plan. It would be worth it all in the end when Hamilton was gone for good and he and Hank were rich.

Once the eggs had been folded into an omelet and cooked to perfection, filling the kitchen

Bitter Reunion

air with an aroma that made his stomach growl, David went to wake up Ben.

There was a new latch on the outside of the bedroom door and the window inside was now nailed shut, but the precautions David had taken in securing the room in which Ben slept had proven to be unnecessary. The child's small body still lay fully clothed upon the bed where David had laid him last night. His head was partially burrowed under a battered pillow, and the pale pink blanket that had been neatly spread over him had been kicked aside and was a ball at the foot of the bed. Evidently there was at least one trait that David shared with his half brother.

His brother.

It was weird. Until this moment it hadn't fully hit him that Ben was really his brother. This sleeping child was part of his blood family, connected to him in a way that nobody else was. For some reason, the revelation was uncomfortable and made David feel somehow unfaithful to Hank. He shoved it from his mind.

Gently, David shook Ben's arm and said his name. Ben's eyes slowly opened.

"David?" he questioned, confused. Suddenly he sat upright and his eyes widened. "Where's Kellie? We were gonna surprise Kellie."

David sat on the side of the bed. "Yes, we were. But you fell asleep at my house last night, Ben. Remember? I didn't want to wake you up, so I called your grandparents, and guess what!"

"What?"

"They said you could stay with me for a couple of days. How about that?"

"I don't know..." Ben said, his bottom lip trembling. "I think I want to go home."

"Naw, come on. We'll have a great time. You just wait and see. I've got all kinds of fun things for us to do together. At least have breakfast with me and then we'll decide, O.K.?"

David didn't wait until Ben could protest. He boosted the boy from the bed and propelled him to the kitchen where the table was already set for two.

Just as David had hoped, it wasn't long till Ben warmed to the idea of spending time with him. He'd just needed to get used to his surroundings. It also hadn't hurt that David had bought a VCR, seven Disney movies and a large assortment of toys with which to bribe him to stay.

"I seen *The Lion King* prob'ly more than anybody else in the whole world," Ben said boastfully around a mouthful of toast. "Don't you just hate Scar?"

"I've never seen *The Lion King*."

"NEVER?" Ben asked incredulously. "Oh boy, you're gonna love it!"

"What's these green things?" he asked, wrinkling his nose. He began to pick them out of the eggs, forming a pile on the side of his plate.

"Those are bell peppers," David replied.

"How come my mom's pepper is really little and black instead of green? I don't like it, either."

"I'll tell you what. Tomorrow morning, I'll teach you how to cook eggs. You can make them just the way you like them, with no pepper at all."

"Wow! I never cooked anything before 'cept cookies. Can we make cookies too, David?"

"Sure. Anything you want."

Bitter Reunion

The rest of the morning went by quickly. Everything was a novelty to Ben, including helping David wash the dishes by hand. He got to stand on a chair and swish them around in warm soapy water full of bubbles. Ben told David that he couldn't understand why his mother didn't do her dishes this way. It was sure a lot more fun than just putting them in the dishwasher and turning it on.

For David, the morning was a revelation. Ben was fascinating. You couldn't help but be captivated by his unique simplicity and innocence. David wondered if all children were like him, or if it was just Ben. Either way, he was finding that he liked the boy, and actually enjoyed having him around. It was going to make the next few days a lot easier to bear.

Seeing how Ben was—so open and trusting—also would have given David added motivation, had he needed it, to kill Hamilton. It was within his power to keep what happened to him from ever happening to Ben. Ben would never need to know what a monster his father really was, and David was glad of that.

Midmorning, Hank showed up as prearranged, to finalize the plan for the ransom demand. David watched as the smile on Hank's face turned to a scowl when he saw Ben sitting in front of the television set.

Hank drug David to the kitchen and gestured to a chair at the table. David sat in one chrome framed, red plastic seated chair, while Hank pulled out another and sat down.

"Is this how you hold someone hostage!" Hank burst out immediately. "Why don't you just put him up at the Ritz Carlton and provide him with room service and a limousine? I thought you understood what the sleeping pills and the rope were for. It's customary to keep a prisoner confined to one relatively small area, such as the bed, or at least the bedroom!" Hank's voice dripped with sarcasm and scorn.

"I know what I'm doing, Pa. Ben trusts me. He's not going anywhere. He thinks he's here for a visit and to have a good time. He likes it here."

"Sure, and in the meantime, he's taking in everything around him. He already knows what you look like and will be able to describe you, but now he's seen me, too. Didn't you hear me when I warned you about that with the Reynolds girl?"

David was momentarily speechless. He hadn't thought of that. Come to think of it, he hadn't even considered how they would return Ben to his mother after the ransom pickup. Hamilton would be dead.

Finally he said, "Why don't we just leave Ben at the airport? We'll get on a plane and be out of the country before they figure out who he belongs to."

With one hand, Hank nervously tapped a salt shaker against the gray Formica table top. "That could work, I guess," he grudgingly admitted. "Then it wouldn't much matter what he remembers about us. We'd be out of the reaches of the law, where I intend to stay for the duration.

"But it's still ridiculous, David, the way you're treating that boy like a house guest. HE IS A HOSTAGE. Nothing more."

David swallowed the urge to remind Hank that Ben was also his brother. Somehow he knew Hank would not be receptive to that fact.

"At the very least," Hank went on, "don't let the kid go outside. A neighbor might see him if he strayed far enough away from the house."

"Despite what you think, Pa, I'm not stupid. I wouldn't let him out. It's still raining, anyway. He won't want to go out. I wish you'd trust me. Just because my methods are different than yours doesn't mean they won't work. I won't let Ben out of my sight. I know how much depends on this."

David was relieved when Hank let the subject drop and went on to another. The ransom.

"I'll be calling Hamilton from a pay phone this afternoon. Before I do, we need to discuss what I'm going to tell him."

Hank reached into his slacks pocket, and David noticed for the first time that Hank looked overdressed. He'd be willing to bet that Hank would be seeing Belinda today.

Hank had removed a small black notebook, which he proceeded to open flat and lay upon the table. It was a pocket-sized daily planner.

"This is today," Hank said, circling the twenty-seventh with a black Bic pen. "The next few days are critical. Timing is everything. We have to decide how long to give Hamilton to come up with the money, and have our flight reservations coincide with that so we can get out of here as quickly as possible after we waste him."

David's eyes were glued to the calendar. He had totally lost track of the days, each one having blended into the next since arriving at Albion. Now, suddenly, with the month spread out before him, he was aware of something that momentarily threw him completely off balance. Then, just as suddenly, the realization snapped into place and seemed completely right, as if he should have known all along that it would be this way. July first, just four days away, was his birthday. On that day he would come full circle.

"...too long." David had missed what Hank was saying. "I think two days ought to do it. The longer we wait, the riskier it gets."

"No!" David said. The assertiveness in his voice caused Hank's head to snap up.

"What did you say?"

"I said, no. We have to wait till the first for the ransom payment. It's important."

"What do you mean, it's important?" Hank stared at David with a mixture of amazement and outrage. He wasn't used to having his statements contradicted, especially by David.

Ben chose that moment to walk into the kitchen.

"I'm hungry, David, and the movie is over. Can I have something to eat?"

"Get out of here!" Hank thundered at the small boy.

Ben stood stock still, eyes registering shock and confusion. Then he whirled around and ran from the room, crying loudly.

"Just great," David mumbled. He rose abruptly, almost knocking his chair over, and followed after Ben.

Ben was curled up on the couch, tears staining his cheeks. The thumb of his right hand was in his mouth.

"I don't like that bad man," he sniffled when he saw David. "I want my daddy."

The words reverberated in David's mind. *I want my daddy...I want my daddy*. He slammed his fist down on the table next to the couch.

"You do not!" David screamed, making Ben cower further into the couch. "You do not want your daddy! *He's* the bad man!"

Bitter Reunion

Ben was crying harder, now. He was nearly hysterical.

David picked him up. Ben struggled hard against him, kicking his feet and pounding his fists. It was like trying to hold onto an angry tiger, but David managed to stagger to the bedroom with him. He dropped Ben to the bed, where the child collapsed in a sobbing heap.

David strode quickly to the door and slammed it hard behind him. Then he slid the latch into place. He stood in the hall for a moment to catch his breath before returning to the kitchen.

By the time David sat back down at the table, he regretted what he had done. So much for having gained the boy's trust. He could try to make amends, but he doubted it would do any good. Everything would be harder now.

Hank, on the other hand, seemed pleased. "That's more like it," was all he said to David about the incident. A half smile, or maybe a sneer, curled one corner of his lip.

"Now, what were you saying about July first?" Hank no longer seemed angry.

"For personal reasons, I need to get rid of Hamilton on the first day of July," David said, a steely note of determination coloring his voice. "I won't do it until July first."

"Personal reasons, huh? There are no secrets between us, boy."

David didn't respond. This once, he wasn't going to let Hank intimidate him.

"Alright, it's a deal. I don't like it, but it's your call. As long as you follow through with your end."

"You don't need to worry about that. Nothing could keep me from it," David said, and he meant every word with all his being.

For half an hour longer, Hank and David discussed details of the plan. Then Hank left, promising to contact David later with Todd's reaction to the ransom call.

The house was quiet.

David walked to the bedroom door and unlatched it. Opening it slowly, he crept inside. Ben was lying on his back, staring at the ceiling. He didn't even glance at David as he approached and stood beside the bed.

"I'm sorry, Ben," David said, kneeling down. "I shouldn't have yelled at you. I just lost my temper. Will you forgive me...please?"

Ben turned his head and looked at David. What David saw in the boy's eyes made his heart sink.

"I just want to go home," Ben whispered. A single tear trickled down his face.

"I can't take you home just yet. Nobody's there," David said. For some reason it pained him to lie to the boy. "Why don't you come on out and we'll make some lunch together. I'll show you how to fix hot dogs and french fries. Do you like hot dogs?"

When Ben continued to stare at David without answering, David said, "Then we can watch *The Lion King*. You can tell me when the best parts are coming. We'll have popcorn and soda pop. Please, Ben." He was practically begging now. "I'm really sorry."

Hesitantly, Ben scooted to the edge of the bed and swung his legs over the side.

"Then will you take me home?"

"Sure," David lied, wondering how he would stall Ben for four more days. It looked like he was going to have to resort to the sleeping pills after all.

CHAPTER 16

The atmosphere in the Hamilton home on the afternoon of June 27th bore a remarkable resemblance to that of a funeral parlor. The air was heavy with unspoken dread, and there was a marked absence of laughter or even normal conversation. The only things missing were the cloying smell of flowers and the sound of organ music. Outside, a sky laden with dark clouds cast little light into a gloomy room. If anyone noticed, they didn't care enough to turn on a lamp.

The living room was hot and stuffy and seemed crowded with too many bodies, all of them but one moving restlessly from place to place without a purpose. A large platter of sandwiches and fruit lay nearly untouched on a coffee table. No one had an appetite. Innocently resting near one corner of an antique secretary desk was the object that had suddenly taken on an uncharacteristic amount of importance. An ordinary black telephone. It was the focus of everyone's breathless anticipation, and its continued silence brought agony to them all.

The Hamiltons and the Reynolds had banded together for support. That morning Lila and Walt had checked Kellie out of the hospital. Then the three of them had come to Todd and Gina's to wait for the promised call from the kidnapper.

Kellie now lay prone on the couch, fighting the desire to sleep. She wanted to be conscious when the call came and had vowed to take no more of the pain pills that knocked her out, even though her head was pounding and her mother kept pressuring her to take them. Not until after the call, at least.

There didn't seem to be a single inch of her body that didn't ache, and she knew from having taken a quick glance in a mirror this morning that she looked even worse than she felt. A large white bandage covered the gash on her forehead that had taken nineteen stitches to close. Besides that one large cut, her face and body bore numerous other smaller cuts and scratches. Some had required stitches and some had not. One eye was blackened, and her arms and legs were covered with ugly bruises, the result of having been thrown from the car to the hard, unforgiving ground. Despite her present physical condition, though, Kellie was very grateful.

She was alive, and she would recover from her injuries. The bullet that had shattered the window of her car had miraculously missed hitting her, and the fact that she had absentmindedly neglected to fasten her seat belt had kept her from being blown to pieces inside a demolished car. There would be few lasting effects of the accident. A scar just below her hairline. The loss of her prized little Chevy. And the memory of that night. It could have been much, much worse.

Mixed with the gratitude, however, was a large dose of guilt, because battered as she was, she was safe now. But Ben—her little Beej, who was as dear to her as a brother—was out there somewhere at the mercy of a would-be killer. The nightmare he must be experiencing didn't bear thinking about. If only she could have taken his place, she would have gladly done it.

She knew from the grim silence that her mother and father and Todd and Gina were involved in their own private battles against despair. It was a lonely feeling.

The afternoon ticked on. When it seemed as if the weight of the silence would crush them all, Lila broke it to encourage them for at least the tenth time to eat something. Heads shook, voices politely declined, and the room returned to its mausoleum stillness. A pendulum could be heard swinging, and the telephone loomed strangely larger with each passing second. Finally, at exactly two-fourteen in the afternoon, it rang. The sound of it was like a scream. Its jarring loudness startled them and alerted them to impending danger.

Todd, seated in the chair nearest the desk, lunged to answer it, hoping against hope that it was the kidnapper. He didn't think he could stand it if it were a chance call from a friend, or a salesperson, or whoever else might decide to call them in the middle of the day.

"Hello!" he said. Too loud. Too desperate.

"Hamilton?"

"Yes," Todd answered, nodding to Gina. This was their man, alright. The one word he had spoken sent a chill through Todd, and he had known instantly.

"Listen carefully, and don't interrupt.

I want five million dollars by Saturday. That should be plenty of time for you to get the money together, so don't even think of stalling for more time. And don't think of letting the cops in on this, either. Not if you want to see your kid alive.

You'll hear from me again Saturday morning as to the time and place to make the exchange."

Todd broke in. "How do I know my son is O.K.? Let me talk to him."

"I told you not to interrupt!" the angry voice bellowed. "I'm the one giving the orders here. Not you! I suppose it's hard for an important man like you to let someone else call the shots. Well, you better get used to it." There was a click in Todd's ear. The conversation was over.

Todd relayed the information he'd been given to the rest of his family, purposely leaving out the underlying threat of the message. It was pretty much as they had all expected, but now it was reality. They were left feeling deflated. There was nothing anyone could do until Saturday, which seemed light years away.

"Five million dollars is a lot of money. Can you get that much?" Lila wondered aloud. The amount had taken her breath away when Todd had mentioned it.

"It's going to take some doing, but yes, I think I can get that much," Todd answered briefly before changing the subject. "We're going to have to try to act normal for the next few days. I know it won't be easy, but we can't arouse suspicion."

"Is there anything we can do to help, Todd?" Walt asked. He hadn't slept at all the previous night, and it showed. His usually sturdy frame sagged and seemed ready to collapse.

"No. I'll take care of everything," Todd said sternly. "I think the three of you should go home and try to get some rest. It's going to be a long four days."

Walt reluctantly acknowledged the logic of Todd's suggestion. He and Lila helped Kellie to her feet and then to the door. After hugs

Bitter Reunion

and promises to stay constantly in touch, they took their leave.

Todd was relieved to have them gone. As much as he loved them, their presence had been a burden. He needed to be alone. He had to think.

"Tell me the truth. Do you think Ben is alright? I can't stand to think of that man with him. And for four more days!" Gina was beside him, her eyes begging him to calm her fears. She leaned into him and wrapped her arms around his chest. He felt as if he were smothering in her need. It was like being in the clutches of a boa constrictor. He couldn't breathe.

"It's going to be fine, Gina. You'll see." He pushed her gently away and turned his back on her. "You need some rest, too, and there are things I have to do. We'll talk later." The tone of his voice was abrupt, and he saw a new hurt in her eyes. It only added to the desire building within him to flee.

He felt like a coward and a criminal for walking out on her, but he had no choice. He had to get away…now.

Alone at last in his den, Todd fell back into his favorite brown leather wing chair and confronted the legion of horrors that filled his mind.

The kidnapper despised him. The caller's message had been delivered in a tone of such undisguised hatred that it had shaken Todd to the core. It made him think of Elaine's last gift to him—the video tape. Her voice on that tape had possessed the same lethal quality. Todd had no confidence that the man would spare Ben's life, even when he'd received the ransom money. If, like Elaine, the kidnapper's key motivation was to make Todd suffer, money wouldn't be enough to satisfy him.

Something else was bothering him, too. Something beyond the obvious that he couldn't quite put his finger on. He thought back over everything that the man had said, but whatever it was remained elusive. It was frustrating. The harder he tried to catch it, the further away it retreated. He let it go.

Todd sat for a long time—he had no idea how long. Time held no meaning for him. It could be morning, noon or dead of night. It was all the same. Reality itself was skewed, unhooked from its moorings and as eerily sinister as an old episode of the Twilight Zone. He couldn't understand it or hold on to it, and it felt dangerously close to slipping away entirely. First, he had to focus, and then he had to fight. It was his only hope.

Nothing was important anymore except one thing. Getting Ben back. He couldn't fail this time around. He had to succeed. Everything depended on it. Everything.

He was thinking more clearly now as if his mind were slowly emerging from a dense fog. He still had four days before the ransom was to be made. That was a break. Maybe it would be long enough for him to figure out who had Ben and make an offensive move of his own.

At some time during the afternoon the sun had decided to make an appearance, and it sent a sliver of light shooting through a small gap between heavy drapes at the window. It cut through the gloom like a knife, dissecting the surface of the large oak roll-top desk behind which Todd sat. A statue coming to life, he stirred and leaned forward to pull out a drawer and remove a small black notebook. He stared at it without really seeing it and weighed his options.

They were far too few. He could call the police and enlist their help, despite the kidnapper's warnings. Or he could follow the kidnapper's instruction to the letter and hope that the man had an ounce of compassion. Neither plan seemed acceptable. That left only one other thing to do.

Todd glanced nervously toward the closed door. He didn't want Gina to know what he was doing. She might not approve and he didn't have the energy to argue with her. It was the first time he'd ever hidden anything from her. It felt foreign and wrong, but necessary.

Todd opened the notebook and flipped quickly through the pages of names, addresses and telephone numbers. It had been at least a couple of years since he had looked up this particular number. He really hadn't thought he would be needing it again.

Carl Grady. The name stared back at him from the page. After only the briefest hesitation, Todd picked up the telephone on his desk and dialed the Portland number beside the name. He hoped Grady was still at the same phone number.

He was.

"Grady Detective Service." Todd recognized the gruff voice.

"Hi, Carl. This is Todd Hamilton."

Something in his voice must have tipped off Carl as to his state of mind, because Grady's next words were, "What's wrong, Todd? Have you found out something about Joey?"

"No, Carl, I'm not calling about Joey this time. It's about my other son, Ben. You aren't going to believe this. He's been kidnapped."

Todd still didn't entirely believe it himself, even as he explained it to Grady.

"You know I'll do everything I can to help you, Todd," Grady said, when Todd had finished telling him everything that had transpired in the last two days. "What do you want me to do?"

"I want you to check out a possible suspect for me. His name is Howard Sneed. If he isn't actually the kidnapper, he may have some idea who it could be." Todd recounted the visit he'd had from Sneed, the threatening notes, and the reference that the kidnapper had made to gay-bashers. He finished with, "So I feel that it's someone from the gay community in Portland, or maybe even Sneed himself. He seemed extremely agitated over what I said to him. Maybe agitated enough to want to hurt me."

There was silence on the other end of the line while Grady assessed what Todd had said.

"Well, what do you think? Will you do it?" Todd asked, when Carl's lack of response began to concern him.

"Yes. I can do that, Todd. Are you sure the perp couldn't be someone you know, though? I mean, more personally?"

"I don't think so. It wouldn't make sense. Besides, I don't know of anyone with a grudge against me. Why?"

Grady answered slowly, weighing his words. "I just thought that, considering the day that the ransom is to be paid, the kidnapper must know your history. It couldn't be a coincidence."

It took a minute for the comment to sink in. The day of the ransom payment. Four days from now. Saturday. July 1st.

Bitter Reunion

That was it! The nagging, elusive something in the back of his mind was identified. Saturday would be Joey's birthday, and exactly eleven years since he had disappeared with Elaine.

Now it was Todd's turn to be silent. How could that have slipped his mind? It must have been the shock of everything else that had happened. But Carl had remembered the day and immediately seen the implications.

But how did it tie in? He thought on that for a moment before he spoke.

"One possibility is that the kidnapper dug into my background. To find out what he could use against me, maybe. I don't know. Then again, maybe it is someone who knows me. Come to think of it, there is one person who could be that angry with me right now."

"Who?" Carl prompted.

"His name is Calvin Manning. He was one of my drivers. I just fired him last week and he took it very badly."

"Did he know about the threatening notes you'd gotten?"

"I don't know. He might have. Some of the people in the office found out about them, and you know how that kind of news gets around."

"Yeah, I know," Carl replied. "I think Manning bears looking in to. I'll start this evening. We don't have a lot of time to follow up on the leads."

Todd interrupted. "I'll take care of checking out Manning myself. I have the time, and I need to be doing something. You just follow up on the homosexual angle for me. That's where I think we're going to find this guy."

"O.K., but be careful," Grady cautioned. "Remember that whoever did this is very dangerous. Don't let Manning find out what you're doing. Listen, Todd, before I go, I've got one more question for you."

"What's that?"

"Are you a hundred percent certain this is the way you want to go with this, Todd? Are you sure you don't want to get the police on it? They'll get the FBI involved and they have far more man power and expertise in these kinds of cases than I do."

"I tried the police once before," Todd said bitterly. "They were worse than useless. I don't trust them. I trust you. You found out more for me than they ever did. I often wondered if I would have found Joey if I had hired you sooner and not wasted so much time thinking that the police would do their jobs. I won't make that mistake again."

"O.K., if you feel that way. You know I'll do everything in my power, Todd. But I just want you to get the best possible help, and I'm not so sure I'm it."

"Well, I am," Todd said with as much confidence as he could muster. He hung up after giving Grady his home and cellular phone numbers and promising to call him if he thought of anything else that could pertain to the kidnapping. In turn, Grady agreed to contact Todd as soon as he had anything to report.

Todd felt somewhat better now that he had spoken to Carl Grady and knew that something was being done to find Ben. The next step was to get together the money for the ransom in case he ended up having to pay it.

Other than his concern for H & H and whether or not it could survive the strain on its capital, the money was a small consideration for Todd. Parting with five million dollars wouldn't devastate him the way it would many a rich man. Maybe he would even be better off without it. He could trace the source of this whole tragedy to money. If he hadn't been wealthy, he wouldn't have been approached by Sneed in the first place. And who would have bothered to kidnap his son if there weren't vast sums of money to be made by it? This whole experience only reinforced what he already knew. Excessive amounts of money could be more of a curse than a blessing.

He had always known that what counted in life couldn't be measured in dollars and cents. His family was his treasure. Nothing money could buy could even begin to compare in value to what they had together—the love they shared. Gina and Ben were everything to him.

The clock on the study wall read five fifty-six P.M. Todd left the room and walked through the house. He didn't see Gina. She must have decided to try to get some sleep. Rationalizing that he didn't want to disturb her, he wrote a brief note saying that he would be at the office. He needed to go over the books before calling the bank tomorrow morning. Softly, he closed the front door behind him.

Twenty minutes after Todd drove away, Gina approached the house on foot from the opposite direction. She hadn't been asleep, as Todd had assumed. She had gone for a walk, driven by a consuming restlessness and a need to escape the four walls that had seemed to shrink in around her. The walk hadn't helped much. Her mind was still in a state of turmoil, but the nervous energy had drained out of her body. It was replaced by a debilitating inertia that was just as bad. Her legs suddenly felt as though they were made of lead, and every step was an effort.

Not often, but occasionally, Gina had nightmares in which she was trying to escape from someone or something. But she couldn't run fast enough. Her motions were slow and drugged. Her limbs were trapped by quicksand or maybe she was under tons of water and that's why they wouldn't move. Panic engulfed her as the danger from behind grew steadily closer. She couldn't get away. That's how she felt now, but this nightmare was no dream from which she could wake up.

When she entered the house, she saw the note on the dining room table. She read it in disbelief. Now, when she needed him more than she had ever needed him before, Todd had left her all alone. Something inside that had been holding on by a thread gave way, and Gina crumpled to the floor. Her body shook with great gasping sobs. She stayed there, unable to muster the energy to get up and continued to cry as she hadn't cried since she was a very little girl.

Much later, when there were no more tears to be shed, Gina slowly arose, wiped her face on the bottom edge of her t-shirt and made her way to the living room. Weak, scattered rays of light were all that was left of the setting sun, and the room was dark. She switched on a lamp and looked around.

It was as though she'd never seen this room before. The tray of food still sat on the coffee table, its fruit now brown and dry. A fly perched undisturbed on one sandwich. He might as well invite his friends. There was more than he could eat, and Gina wasn't interested in sharing it with him.

Bitter Reunion

She wandered through the rest of the house alone, switching on lights as she went. It was the same in each room. She'd always loved her house, but now suddenly it was a cold, uninviting place. It didn't seem like home anymore.

Ben's room was the worst. Smokey was there, lying forlornly on the floor. Usually, he slept up on the bed, often with his furry head upon the pillow only inches from Ben's. Tonight there was no small boy to invite him up, so Smokey would stay on the floor until morning, faithfully guarding the room and keeping watch for his master. Gina wondered if anyone had thought to feed the little guy. It now seemed to take extraordinary effort to remember to do ordinary routine things.

Toys lay scattered on the floor, awaiting their owner's imminent return from whatever interruption had taken him away. And the room was quiet, as it never was when Ben was present. No vroooom of imaginary race cars or roaring of imaginary lions. Gina absent-mindedly ran her hand along the surface of Ben's bed. Was it really just yesterday morning that she had lost her temper with him in this room? She flinched, thinking of it.

It had happened just before they had left for Mom and Dad's. After having packed Ben's bag, she had been helping him make his bed when she had discovered a big glob of white glue that ran down one side of the bedspread and formed a hardened puddle in the carpet below. She herself had become unglued at the sight of the plastic bottle, lid removed, lying on its side near the edge of the bed.

"What is this doing here like this?" she had demanded of Ben, holding the sticky, empty bottle up accusingly.

"Must have fell over," Ben had said.

"Why did you take the lid off, Benjamin?"

The use of his full first name had cemented the knowledge that he was in deep trouble. "I couldn't get the glue out, mommy. I squeezed real hard, but it wouldn't come out. So I had to take the lid off and then it came out too much."

Gina had gotten out the carpet cleaner and gone to work on the glue, but it was hopeless. It had dried as hard as rock. The carpet was new, Gina had been rushed, and the more she'd scrubbed, the madder she'd gotten.

"Don't EVER take the lid off of the glue, again! And you are NOT to use glue or paints or ANYTHING messy in this room without asking me first!" She'd known the tone of her voice was unreasonably harsh and strident, and before they'd left the house Ben had been in tears. He had still been sullen when they parted. And now the memory of the way he had looked haunted her. What if that was the last time she would ever see him? She couldn't bear the thought.

Dear Lord, why hadn't she apologized? Why had she been so angry with him? He was just showing the normal irresponsibility of a child his age. If only she could go back in time. Yesterday she hadn't realized how much she had that she took for granted. She'd been more concerned about a stupid carpet than the feelings of her precious child. She could no longer stand to be in same room where she had yelled at Ben and made him cry.

Leaving all the lights burning brightly behind her, Gina went at last to the bedroom. Their bedroom—hers and Todd's. Two windows were open, and a cross-current of cool night air sought to bring relief after the heat of

Bitter Reunion

the day. It only added to the chill that already permeated Gina's body.

Fully clothed, she climbed under the covers of the bed. She took up such a small space on its king-sized mattress. Todd should be lying here beside her—how she longed for him! But somehow she knew he wouldn't be returning for some time yet. She had never felt so alone.

She lay willing herself to sleep, but sleep wouldn't come. Only nightmares. Maybe she still had some of that codeine cough syrup around from when she had bronchitis. It always seemed to put her to sleep, and maybe it would do the same thing even if she didn't have a cough.

She sat up in bed and swung her legs over the side. Her right foot hit the leg of the night stand beside her, and she heard a thump as something fell from it to the floor. Bending over to pick it up, she discovered that it was her Bible. It had fallen open to the spot where she had last read, and she saw the familiar passage imprinted on the leather bookmark which had resided in her Bible for years. "Cast all your anxieties on Him, for He cares about you."

Forgetting all about the cough syrup, Gina began to read. The words were like bread to a starving person, and in them was the comfort she so desperately needed. Hours later, when Todd returned home, he found her in a deep dreamless sleep in which there were no demons.

CHAPTER 17

Wednesday, June 28

When Hank woke up Wednesday morning groggy and disoriented, he had no idea where he was. Then he heard the loud wheeze-whistle-grunt of Belinda's unique brand of snoring and his eyes began to focus on frilly pink ruffles. He remembered now—only too well.

He really didn't need this con, he told himself, lying still so as not to wake Belinda up. Hamilton's ransom payment would make what Belinda was going to give him seem like chicken feed. But still, the con was in his blood and it had been a way to kill time while in this hick town. And he just loved the feeling it gave him when he pulled it off—when he walked away with someone else's money. It was even worth waking up beside Belinda now and then. He chanced a glance in her direction. She was lying on her side, her mouth open wide, saliva making a dark, damp stain on her pillow. It would be a distinct pleasure to rip her off.

Belinda began to stir. One eye opened slightly. Hank got out of bed before she was fully awake and retreated to the guest bathroom where he showered, shaved and dressed. He always felt uncomfortable here in Belinda's house. It was probably one of the most expensive homes in Albion, and could have been stunning if it had been tastefully decorated. But Belinda had done the interior herself and it was atrocious. The whole place looked like a pre-adolescent girl's bedroom. Pink and purple, lace and ruffles, pillows, hearts and flowers. Everywhere. At the moment, his stocking feet were sunk three inches deep in fluffy pale-pink carpet, and he gazed at his reflection in a heart-shaped mirror. A few days in this environment could completely deplete a man of testosterone. It was a good thing he smoked. It gave him lots of excuses to step outside where he could escape Belinda and her house. Hopefully, this would be the last day he would have to spend any time at all here, he thought.

By the time he entered the kitchen, Belinda had breakfast cooked and waiting for him. That was Belinda's only redeeming quality as far as Hank could see. She was a great cook, maybe even better than David. This morning she had made his favorite, eggs benedict.

"This is excellent, pumpkin," Hank raved as he ate, using the idiotic endearment because he secretly thought she actually was a lot like a pumpkin. Big and round and reminiscent of Halloween. He was going to pour on the charm this morning and get that check she had been promising him. The one he was going to invest in a sure-fire land deal for her, or as she put it, for them and their future together. Then it would be sayonara, baby. He would never have to look at her face again.

They ate in near silence, both enjoying the food too much to talk. Hank had to admit that he would miss her eggs benedict.

"So, what's the latest Country Club gossip?" Hank had eaten the last bite of his breakfast and felt it was time to be congenial. He could start out slow and then ease into the subject of the land deal.

Belinda laid down her fork and shifted in her chair. She was wearing hot pink shorts that were too short and too tight. She adjusted them where they had bunched up between her large thighs. That done, she considered his question.

"Oh, I forgot to mention it last night," she said, her face becoming animated at the thought of the juicy little tidbit of news that she had to share. There was a hint of drama in her voice. "But maybe you know about it already." She paused to heighten the suspense, and Hank played along, pretending to be curious.

"About what?" He leaned forward as if he couldn't wait to hear.

"Did you hear about what happened to Kellie Reynolds?"

So that was it. Maybe this would be mildly interesting after all. He shook his head sorrowfully. "Yes. It's awful isn't it? How is her family taking her death?"

"What?"

"It must have been a shock to learn of her death."

Belinda's mouth was hanging open again, and she had a perplexed expression on her face.

"You must of got your wires crossed, Thomas. Kellie was in a bad wreck, but she isn't dead. Where did you hear that?"

He was speechless. He scrambled from the chair and began to clear the table of dishes in a clumsy attempt to cover his confusion and dismay. "Well, I heard about her accident and I guess I just assumed it was fatal. Sounded like a bad one."

"It was! I found out about it from the mother of one of Kellie's friends. Kellie's real lucky to be alive. Her car exploded!"

"So how *did* she survive?" Hank asked, no longer having to act at being interested. Belinda had his full attention now, and she was basking in it.

"She got thrown out before the explosion. Can you believe it? She's already out of the hospital! She didn't have a single broken bone or anything!"

"That is amazing," Hank responded, trying to sound sincere.

Belinda began to help him with the dishes, stacking them on the pink marble counter top as Hank crammed them into the dishwasher. She prattled on happily about this and that, and Hank made a show of listening. But his mind was a million miles away.

He'd been unforgivably careless. From the time he had called the Reynolds girl on his cell phone till he'd seen her car disintegrate in flames, everything had gone so smoothly that he hadn't bothered to check it out any further. If he had followed up, he would have discovered her where she had landed, and she wouldn't be alive and potentially able to blow things sky high—the way she should have been herself. In fact, he'd been so confident, that once David had informed him that there was no mention of the kidnapping in the news, he hadn't thought to check the paper or listen to the radio for an account of the accident.

Fuming at himself, at fate and at David for having made Kellie Reynolds a problem in the first place, Hank considered the implications of this latest development. There were still three days to go until the ransom payment was to be made—plenty of time for Kellie to suspect David and then to remember that David and he had been together at the park. Plenty of time to send the authorities out looking for him. Hank dumped a half-full cup of coffee into Belinda's lavender sink and turned on the faucet. Then he watched as the brown liquid was rinsed down the drain. That's what could very well happen to all his carefully laid plans. They could go right down the drain.

There was no way around it. He was going to have to make some immediate defensive plays, the first of which would be to move out of the apartment and into the house with David. The rental transaction on the house had been done entirely by phone and mail under an assumed name. They should be relatively safe from discovery there.

It was risky and went against all common sense, but he was also considering another crack at the Reynolds girl. It was a matter of pride now, as much or more than a matter of safety. Whether she'd meant to or not, Kellie Reynolds had beat him at his own game and made him feel like a fool. And no one made a fool of Hank and got away with it. Especially not some young female relative of the man he had come to think of as his personal enemy.

Oh yes, he desperately wanted her dead.

"You haven't heard one word I've said." Belinda's high pitched complaint intruded on his thoughts. She was really beginning to grate on his nerves, and he wanted nothing more than to wrap his hands around her throat and squeeze.

"I'm sorry, darling," he said. "It's just that I've been so preoccupied, thinking about us."

Hank forced himself to draw her close in a romantic embrace. He caressed her cheek with his forefinger and leaned over slightly to whisper in her ear. It was his famous Don Juan technique, and he had mastered it to the point of perfection.

"I have to make that trip to New York right away. I'm flying out first thing tomorrow morning. It's going to be torture being without you, but it will only be for a couple of days. When I get back, I think we should be married."

"Thomas!" Belinda squealed, her eyes sparkling with joy. "Is this a proposal?"

No, you idiot, it's my way of saying good riddance, he thought. "Yes, darling. I don't have a ring yet to put on your beautiful finger…but will you marry me?"

"Yes, oh yes," Belinda gushed. "I love you, Thomas." Her face was flushed and there were tears glistening in her eyes. Her arms tightened around his neck till he was afraid she might strangle him.

The proposal had been a sudden inspiration, but it also turned out to have been a stroke of genius. Everything that came after was easy. Belinda was in such a state of euphoria, she hardly hesitated at all when he told her he needed a check for the five hundred thousand he was going to invest for her while in New York. She scribbled out the amount, signed her name and handed it over to him. It was a beautiful sight, that three by six-inch piece of paper, even if it was cotton candy pink with bows and hearts imprinted all over it. The six figures written on the amount line made it a work of art.

Before he left her house for the last time, Hank took Belinda in his arms again and kissed her long and hard with a passion she had never realized he felt for her. He truly does love me, she thought, and her heart soared at the realization that her days of loneliness and longing for someone to care about her were over. Then she escorted him to his car and watched as he drove away, exiting her life as completely and suddenly as he had entered it.

CHAPTER 18

"I'm still not sure why you want to talk to me without Cal, Mr. Hamilton," Tanya Manning said, as she sat across from him at her kitchen table. She held a toddler on her lap, and there were five other children in the next room, watching Sesame Street on the television. Todd could hear snatches of a conversation between Bert and Ernie.

"Is he in trouble? Is it the drinking? Because if it is, there's nothing I can do. Believe me, I've tried to get Cal to see that he has a problem, but he won't listen to me. It's like talking to the wall, only a lot more frustrating."

Todd was beginning to get the distinct impression that Tanya hadn't been informed of Cal's termination, and he hated to have to be the one to tell her. That was her husband's job. But then, Cal Manning didn't seem to be performing any of his jobs too well lately.

Neglect was the word that had come to mind the minute Todd had set foot on the Manning's property. He'd walked through a weed-infested, toy-cluttered yard and immediately encountered a broken doorbell.

His knock had been answered by Tanya, who had been balancing a runny-nosed child on her hip, and when she invited him in, he had seen that the inside of the house was no better off than it's exterior. Everything seemed to be in a state of disrepair or cluttered beyond recognition. And there were children everywhere.

Tanya, though–that was a different matter. It was the first time Todd had seen her when she wasn't with her husband. Cal was the

Bitter Reunion

domineering type who had a way of overshadowing those around him. Todd was finding out that there was more to Tanya than he had suspected.

Of average height, average weight, nondescript features and hair that could be described as either dark blonde or light brown, she was a woman you would never look twice at on the street. But there was a strength, a steely determination in her eyes that Todd had never noticed before.

"Is that it? The drinking?" Tanya prodded, when Todd's silence went on too long.

"He didn't tell you that I fired him?"

"No." She didn't look surprised, and if she was upset, Todd couldn't tell. It wasn't the reaction he had expected. He didn't know whether to be relieved or not.

"Excuse me for a moment," Tanya said.

She packed the baby out of the room, and came back five minutes later without her. Todd could hear the child howling in the background, and Big Bird's voice grew louder.

"She'll go to sleep before long. She always has to cry a little before dropping off," Tanya explained, as she poured herself a cup of coffee.

"Would you like some?" she asked.

Todd shook his head. He didn't need caffeine—he was already jittery enough. All he wanted to do was to get on with this investigation into the recent activities of Cal Manning.

Tanya poured three teaspoons full of sugar into her steaming cup and returned to the table.

"I don't blame you. For firing him, I mean. I knew it was only a matter of time before you either let him go or he got in an accident on the road."

"I really hated to have to do it," Todd said. "I know it's going to make things difficult for you."

Tanya shrugged her shoulders. "For Cal, maybe. Now he won't have a paycheck to blow on booze and gambling. Let me tell you something, Mr. Hamilton. Cal hasn't contributed anything to our marriage for a very long time. Have you ever heard the old saying that alcoholics don't have friends, they just have hostages? Well, I'm Cal's hostage. But not for long."

The word hostage jumped out at Todd. There were questions he wanted to ask Tanya, but she wasn't giving him the chance. She had things to get off her chest, and he was a listening ear. Spending her days with small children made her hungry for someone to talk to.

"I'm saving my money," she went on. "I babysit and do sewing and other odd jobs. As soon as I have enough for plane tickets for me and the kids, we're out of here. I'm taking them and going home to Pennsylvania. My mom will help me with the kids, and I intend to go back to college and get a degree. I've got to pull my life together for the children's sake. And for mine."

"I still love Cal," she said, with the first hint of regret. "He's a wonderful man, underneath it all. He started out just like me, drinking an occasional beer. You know, no big deal. And then one day, he couldn't stop at just a few. Before I knew it, alcohol became his life."

"I understand," Todd said. It sounded exactly like Elaine. "I've been there, too. My first wife was an alcoholic.

"It's hell, isn't it?" she said.

Todd nodded.

"So, when did he get fired?"

"Last Friday."

She laughed, a mirthless, derisive sound. "He never said a word. He's been gone for two days. I just figured he was driving truck. Guess not."

Her words caused Todd to sit a little straighter in his chair. If Manning hadn't been at home, where was he? Could he be with Ben right now? Had the loss of his job forced him to invent other ways to get money for his addiction?

"I need to find him, Tanya. You don't happen to know where he could be?"

"I have a pretty good guess," she answered. "Try the Tally Ho bar on Hawthorne Boulevard. It's his home away from home. In fact, he's probably there more than he's here."

Before Todd left for the Tally Ho, he wrote out a check and handed it to Tanya. She looked at it, and her eyes widened.

"I can't take this," she protested and tried to give it back, but Todd was already walking toward the door.

"It's for the kids and that new life in Pennsylvania," he said, just before the door closed behind him.

Todd wondered if he looked as out-of-place as he felt. As soon as his eyes adjusted to the darkness, he knew that he did. The Tally Ho was obviously a tavern that catered to the serious drinker, because a sober person would have no desire to hang out here. It wasn't one of those trendy spots with psychedelic lighting, loud music and dancing or the type of place where people came to do their social drinking and watch a football game on a large screen T.V. It was a dive, with absolutely no atmosphere save that of a dirty, darkened dungeon. A jukebox in the corner provided the only diversion, other than the alcohol. It offered up plaintive words of loss and desperation to a mournful tune.

Being here gave Todd the creeps. The only times he'd ever been in a bar had been the numerous occasions when he'd gone in search of Elaine, but that had been years ago. He wasn't a drinker. Period. Not wine, not beer—nothing. It wasn't that he thought moderate drinking was necessarily an evil. It was just that he couldn't see the point. He knew what alcohol could do to people. He knew where moderate drinking could lead, and to his way of thinking, the momentary pleasure of a slight buzz wasn't worth the risk. There were plenty of other ways to have a good time.

One thing was for sure. The clientele in this place didn't seem to be enjoying themselves very much. Most of them sat alone, morosely hunched over their drinks.

Todd stood just inside the door and looked around, searching for Manning. A muscular giant of a man sporting a prolific full beard and handlebar mustache, Manning was about as inconspicuous as Hulk Hogan, and it wasn't long before Todd spotted him sitting at the bar beside one of the few women in the room. The two looked cozy.

I'll bet Tanya doesn't know about this, either, Todd thought, as he advanced to the bar and took a seat on Cal's other side.

"What'll it be?" the bartender asked in a bored voice.

"I'd just like a cola, please," Todd answered.

Bitter Reunion

The man grunted and lifted thick eyebrows in what could have been surprise or irritation before wordlessly retreating.

"Well, if it isn't the boss man! Or should I say EX-boss man?" Cal boomed, staring straight at Todd with murder in his eyes. "You want to beg me to come back to work? Huh? Is that what you're doing here? 'Cause I wouldn't work for you if you were the last man on earth!"

"It's O.K., Calvy," the woman said, leaning across Cal to glare at Todd. "Can't you leave the poor guy alone?" she asked Todd. "Haven't you already done enough to him?"

Todd noticed that his cola had appeared, as if by magic, on the counter in front of him. He took a sip and tried to decide what he was going to say to Cal. He couldn't exactly come right out and ask if Cal had kidnapped his son. Then again, if Manning had taken Ben, he probably suspected why Todd was here.

"Butt out, Judy," Cal snapped. "This is between the boss man and me!"

Judy's full, bright red lips formed into a pout. She turned back to her drink.

Todd lowered his voice, hoping Cal would do the same. Engaging in a public shouting match was the last thing he wanted to do.

"Where have you been for the last two days, Cal? Tanya thinks you've been out driving. Don't you think you owe it to her to let her in on what happened?"

"Why? So she can nag me and show me how disappointed she is in me? Who needs it? There are some places where I'm still appreciated."

"She loves you, Cal, but you're going to lose her if you don't get some help. You're going to lose everything. The alcohol is going to ruin your life."

What was he doing? Todd wasn't saying what he'd planned. What did he hope to accomplish by making Cal angry?

To his surprise, instead of jumping to his feet and shouting obscenities, Cal said nothing. Instead, he looked away from Todd and took another swig from the glass in his hand. It was a long moment before he spoke again.

"It's too late," There was no longer anything in his voice but remorse.

"It's never too late. You can get help. Alcoholics Anonymous."

"No, you don't understand."

Todd had to lean closer to hear.

"I have gambling debts I can't pay. People are after me. There's Judy…and there's the need. There's always the need. I can't get away from it, Todd."

"Just admitting that you need help is a start. You can work your way out of this a little at a time. Tanya will help you, and if you want, I will too."

"I'll think it over." There was no conviction in the statement.

Cal set his empty glass on the pock-marked wooden bar. He slowly got to his feet, and without saying another word, headed for the door.

"Cal! Wait for me!" Judy, suddenly aware that he was leaving without her, moved to snatch up her purse.

Cal seemed to see her for the first time. He shook his head and held up his hand to stop her.

"I'm tired," he said. "I'm going home."

When he had left, Todd moved to the seat beside Judy. She had been staring at the door, a shocked expression on her face, but now she whirled to face Todd, her eyes full of spite.

"What did you say to him?"

"Nothing much. I just reminded him that he's a married man."

"It's none of your business what Calvin does! He happens to be in love with me!"

Despite himself, Todd felt sorry for the woman. She was probably only in her twenties and was relatively attractive, in an overdone way. Her long chestnut-colored hair was lacquered and teased, and her fingernails could have been lethal weapons. She wore skin-tight black pants with a midriff top that didn't sufficiently cover her ample chest. It was sad that the girl had so little self esteem that she found it necessary to dress this way and to settle for a relationship with a married man.

"Listen, Judy, I'm not here to argue with you. Just answer one question for me, and I'll go away and leave you alone."

"What?"

"All I want to know is where Cal has been the last two days, and what he's been doing."

"Why? I don't want to get him in any trouble or nothing. Besides, why should I help you out? You ain't exactly done anything for me."

Todd reached into his pocket and got out his wallet. He pulled out a fifty and waved it in front of her eyes. He'd probably be arrested if a policeman happened to walk in right now. Who in his right mind would believe he was just paying her for information?

The bill was gone in a flash.

"Now you're talking my language," she said, tucking it daintily into her purse. "I got other things that are worth paying for, too, ya know."

She must have read his mind. "Just tell me about Cal," Todd said.

"O.K. Your loss." She smiled, revealing teeth that needed some dental work. "This is too easy. Cal has been with me for the last few days. We went to Raven River to gamble on Monday morning and just got back last night. I think we kind of wore out our welcome, if you know what I mean."

Todd supposed he did. He also supposed it would be easy enough to verify Cal's whereabouts. Raven River gambling casino was located on an Indian Reservation not more than a hundred miles away. A call or a visit would be easy to make. He wasn't sure he'd even bother, though, since Judy's statement had the ring of truth to it. He'd never seriously believed that Cal was the kidnapper anyway.

"Thanks, Judy," Todd said, and began to get up.

"Hey, aren't you going to buy me another drink?" She put her hand on his arm, the touch ripe with invitation.

"You've got fifty dollars. Buy your own drink if you want, but there are better things you could do with the money."

He had to get out of this place which was starting to make him feel claustrophobic and dirty. Todd pulled away from her, and struggling to breath normally, practically bolted for the door. Bursting into the surprising brightness of the day, he paused only long enough to thirstily drink in the fragrance of fresh air and feel the warm sunshine on his face before getting behind the wheel of the Grand Am and speeding away from the Tally Ho Tavern.

CHAPTER 19

"Mom, it's for you!"

The telephone again. It had been ringing steadily all day, mostly well-wishers calling to say they'd heard about Kellie's accident and wanting to know how she was. It was nice that people cared, but it was getting harder and harder for Lila to avoid mentioning anything about Ben. Deception wasn't in her nature. It was hard enough for her just to keep Christmas and birthday secrets.

If it weren't for the fact that she had to keep the line open for Gina and Todd, she would be tempted to take the phone off the hook. She'd already spoken to Gina earlier this morning and tried to convince her to come over, but Gina had declined, saying she needed to stay at the house in case the kidnapper happened to call. When Lila had offered to come to Gina, Gina had urged her not to. "Please don't be offended, but Todd doesn't want company right now," she had said, and there had been a strained sadness in her voice. Lila was worried about them both. She couldn't bear to think about what it would do to them if anything happened to Ben. He was the light of their lives.

Taking the phone from Kellie, she heard Charlene Monroe's familiar voice and knew this would be the ultimate test. Charlene had been a close friend for years, and she was the type of person you instinctively opened up to. That was why she was so well suited to the work she did at the Pregnancy Center.

Fortunately, Charlene had other things on her mind besides Kellie's accident, so after expressing her concern and relief that Kellie was alright, she went right on to the other reason for her call.

"I know this might be a bad time, Lila," she said. "But I'd like to send someone over to talk to you. Her name is Sylvia. Gina spoke to her on the hotline last Friday. She's about the age you were when you gave birth to Kellie, and she thinks she's too old to have another child. There are some other issues involved, too." Charlene went on the explain about the infidelity and the fact that Sylvia wanted to save her marriage but was afraid she couldn't do that and raise her ex-lover's child.

"I'm sorry, Charlene. I just don't know how I could see her today." Somehow Lila was having trouble mustering up any sympathy for this woman who had made such a mess of her life. All she could deal with right now were the problems of her own family. "Could it wait until next week? Things are…hectic around here for the next few days."

"Well, if necessary, but I think Sylvia is on the verge of getting an abortion. I talked to her on Monday, but I don't think I got through to her. It surprised me that she even agreed to talk to you. A few days could be too long."

Charlene always made it so hard to say no. Besides, Lila knew she was right. A delay would most likely result in an abortion. If there was anything she could say or do to prevent that, she had to try, regardless of what else was going on in her own life.

"When you put it that way, I guess I can't very well refuse, can I? When and where do you want us to meet?"

"I knew I could count on you. I'll bring Sylvia out to your house so you won't even

Bitter Reunion

have to leave home. How about around three-thirty?"

Lila agreed to the time. She wasn't planning on going anywhere all day anyway.

"Thank you, Lila. I really don't know how the center would make it without women like you. And I don't know how I would make it without a friend like you."

It was the moment Lila had dreaded. The one in which she wanted so badly to confide in her friend that she could taste it. "I'll see you this afternoon," was all she said, and then she hung up.

It's funny how much we take for granted, Lila mused, stepping away from the phone and walking to the window. All the innumerable blessings that fill our lives every day. Why don't we fully appreciate them until they're gone? The things that had troubled her just last week suddenly were of no consequence at all. Three months ago, Walt had been laid off at the factory where he had worked for over twenty-five years, throwing them into a financial tailspin and causing them to have to face some tough decisions. Should Walt swallow his pride and accept Todd's offer of employment at "H&H", or should Lila go looking for work herself? Would they be able to help Kellie with college expenses, or yet again fall back on Todd and Gina? Suddenly, it didn't seem to matter. All false pride had been swept away on the wind of the crisis that now dominated their lives. Last week, unbeknownst to Lila, she'd had it all.

Lila sighed and tried to wrench herself away from the intolerable thoughts on the edge of her consciousness. If only she had something to immerse herself into and to take her away from the moment-to-moment battle against fear and depression that she was experiencing.

She knew Walt was having the same problem. She could see him on the other side of the big picture window pushing the lawn mower around, sweat dripping off his forehead. The lawn had been mowed only a couple of days ago, so it wasn't necessity that prompted him to do it today. It was either stay busy or curl up in a ball and shut out the world.

Lila headed for the cleaning closet.

Kellie, too, was restless today. She had slept most of the day before, but was feeling better now and had quit taking pain pills, which was a mixed blessing because sleep had been a refuge.

Her body was still too sore to do anything strenuous, so she tried to distract herself by watching television, something Kellie almost never did in the middle of the day. Flipping through the channels by remote control, she found that the only thing daytime TV seemed to offer was gloom, doom and woe, of which she already had plenty. It was either soap operas or talk shows, and at the moment none of the talk shows were of the "mindlessly trivial but benign banter" variety. Instead, the common thread running through them was a seemingly blatant attempt to show humanity at it's worst.

"My mother slept with my lover."

"Jerks and the women who love them."

"My daughter is a prostitute."

Each program tried to be more outrageous than the last. Kellie channel-surfed in fascinated revulsion. How could people parade their personal problems in front of the whole country like this, she wondered. Where was their self respect? One woman and her grown daughter spouted such a torrent of horrible, hurtful accusations at each other that it made Kellie cringe. She couldn't imagine any motivation that could ever cause her to publicly confront her mother in such a way. The things these people had done to each other was bad enough, but to air it on television took them to an even deeper level of degradation.

Sensationalism, that's what they called it. Kellie pushed the power button and turned off the television. She'd felt like a voyeur, listening to what should have been kept private within the confines of a person's home or maybe even their bedroom. There was no way she wanted to increase the viewer ratings of any of these programs any longer.

No wonder the country was in such deep moral trouble these days, she thought. The media had to be at least part of the problem. This daily flaunting of the bizarre, corrupt and deviant was bound to have an effect, if only in that it desensitized people, making it seem as if the abnormal were the norm. And maybe it truly was beginning to be. Kellie didn't want to believe it, but considering what had happened to Ben and her, it was easy to think evil was running rampant. She didn't know if she would ever feel the same way about the world again. It scared her.

She rose gingerly from the couch and walked with a slight limp to the kitchen, noticing as she went that she had never seen the house this clean before. Between phone calls, Mom had been on a cleaning rampage, one she was still engaged in. Kellie found her at the stove, scrubbing the drip pans under the burners, attacking them as furiously as if they were her mortal enemy, a grim determination in the set of her mouth. As though she thought that if the house sparkled, Ben would be safe.

"I've decided to go in to work for a couple of hours," Kellie said.

Lila turned to look at her with haunted eyes.

"But Kellie, you just got out of the hospital yesterday. I wish you'd take it easy a little while longer."

"I'm fine, Mom. Really. Carol called and said the same thing, but I told her I'd be there. Travis is on vacation this week, so they're short staffed, and I need to get out of here for a few hours anyway. I'm going absolutely nuts."

Before her mother could object, she went on. "All I'll have to do is stand behind the counter and make sandwiches. I think I can handle that. And don't worry. I'll be careful about what I say."

Lila knew it was useless to argue with Kellie when she had her mind made up. Besides, she understood exactly how her daughter felt. Before she had a chance to respond, the doorbell rang.

Two uniformed policemen stood at the door when Lila opened it. Her heart pounded with apprehension as they introduced themselves. Officer Smith was disarmingly young, with an open, sincere face and a broad smile. Officer Huntington was older, probably around forty-five and looked infinitely more worn and street wise, no doubt the result of his many years on the force. It was Officer Smith who explained that they were there to question Kellie about the accident.

Lila politely offered them a seat and asked if they would like a glass of iced tea. Both

Bitter Reunion

men declined, and Lila excused herself to go and get Kellie.

"What am I going to tell them?" Kellie asked with dismay when Lila told her who was waiting in the other room. "I just don't know if I can sit there and lie to them! What if I screw everything up and make them suspicious about the accident? Things will be even worse for Ben than they already are if that crazy person who has him thinks the police know about the kidnapping."

"We knew they would question you, honey. We already talked about this." Lila's voice was low, just above a whisper. "Tell them as much of the truth as possible. Just don't tell them all of it. You'll do just fine."

She took her daughter's hand and walked beside her until they had joined the policemen. The sight of them made Kellie's stomach flutter, and she wished she could turn around and flee the room. By the time Lila had introduced the officers to Kellie, she had begun to calm down, and the questioning went better than she had dared to hope.

Officer Smith was warm, friendly and easy to talk to. She found that by telling him everything that had transpired on the road and simply omitting the part about the bullet through the window, it sounded as though she'd been the victim of a drunk driver. She could honestly say she hadn't been able to see what the other car looked like and had no clue who its driver could have been. The good-looking policeman nodded his head as if he wasn't surprised and seemed completely satisfied with her answers.

Officer Huntington made her a little nervous, though. He had scarcely said a word since the first "Hello." He sat quietly, occasionally jotting something down on a note pad that was balanced on one knee. He seemed bored and distracted, and his gaze continually strayed to the window. Kellie wished she knew what he was thinking.

"Where were you going?" Huntington asked abruptly.

The conversation had wound down to the point where Kellie had thought she was out of the woods, and the sudden question took her off guard.

"Pardon me?" There was a little squeak in her voice. She hoped he hadn't noticed.

"She was going to pick up her nephew," Lila broke in.

Kellie thought Officer Huntington looked skeptical. Her face was hot, and she could swear he knew they were holding something back. She felt herself squirming in her chair, and she had the sudden urge to blurt out everything.

"Bad night to have been out," he said. Then he smiled and stood up. "If you remember anything else let us know. He gave Kellie a small pat on the shoulder and took a step toward the door. "We're real sorry about your accident but glad you made it out alive. I wish we could say that we thought we'd catch the culprit responsible, but it doesn't seem too likely. The sad thing is that someday he probably will kill someone."

Officer Smith shook her hand and thanked them for their co-operation, and then the two men were gone. It was over. And she hadn't had to tell a single lie. Kellie breathed out a long sigh of relief and hugged her mom.

"I almost blew it. I felt just like a criminal. If you hadn't been there, I don't know what I would have done."

Bitter Reunion

"The Lord would have seen you through," Lila said.

The policemen's visit had taken more time than Kellie had realized. Carol would be expecting her soon.

Kellie got out her key ring and made sure she still had a set of keys to her mother's car. Then, after saying goodbye and overriding more protests about going in to work, she left the house.

She was a little nervous about getting behind the steering wheel of a car again so soon, but she knew that the old adage about getting back on the horse was true. She might as well confront her fear of driving now and get it over with. It even occurred to her that something good might have come out of the accident. She felt completely cured of her love of driving too fast. It would probably be a very long time before she earned another speeding ticket.

As she walked stiffly down the steps, a car she recognized as Charlene's pulled up in front of the house and stopped. Charlene emerged from the driver's side, and another woman got out on the passenger side. The other woman was strikingly attractive for someone Kellie considered "older". Her sleek jet-black hair was lightly touched with gray and worn swept away from her face in a french twist. She was tall and willowy in a flowing peach tunic and matching pants.

Kellie met the two women on her way to Lila's car. She greeted Charlene and gave her a warm hug. Kellie had known her for as long as she could remember, and Charlene was like a member of the family.

"Kellie, this is Sylvia," Charlene said, introducing the other woman. Up close, Kellie could see that Sylvia's eyes were dark like her hair, and fringed with long, thick lashes. Her skin was flawlessly smooth and creamy white, in stark contrast to the color of her hair and eyes, and her rose lips were full and perfect. There were simple pearl earrings at her ears. Even now, at her age, this woman could be a model.

Sylvia said hello and tried not to stare at the bandage and Kellie's black eye.

"It's nice to meet you," Kellie said, self-consciously. "I'm sorry I look like Frankenstein. I was in a car accident the other day."

The statement brought sympathetic comments from Charlene and resulted in a short conversation about the accident. At last, Kellie managed to extricate herself and make it the rest of the way to the garage.

Moments later, inside the house, Lila had much the same reaction to Sylvia upon being introduced by Charlene. Her beauty was a little intimidating, but she seemed like a genuinely nice person. Lila brought out cookies and iced tea. After being comfortably seated and making a few moments of small talk about the weather, Charlene brought them to the reason for the visit.

"Sylvia, I've explained your situation to Lila. And while Lila didn't face all the same circumstances that you do, she also found herself pregnant at a time when she'd thought her child rearing days were almost over. At least in that, she can identify with you. So I'm going to just let Lila tell you how it was for her."

Bitter Reunion

Lila toyed with her napkin for a moment, unsure of how to begin. This was harder than usual. She wasn't quite sure why.

She pointed to a framed picture on top of the piano. "That's my daughter, Kellie. It's her senior picture."

"Yes," Sylvia said. "We met outside just a moment ago. She seems like a lovely girl."

"She's the reason I'm talking to you right now," Lila went on, uninterested in exchanging meaningless pleasantries. "I want you to know that I do understand how it feels to suddenly discover that your life is about to take a completely unexpected and unwanted turn. Gina was sixteen when I found out I was pregnant again at thirty-nine. It hit me like a ton of bricks. The thought of midnight feedings, potty training, and ear infections all over again, and this time around I would be older… more worn out. It overwhelmed me, and believe me, I shed a lot of tears. I just couldn't imagine another eighteen years of the kind of round-the-clock responsibility it takes to raise a child."

"Did you ever consider an abortion?" Sylvia asked. Her eyes were riveted to Lila's face.

"No," said Lila. "I never did. Because of my belief in the sanctity of life, it was never an option for me. And also, I loved my daughter Gina and I knew that I would love the child I was carrying just as much. I just didn't expect to enjoy her as much as I have. I thought I was making some kind of noble sacrifice to give birth to her, but I was so wrong. Instead of a burden, Kellie has been one of the biggest blessings of my life. I have never for even one second regretted having had her, and now I can't imagine life without her."

"I'm glad things worked out so well for you, but things are different in my case. They're more complicated."

"I know that," Lila said, with a hint of impatience in her voice. She weighed the merits of what she wanted to say and then made a decision.

"Sylvia, part of you must not really want to abort the baby you're carrying, or you wouldn't be here. You must have known I would try to talk you out of it, and that is exactly what I'm going to do. I hope you won't be offended, but I'm going to be blunt."

Sylvia's eyes widened and even Charlene looked surprised. There was an intensity about Lila that she had never seen before.

Lila went on, not bothering to choose her words carefully anymore, but just saying what was on her heart. "I almost lost my daughter this week. If I had, it would have been the biggest loss of my life. And if I had aborted her before she was born, it would have been an even bigger loss, because I wouldn't have had the privilege of having known and loved her for the last eighteen years. LIFE IS PRECIOUS." She emphasized each word. "I've never seen that quite as clearly as I do since Kellie's accident. What gives you or me or anyone else the right to take it at ANY stage along the way?"

Sylvia was silent, her head bowed. For the first time, Lila almost felt sorry for her—but not quite..

"If you truly can't raise your child, I can understand. But that is still no excuse for an abortion. Please, give someone else the chance to love him or her. There are so many who would give anything to be able to have a child! Gina, for instance, has one son, and

Bitter Reunion

would love to have more children, but she can't." And she may lose the son she has, Lila thought, and the injustice of it ignited the fire in what she said next.

"Choice. That's what it's all about, isn't it? You can choose life, or you can choose death. Legally, it's your decision, and nothing I say can change that. And if you choose death, don't mask that choice behind the guise of a woman's right to govern her own body. Be honest. It's about selfishness and the poor choices that have already been made."

Lila had no more to say. An uncomfortable silence hit the room like a cold blast of air. Sylvia opened her purse, extracted a Kleenex and dabbed at her eyes, while Charlene sat in a state of stunned disbelief. What was the matter with Lila? Was it Kellie's accident that had caused her outburst, or was there something more? Charlene wished she had taken Lila's advice and waited until next week to bring Sylvia over.

Sylvia was already in tears, and Lila looked as though she was about to start crying, too. Charlene decided she'd better get Sylvia out of here, before things got any worse than they already were. She would talk to Lila later and get to the bottom of what was bothering her. As tactfully as she could, Charlene brought the visit to an end and ushered Sylvia away.

Twenty minutes later, Walt found Lila still sitting in the chair where they had left her, staring blindly at the uneaten cookie on her plate and the twisted powder-blue napkin beside it.

He sat down beside her. Neither one spoke, but both were comforted by the presence of the other. When she was able to, Lila told Walt of her conversation with Sylvia and how she had lost control of it. He was sympathetic, as she knew he would be, but she still felt awful. And she surely didn't need anything else to feel awful about. She guessed she was just going to have to leave it to the Lord to undo any damage she might have done. With a sigh, Lila patted Walt's hand. She had to try to get a grip on her emotions, for his sake and for Gina's. Vowing to pull herself together, she reached for the phone to call Gina again. Maybe there was news about Ben since the last time they'd spoken.

CHAPTER 20

The room seemed fuzzy and it was a few minutes before Ben knew he was really awake. He was so sleepy! And he couldn't remember or even think very well. Maybe he was sick. That must be it. He was sick—and he wanted to be home in his own bed with his mom right beside him, giving him some of that pink medicine and rubbing his back.

But this wasn't his bed. It wasn't as soft, and the blanket was scratchy. Where was his teddy..and Smokey? And where was Mommy? He was scared, and he wanted to cry, but he was too tired…just too tired. The room faded out again. He dozed, then came awake once more. This time he remembered that he was still at David's house. He didn't know how long he'd been here—that part was too hard to figure out. It made his head hurt to try.

A lot of other things were hard to figure out, too. Like how come David wouldn't let him go home, and how come he kept on falling asleep. He would wake up just a little and David would give him something to eat or drink and then he would fall asleep again. And every time he woke up, he was still here. Why didn't Mommy and Daddy come and get him? Or Kellie or Grandma and Grandpa? Didn't they miss him?

He wasn't going to cry any more. It just made David mad. And he wasn't a baby, anyway. Maybe he would just get up and go home. He sat up and slipped over the side of the bed. His legs felt funny as he walked to the door. They were sort of tingly and wobbly. Everything else on him felt funny, too. Yep, he must be sick, alright.

When he finally reached the door, Ben held his breath and turned the knob. Whew! It wasn't locked, like it had been the last time. He had cried really hard then.

The door creaked as it swung open. "SHHH," Ben cautioned it. "Be quiet."

He tiptoed down the hall and peeked into the living room. Empty.

Where was David?

Ben moved quietly to the front window and carefully looked out. The blazing sunlight hurt his eyes. He blinked and squinted, and then he saw David. He was sitting in a chair under a shady tree, reading a book. Ben looked longingly at the tall glass David had in his hand and licked his parched lips. He sure was thirsty! And it was hot in here! That must be why David was out there.

Ben moved as quickly as he could to the kitchen and the back door. His hand grabbed the knob and twisted. It wouldn't budge. He was stuck. He could feel the tears trying to push their way out of his eyes, but he wouldn't let them.

There had to be a way to get out of here without David seeing him. He went back to the living room, but he couldn't go out the front door, even if it wasn't locked. He knew David would see him from where he sat and then he would be mad.

What was he going to do? He had to get out of here! He looked frantically around the room.

The telephone! Ben knew how to use the telephone, and there was one right there on the table by the couch. His pulse quickened. He even knew his own phone number by heart. That and his address. Mommy had taught him a song to make it easier for him to remember.

Bitter Reunion

Boy, was he glad, because now he could call her and then she would come and get him.

This telephone was different from the ones he had used before, though. Perplexed, he studied it. Instead of being on buttons, the numbers were under a big round thing with holes in it, and Ben almost gave up before he figured out how to make the thing work. He had to struggle to pull each hole around with his small forefinger. When that was too hard, he gave up and used his thumb. Finally, he was pretty sure he had dialed all the numbers right, but it still didn't work. He knew the brrr...brrr...burr sound that meant the phone was ringing, but all he heard was a beep...beep...beep. It just went on and on.

He was pretty sure the beeping meant he'd done something wrong, but what? Beep...beep...beep.... Should he hang up and try it all over again? Hot tears of frustration and fear finally spilled onto his cheeks.

Ben was still holding the receiver to his ear when the front door opened.

"I'm sorry, David," he started to say, turning toward the new sound, but the words got stuck in his throat.

It was the bad man!

Ben let the phone drop and ran for the door, but he couldn't get around the man, who was standing right in his way.

"I want my MOMMY!" he screamed, as the man grabbed him hard by the arm and jerked. Then the man's other hand drew back and came toward his face, fast. Ben squirmed and twisted, and the fist missed him, but he couldn't pull loose from the iron grip of that huge hand around his arm. Shutting his eyes real tight, he waited for the blow that he knew would come.

"Don't!" Ben heard, from the direction of the door. "Don't hit him!"

Ben dared to open his eyes and see David beside him, yelling at the bad man.

The man was still holding his arm. It hurt.

"I mean it, Hank," David said, and his eyes were hard. "Let go of him."

Abruptly, the man pushed and let go all at once. Ben fell hard on the floor. Whimpering, he scuttled backward away from the men, scarcely even noticing the little red pinpricks of blood appearing where the skin had been scraped from his knee.

"So now YOU'RE giving the orders?" Hank thundered at David.

"We agreed that the boy wouldn't get hurt, or anyone but Hamilton. If you go back on your word about that, then why should I keep my part of the deal?"

"The kid was trying to use the phone when I came in! What the…I thought you had him drugged! How did he get out of the bedroom?"

From the floor by the end of the couch, Ben noticed that the bad man's face was kind of purple, his hair poked out in a weird way and there was even a little bit of spit on his bottom lip. For some reason, instead of looking funny, it looked scary. Real scary.

"He HAS been drugged. He's been sleeping all the time, but I'm not sure how much of those sleeping pills to give him. He's just a little kid, and I don't want to overdose him. I guess I didn't give him quite enough the last time. And I know I should have locked the door," David said. "I won't forget again."

"You don't need to worry about that. I'm moving in with you, and I won't let you forget. My bags are in the car. After we bring them in, I have to go out for awhile. And

Bitter Reunion

after that, it'll be the three of us. All for one and one for all. Until we have our hands on that money and we can ditch the third musketeer over there."

"Now, go mix something up that will knock him out for a good long time," the man said, nodding toward Ben and making Ben turn and hide his face in the cushion of the couch behind him.

"Make it at least twice as strong as last time. Because if he gives me any more grief, I won't be responsible for what happens to him."

When David had left the room, taking Ben with him, Hank made a couple of quick phone calls and found out what he needed to know. The information invited an evil smile that curled the corners of his lips. He would make a trip to the bank to convert Belinda's check to a cashier's check. And then he would pay Kellie Reynolds a little visit.

. . . .

"Are you O.K.?"

Kellie looked up to see Carol staring at her.

"My head's aching again. Maybe I shouldn't have tried to come in today, after all."

It was true. She had overestimated her ability to spring back from the accident. She didn't feel at all well. Then too, there was Ben. She couldn't stop thinking about him at the deli any more than she could at home. And it was hard not being able to say anything to anybody, especially Carol who had to be able to see as plain as day that something was bothering her.

The deli had been slow, which was a blessing because Kellie couldn't concentrate. It seemed like all she did was apologize to customers for mixing up their orders, charging them the wrong amount or making them repeat themselves. The worst had been the family with the little boy who looked a lot like Ben. Seeing him had upset her so much that she had spaced out everything they'd said. They had to repeat their order three times before she got it straight, and she'd been so shaken by then that she could barely keep from crying.

Thank goodness her shift was nearly over. The doors to the deli were already locked, and she and Carol were almost finished cleaning up for the evening. Kellie couldn't wait to get home and collapse.

Carol set down the sponge she had been using to wipe down the counter and joined Kellie at the refrigerator. She put her hand on Kellie's shoulder.

"Listen, Hon, why don't you go ahead and leave? I'll just finish up on my own. We're almost done anyway."

"You don't mind?" Kellie asked gratefully. She really was exhausted and feeling worse by the minute.

"No, of course not. Take off. And don't you dare come back tomorrow unless you're feeling up to it, you hear me? I'm sure Tammy wouldn't mind working some extra hours."

"O.K., and thanks, Carol. I really appreciate it."

The pain behind Kellie's eyes was gathering momentum now. There was a pounding as of countless Indian braves beating an ominous war-dance in her brain. She contemplated having her mom or dad come to pick her up, but decided against it. She could hang in there

Bitter Reunion

long enough to drive home. Then a pain pill and bed.

She snatched her purse from a cupboard near the back door and fumbled through it looking for her car keys. I don't have the patience for this, Kellie thought irritably, and berated herself for letting her purse become a final resting place for everything from candy wrappers to empty bottles of hand lotion. Maybe it would help if she got a smaller one next time.

As usual, the item she was looking for had somehow made its way to the very bottom of the garbage heap, even though it was the last thing she had stuck in there. She pulled out the keys, jerked open the door and emerged into the darkening, shadow-filled parking area behind the building. Pain wiped out every thought except for the need to get home, and she didn't see the shadows shifting between her car and Carol's as she approached them.

Inside the deli, Carol paused from putting away the last of the sandwich makings. It was so peacefully quiet here with the doors locked and everybody gone. In her busy life, solitude was a treasure to be savored. All too soon she would return to the chaos of her small apartment and the arduous chore of getting the kids to bed. Why rush it?

Carol retrieved a bottle of Snapple from the cooler and headed for an empty stool. As she did, she noticed something out of place on the floor next to the back door. Taking the bottle with her, she went to see what it was.

"Oh, no," Carol thought aloud, as she bent to pick up the small black clutch wallet at her feet. "This must have must have fallen out of that feed-bag Kellie calls a purse."

Realizing that the wallet most likely contained Kellie's driver's license and her money, Carol quickly picked it up and rushed to open the door, hoping to catch Kellie before she drove away.

In the same instant that Carol reached for the doorknob, Kellie struggled to insert a key into the locked door of her mother's car. The darn thing wouldn't go in right. Maybe she had the wrong one. There were so many keys on the ring, and it was so dark it was hard to see for sure which one she had. She groped through them impatiently and then managed to let the whole ring of keys slip through her fingers. She heard it jangle as it hit the concrete. Great, just great, Kellie thought, while bending over to pick it up. The evening just kept getting better and better. She was in a crouched position, her hand around the black tube that was part of the key ring.

"Don't make a sound." A voice erupted from the night, sending shock-waves through her brain and causing her body to go rigid. A scream died in her throat. She could taste it in her mouth, bitter like bile.

"Get up real slow," the whispered voice demanded from somewhere just behind her and to her left.

Kellie could feel the hard, cold steel of a gun barrel in the small of her back as she stiffly and painfully got to her feet. Her mind raced. She knew instinctively that the voice belonged to the man who had run her off the road. He was here to kill her, and if she didn't think of something within the next few seconds, he would probably do it.

"Now, unlock that door, get inside the car and scoot over to the other side. Real easy."

Suddenly, Kellie was furious. If this man was going to take her life, at least she wasn't going to make it easy for him. Frantically, she searched her memory for any of the moves she'd learned in that self-defense class she had taken last summer. None came to mind. The point of the gun kept prodding at her, reminding her of her vulnerability and making it hard to think.

"I said, move!"

I could throw the keys, Kellie thought. If he doesn't want to kill me right here, it will at least buy me a little time and maybe I can get away while he looks for them. Her fingers tightened around the keys in preparation, ready to fling them in one sudden movement, when suddenly all the angry, frightened, chaotic fragments of her mind coalesced into a solid realization.

Of course! The key ring! She had a weapon right in her hand! The smooth three-inch tube she now gripped so tightly her fingers hurt was actually a small container of pepper spray in an imitation leather casing. Daddy had given it to her for Christmas and insisted she attach it to her key ring. She had laughed and called him overprotective. It had never occurred to her that she might actually need it someday, and now that she did, she'd almost forgotten she had it. But dear Lord, how could she possibly use it on her assailant when he had a gun to her back?

"Are you deaf, or are you just trying to commit suicide?" the man snarled, so close to her ear that she could feel his hot breath and the spray of his spittle against her neck.

A thought…insane in this moment of life or death. She wished she'd worn her hair down so it might have shielded her from the wet foulness that issued from the creature's mouth.

She was no match for this Goliath behind her. Even unseen, his presence exuded an essence of power, a malignant evil force. And like the simple shepherd boy, she could only trust in God.

"No!" Her voice shook, but it rang with authority.

"You asked for it," the man said, his voice a low growl. "I was going to give you a break, but if you don't want to prolong your life, so be it."

Kellie silently but quickly unsnapped the top of the tube and managed to get her thumb positioned over its plastic trigger. Then, holding her breath, she steeled herself to break away and to feel the blast which was sure to follow.

Then she heard a THUNK, and her assailant cried out. At the same time, she heard the sound of breaking glass and another voice rang out.

"Run, Kellie! Run!"

But she didn't. Instead, she whirled around with all the momentum she could muster and pressed her thumb down on the trigger of the small weapon in her hand. She heard a scream, but it wasn't her own, and then she ran. Ignoring the pain in her limbs, she ran for all she was worth, as if she were competing in an Olympic track event in which the prize was her life. Within a few strides she realized she wasn't running alone. Carol was right beside her, and neither one slowed until they were safely behind the closed and locked door of the deli.

Bitter Reunion

For a moment, they clung to one another, both too shaken to speak. Then, realizing they might still be in danger, Carol called 911.

"We did it," Carol finally panted, as she and Kellie cowered behind the counter waiting for the police to arrive. "I've never been so scared in my life!"

Having partially recovered from the state of shock she had been in, Kellie finally was able to speak. "I can't believe you came along when you did. You saved my life. What did you do out there?"

Despite the seriousness of their situation, a grin touched Carol's lips. "When I got close enough that I was pretty sure I could hit him, I threw a full bottle of Snapple at the guy. I don't like to brag, but I was the star pitcher for my high school girl's softball team. That bottle really packed a wallop. Oh, and here's your wallet. You dropped it before you left. That's why I came out after you."

"Thank the Lord that you did! And that the bottle stunned him long enough for me to spray him with pepper spray."

"So that's what happened! All I knew was that the guy screamed and doubled over. I couldn't figure out why."

"Yeah. I always wondered if this stuff would really work if a person needed it to. I mean, what if it had malfunctioned?" Kellie stared in wonder at her key ring. "I must have gotten a whiff of it myself. My eyes are burning like crazy. Remind me to thank my dad for forcing me to carry it, will you?"

"I think I'll get one, too," Carol said. "A bottle of Snapple is a little too large to fit on my key chain." Kellie laughed and then Carol joined in. Soon tears were streaming down their faces and they couldn't catch their breath. The laughter echoed throughout the cavernous depths of the dining room, bouncing off empty tables and chairs. There was an edge to the sound, something slightly off-kilter. Fear and spent adrenaline had turned to hysteria. By the time they managed to get themselves under control again, they could hear the sirens from approaching police cars.

They hadn't told the half of it, all those stories he'd heard in prison. About how your eyes burned and ran with tears, while mucus streamed from your nose like a river. How for a half-hour, maybe longer, you'd want to tear your eyes out.

Hank sat in his car recovering from the pain and the humiliation of his encounter with Kellie Reynolds. It was still hard to see, and the burning was nearly unbearable. He had no idea how he'd even made it to his car, parked several blocks from the deli, but somehow he had, and then he'd even managed to drive to Lonsbury Park where he knew there was a water fountain. Once there, he'd splashed the cool, soothing liquid into his face and eyes until he'd felt he had no choice but to move on.

The excruciating pain in his eyes was nothing next to the knowledge that she had done it again. She had beat him. She was still alive, and he was the one forced to flee like a dog with its tail between its legs. And he'd been so close! Just one small pull of the trigger away from blowing her into the next world.

His hands repeatedly opened and closed in frustration and anger as Hank sat, head back against the seat of the car and eyes closed, waiting for the pain to subside. Only one thought now filled his mind. It played over and over again like a broken record. She would pay. All of them would pay.

CHAPTER 21

Thursday, June 29

Gina hadn't seen much of Todd since the call from the kidnapper. He was gone much of the time making 'financial arrangements', and even when he was home, he was cold and distant. She could see how much he was hurting and she wanted to comfort him and to be comforted, but he wouldn't let her near. Their needs were driving a wedge between them. The more he retreated into himself, the more she longed for him and the wider the distance between them grew.

Gina tried to understand. Men handled fear and grief differently than women did, and there was the fact that Todd had been through this nightmare before. Joey had never been found, and that had to be preying on his mind. It was bad enough for Gina. She could only begin to imagine how Todd must be feeling. What concerned her the most was that he was trying to deal with all of it alone. Too proud or afraid to open up to her or to anyone, he was pushing his feelings down, trying to hide them even from himself. She knew they were there, though. The love they shared for Ben was a common denominator allowing her to know the depths of his despair, whether he wanted her to or not.

The news they received last night had only added to their anxiety. Someone had made another attempt on Kellie's life. It made no sense. Why would the kidnapper risk exposure now that he had Ben? Everyone had thought that driving Kellie off the road had been a one-time show of violence, a way of saying that he

Bitter Reunion

meant business. They had assumed the only one in danger now was Ben. It was an assumption that had almost cost Kellie her life. And the fact that the kidnapper seemed determined to kill someone didn't bode well for Ben's chances of making it back to them alive. Facing that fact was the hardest thing Gina had ever had to do.

For the last two days she had stayed within the confines of the house out of a sense of loyalty to Todd. She'd wanted to be accessible to him should he need her. But now, suddenly, she wondered if the best thing she could do for Todd and for herself would be to give him some space. She needed company so desperately—someone to talk to and to share her burden with. Alone with her thoughts, the days were so long. It was as if the hours that drug by were some medieval torture device from which there was no escape. She needed her parents and her sister. And they needed her, especially after last night. Todd didn't want them here, so her only option was to go to them.

Once she had made up her mind to go, Gina wasted no time. She hastily wrote a note for Todd, who had already left the house, to let him know where she would be. Then she headed for the garage. As she backed the van out into the blazing noon-day sun, she wondered if there was anyone watching her. Maybe she would be the next victim on the kidnapper's list. Somehow, the thought didn't really disturb her. She wasn't afraid for her own safety. It was Ben and Kellie that she was worried about.

Years ago, Gina had heard a statement in a sermon that had stayed with her ever since. The pastor had said worry was unconscious blasphemy. And she supposed it was, in a way.

To worry was to doubt God's absolute control and His ability to see her through any situation. Most of the time she didn't consider herself much of a worrier anyway. But now worry was her constant unwanted companion tempting her to believe that the worst was sure to happen, and she would never be able to endure it.

As she drove across town, the darkness of her thoughts threatened to smother her. She turned on the radio, which was always tuned in to the local Christian station, hoping for a distraction. Instantly, the van came alive with music, and as always, it was a balm for her battered soul. She knew the song well. It was one of her favorites. Its message was simple and yet profound.

When life doesn't make any sense, when we don't understand God's design, there is nothing for us to do but to cling to the One who holds all the answers. Radio waves carried the words and the melody to her, but Gina knew the message was straight from the Lord. It gently wrapped itself around her in a cocoon of comfort, and assured her that whatever happened, He was there. Just like He had always been and always would be. And that, for now, was all she needed to know. Tears streamed down her face, but they were tears of release. Whatever the future brought, it was in the hands of God.

Minutes later, she turned into the driveway of her parents home, still red-eyed but feeling better than she had since first hearing the news about Ben. She parked beside a black car she had never seen before. A Lexus, no less. It gleamed in the sun, and she could see her reflection in the perfection of its wax job. It was an expensive symbol of the "good life" which so many sought. And which was so empty.

Gina was surprised to find out that her mother was entertaining company and even more surprised when she found out who the visitor was. So this was Sylvia, the woman she had talked to at the Crisis Pregnancy Center last Friday. Was it really only last Friday? She marveled as she shook the lovely woman's hand and was introduced by her mother. It seemed like a lifetime ago—so much had happened since then. She had all but forgotten that conversation, but now that she was reminded of it, she wondered what Sylvia had decided.

"It's nice to meet you," Gina said, taking a seat beside her mother on the sofa. "I hope I'm not interrupting anything. I didn't mean to barge in on you like this."

"No, no. I'm really glad you showed up here when you did, Gina. I was just getting ready to tell Lila something that concerns you, too."

"You were?" Gina was glad for the momentary distraction from her own troubles.

"Yes. But first, I would like to thank you both for what you said to me."

"I'm surprised," Lila said. "To tell you the truth, I didn't expect to ever hear from you again after our last visit. I was upset and less than tactful. I apologize."

Gina hadn't heard about that visit, but then with everything that had gone on, it was no wonder her mom hadn't mentioned it to her.

"Please don't." Sylvia uncrossed her long, shapely legs and leaned forward. "I've never been one to beat around the bush myself, and I appreciate the same quality in others. Believe it or not, you said exactly what I needed to hear. It shocked me into taking a good hard look at myself, and I didn't like what I saw. For far too long, I've been thinking only about me, and look where it's gotten me. It's time I started thinking of someone else's welfare for a change. Like my husband's...and my baby's. I've decided not to have an abortion."

The relief in the room was almost a physical presence.

"That is very good news," Lila said. "You're making the right decision, Sylvia."

"That's not the only decision I've made," Sylvia went on. "Somehow I managed to find the courage to talk to my husband. I told him everything last night. He took it pretty well, considering. It's too early to say for sure, but I'm hopeful he will forgive me in time and that our marriage will survive what I've done. But I know he'll never be able to accept the baby. And if Larry leaves me, I can't raise this child alone. I wouldn't give him the love he deserves to have. I guess I'm still too selfish to handle that.

"So I've decided that I want to give my baby up for adoption." She paused and looked from Lila to Gina. "And I want you to be his mother, Gina. I want you and your husband to adopt him...or her."

Gina was speechless.

"You don't have to give me an answer yet. I know I've sprung this on you out of the blue. But will you think about it?"

The impact of what Lila had said began to sink in. "Wh..why me?" Gina managed to stammer.

Sylvia's eyes met Gina's. "Because when you spoke to me on the phone last week, I could hear the conviction in your voice. Your love for children came shining through. You're the kind of mother I would want this baby to have.

Bitter Reunion

Lila told me how much you would like to have another child. I think you should, and I'd like to be the one to make it possible."

"I…I'll think about it," Gina said.

She was confused. Why was this happening now? Any other time she would have been overjoyed to hear what she had just heard— but not now. All she could think about now was Ben. He was the only child she wanted. His face filled her mind, and there was no room for another.

"Are you alright, honey?" Lila was looking at her with concern.

"Um, do you mind if I excuse myself?" Gina asked in reply. Without waiting for an answer, she bolted from the room.

The rest of Sylvia's visit was an ordeal for Lila, but she smoothed things over the best she could. When Sylvia finally left, Lila went searching for Gina. She found her in the bathroom washing her face and trying to eliminate the evidence that she had been crying once again.

"I'm sorry, Mom," she said when she saw Lila at the door. "I want to be strong, but every time I think I have my emotions under control, something happens to set me off again. When I walked in the door just a few minutes ago, I was fine. I had just turned everything over to the Lord." Her voice quivered, "And then—it hits me as if for the first time. I may never see my baby alive again.

"It was so hard when Brad died…letting go of him, you know. Accepting that life would have to go on without him. But this is even worse. Ben is my child! He may be suffering, and he needs me! And, oh God, how I need him. I feel as if part of my very soul is missing, Mom. Why can't I have faith?"

Gina sat down on the toilet lid and buried her face in her hands. Lila took a seat across from her on the edge of the white porcelain bathtub. Neither one noticed their surroundings.

"It's alright, honey," Lila said softly. "Any parent would feel the way you do. I'm sure God understands. He once saw his only Son suffer and die."

"But why can't I just trust in God? Why do I keep falling apart like this?"

"Because you're human, just like the rest of us. God gave us emotions, and there are times when we need the tears. Let yourself grieve, and don't feel guilty about it. It doesn't reflect a lack of faith, only a deep love for your child."

"Thanks, Mom," Gina sniffed. "I don't know what I would do without you. You're always there when I need you, and you know just what to say to make me feel better."

Lila shrugged. "That's what mothers are for, honey."

"I feel bad about Sylvia, though," Gina continued. "She must think I'm a nut case, going off the deep end like that when she probably thought I'd be ecstatic."

"Don't worry about that. Maybe I shouldn't have, but I told Sylvia you were very worried about Ben right now, and that was why you were so upset. Fortunately, she accepted what I told her without asking me to elaborate. I said that once Ben was out of the woods, you would get back to her about her proposal."

"I just can't think about it right now," Gina said despondently.

"I know."

Gina pulled a length of toilet paper off the roll beside her and blew her nose.

"How's Kellie doing? I haven't seen her since I got here. You didn't let her leave the house, did you?"

"She's pretty shaken up and still sore from the accident, but otherwise fine. She's in her room, resting." Lila shook her head. "This whole thing is so crazy, Gina. I don't understand what's going on. Why Kellie? Why did that man try to kill her again? What does he have to gain by her death?"

"I don't know, Mom. But I think we'd better keep her under lock and key. Did she recognize the man?"

"No. It was dark, and most of the time he was behind her. She doesn't remember seeing his face at all."

"What did she tell the police?"

"She made it sound like an attempted carjacking, but they must wonder about it. What are the odds that the same person would almost be killed twice in less than a week? I have a feeling they'll be back for more questioning."

"Sometimes I think we should tell them everything and let them take over," Gina said. "But Todd just won't hear of it. I pray we're doing the right thing, Mom."

"Me too. And that's all we can do."

"Now, come on. Let's go out on the patio and find your father. He'll be glad you're here."

CHAPTER 22

Cruising along Interstate 5 and deep in thought, paying attention to the speedometer was not a priority. Todd pushed eighty on the outskirts of Portland, but his mind raced faster, searching for answers to too many questions. One of them concerned the way he had been behaving and what it was doing to his wife and their relationship.

The worst of it was that he had no idea why he was pushing her away. He only knew that her need threatened him. He couldn't talk to her about his feelings, and he knew she disapproved of the way he was handling the situation.

Gina said he was running away, trying to avoid facing it. Well, he wasn't! He was the only one doing something about it! That was the reason for this trip to Portland to meet with Carl Grady. Hopefully he would learn something about who was behind the kidnapping and the attempts on Kellie's life. And then maybe he could do something to get his son back, before it was too late. What did Gina want him to do? Just sit by and watch his life fall apart around him?

He had seen her reading the Bible and praying. She wanted him to join her, but that was another thing he couldn't seem to bring himself to do.

Pray, and everything will be alright. Live your life for the Lord, and nothing terrible will happen to you. It was too simplistic. If it were that easy, everyone would be a Christian.

While he believed it was true to a point that the decisions he made determined the life he lead, he knew beyond a doubt things happened over which he had no control. The rain fell on the righteous and the unrighteous alike. He'd had enough rain in his life already to prove it, and so had Gina. O.K., so maybe the loss of Joey could be traced back to bad decisions on Todd's part, but what about Gina? Her first husband hadn't had a miraculous cure from cancer, even though both Gina and he had been committed Christians. Todd had never known Brad, but from all accounts, he'd been a great guy. Not only that, but he'd been only months away from graduation at the seminary where he was studying to become a pastor when the cancer had struck. Now, there was injustice for you. Without presuming to second-guess God, Todd couldn't understand his death, because if anyone was worthy of a miracle, if anyone could have made a difference for the Lord had he been allowed to live, it was Brad.

Yet there was Gina, down on her knees, as if she could control Ben's fate simply by offering up fervent and frequent prayers. Well, that wasn't the answer for him. "The Lord helps those that help themselves," was a philosophy that was more to his way of thinking at the moment.

A red convertible with its top down braked unexpectedly in front of Todd, jerking him out of his reverie. He was getting near his destination now, and traffic demanded his full attention.

Twenty minutes of bumper-to-bumper, horn-honking city driving later, he found himself on 127th Avenue. Then it took another ten minutes and five times slowly around the block to find a parking space. At last, a yellow Honda vacated a spot just as he was approaching, making him the lucky recipient of it.

Grady's office was a little less run-down than the other buildings in the derelict section of Portland in which it was located. There were bars across the windows of the box-like cinder block structure, and no effort had been made to enhance its drab appearance. Half a block away, on the street corner, three unkept men with glassy-eyed stares and nowhere to go, loitered.

It had been at least five years since Todd had last been here, but nothing much had changed. The same tired bell announced his entrance as he walked through the door and once inside the room, he was greeted by the same shabby gray carpet and walls the color of dirt. No abstract paintings or plants on end tables. A calendar with the words "Sully's Paint and Glass" hung on one wall. Looking out of place in the corner, like a diamond ring in a Cracker Jack box, stood a table upon which resided a computer, printer and fax machine. The electronic age had invaded even the remote reaches of Carl Grady's office.

Carl Grady himself sat behind a nondescript desk smoking a cigar. He was a beefy man, built much like a heavyweight boxing has-been. At forty-six, he was still muscular, but now there was a thick layer of fat around his middle that hadn't been there in his youth. A twice-broken nose and two missing teeth gave testimony to the fact that he'd been in his share of fights, but they had not taken place in a boxing ring. His had been on the streets and in the alleys of Portland, Oregon.

"Have a seat," he said, gesturing to a brown Naugahyde arm chair that had seen better days. It had been patched up with duct tape so many

Bitter Reunion

times that there was little of the original upholstery left to be covered.

"I wish I had better news for you, Todd, but like I told you on the phone—nada. I wish you hadn't driven all the way up here just to hear me say it again."

"Then I want you to give me Howard Sneed's address," Todd said. "Maybe if I talk to him myself, I can get something out of him that you couldn't. He has to have an idea who could be behind this!"

Grady shook his head and removed the cigar from his mouth. "Don't waste your time. I'm telling you, the guy is clean. He's been thoroughly checked out. Believe me, he isn't involved in a kidnapping. How about Manning?"

Todd shook his head. "He has an alibi. I checked it out, and it's iron-clad. Besides, he's been too out of it lately to have done it. It wasn't Manning."

"Then we're back to square one."

"It may look that way, but you can't know for sure that it wasn't Sneed, Carl. I still think he at least has some idea about who could have kidnapped Ben."

Grady's gravely voice was gruff, but there was concern in it. "Listen to me. You haven't got much time left, Todd. Give up on this. I think you're barking up the wrong tree here, especially since you told me about what happened to your sister-in-law last night. Someone really wants her dead, either because they hate her or she's a threat to them, and that doesn't fit in with your theory about Sneed.

"There's more behind this than meets the eye. I can feel it in my gut. But I don't have the time to unravel it." He paused. "I know you don't want to hear this, either. I think it's time to call in the police."

Todd jumped to his feet. "So you're giving up on me?"

"It's for your own good. I don't want to be responsible for a death because I agreed to do something that I know I can't."

Todd stood where he was for a moment, as if undecided about what to do next. Then he held out his hand, palm up. "I want that address. It's the least you can do for me, if you aren't going to stay on the case."

It was useless to argue. Grady knew if he didn't hand over the address, Hamilton would just go to the phone book and look it up. If the guy was determined to chase a wild goose, Grady couldn't stop him. Reluctantly, he leaned across his desk and picked up a notepad. He tore off the top sheet of paper and wrote something on it. Then he stood and approached Todd.

"I think of you as a friend, Todd," he said as he gave Todd the slip of paper. "And I wish there was more I could do for you. I truly do."

"I know," Todd said.

Howard Sneed lived in a bedroom community of Portland that was known for its up-scale housing. Todd followed a steep twisting road that gradually made its way up a hillside covered with small palaces owned by doctors, lawyers and corporate CEO's. Most of the homes offered only a glimpse of their splendor behind high fences and hedges that shielded them from the harsh realities of the outside world.

Bitter Reunion

Unlike many that Todd had passed, Sneed's property was accessible without having to buzz at a gate, and there weren't any guard dogs or elaborate security systems in sight. His house, too, was surprisingly modest considering where it was located. Its architectural style was modern, with massive windows to let in the sun, which was momentarily hiding behind an ominous black cloud. Constructed of redwood and stone, it seemed to blend into the lavishly landscaped acre on which it stood. It had the look of a cabin in the mountains but on a grander scale.

Todd rang a doorbell and listened impatiently to the melodic chimes from within. After a moment the door was opened by a pretty, slightly plump woman. She wore a cheery red and blue print apron over blue jeans.

"I'm Todd Hamilton, and I'm looking for Howard Sneed."

She smiled, showing dimples in her cheeks and making him think of Shirley Temple. "Then you're in luck. He just happens to be home today. Is he expecting you?"

"No, but I really need to talk to him," Todd said. "It's urgent."

"Then come on in," she said. "I'm Howard's wife, Nancy, and I'd shake your hand, but mine are covered with flour. Making bread the old-fashioned way," she elaborated. It's relaxing, and I still think the taste of homemade beats a bread machine—something about kneading it yourself."

She lead him inside to a giant overstuffed sofa made of a tweedy fabric in a neutral shade of beige. All the furniture here was Paul Bunyan sized and yet it was still dwarfed by the dimensions of the room where Todd found himself. An entire east wall was a window soaring two-stories high to meet a beamed cathedral ceiling. And outside the window reigned a breathtaking view of Mount Hood.

"It's lovely, isn't it?" Nancy Sneed said, seeing the direction of Todd's gaze. "You should see it on a really clear day. I guess you could say the whole house was built around that view. Enjoy it, and I'll go get Howard."

As she left, Todd began to inspect his surroundings. Evidence of children was everywhere. A doll with ratty hair and a missing shoe, a pair of roller blades beside the front door, and pictures scattered about of a boy and two girls in various stages of their lives. Todd rose from the sofa, sidestepped an abandoned bicycle helmet, and walked to the window. To one side of the sloping yard, he could see a swing set at which three children played.

This whole scenario was nothing like he had expected. Howard Sneed was obviously a married man with three children—a far cry from the man Todd had assumed he was. As Todd wondered how many other false assumptions he had made, Sneed himself appeared, looking very little like Todd remembered him from their first meeting. Today he wore a casual knit polo shirt in a soft shade of sage and tattered jeans.

"So, which is the best part of the view," he asked, coming to stand beside Todd, "Mount Hood or the kids?"

"Not even close," Todd said. "The kids."

"Excellent answer."

"Now, what can I do for you?" he asked, reverting to the abrupt manner that Todd had seen in their previous encounter. "Have you reconsidered that donation?"

Bitter Reunion

It was then that Todd decided Grady was right. He suddenly knew with certainty that Sneed wasn't the kidnapper. Now his only hope was that the man could lead him to the person who was. Todd decided to level with him.

"I know we didn't part on the best of terms, but I'm in trouble and you're the only one I know who can help me."

As Todd explained all that had happened, from the threatening notes through the last attack on Kellie, Sneed listened silently without interrupting.

"You already know that I thought you wrote those notes. I'm embarrassed and ashamed to admit it, but I also thought you might be the one behind the kidnapping," Todd confided, when he had finished. "I'm sorry, and I hope you'll forgive me. I don't believe it any more."

"Good, because depriving a man of his child is the last thing on earth I would ever want to do," Sneed said. "And I suppose I owe you an apology, too. I overreacted at our last meeting—I don't usually do that. I have to admit that I can see why you might have suspected me. What can I do to help?"

"I was hoping you'd be able to give me the names of anyone who might have found out that I refused to donate to the AIDS charity—especially anyone who has a volatile personality or a history of harassment."

"In other words, the lunatic fringe," Sneed supplied. Todd nodded agreement.

"I wish I had names to give you, but I honestly don't have a clue who could have done such a thing. I didn't publicize your refusal to donate. In fact, I didn't tell anyone."

It wasn't what Todd wanted to hear. It meant a dead end in his effort to find a new suspect.

"Are you sure there isn't any way someone could have found out?" There was an edge of desperation in his voice.

"None I know of. And I would tell you if there was. We may not see eye to eye on some things, but I understand about being a father, and I know something of what you must be going through. It has to be a living hell." He surprised Todd by putting his hand on Todd's shoulder in a gesture of support and compassion.

"See that sweet little thing out there? The one wearing red shorts?" Sneed was pointing to one of his daughters through the window. She was a thin, frail-looking girl of about six, with wispy blonde hair.

"She has AIDS, and unless there's a cure in the next few years, I know I will lose her. It hurts every day. Every single day." The note of despondency in his voice echoed the way Todd felt, only now he felt shame as well. How wrong he had been about this man!

"I'm sorry," he said again. It was all he knew to say.

"Her name is Abby. My wife had a blood transfusion years ago, before Abby was even born. When Abby got sick and was diagnosed with AIDS, we discovered Nancy was HIV positive. She hasn't developed the disease yet, but she could at any time. The other two kids, Jenny and Matt, are fine. Thank heaven at least for that."

In a detached monotone, he continued, "The day I met with you was one of my low days. I was frustrated by the fact that AIDS and homosexuality are so linked in people's minds,

Bitter Reunion

that many of them won't even consider backing the cause. It's almost as if they don't want to see a cure because they feel that anyone who gets it deserves to have it. I lashed out and called you a homophobe. Later, I was sorry I did that. I thought about the things you said and some of them made a lot of sense. The advertising for abstinence and faithfulness in marriage. It's a good idea, but there will always be those who disregard it. Unfortunate, but true. And I've been angry about the way AIDS is spread, too. It was probably the blood of a drug-user or a homosexual that my wife got in the transfusion. Because of someone else's lifestyle, I will probably lose my child and maybe my wife. Yes, it angers me, but I can't let the anger stop me from doing all I can to find a cure. I've seen people die from AIDS. Nobody deserves that; not my daughter or anyone else."

Todd had to admit there was truth in what Sneed had said. Suddenly he was seeing things he hadn't before, like the fact that maybe he did judge the homosexual for his sin more harshly than he judged others. Wasn't he, after all, the one who had preached to Sneed about all sin being alike to God and all people being sinners? What made anybody more worthy of death than Todd was himself? Without the Lord no one had the power to change. And how could anyone find the Lord without being shown compassion and love just the way they were? These questions ran through Todd's mind in a flash, humbling him. He would need time to sort them out.

"You've given me some things to think about, too," Todd told Sneed. "I misjudged you. We have a lot in common."

"Yes, we do," Sneed said, and Todd could feel a bond being forged between them as they stood side by side and watched the children play.

"I shouldn't have burdened you with my problems," Sneed said at length. "You have enough on your mind."

"Maybe I needed to hear it. If you can't help me, maybe I, at least, can help you. I think I'd like to make a donation after all—to pediatric AIDS. I'll call you next week with the details."

Sneed thanked him and the two men shook hands warmly.

"I hope when you call you'll be able to tell me your son is safe and sound," Sneed said. "If there's anything I can do to help, now or later, please let me know. And I truly am sorry if our meeting had anything to do with his kidnapping."

He walked Todd to the door. With one foot already on the threshold, Todd had a thought. There was another way he could help this man who now seemed like an old friend.

"Do me a favor," he said, "in return for the donation I'm going to make."

"Sure, anything."

"You know what I said before about the Bible?"

Sneed nodded.

"I still stand by it. And I'm asking you to read it for yourself, starting with the New Testament. That's all…just that you read it."

Howard seemed to consider for a moment and then said, "O.K., it's a small price to pay for a worthy cause. You've got my word that I'll read it. Just make that donation sizeable."

CHAPTER 23

An empty house and defeat.

Todd had read the note from Gina as soon as he got home, and he'd thought it would be easier with her gone. But he was wrong. The house seemed to scream with silence.

It was over. There was nowhere else to turn. Nothing else he could think of to do. He had never felt so helpless or been so low in his life. His son was counting on him, and he had failed. Again.

He hadn't eaten anything since an early breakfast of coffee and toast. Not that it mattered. He wasn't hungry. He was just weary.

Maybe all he needed was to rest. He hadn't slept more than a few hours…in how many days? He couldn't remember. Couldn't think. Maybe with a few hours of sleep, he'd be refreshed and able to come up with another plan. Maybe.

Todd fell heavily onto the sofa, and suddenly Smokey was there beside him. He hadn't even realized the dog was still in the house. Smokey seemed to know Todd was too despondent to enforce the house rules and make him get down, so he pawed and sniffed and finally settled himself comfortably in the soft woolly folds of a hand-knitted afghan. Todd stroked the dog's shaggy head with one hand and leaned over to remove his shoes with the other. His head came level with the coffee table, and he saw Gina's Bible lying on it. A word entered his mind and lodged itself there.

Hypocrite.

He tried to push it out, but it wouldn't go away.

Hypocrite.

Deborah Barlow

What business did he have telling Howard Sneed to read the Bible, when he hadn't picked one up in the last five days?

There were reasons, he told himself. He'd been too busy contacting accountants and bankers to get the ransom money together. Too busy dealing with Grady and Sneed and Manning. There hadn't been any time.

So, what's your excuse now?

I'm tired! Leave me alone! Todd ordered the voice in his head, but it only became more insistent.

You know what you need to do. Do it.

He was too broken to wage the war against his conscience any longer. Giving in to the truth it whispered in his heart, Todd picked the book up off the table. He had no idea where to read. It took too much effort to think of a particular passage to look up, so he just let it fall open at random.

It opened to Isaiah, chapter 31, a marked page. Gina must have been reading here—there were lines highlighted in fluorescent yellow. He read them.

"Woe to those who go down to Egypt for help, and rely on horses, and trust in chariots because they are many, and in horsemen because they are very strong, but they do not look to the Holy One of Israel, nor seek the Lord!" And further down the page, "Now the Egyptians are men, and not God, and their horses are flesh and not spirit."

It pierced him like an arrow as he saw with perfect clarity the parallel. Instead of turning to God, he had ignored Him in favor of Carl Grady, a mere man. If he had been ashamed in the light of today's revelations concerning Howard Sneed, it was nothing compared to the shame and guilt he felt now. How could he have been so stubborn and proud?

There were two more marked pages in Gina's Bible. She had done the groundwork for him, and all he had to do was follow her lead. He turned back to the first one. It was in Exodus 14.

"Do not be afraid. Stand firm and you will see the deliverance the Lord will bring you today….The Lord will fight for you; you need only to be still."

And then the last passage, Romans 11: 33-36.

"Oh, the depth of the riches both of the wisdom and knowledge of God! How unsearchable are His judgments and unfathomable His ways! For who has known the mind of the Lord, or who became His counselor? Or who has first given to Him that it might be paid back to Him again? For from Him and through Him and to Him are all things. To Him be the glory forever. Amen."

Suddenly the truth was there in bold black and white, with no shades of gray. At last, Todd faced head on what he'd really known all along-that his trust should be in God and not in his own frail resources. Like Jonah of old, he had chosen to ignore God's voice and run in the opposite direction. That had been his real failure. Only now, in the stark light of his impotence had he been driven to seek the Lord.

"Lord, I'm sorry," Todd said aloud, sliding to his knees on the floor. "I'm so, so sorry. I've been angry with You for letting this happen to me again. And I've been afraid to pray, because I know You aren't some genie who will give me everything I ask for. I knew there wouldn't be any guarantees, and I was afraid that I'm too weak to bear it if I lose Ben the way I lost Joey. But you brought me through the loss of Joey, and You gave me joy again. I know that no matter what happens, You are in control. You may not take away this trial in my life, but you will guide me through it. Help me to trust in You."

With that short prayer, Todd relinquished it all. He laid his burden at the Lord's feet and felt its weight replaced by lightness. Focusing on the power of the Almighty God, he was fortified, and he knew what had to be done.

First, he made a phone call. He dialed a familiar number and asked to speak to Gina.

"Hi, it's me," he said when he heard her voice. "I've finally come to my senses. You were right. I was running away. But I'm not running any more, Gina. From now on, we're going to do things God's way. The right way."

Then he explained what he wanted her to do.

It was a somber group that met at the Reynolds house that evening. It was the first time the K-Group had been called together for a reason other than a regular meeting. Todd's and Gina's voices over the phone had alerted them that this was an emergency, and every last couple dropped whatever plans they had in order to come. Along with the usual members and Walt, Lila and Kellie, there were two additional couples who showed up, Pastor David Smith and his wife, Sandy, and Charlene Monroe with her husband, Meryl.

Walt and Lila's living room was crowded to overflowing. The air conditioning worked overtime sending out ferocious blasts of icy cold, but the room was still hot and stuffy. No one noticed. All eyes were glued to Todd's face and an expectant hush had fallen.

Bitter Reunion

Todd cleared his voice and looked around at all the familiar faces. It was time to begin, but he didn't know quite how or where to start. At last, his gaze rested on Gina, sitting to his right. Her eyes met his, and in that moment he realized how much he had missed her, how close he had come to making one of the biggest mistakes of his life. She reached for his hand and smiled her encouragement.

"Thank you for coming," he said. "Gina and I knew we could count on you."

"What is it, Todd? What's wrong?" Pete could never be patient for long. "You know we're here for you, buddy."

It was true. He'd be willing to trust his life to anyone in this room. It came to him then that, in a way, it was exactly what he was going to do.

"What we need is your prayers," Todd said. "Probably more than we've ever needed anything before."

Then he told them. As with Howard Sneed, no one said a word until he was finished, not even Pete. When it was clear that he was done, though, the voices all came at once—expressing outrage, shock and concern.

"I think you should call the police," came from John Nesbaum, with echoing sentiments from several others.

Pete was on his feet, offering to go with Todd to make the ransom payment and ambush the kidnapper from behind. His choice of terminology for the kidnapper was overlooked by the group. They had weightier matters to contend with.

Todd held up his hand to silence them. "I'm not exactly sure why," he said, "but I don't want to get the police involved. There are times when they should be, but for some reason, I don't think this is one of them. You may think I'm making a mistake, but I hope you will all honor my request that you don't contact them about this yourselves. Whatever happens to Ben is in the Lord's hands at this point. And that's exactly where I want to leave it."

"What we need right now," Gina interjected, "is just to know that you will all be praying for Ben and for us. From now until this is over, one way or another."

"You know we will be, Gina," Carolyn said. The rest nodded in agreement.

"There is one other thing that I haven't mentioned yet," Todd said. "The day after tomorrow is also the anniversary of the day I lost Joey." His voice cracked, and suddenly it was as if he were talking straight to God, and no one else was in the room. "I…I've never really stopped missing Joey. He was my firstborn, my Joseph. We were so close, just like Jacob and Joseph in the Bible. I used to read that story to him. He never got tired of it. Later, I read it to Ben." He dropped his head, a faraway look in his eyes. "I love him so much, just like I do…did… Joey. And now, I might lose them both…Joseph and Benjamin." He looked up at the group again. "I just don't know if I could take it." Unable to go on, he sat back down.

Pastor Dave spoke up. "Let's pray, now. Let's take all these things to the One who is able to deal with them. If you feel like kneeling, go ahead. And let's pray for the man who has taken Ben. There's a horrible bitterness eating away at his soul. Let's ask God to deal with that, too."

CHAPTER 24

Friday, June 30

A heavy stillness blanketed the afternoon. Black thunder clouds seemed to be hovering, waiting for the right moment to join forces in a mass assault on the earth below. Tense anticipation...it was the same feeling that permeated the Hamilton's house. It was the day before D-Day. Within twenty-four hours or so, it would all be over.

Todd had spent the morning at the office, trying to catch up on some things he had let slide the last few days, but he had given up before he was half done. He hadn't been able to concentrate. He was probably making it hard for his employees to concentrate, too. It was impossible to miss the concerned looks on their faces when they glanced in his direction. They weren't accustomed to the quiet, distracted man that he had become of late. Claiming, not untruthfully, that he wasn't feeling well, he'd left for home.

Now that he was here, he wasn't sure what to do with himself. He was used to being a man of action. Standing in the wings wasn't his style.

Kathy Simon was here, talking in hushed tones with Lila and Kellie, while Gina sat in the corner with a telephone to her ear. In another corner, Walt dozed fitfully in a recliner.

Curiously, despite the circumstances and the inherent tension they created, a kernel of peace remained imbedded in the core of Todd's soul. He was reminded of the time in the eighth grade when he had struggled to grasp the concept of algebra. An excellent student, he had been embarrassed because he just couldn't seem to get it. For at least a month, he had tried on his own to figure out how those A's and B's equaled C's, all the while hiding the prominent D's and F's on his test papers. Then one day, knowing he was in over his head, he had told his dad of his problem.

After all this time, he could still remember his dad's response. He hadn't gotten the look of disappointment and the stern lecture he had expected. Instead, Dad had sat down beside him at the kitchen table and patiently explained whatever equation it was that Todd hadn't understood. In a matter of minutes, the problem that had plagued him for so long was gone. Just like that. And then Dad had said, "I wish you hadn't waited so long to tell me about this, son. You didn't have to battle this all alone. I'm always here to help you."

It was that way now. He wasn't fighting alone anymore. He'd taken the problem to his Father. Like he should have done from the first.

"Todd," Gina said, interrupting his thoughts, "that was Carolyn on the phone. I want you to listen to this." The last comment was intended for everyone in the room. They all gathered around Gina except Walt, who continued to sleep in the corner. Knowing he'd been battling insomnia, no one had the heart to wake him.

"She confided in the twins. About Ben. They really love him, and she thought they should know so they could be praying for him. Anyway, the point is that the girls remembered something from the day they baby-sat him. Last Friday. Both Melody and Melissa noticed someone driving slowly by the house several

Bitter Reunion

times. They figured he was just lost, but hearing about Ben made them think it might have been more sinister than that."

"I'll bet it was the kidnapper!" Kellie exclaimed. She edged forward on her seat. "He was probably watching Ben, just waiting for a chance to get him."

"Do they remember what the car looked like?" Lila asked.

"Even better than that," Gina answered, excitement in her voice. "Apparently they remember the car and its driver in vivid detail. Melody, who is completely boy crazy, had a good description of the driver. She said, and I quote, "He was this gorgeous hunk." She got a close look at him when she went out to get the mail. Said he stared right at her. Early twenties or late teens, blonde hair and, as I said, good looking. I'm sure that's why she remembers."

"What about the car?" Todd asked.

"Red and sporty with an Idaho license plate. They didn't know the make or model."

It took only a second to connect. "What?" Kellie asked as if she hadn't heard. But she had heard, and she knew someone who owned a sporty red car with an Idaho license plate. Someone she had just met last week. Someone she hadn't seen since the day Ben was taken. *Someone she had liked...a lot.*

Disturbing thoughts bumped and whirled in Kellie's head as the conversation went on around her. Unobtrusively, she got up and walked out of the room. She needed to think. Making her way to the patio, she took a seat on a white wooden glider. The first large drops of rain splatted heavily on the roof over her head. She could hear faint, far-off thunder, and it seemed to be part of the workings of her mind, echoing the disquiet that lurked there.

The description fit David in every way. The rest fit together, too. David's reluctance to talk about himself. His interest in Ben. The distant way he had acted on Monday when he'd told her that he was leaving. Oh yes, it fit only too well. He had been using her so he could get to Ben. And she had made it easy for him. Practically handed Ben over on a silver platter.

He should have been an actor, Kellie thought bitterly. She had honestly thought he liked her. Last Sunday, she could have sworn he had enjoyed their day together…almost as much as she had. What an idiot she had been! He had tried to kill her twice since that day. It made her feel sick to her stomach to think about it. Carol had been right about David. And Kellie had been a naive fool. How could she ever trust her instincts again?

There was still something she didn't understand, though. If she was right, she knew who had kidnapped Ben and tried to kill her… but why? Why? What could Todd possibly have done to have made David hate him so? What had she done? And who was David, anyway?

As the approaching storm loomed ever nearer, Kellie tried to replay the conversations she'd had with David, searching for clues to his identity, his motives. If David were really the kidnapper, there had to be a reason. She needed to make sense of it.

The first time she'd seen him had been at the deli. That, too, must have been set up just so he could meet her, but she couldn't think of anything he'd said that was out of the ordinary. Just that he was from California, which was probably a lie, in view of the license plate. And that he was in Albion to attend college—another lie.

Then on Friday, she'd run into him at the concert. It had seemed coincidental, but now she knew otherwise. What had he told her when they had talked? She struggled to reconstruct the scene and hear again his words. Start at the beginning, she thought.

He'd seemed surprised to see her, almost as if he couldn't place her at first. Yes, he was definitely a good actor.

She had introduced him to Ben, and then…

Thunder clapped, and in the same instant it came to her. The prayer meeting last night, when Todd had spoken of his two sons—it had tickled a memory. She hadn't been able to pin it down then, but now…

Ben's voice. "My name is Ben, short for Benjamin."

Then David. "Benjamin, Joseph's younger brother."

Ben. "You know that story, too?"

David. "My father used to read it to me when I was younger."

No. It couldn't be. Could it? Kellie's heart was pounding so hard she could barely breathe. An answer had presented itself so suddenly and so clearly that it terrified her.

David was Joey.

Yes, that had to be it! David was really Joseph Hamilton! It was like finding the missing piece to a puzzle, but discovering that once it was inserted, the whole picture was completely different than it had been only a moment before. Kellie had no idea what to make of it.

They were all still gathered in the living room when Kellie returned, walking on shaky legs. She didn't want to tell them what she suspected yet. What if she was wrong? There had to be a way to verify what she was thinking.

Gina looked up as she approached. "Are you O.K., Kel?" she asked. "You look pale. Have you got another headache?"

"No, I'm fine," Kellie said. "Just upset about Ben, I guess."

"Maybe you should lie down, Kellie," Todd said. He sighed and wearily combed his fingers through his hair. "It still hasn't been that long since the accident, you know."

He was looking at her, expecting a response of some kind, but Kellie hadn't really heard him. She'd been caught unexpectedly by a new revelation. That mannerism of Todd's just now had reminded her of David. He'd had the same way of distractedly running his fingers through his hair. Now, looking for other similarities in the two, she saw them. David's hair and eyes were lighter, and their noses were shaped differently. But they shared more than just a passing resemblance. Or did they? Maybe she was just conjuring up something that wasn't there at all. She couldn't be sure.

"Todd, do you have any pictures of Joey? I'm curious about what he looked like."

"You want to see one right now?" Todd asked, surprise showing in his voice.

"Yes. If you don't mind."

Todd left the room and returned shortly with a photograph album. He wordlessly handed it to Kellie and left her to browse through the pictures alone. She could understand his reluctance to look at them, especially now. She hoped he didn't think she was too insensitive to have asked to see them. She

Bitter Reunion

took the album to the dining room table where she could be alone with Joey and the past.

The album was large and heavy with a thick blue cover that bore the word "Memories" in faded gold letters. It was worn-looking, as if it had been handled a lot, and Kellie could imagine Todd pouring over its pages time and again in search of those memories, his only link to the son he had loved so much. Feeling somehow like an intruder, Kellie slowly turned the cover over.

The first page was covered with pictures of a little boy who looked a lot like Ben…but then of course, they were half brothers, weren't they? She tried to see David in the young, smiling face, but she couldn't find him there. Twelve years or more had passed since these pictures had been taken. The little boy was now a young man. Whether or not that man was David, she still couldn't tell.

Two more pages. More pictures of Joey. More uncertainty. Then, on the third page, Kellie found her answer.

The first thing she noticed was that one of the pictures included a woman. She was standing beside Joey and squinting into the sun. And it was in her face that Kellie saw the first sign of David. She had his eyes and his nose. She had the same Nordic blonde beauty.

It must be Elaine, Todd's first wife. She stood on a sandy beach, the wind blowing her long hair back from her face. Kellie stared at her, mesmerized. How could David not be this woman's son? Still, did the fact that he looked like her really prove anything?

She tore her eyes away from Elaine and focused instead on the child at her side. Joey must have been around six in the picture. He looked up at his mother, a wistful expression on his face. They were not touching. He was carrying a bright green plastic pail and wore only a pair of swimming trunks. The child was lanky, his bare legs like twin toothpicks.

Kellie's eyes locked on those legs, and her heart skipped a beat. She knew now that it was true. The boy in this picture was Joey Hamilton...and he was David Ross. The evidence was there, right before her eyes, so conclusive that there was no arguing it. On the right leg just above the knee, the small Joey of so many years ago bore a large reddish-brown birth mark. She had noticed an identical birth mark on David's leg when they had played tennis together on Sunday. She remembered thinking that it was probably the only imperfect thing about him.

It was one thing to suspect that David was Joey and another to know it. She was overwhelmed by the magnitude of what she had discovered. It meant that Todd's own son, whom he had grieved over for years, was trying to kill her and was holding his own brother for ransom. What kind of sense did that make? As far as she could see, none at all.

There was only one thing she knew for sure. She had to tell Todd.

He hadn't believed it at first. Even when she'd shown him the picture and explained about the birthmark, he'd fought against admitting that Joey was the kidnapper. And now, hours later, Todd still couldn't fully grasp it.

He'd prayed for this day for so long, but now that it was here, he was in a state of shock. It wasn't the way he had dreamed it would be. He was scared, and he wasn't even

Bitter Reunion

sure what scared him the most—the thought that Joey had such a deep-seated hatred against Todd that he had taken Ben because of it or the possibility that somehow Kellie was wrong and the kidnapper wasn't Joey after all.

Either way he hadn't really found his son, had he? Not the loving child he remembered. In Todd's mind, Joey was still eight years old, with freckles on his nose and teeth missing. It had been so long ago, yet it felt like yesterday. He and Joey playing baseball in the back yard. Reading a bedtime story and listening to his son's innocent prayers. Riding bikes together. Hearing his boy say, "I love you, Daddy." There simply wasn't any way to bend or twist those images into one of an angry young man with murder in his heart. It was unbearably painful to imagine what kind of life Joey must have led to have caused him to do what he was doing now.

Todd's emotions were a confusing rollercoaster of highs and lows that all lead to the same place—the realization that Elaine's plan had worked all too well. His son despised him.

"What are you going to do, honey?" Gina asked quietly, voicing a question he had already asked himself a dozen times. "How are you going to convince him you didn't abandon him?"

It was late. Todd and Gina rocked slowly in the same porch glider where Kellie had sat earlier, but the storm had passed over and the black night sky was filled with bright, glittering stars. Eternity seemed so close, as if you could reach out and touch it with your hand. How Todd wished he could see tomorrow from its other side and know the outcome.

"I don't know," he said. "I just have to pray that I'll find a way."

Deborah Barlow

They sat intertwined, letting the sounds of the night ease their souls. A dog barked at some imaginary threat to his domain. Smokey, who lay at their feet, responded with one short "woof" of his own before closing his eyes again. A cricket chirped. A distant train rumbled by, its whistle piercing the soft stillness.

Sometime after midnight, an early morning chill forced them from their sanctuary, and they went inside.

CHAPTER 25

Saturday, July 1

Blessedly, the call came before noon. It seemed much later to Todd and Gina. They had slept little and risen shortly after dawn. They were exhausted, yet keyed up and ready to face whatever came next. The sooner it happened, the better.

"It's me again."

The voice was immediately familiar, and yet now that Todd knew who it belonged to, it threw him. It didn't sound like a young person's voice at all. It was very deep, hard and mean. He felt no connection to the one behind it. Only a sense of repulsion. The thought crossed his mind that maybe it wasn't Joey after all, but he discarded it. Joey must be disguising his voice.

"Are you ready to deal? Have you got all the money?"

"Yes," Todd answered. "But I'd like some assurance that my son is still alive. Please, just let me hear his voice."

"I'd like to oblige you, Hamilton. I surely would, but the kid's taking a little nap right now. I'd hate to disturb him." There was laughter, as if the kidnapper had said something funny. "You're just going to have to take my word that he's unharmed. And you can also believe me when I say that he'll be dead if anything goes the slightest bit wrong with the ransom. Do you understand me?"

"Yes."

"Good. Now here's what I want you to do. There's a burned out barn off the south side of highway 20 about eight and a half miles west of Albion. You can barely see it from the road."

"I know the place," Todd said.

"I'll be waiting there for you. Come alone and bring the money. No one else is to know where you're going. Drive around to the back of the barn and park your car at the end of the dirt driveway. Then get out and walk toward the barn with the money. I'll see you coming. Drive the Grand Am. I've got binoculars and I will know if it isn't you behind the wheel. I'll also be able to see any other cars that approach that barn, so don't try a sneak attack. It won't work. And no cell phone."

"Don't worry. I'll do just as you say. All I want is to get my son back." All I want is to get both of you back, Todd thought. He ached to tell his son that he knew who he was and he'd never stopped loving him. Todd held back, though. He had to confront Joey face to face. It was the only way. "What time should I be there?"

"Two o'clock. On the dot. And you better not have car trouble, because if you aren't here by two fifteen, the whole thing's off and the kid is dead."

Todd started to protest, but he heard a click and knew it would be futile. The conversation was over.

A wave of dizziness swept over him, and he wondered if he was going to be sick, but the moment passed. Todd slowly placed the receiver back on its cradle and turned to face Gina.

"What is it?" she asked in alarm when she saw his ashen face. "Is Ben alright?"

"I hope so. I really don't know," Todd answered. He rose from the desk chair to pace the floor. "I can't believe that was my own son that I just spoke to. If only you could have heard him, Gin. He sounds so…evil. I don't know how else to describe it. It worries me. I'm not so sure I'll be able to convince him that he's been wrong about me all these years. He'll probably just think I'm making something up to placate him."

"You have to think of a way, Todd. You just have to. This may be the only chance you will ever have to reach him." A new and startling possibility had occurred to Gina. "Do you think you might be in danger yourself?"

"I wish I could say I didn't, but I honestly don't know that either, honey. All I know is that I have to go. I don't have a choice. If I don't show up at the meeting place by two fifteen, he will kill Ben. That's what he told me, and I don't think he was bluffing. He holds all the cards."

"It may look that way to us, Todd, but the Lord is on your side. Don't forget that. It changes everything."

"I know. You're right." Todd wished he were more confident, but he couldn't erase the sound of that voice from his mind. It had been full of a venomous hatred that had sent chills down his spine. The fire of that kind of hatred would be hard to quench.

Except for the location of the meeting place, Todd told Gina the details of the ransom meeting, and she went to the telephone to call her parents. They, in turn, would contact everyone who had been at the prayer meeting to let them know what was going on and when to be praying. As she spoke to her mother, Todd escaped to the den to do some praying of his own. If ever he had needed to draw upon the power of God, it was now. He had never felt so helpless.

David couldn't wait to be gone, but Hank insisted on going over the plan again for about the twentieth time. All this talk was really beginning to bug David. He sat at the table and fiddled with the gun that lay there in front of him, thinking about the freedom it was about to bring.

Hank's lips moved, but David wasn't listening to the words they formed. He was seeing it again, all in slow motion. The way it would be.

The gun is recoiling in his hand.

Hamilton's head is snapping back and his body is falling.

He twitches once, then lays still.

He's dead.

"Did you hear me? I said, quit messing with that gun! It's loaded, and I don't want you blowing yourself away before you even get a chance to blow Hamilton away!"

"Not likely. The safety's on," David retorted. "And I'm not some ten-year-old kid playing with daddy's gun. It's going to be mine, remember?"

Hank slammed his fist down on the table. "I ought to go and off Hamilton myself! I'm sick and tired of your attitude! You think you can talk to me like that just because I'm counting on you to do the killing. Well, think again! I'd just as soon do the job myself! It was only as a favor that I offered to let you do it in the first place!"

David dropped the Colt 45 two inches to the table top and raised his hands in a sign of surrender. He scraped his chair away from the side of the table and the fury of Hank's verbal onslaught.

"Sorry, Pa. I guess I'm still a little mad that you didn't let me make the ransom call. You know how much I wanted to hear Hamilton grovel."

"Your turn's coming, if you don't screw it up. And it's going to be a whole lot sweeter than a phone call."

Hank stood up and walked across the room. He opened a cupboard door, looked inside and pulled out a tin can with a green label on it. He held it for a second. Then, unexpectedly, he drew his arm back and threw it across the counter where it hit the ancient radio with a crash. Pieces of plastic flew.

"There isn't a decent thing to eat in this whole kitchen!" he ranted, as he slammed the cupboard door forcefully. It popped back open, and he slammed it again. "This job can't be over soon enough for me. I want out of this lousy, rotten town and this lousy, rotten shack! Why did I let you talk me into waiting until two o'clock?"

"It's important to me," David said. "I won't hassle you about anything else, I promise. And I really do appreciate it."

"You'd better, boy. 'Cause you've been just about more trouble than you're worth."

Hank looked at his watch. "You should be leaving now," he said. "We want to make sure you get to the barn well before Hamilton does."

David stood and picked the pistol up off the table.

"One last time," Hank said before David could take a step. "Are you absolutely sure you can do it? Because if you aren't, I want to know it now. Otherwise, I'd better not see you again until Hamilton is dead."

David looked him square in the eye. "I'd rather die myself then let him live."

Hank was satisfied with the answer. He stood aside and let David pass him as he walked toward the back door. Then he said, "Good luck, Son."

As David eased himself into the front seat of the Camero, he glanced back at the house and saw Hank still standing at the door wearing the scowl that had been there since the night that Hank had moved in with him. David had no idea what might have ticked him off, but he was still sullen and angry over something. David had been walking on egg shells, afraid of setting him off. He just hoped that Ben would sleep soundly while he was gone, because there was no telling how Hank would respond if he had any trouble with the boy—especially when he was in such a bad mood.

Having to drug Ben was the worst part of this whole business. It worried David, because he didn't really know what he was doing. The matter of dosage was trial and error. If he gave the child too little, he would wake up too often, and Hank would be in a rage. If he gave him too much, he could kill him by overdose. That had been his biggest fear. Consequently, he'd given Ben smaller doses than Hank would have liked and then watched for the first sign that Ben was stirring, so he could give him more. Today, though, he'd increased the dosage because he knew he would be gone for a couple of hours. He hoped he hadn't increased it too much.

David drove out onto Sherman street and shrugged off his anxiety about Ben. The boy would be fine, and soon David would be, too.

Bitter Reunion

Everything was going to go exactly the way he had imagined.

Minutes later, David left pavement for gravel, then parked his car out of sight from the road in a thicket of trees behind the old barn. Rolling the windows down, he settled in for a wait. He had about forty-five minutes to kill before Hamilton would be arriving. The thought made him smile. First he'd kill time, then he'd kill Hamilton.

It was a good day for a killing.

The sun had decided to grace the sky with its brilliant presence again, after the latest spell of stormy weather, and no clouds dared to infringe on its domain. A warm gentle breeze ruffled the tall grass that blanketed the ground. Birds chirped and butterflies flitted playfully about. It was probably a day much like that one twelve years ago. David could still remember the feel of it before it had all gone bad. There had been a sense of hope and joy that he had not experienced since then, but he could recapture it. It was there to be had, just beyond his reach.

"Happy birthday to me." He liked the way that sounded. Nobody had said those words to him for over a decade. It was about time someone did, even if it was only himself. He was about to give himself a present, too. The gift of sweet revenge.

He checked the time. It was one-thirty. David wouldn't be left to wait and watch for someone who never intended to come. Not today.

Or would he? A small doubt presented itself. What if Hamilton didn't show after all? What if he didn't care about Ben any more than he had about Joey? It was a possibility wasn't it, even though Hank had been sure that he would come? David couldn't stand to think about it. He would come. *He had to come.*

David removed the Colt 45 from his glove compartment. Then he got out of the car and crossed the grassy stretch that led to the barn. The building was a structural hazard. It looked as if it had once been a proud, towering edifice, but now portions of the roof were gone, leaving gaping holes in their place. What was left of the red paint had weathered to a dull watery pink. One side of the barn leaned precariously, held up by a remnant of wall that had managed to escape the flames which had blackened and burned the rest of it. David could see exposed beams inside the cool darkness of the building.

Standing there alone, the barn was a picture of solitude. No other buildings were in sight. If there had ever been a farmhouse that went with the barn, it must have burned completely down. There were no cows or chickens, no crops of any kind. No children going about their daily chores. All that remained of days gone by was a rusted-out green tractor standing as discarded as the barn. David was at one with his surroundings. He knew about being discarded.

As he carefully stepped inside, something low to the ground darted from the shadows and streaked past him. The suddenness of the movement startled him, but it was only a mangy yellow cat who had taken a break from poaching mice to nap in the shade of the barn.

Finding a vantage point where he could watch for Hamilton proved to be easy. There were lookout holes everywhere created by the fire. David spotted a grease-stained wooden barrel and rolled it over to a place where he could see the road through charred edges of siding.

Righting the barrel, he brushed a thick layer of dust off the top, and then sat down on it.

It shouldn't be long now. His heart raced. Two o'clock was approaching.

His own personal witching hour.

CHAPTER 26

The prayer warriors had assembled. Instead of marching, they knelt. Instead of standing at attention, they bowed. Their ranks numbered in excess of one hundred. Three church prayer chains had been enlisted, and they faced their mission with tenacity, not underestimating the opponent. They fought against Satan, not merely his human pawns. Evil was his realm, and he was the commander-in-chief.

Their power was far greater than could be imagined by looking at their frail physical bodies, few of which were in combat condition. They were just ordinary people with the ultimate weapon at their disposal. Clad in protective armor, their swords at the ready, they charged.

Gina had intended to be engaged in the battle along with them, but instead found herself standing on the immense flagstone doorstep of a house she'd never seen before. Kellie stood beside her, bouncing up and down on the balls of her feet, not bothering to try to stifle her impatience. The house looked deserted. Curtains were drawn shut, and the place was quiet as a tomb.

It was Belinda Montgomery's house.

They were here because Kellie had recalled an encounter she had seen between David and a man at the park. The memory had come on the way to Todd and Gina's, and by the time she and her parents had arrived, she had even remembered where she had seen the menacing-looking man before she'd seen him with David.

Bitter Reunion

He'd been sitting in the Country Club dining room sharing a table with a blonde woman who Kellie had met before. Belinda Montgomery.

What was frustrating was that Kellie may have remembered too late to do any good. Todd was already gone, and there was no way to let him know there was probably a second person involved in Ben's kidnapping. Todd was only prepared to deal with Joey, and now who knew what kind of situation he would be walking into?

Finding out about the incident in the park had only made Gina more afraid for her husband than ever.

When Kellie told Gina about Belinda, Gina had immediately tried to call her, but the line was busy. So, without stopping to think it through, Gina had asked her mother to stay and wait by the phone, then grabbed up the telephone book and whisked her dad and Kellie out the door and to the car.

Now Gina stood beside Kellie facing Belinda's intimidating fortress of a door and chided herself for having been so impulsive. She had no idea what she was going to say to Belinda Montgomery.

"Excuse me, I was wondering if you've been dating a kidnapper?"

Or how about this one? "Is there any chance that your boyfriend may have tried to kill my sister?"

It was only minutes away from the appointed time for Todd's meeting, anyway. What was there to gain by finding out anything more about Joey's accomplice now?

As Gina looked nervously around, Kellie punched the doorbell over and over, like a pre-adolescent prankster getting ready to run.

Walt waited in the car, prepared to join them at the first sign of trouble.

"Come on, Kellie, let's go. This was a bad idea. Maybe it's a good thing nobody's home. What if that guy had been here when we showed up? He could've shot us right where we stand."

Kellie pulled her hand back from the door as if it was charged with electricity. "Oh! I didn't think about that! Why do I suddenly feel like there's a huge red bull's-eye painted on my back?"

"I know," Gina said, uneasily. "It only just now occurred to me, too." She made a move to turn around when half of the massive twelve-foot double door opened.

Belinda stood there, and it was apparent to both Kellie and Gina that something was wrong, because the woman looked worse than horrible. At one forty-five in the afternoon, she was still attired in a wrinkled and food-stained pair of purple pajamas and a fuzzy pink robe. Even more revealing, her eyes were rimmed in red and her complexion was splotchy. She wore no makeup. Gina barely recognized her, even though she'd seen her many times at social events.

"Wha' ya want? 'M not feeling well. Leave me 'lone." A strong smell of alcohol explained the slurring of her words.

Now that she was face-to-face with Belinda, Gina was at a loss for words. Belinda started to close the door.

"No, wait," Kellie blurted out. "Please just give us a minute. We're looking for a man that I've seen with you at the Country Club. I don't know his name, but it's important that we find him."

The door stopped in mid swing. Belinda stood there for a moment, as if she were trying to remember where she was. Then she said, "You wan' Thomas? Join the crowd. He's gone. He took my money, 'n took off. He never called, so I tried to call him. He never checked in at that hotel," she told them as if they should already know what she was talking about. "An' then I foun' out he already cashed my check an' closed out our joint account." She began to laugh, and then to their dismay, her laughter turned to tears.

Gina felt terrible pressing the point when the woman was obviously so distraught, but she tried anyway. "Can you tell us where he lives, or lived?"

Belinda shook her head. "Ne'er went there. He always came here. Wha'd he do, anyway? Rip you off, too?"

Gina dug in her purse for a piece of paper and a pen. Why did it seem like she could never find anything in there when she needed it? Finally, frustrated, she pulled the checkbook out of her purse and hurriedly ripped a deposit slip containing her name and telephone number out of it.

"Here," she said, handing it to Belinda. "Please hang on to this, and call me if you think of anything that could help us contact…Thomas. Will you do that?"

Belinda stared blankly at the paper in her hand and didn't answer. Then she backed away and softly shut the door. They could hear the sound of a dead bolt being engaged.

"I don't know about you," Kellie said to Gina, "but I think we've just found another victim of David's friend."

Gina wasn't listening. She was already on her way to the car. "Hurry, Kellie. We need to get back. It's almost two.

....

"Hello!"

Lila answered the phone on the first ring.

"I...I'm trying to call Gina...Ham..Hamilton," a female voice said hesitantly.

"This is her mother," Lila said impatiently. "She isn't home right now, and I really need to keep this line open. Could you call her back tomorrow?"

"Sure, I guess. Jes' tell her B'linda called."

"Wait, don't go! She's walking in the door now." Lila gestured frantically to Gina, beckoning her to the telephone.

The line was silent.

"Are you still there?"

"Yes." Belinda sounded timid, ready to hang up at the slightest provocation.

"I'm sorry. I didn't mean to be rude. I'm sure Gina would want to speak to you. Here she is."

Lila handed the receiver to Gina, who by now was leaning over her mother's shoulder. "It's Belinda," Lila whispered.

Gina put the receiver to her ear. "Hi, Belinda. Thanks for calling so soon. Did you happen to remember something that can help me get in touch with Thomas?"

"Maybe. 'M not sure. He's prob'ly skipped the country by now, anyway."

"Maybe not," Gina said. "I have a feeling he's still around."

"Well, you see, there was this one day when I was getting rid of old newspapers. You know, bundling them up to put out for reshy..cycling. 'Nyway, one of them had the..oh you know...the want ads.."

"The classifieds?" Gina supplied.

"Yeah, those. They were showing, and one of 'm was circled in ink. It mushta been Thomas that done it,'cause it wasn't me. It was a rental house on Sherman shtreet. Couldn't figure out why Thomas would of been int'rested in it. Sherman street's a real slum. Not his kinda place."

"You don't happen to remember the address by any chance?" Gina asked, her voice raising in excitement.

"'S a matter 'a fact, I still got the ad. Don't know why I kept it. Guess part of me never did trusht him completely. Wish the resht of me woulda paid 'ttention."

Belinda began to giggle, and Gina was afraid she was going to lose her completely.

"What's the address, Belinda?" she asked loudly and firmly, trying to reach Belinda through the sound of her drunken laughter. "Do you have the advertisement there with you? Tell me the address."

The giggling lessened and turned to hiccups. Finally Belinda got control of herself and was able to speak again.

"1359 Sherman. The Harlem of Albion. He desherves to live in a place like that—but prison would suit him better."

"Thank you, Belinda. Thank you so much! You don't know how much I appreciate this," Gina said, vastly relieved to have gotten the information she sought. Talking to Belinda was worse than trying to converse with a small child.

"My pl…my pleasure," Belinda replied bitterly, taking pains to enunciate the words clearly and precisely. "Just find that snake, and I'll help you nail his slimy hide to the wall."

....

Belinda was glad that someone was going after Thomas. She would do it herself, but she couldn't face him quite yet. Maybe it would be a long time before she could. Maybe never.

She padded across pristine white carpet to the master bathroom. Avoiding looking in the mirror, she opened the medicine cabinet and withdrew an amber-colored round bottle, noticing at the same time that she still had the scrap of newspaper containing the ad in her other hand. In a symbolic gesture, she lifted the toilet lid, crumpled the piece of paper into a tight little ball and threw it into the bowl. Then, flushing, she solemnly watched as it swirled round and round and finally disappeared. If only it were that easy to erase all the feelings she'd had for Thomas.

Belinda Montgomery. The name was well-know in the town of Albion. It brought to mind most of the things that other people ran after but could never quite lay hold of. She was filthy rich, a socialite in impeccable standing. She lived in an eight-hundred-thousand dollar home and drove a Mercedes. She could call the governor of the state by his first name. Yet despite all this, down deep inside of her there was this tremendous, gaping void. Ever since she could remember, all she'd ever wanted was to be loved. It was the one thing that had eluded her.

She'd spent her whole life searching for the man who would want only her. A man who would see the real Belinda beneath the rolls of flesh and the trappings of wealth that surrounded her and who would accept her just as she was. Three failed marriages and a string of men who had used her was all she had to show for her efforts. The man of her dreams simply didn't exist. She had nothing to offer; there was nothing about her that was worth loving. Belinda Montgomery knew with sudden clarity that the gnawing loneliness which had always plagued her would be her closest companion for the rest of her life.

Clutching the small bottle tight, as if it might try to escape from her hand, she carried it back to her bedroom and set it down beside a much larger bottle of Vodka already on the night stand beside her bed. A little more booze and a few sleeping pills. That ought to do it. She was going to drown out the image of Thomas Kellog, or die trying.

CHAPTER 27

So, Dad, you made it right on time. I'm so glad you've finally learned to be punctual.

David held the small binoculars to his eyes and followed the progress of the lone green car inching along the lane that led to the barn. It was Hamilton all right. David's blood ran cold at the sight of him, and yet it was a tremendous relief to know that he'd come. The first hurdle was over with. Now that Hamilton was here, the rest should be easy.

He placed the binoculars back in his pocket and watched the car until it was within only a few hundred feet of the barn. Gripping the gun firmly in his right hand, he left his lookout corner and crossed again to the back end of the barn. There he stood just beneath the sagging overhang of the roof, where sunshine and shade met, forming a line in the dirt.

He was in no hurry. He'd waited twelve long years for this moment, and he could afford to take his time. He wanted to imprint on his memory every detail, every nuance. He wanted to remember forever exactly how this moment had felt.

Hamilton parked the Grand Am and got out. Standing beside it, he shaded his eyes with his hand and turned his head toward David. The handle of a small soft-sided brown suitcase was in his other hand. Hesitantly, he took a step.

"Are you here?" he called out. He took another step.

David moved out from the shadows. Hamilton saw him and stopped.

David raised the Colt 45 and pointed it at Hamilton's heart. "Walk slowly," he said, "and bring the suitcase over here."

Hamilton stood rooted where he was. There was an odd expression in his eyes as they bored into David.

"I said, MOVE!"

"Joey." Hamilton said the word softly, but to David it sounded like a canon going off in his head. "Joey. It really is you. I was afraid to believe it."

"My name isn't Joey! It's David!"

Hamilton was walking slowly toward him now. His eyes never left David's face. "I didn't leave you, son. I would never have done that. Your mother tricked you into believing it."

"Shut up!" David screamed. The hand that held the gun shook. He released the safety and tried to steady it, his finger tightening around the trigger.

"Joey, you have to believe me. I never stopped loving you. I've been looking for you since the day you disappeared."

The sun was still shining. It touched David, but he couldn't feel it. Something cold and dark had him in its grip.

"If you don't shut up, I'm going to blow your brains out. AND MY NAME IS NOT JOEY! JOEY IS DEAD!"

Rage exploded from the depths of David's being. He hadn't expected Hamilton to know who he was until he himself chose to divulge it. He'd counted on exulting in that moment of revelation...the moment when Hamilton would discover that the cast-off child of his youth had come back to haunt him. How sweet it would have been.

The man had stolen even that from him! How had he known? What had David done to give himself away?

The leopard hadn't changed his spots. Hamilton stood there lying to him just as he always had before with the same disarming look of sincerity that had fooled Joey. It wasn't going to fool David.

"Joey, I know how devastated you must have been. Please, just give me a chance to explain." Smooth and silky, the words were a snare tempting David to believe, beckoning to him like a prostitute by the side of the road, making him crave what they promised to deliver.

"You know I loved you. Remember how it was between us, Joey? All the great times we had together." Hamiltons's voice cracked but he kept talking. "I enjoyed them as much as you did. In your heart, you must know it."

The words kept coming, pounding at David, wearing him down, weakening his resolve. But then a picture, fortifying in its sudden clarity, flashed through his mind. A small boy sat alone on a doorstep and watched the road. Watched and waited and felt hope diminish with each passing minute, until it was gone. And then nothing but a cold emptiness; one that went on and on, year after year until this very moment.

David was drowning in the depths of emotion that flooded over him. It was more than he could bear. In pure reflex to the pain, his finger acted of its own accord and squeezed the trigger of the gun. There was a deafening blast, bringing an end to the words and the buzzing in his head. It echoed, and then a blessed quiet descended.

Bitter Reunion

He was in control again. The shot had gone over Hamilton's head, and now David lowered his arm back down to chest level. He'd almost done it…he'd *needed* to do it, but Hank had made him promise he wouldn't kill Hamilton until he'd seen the money and was satisfied it was all there.

"Don't say another word, or you will never see your precious Benjamin again! Now put the suitcase down and back away from it. Then stand still with your hands in the air," David said, his voice firm.

Hamilton did as he was told. The suitcase rested in the grass between them. Checking its contents would take only a second, and then David would end it. He would blow Hamilton into eternity and then return to Hank and a new life. In four strides, he was beside it. He knelt and flipped the latches on the lid while holding the gun on Hamilton. In a sudden movement, he threw back the lid.

NO!

The first thing that registered was that there was absolutely no money in the case, and then colliding with that realization and overpowering it was the recognition of what he was seeing in its place.

It was a black baseball mitt with the name "Willie Mays" scrawled across it in electric blue letters. It looked as though it had been purchased just yesterday, but it was resting on top of a white paper bag that proved otherwise. The bag said "McLain's Sporting Goods".

It flashed through David's mind in an instant. He was at Ellie's Edibles again, hearing Kellie's voice. "McLain's Sporting Goods was right here. The building was remodeled. Old man McLain sold out years ago."

David knew what it meant, but his mind refused to process the information. Overhead, the birds stopped singing, and the warm afternoon breeze stilled. Suspended in time, the moment stood motionless and silent, starkly void except for one thing.

The glove.

It was in his hands now, the gun discarded on the ground. Echos of the past suddenly reverberated all around him, bouncing off the trees, the walls of the old barn, the ground beneath his feet; and yesterday's reality began to play again on the screen of his mind.

McLain's had been his favorite place to hang out when Elaine wanted him out of the house. Day after day, he'd ride his bike there and spend hours admiring all the sports equipment, imagining himself a famous major league player in need of some new gear. Mr. McLain hadn't seemed to mind.

Once he'd seen the glove, it made all the other stuff seem like junk. It was all he wanted, all he could think about. In that far-away time when he'd known how to dream, it had been the ultimate object of his burning boyhood desire.

And now, it was here. He was touching it. It felt and looked exactly the way he'd thought it would. An eight-year-old's dream come true.

Hamilton had lowered his raised arms. David didn't notice.

"I bought it for you that day," Todd said, daring to speak. "I've had it ever since, hoping some day I could give it to you. Happy birthday, Son."

David was confused. In the blink of an eye, everything he had held to be true was turned upside down, and yet it was the first time in over a decade that anything had made any sense at all.

David raised his eyes from the mitt. His father was standing there, tears streaming unchecked down his face. And then David was standing too, and suddenly he felt strong arms around him. There was a great wrenching inside as something hard and barren tore loose, and a loud wailing assaulted his senses. It was the sound of anguish and despair, of someone's heart breaking in two. He wanted to tell his father not to cry, but he couldn't speak. And then he knew why. The sobbing he heard was his own.

All the tears David had stored up for so many years were at last set free in a rushing torrent of hurt and pain mixed with something new and so powerful that it transcended everything else. It was love. His body shook as he rocked in Todd's embrace.

Joey was home. He clung desperately to Todd, as though afraid that if he let go, he would wake up and find that all this had just been a dream. A wonderful, but transient dream.

"Thank God, thank God," Todd was muttering as he held his son. "I didn't know if you would believe me. I didn't know how to convince you that I never stopped loving you. The day you disappeared was the worst day of my life. I bought you that mitt you wanted so much, and I couldn't wait to pick you up. But when I showed up to get you, nobody was there.

"I couldn't believe what she'd done. Elaine had decided to take you with her, because she knew it was the worst thing she could ever do to me. She even left a video tape explaining how she fooled you into thinking I had abandoned you. I still have it, Joey. If you have any doubts left, it's proof that what I'm saying is true." Todd continued to explain, "I hated her for a long time for what she did, so I know how you must have hated me."

As David's sob diminished, Todd backed off a step, removed a handkerchief from his pocket, and handed it to his son.

"I'm sorry. I'm so sorry…Dad," David said when he could speak. "I almost killed you! Oh, God, what if I had killed you and never even found out what Elaine did?" It terrified him to think how close he had been to doing just that. Only a breath away.

"It's God that we both have to thank for this moment, Joey," Todd said. "He never stopped loving you, either. Right now there are people all over this town praying for you—and for me and for Ben."

"Oh, no!" David said. With everything that had happened, he'd forgotten all about Ben and Hank and the ransom money. What was he going to do now? How could he explain to his dad—how good that word sounded! —that his other son was still in danger?

"What is it?" Todd asked, alarmed. "What's wrong? Is Ben O.K.?"

"I think so," David said, looking miserable. "He's not here with me. I left him with Hank."

CHAPTER 28

The kid was still sleeping soundly. There hadn't been a peep out of him since Hank couldn't remember when. He leaned over the bed and checked the boy's pulse. Still alive, at least for now.

Hank intended to remedy that situation before he and David took off for Rio de Janeiro. The thought gave him some satisfaction, but not enough. It was the girl that he really wanted. It was the first time he'd ever wanted to kill someone bad enough to risk the consequences—and money wasn't even the reason. It was hate, pure and simple.

Only the fact that he was so close to getting his hands on five million dollars kept him from going after her. Ben would be a substitute, the best he could do under the circumstances. He only hoped that she would grieve. David seemed to think she really cared for the kid. Maybe Hank would leave her a note to let her know that Ben had died in her place. The idea caused him to smile, but the smile never reached his eyes. They were as hard and soulless as flint.

As Hank left the bedroom and closed the door behind him, he looked at his watch. Where was David? He should have been back by now. Hank felt a stab of anxiety. What if something had gone wrong? He was beginning to wish he'd trusted his instincts and gotten rid of Hamilton himself. If David didn't show pretty soon, Hank was going to have to leave without him or the money. It would be a bitter pill to swallow, but better than rotting away in prison. He'd let David do that for him—maybe it would toughen him up. In any case, there was a flight to catch, and Hank intended to be on it.

....

 The minutes turned into an hour, and still there was no word from Todd. Something must have gone wrong.
 This was the worst kind of agony. The waiting never seemed to end. Gina couldn't stand it. Now that she knew where Ben might be, she had to try to go to him. If she stayed here for one more second, not knowing what was happening to him, she just knew she would go completely, stark-raving mad. Her child needed her, and she needed to be with him, no matter the cost.
 She knew Mom and Dad would insist on going along if she told them what she was planning, so she didn't explain. She simply said that she wanted to be alone, then snuck out the side door to the garage and was driving away before they realized she'd left the house. They would worry, and she regretted that, but she wasn't going to jeopardize their lives if she could help it. She would go alone.
 Gina was half way to Sherman Street before she realized they would probably figure out where she'd gone. Even though she hadn't divulged the address to them, they would call Belinda back and get it for themselves. But she couldn't worry about that right now. There was only room in her mind for one all-consuming obsession. She had to find Ben. The driving force of it shut out even her anxiety for Todd. Like a mother bear protecting her cub, nothing else mattered. Nothing at all.
 Belinda had been right. Sherman street was as close as Albion got to a slum. Gina drove

Bitter Reunion

down it slowly, trying to find house numbers on hovels that didn't seem to bear any. Finally, she spotted one and realized that she was getting close to her destination. It was time to park the car and approach on foot. No sense in alerting the occupants of her arrival.

The problem was that there didn't seem to be any place to park the van where it wouldn't stand out like a sore thumb, and in doing so, invite half the neighborhood to strip it clean. Gina turned around and headed back in the direction she had just come. Touring a five block radius of Sherman Street, she searched for a better place to leave the van, and settled on Columbus Street, just two blocks east of Sherman. At least on Colombus, every other car wasn't rusted out or sitting up on blocks. Children played in yards that were mowed, in front of homes that, though modest in size and architectural style, bore the proof that someone took pride in them.

After locking the Windstar, Gina sprinted back to Sherman, wondering as she went exactly what she was going to do once she got to the residence Thomas had circled in the paper. She didn't have a plan. All she had done was to answer the insistent call from within that urged her to join her son. But what if he wasn't even there? What if Thomas hadn't followed up on his interest in the ad, or what if the place had already been rented out by the time he had?

Doubts and fears assailed Gina's mind, and she was developing a cramp in her side from running. The day had grown hot and sticky. She felt her clothes clinging damply to her body. Sweat ran down the side of her face. Her head began to pound.

I'm coming, Beej. Please be there. Please be alright. Mommy's coming. It was a chant of despair, longing and hope. It was a prayer.

She didn't break stride until she reached the end of the road and had no choice but to stop. Panting from exertion and the heat, she looked around in confusion. There was no 1359. It was a dead end. Her heart plummeted. She felt like screaming or crying. Or just letting herself crumple to the ground, never to get up. Then, as she was about to retrace her steps, thinking it was possible she had missed the number somehow, she saw it. There was actually a break in the undergrowth and foliage that she hadn't noticed at first. It was a driveway of sorts, and it must lead to the house she was looking for!

With renewed energy, Gina ventured ahead. Careful now to avoid being seen, she crept along, staying well to the side of the dirt lane within the dense thicket of trees, bushes and vines. Her cover was a mixed blessing, because while it hid her from whoever might be watching from the small white house that had come into view, it also made her progress slow and painstaking. Dead roots and treacherous blackberry brambles reached out from nowhere to trip her sandaled feet or grab her around bare legs. The last thing she needed was to fall and sprain an ankle. She was so close now.

Halfway to the house, Gina paused to peer through the branches of an overgrown Rhododendron, its broad leaves scorched by the sun. What she saw made her pulse quicken. The car that was parked beside the house wasn't red, but it had an Idaho license plate attached to its rear bumper. It must belong to Thomas. She knew it! He was here!

But Joey wasn't, and neither was Todd. The white car was the only one around. So did that mean that Ben was here or somewhere else? There was only one way to find out. Gina let the branch fall back into place and continued on. Finally, parallel to the carport side of the house, she broke cover and dashed from the bushes to the house. There were no windows on this side, but nevertheless, she felt exposed and vulnerable. There was a door on the other side of the car. It could open, and Thomas could come walking out at any moment. Quickly, Gina made her way to the back of the house, where it was less likely she'd be discovered. She hoped.

There were no doors back here, only three windows. She stood just to the side of the first one she came to, and stopped to catch her breath. Then, slowly, touching the white cedar siding with one hand and poised to run if necessary, she peeked through the window and into the room on the other side. It was a kitchen, and it was empty. She wasted no time inspecting it, but moved to the next window. It was covered by closed white mini-blinds, but she could see enough through a space at the edge of the blinds to be able to tell that it was a bathroom. Likewise empty.

That left one window. It was dirty, and there was a chartreuse curtain hanging behind it that blocked most of the view from outside. As with the bathroom window, though, there were places where the fabric didn't quite cover all it was meant to. Maneuvering to a position from which she could see through one of those places was another matter. It was awkward, because there was a large and prickly bush directly below most of the window. Gina had no choice but to wade into it. Ignoring the stab of hundreds of tiny needles to her already thorn-ravaged legs and feet, she stood in the midst of the bush and pressed her nose to the window.

The gloom inside made it hard to make out much more than the fact that it was a small bedroom she was looking at. She squinted and strained her eyes in order to see better, and details began to emerge from the dark recesses of the room. She could see a dresser with a round mirror above it on the wall across from her, and what she saw sitting atop it caused the breath to catch in her throat. It was a pair of shoes. They were small, red canvas tennis shoes with rubber toes and white laces. She knew those shoes. She'd bought them for her son.

Her focus jumped quickly now to the bed that occupied the wall to her left. He was there, curled up on top of the covers. Her baby. Gina's lips formed a silent word. Ben.

Please, Lord, let him be alright. He lay so very still, and his small body looked so fragile. As if to allay her fears, at that moment he stirred in his sleep and rolled onto his back. At least he was alive.

Gina rested her forehead on the glass of the window and thanked the Lord that she had found her son. Now if only she could get in to him and then get him away from this place! Bracing her feet as best she could, she tugged and pushed at the window frame with all her strength, but it wouldn't budge. She thought briefly about breaking the glass with a rock, but she knew it was a foolish idea. The sound of breaking glass would alert Thomas for sure.

Ben lay not more than five feet away from where Gina stood, but he might as well have been in the next county for all the good it did her. She felt hot tears of frustration behind her eyelids. There had to be a way of getting inside that room!

Gina stepped back from the window, disengaging herself from the bush. Her legs were on fire, covered with bleeding scratches. She looked at them as if they belonged to someone else and then dismissed them from her mind.

If she could just get INSIDE the house anywhere, maybe she could get to the bedroom where Ben lay without being detected. She would have to try. Gina bent over and removed her rafting sandals. They only got in her way. Then she walked barefoot back to the bathroom window.

It was open. Two or three inches separated the bottom half of the window from the sill. This window, however, unlike the bedroom window, had a screen between it and the insect-populated outdoors. It seemed to be latched from the inside, but there was a small tear in the mesh. Gina hooked her right forefinger into the tear and gave a quick, hard jerk. With satisfaction she saw the screen rip several more inches, enough for her to reach her hand through to the latch. It was tight between the window and the screen, but there was just enough room for her fumbling, shaking fingers to work the latch out and free the screen at the bottom. After that, it was just a matter of lifting it up to release it from the mechanism that held it at the top, and the screen was off. She leaned it against the house, and turned her attention back to the window itself.

Gina could see that the bathroom was still empty, and the door from it to the rest of the house was closed. Praying that it would stay that way for awhile longer, she pushed upward on the bottom of the window fame. It didn't move. Straining, sweating and grunting, she pushed harder, giving it every ounce of strength she possessed. With a grating noise that made her flinch, the window protested before suddenly giving up its battle and jumping open. Gina raised it as high as she could get it to go. There would be more than enough room for her slight body to pass through it.

She was in a hurry, now. Time was running out. Something was going to happen soon. She could feel it in every nerve and fiber of her body, and with each passing second the feeling intensified. She was going to be discovered, or Thomas was going to hurt Ben, or… She wouldn't let her mind finish the thought.

She grabbed on to the window sill with both hands and tried to boost herself up, but to no avail. She was too short—the window hit her at chin level.

Gina looked frantically around the yard for something..anything to stand on. Her eyes lit on a large rock beside a tree. It would do. When she rushed to get it, though, she found that it was much heavier than it looked. Rather than carry it, she was forced to push and roll it along the ground, and it seemed to take forever to get it positioned underneath the window.

At last, Gina stepped up onto the rock. She grabbed the frame again and, hopping and lunging all at the same time, managed to propel herself up onto the sill. Then she was falling through the blinds to the other side.

Oh, no, he's going to hear me! It was all she had time to think before she heard the THUD and felt the hard linoleum floor beneath her. Unhurt, she scrambled to her feet and stood behind the bathroom door, listening intently for the sound of approaching footsteps. Besides the wild beating of her own heart, the only sound was that of a television in the background—loud gunshots, yelling and suspenseful music. Thomas must be hard of hearing. Gina breathed out a shaky sigh of relief. Now, if only mother nature didn't call him before she could get out of here!

Slowly, she opened the door and peeked out into the hallway. To her right, she could see part of the living room, but not enough of it to know for sure whether or not Thomas was there. To the left were two closed doors. Her son was behind the one off her side of the hall. She stepped through the bathroom doorway and crept noiselessly toward that other door, feeling like a mountain climber on the verge of reaching the top of Everest. She was almost there, but she could hear the faint far-off rumble of an approaching avalanche. The hair on the back of her neck stood at attention. She glanced quickly behind her, expecting to see the evil specter that had tried to destroy her life. His presence pervaded the house, filling it with the oppressive heaviness of doom. Unseen eyes seemed to bore into her. Hurry, her mind screamed. Hurry!

The door was locked from the outside, but with just a slide lock that didn't require a key. Gina opened it and was inside. Then she closed it softly and rushed to the bed.

Oh, yes. Mommy's here.

Gina scooped her son up into her arms, and held his warm body close. Nothing had ever felt better, and she knew that this side of heaven, nothing ever would. Tears coursed down her cheeks, and her heart felt as if it would burst with joy.

"Thank you, Lord," she whispered, as she rocked Ben in her arms just as she had when he was a baby and covered his face with her kisses.

Ben muttered something, but didn't wake up. They must have drugged him.

Her little boy looked like the poster child for some third-world, war-ravaged country. His hair was matted to his head, his eyes were sunken, and his skin bore a sickly pallor. His small body was burning up. The room was stifling.

They weren't out of the woods yet, but at least Gina was whole again. She would rather be here with Ben and risk death than to be without him. Whatever happened now, they would face it together. Ben was no longer alone. She didn't intend for them to die, though. She intended to get them out of this house and to the car without being discovered. Tenderly, she laid him back down on the bed and walked to the window, expecting to be able to open it from the inside so they could escape. Her eyes widened in shock and her stomach flip-flopped. The heads of four large nails protruded slightly from the frame. The window was nailed shut.

CHAPTER 29

David looked at his watch and winced. He was already late. Hank would be getting nervous, and if Hank got too nervous, he'd be dangerous. He might even hurt Ben.

The hardest thing David had ever done was to leave his father to go back to Hank. Even knowing that it was only a temporary separation didn't help much. Todd had wanted to come with him, but David had talked him out of it. The sight of Todd would have infuriated Hank. For that and a lot of other reasons, this was something David had to do alone.

As his car sped along the highway, David's mind raced alongside it. He was still trying to digest the events and revelations of the day. It had all turned out so different than he had imagined and yet the result was what he had longed for. He had been set free.

The hatred he had felt for his father had been the real source of his bondage. He now thought of it as a cancer that would have eaten away at his soul until the day he died, and killing his father would never have changed that. It still scared him to think of how close he had come to destroying the only person who had ever really loved him. What his bitterness had already driven him to do was bad enough. He had caused his father so much needless pain, and he didn't know if he could ever forgive himself. The amazing thing was that Todd had. It was beyond David's comprehension.

A miraculous change had occurred in David over the course of the last two hours. It was as though he had been blind, and then had suddenly received the gift of sight. Every detail of his life, every emotion and thought had been transformed by a radiant light that went beyond the power of mere words to describe. He was a new person, or maybe just the old one, reborn.

He and Todd had been overwhelmed by all they'd wanted to say to each other. There was so much to catch up on. Eleven years. They could have talked for hours, but because of the circumstances, they'd only had time to share the most crucial details. Todd had learned of Hank's existence, and David had learned that someone had tried to kill Kellie twice.

It had to have been Hank. At least David was able to assure Todd that he hadn't been responsible for that. As he drove, he thought of her— so beautiful in her simple trusting kindness. He could never have hurt her.

David didn't realize until he saw the traffic light that he'd reached the outskirts of town. He had to slow down. It wouldn't do to get stopped by a policeman now.

Hank had tried to kill Kellie. For some reason, the realization didn't shock David as much as it should have, but it did worry him. It was more evidence that Hank was dangerous. He wasn't going to be happy to find out that the kidnapping was being called off, and David had no idea what his reaction would be. All he wanted was to be able to convince Hank to forget the whole thing and leave town. Just take Belinda's money and go.

David felt a wave of guilt pass over him. Hank had done so much for him. He had given him a home and watched out for him all these years. How was he going to be able to tell Hank that he didn't want to be a part of his life anymore? He had to find a way, and he had

Bitter Reunion

to do it now. The Camero had found its way to Sherman street without David being conscious of it.

The white Tempo was still parked in front of the house. Part of him had hoped Hank would be gone, and Ben would still be sleeping peacefully in the small bedroom. It would have been so easy.

For a brief moment, David sat behind the wheel and pulled together his resolve. Whatever else happened, he was determined to get Ben back to Todd safely. He'd be willing to stay with Hank, if necessary, or even to die. The one thing he couldn't do would be to return to Todd without Ben. He got out of the car and began to walk, his heart pounding.

Hank had already seen the Camero pull up and was at the door before David was.

"You're late! I was getting worried. Where's the money? Is it all there? Are we safe? Nobody followed you, did they?" He fired off the questions like a machine gun, and then he paused, seeming to notice that David wasn't responding as he should be. He was just standing there, a solemn expression on his face.

"We need to talk, Hank," David said. It was time for the showdown.

"What do you mean, we need to talk?" Hank asked incredulously. "What we need to do is get out of here! You do have the money, don't you?"

"No," David said quietly. "I don't."

Hank stared wordlessly, willing David to keep on talking. The silence was unnerving. Hank was making him feel like a bug under a magnifying glass.

"It didn't go the way we planned, Hank. Somehow, Hamilton knew I was behind the kidnapping, and he didn't bring the ransom money."

"So you killed him, right?" Hank demanded, his face turning a strange shade of purple.

There wasn't any way to break the truth except straight out. "He…uh…he explained some things to me that I never knew before, Hank. He didn't abandon me, after all. Elaine tricked him—and me. My father still wants me. He always has."

"I can't believe you were stupid enough to buy his story! Didn't you know he would try to get off the hook by feeding you a line?" Hank was livid. "You're telling me that Hamilton is still alive, and you have come back here without a dime from him?"

"He had proof, Hank. I know that what he told me was the truth."

"So what? What if it was the truth? It doesn't change anything. We came here to get that money from Hamilton, and I'm not leaving until we have it!" Hank yelled, obscenities punctuating the sentences.

"The whole reason we decided to kidnap Ben was for revenge, wasn't it?" David asked, trying to reason with Hank but knowing it would do no good. "I don't want to take his money now. He never did anything to me, after all. Don't you see? We were wrong, Hank."

"Well, I still want that money!" Hank raged, furiously. "He owes it to me. I raised you! You are still my son, not his! Do you understand me, David? I WILL HAVE THAT MONEY, AND I WILL HAVE YOU!!"

David backed away, suddenly afraid. He had seen Hank angry many times before. He had seen Hank in a rage, and he had seen Hank violent. But he had never seen Hank like this. It came to David then that it was blood-lust he was

Bitter Reunion

witnessing. Hank wanted to kill. David retreated further until he could feel the hard surface of the wall behind his back.

Hank had a gun in his hand now, and he was advancing on David. When he stood within three feet of David's face, he continued. "We have a new plan now, Son. This one is going to work. Do you understand?" His voice was calm, almost soothing. David nodded.

"You will go to Hamilton and convince him to bring the ransom here to the house. By six o'clock. If he doesn't show, I will take Ben and go. Ben will be my son, just the way you are, and Hamilton will never see him again."

"And what about me?" David asked.

"I already told you. You're mine. You always have been. You will come here with Hamilton, and after the ransom exchange is made, you will leave with me."

"But I don't want to go. I want to stay here with my family. I want to get to know my father again and my brother."

David felt the blow before he saw it coming. His right cheek stung.

"I'll see you dead before I see you with him! How many times do I have to say it? You are mine! Now go," Hank said, and stepped aside so David could pass.

There was one more thing David wanted to know before he left.

"Why did you try to kill Kellie Reynolds?" he asked.

Hank said nothing, but the answer lay somewhere in the depths of his cold, staring eyes. David turned and walked away.

From behind a closed door down the hall, Gina had heard nearly every word of Hank and David's exchange. Just as she had been about to attempt a trip back to the bathroom window, this time with Ben in her arms, David had shown up, and she had been afraid to proceed any further. She could tell by their raised voices that the men were moving around in the living room, and the bathroom door was visible from part of it. She wasn't going to chance being discovered now.

Their conversation had added to her paralysis. She didn't know what to make of it all, but certain facts had become saliently clear. Her heart had soared when she had learned that Todd was unharmed and had been reunited with his son. Joy had been short-lived, though, turning abruptly into a numbing fear. This Hank, or Thomas, or whatever his real name was, was most definitely an extremely dangerous man. The tone of his voice had sent chills down her spine. There was something in it that went far beyond greed, and she had understood for the first time the true nature of the peril they were in. She and Ben were trapped in the same house with a madman.

Gina left the door and returned to the bed for her son. He was so thin and frail, so why was he so heavy? She staggered under his weight. For days, she had eaten next to nothing, and the heat and exertion were also taking their toll. The room was a sauna! What she desperately needed was to rest and have something cold to drink, but there was no time for the luxury of even another moment of inactivity. She would have to draw on sheer determination spiced by fear to fuel her tired, weakened body.

"Come on, baby," Gina whispered. "Hang in there. Mommy's going to take you home now."

She repositioned Ben's slack body one more time, relieving pressure on her left hip. That fall in the bathroom must have done more damage than she'd thought at the time. An elbow was scraped, and for some reason, she couldn't seem to walk without limping.

She was looking at the door, wondering how she was going to open it without dropping Ben, when the problem suddenly and frighteningly rectified itself. In stunned horror, she watched as the doorknob began to turn on its own. She couldn't move or breathe—it was the quicksand nightmare again. Thick brown sludge seemed to hold her fast in its ever tightening grip, as the door swung toward her in sickening slow motion.

She'd expected a towering hulk of a man to appear before her, but he was not large. A fleeting expression of surprise crossed the craggy features of his face and then was quickly replaced by a smile. He looked almost happy to see her.

"Well, well, what have we here?" he said.

The quicksand threatened to suck her under.

. . . .

"She just took off, Todd. Believe me, I never would have let her go without me, if I'd had any idea that's what she planned to do. I guess that's why she didn't tell us." Walt shook his head miserably, unable to meet Todd's eyes. "She was worried when you didn't come right back, afraid something had gone wrong. I think Belinda told her where to look for Ben, and that's where Gina is now."

"Then we have to go after her," Todd said, drowning in his own sea of misery. "I have a bad feeling about Hank. I'm not so sure Joey can handle the man. After all, he did already try to kill Kellie, and if he's capable of that, the man's capable of anything. I never should have let Joey face him alone, either."

He'd gotten his son back only to watch him drive away again almost immediately. At least Joey hadn't been in any danger before this afternoon, but who knew how Hank would respond now that he wasn't getting what he wanted? He would want to get even, wouldn't he? And what better way than to carry out his threats concerning Ben and then go one step further?

Why had he let Joey convince him that Hank would listen to reason? Did a killer care about what was right? And was the relationship Joey had built with Hank strong enough to be used as leverage to free Ben? Todd wanted to think so, but he didn't.

Walt, Lila and Kellie were watching him, trying to gauge his expression. They were afraid, he could tell. Like him, they'd been ecstatic about what had happened with Joey, but uncertainty over Ben's fate remained a dark shadow that robbed them of celebration. And now Gina was probably in danger, too. Would this ordeal never be over?

"We have to call Belinda back and get her to tell us where Gina went!"

Why didn't they move? Why weren't they already on the phone with this woman they'd told him about? The one that Joey had mentioned, too, as having been Hank's latest prey besides them.

Todd marched across the room, heading for the telephone himself.

"We already tried, Todd," Kellie said. She bit her lip to keep it from trembling. "She doesn't answer the phone."

"I thought you told me that she was dead drunk!"

"She was," Lila jumped in, the tone of her voice reflecting her consternation over being unable to contact Belinda. "She wasn't even dressed. She still had on her bathrobe. I can't imagine her having gone anywhere in her condition, but she sure isn't answering her phone."

Walt and Todd exchanged a glance. They were thinking the same thing.

"You two stay here," Walt said, heading for the door.

Todd was right behind him. "We're going over to Belinda's."

Walt drove with little regard for the speed limit, and in no time he was pulling into Belinda's driveway. The house looked exactly as it had earlier in the day, but minutes later, he and Todd had concluded that this time Belinda would not be answering her door. She would have to be deaf not to hear the repeated knocks and rings of the doorbell. That meant she was gone, passed out, or purposefully avoiding them, and whatever the case, Todd wasn't ready to leave yet.

He tried the door. It was locked.

"Let's go around to the back," he said, and Walt nodded in agreement.

They raced around the sprawling exterior of a house that resembled an English manor, dodging hedges and scaling a fence, then making their way through an obstacle course of lavish gardens, swimming pool and patio furniture.

At last the winded pair made it to a secluded veranda and the double french doors that gave access to the back of the house. They, too, were locked.

Todd backed off a few steps and muttered under his breath, "Here goes nothing."

He lunged, brought his leg up, and kicked, catching the doors where they met with the bottom of his right shoe. They held fast. He kicked again and again. Finally he heard the satisfying sound of wood splintering and glass shattering, as they buckled and swung inward.

"Come on!"

Walt didn't move. He looked suddenly uncertain. "I don't know about this, Todd. Do you realize that we're breaking into someone's house? That's a serious crime."

"Right now, getting caught for breaking and entering is the least of my concerns." Todd didn't wait for Walt to respond. He was already inside the house.

Walt followed, and the two moved from one pink room to another, feeling as if they'd dropped into a gigantic bottle of Pepto Bismol. The place seemed to be abandoned.

They were beginning to believe that Belinda had indeed left the house, when they found her. She was in the room at the farthest reaches of the house, a monstrously proportioned bedroom. The brass bed on which she lay was huge, dwarfing her body and emphasizing her vulnerability. One arm rested across her face, as if she were trying to hide from the world.

As soon as they saw her, they rushed to her side. Todd took her wrist and frantically felt for a pulse, while Walt inspected the frightening evidence of the woman's loneliness and despair. An empty vodka bottle lay on its side and there was a prescription bottle on the bed near the tips of her limp fingers. He

Bitter Reunion

picked it up and shook the three remaining pills out onto his palm. They were small and white, and he had no idea what kind they were, but the label on the bottle instructed that they be taken at bedtime.

"She's still alive," Todd said, answering Walt's unasked question. "But her pulse seems weak to me, and she's not waking up."

Walt held up the pill bottle, and Todd caught its implications immediately. Wondering if they had discovered her in time, he snatched up the receiver of a pink cordless telephone and dialed 911.

As Todd relayed crucial information to a dispatcher, Walt began a frantic search of the premises, hunting for the newspaper ad. Gina had told him about it, while leaving out the address of the rental house that it described. Never expecting her to go there, he hadn't thought to ask for it. If only he had, they wouldn't be wasting time having to search this monstrous pink palace.

But then you wouldn't have discovered Belinda, he thought, and he wondered if he'd had to make the choice, whether he would have sacrificed the life of this stranger for the chance to rush to the aid of those he loved.

Dumping out a waste basket in the bathroom and scattering its contents on the floor, Walt searched frantically, only to find the usual assortment of discarded debris. Quickly, he moved on. That ad had to be here somewhere! He rifled through a small stack of newspapers he came across, but they were all too current to be the one that had carried it.

Some time later, Todd found him still searching, leaving a trail of garbage in his wake.

"What are you doing, Walt?"

Deborah Barlow

"I'm looking for the ad I told you about. It has to be here in the house somewhere, but I can't seem to find it! Somehow we've got to get that address!"

"Listen, you keep on looking. We can't leave Belinda anyway. I'm going to stay beside her until the ambulance arrives. Maybe you'll find it by then."

Todd returned to the bedroom and Walt went on searching. It was a big house, and there must be countless places where a piece of paper could hide. He couldn't think about that, though, or he would be tempted to give up, and that was something he couldn't do. The lives of too many people depended on him.

CHAPTER 30

David drove aimlessly. His head pounded, and the side of his face where Hank had hit him throbbed dully. Only when he'd put enough distance between himself and the house on Sherman Street to feel his breathing return to normal was he able to see his surroundings clearly. It surprised him to find that he had driven to the park where the concert had been last week—where he had sat on the ground and talked with Kellie and Ben.

Oh, how he wished he could turn the clock back to that evening and experience again the magic of the music and the sunset, and most of all, of being with Kellie. He had never known living could feel like that, but even that moment hadn't been able to compare with the one in which he'd known that his father still loved him. A new horizon had opened up, ripe with the promise of endless tomorrows full of exciting possibilities. Then, just as suddenly as it had been given, it had all been snatched away again.

He had ruined it with his sick desire for revenge. He could have had it all—a family, a home and maybe even a girlfriend, but if Hank had his way, David would never see his father or Kellie again.

The park drew him. Making a sudden decision to stop, he pulled the Camero into a parking space, turned off the ignition, and got out. Following one of the winding bike paths that laced through the park, he was lead to a bench by the bank of the river. There, he sat and watched the Calapooia roll by, flowing without reservation or choice toward its destiny—to be at one with the ocean. If only it were that simple for him. If only he knew what to do, what choice to make. He closed his eyes, waiting for an answer to present itself. None did.

There was no way out that he could see. If he went to Todd, he knew that Todd would gladly pay the ransom for Ben, as Hank had demanded. The trouble was that David was certain that Hank would never rest now until Todd was dead, and nothing would prevent him from shooting Todd once he had the money. If David took the money to Hank without Todd, Hank would feel cheated and probably kill Ben.

He might even kill David, too. Whatever bond had existed between them had not been forged from love and had probably been weakened beyond repair by David's admission that he wanted to stay with his father instead of Hank.

The only other option was to not show up at all, in which case he would be sealing Ben's fate for sure.

What about ambushing Hank? As quickly as the idea presented itself, David discarded it. He'd never be able to pull it off. He was no match for Hank, and even if he had been, he'd never be able to hold a gun on anyone again.

There was nothing he could do, and yet he had to do something.

"Run away," a voice inside of him seemed to be saying. The river was right there, its waters hypnotically soothing, whispering his name. It invited him to join it, to let its cold, numbing depths wash away all guilt and confusion. It promised sweet peace. "Just wade out and let the current take you."

No. He couldn't.

He couldn't give up—not as long as there was a breath in him. Not as long as there was the

Bitter Reunion

slightest glimmer of hope. It came to him then that Todd had been in much the same type of situation that he now faced. No one, least of all David, would have guessed that Todd could have made it out of that meeting at the barn alive. And yet, he had. Todd had claimed it was because of God. He'd said people were praying, and that he had prayed himself because he knew that no one but God could help.

Was Todd right? Was it God who had turned the day around and kept David from making the biggest mistake of his life? David searched within himself for the answer to a question he was suddenly afraid to ask. Did he believe in God? Yesterday, he would have said no, but now everything was different.

Hesitantly, he walked to the water's edge and got down on his knees. There was nothing to lose and no other way out. He would do as Todd had done and pray. It had been so long since he had talked to God, though, that he didn't know how to begin. His mind was a blank, and he felt like an unworthy beggar. After all the years of ignoring Him and claiming He didn't exist, what right did he have to ask anything of God?

"I deserve whatever I get, God," David finally said. "But Ben and my Dad don't deserve to get hurt because of me." The words seemed to hit the surface of the water and boomerang right back to him.

I can't pray, he thought. I can't even pray. He felt like giving up, but this was his last resort, and he wouldn't quit until he'd given it everything he had. Maybe there was another way to begin.

"I'm sorry," he whispered. "I've shut You out for a long time, and even now I'm not sure you're really there. I want to believe. I just don't know if I can. Help me."

He didn't know what else to say, so he said nothing. Instead, he let the ensuing stillness wash over him, and in it he found a grain of faith still there in the far reaches of his soul, buried under an accumulation of years but not lost. It was enough. As he waited with bowed head, it began to blossom, and he found his focus moving unswervingly away from himself and onto the Lord. Feelings of helplessness and guilt were swept away in a flash of understanding. Almighty God, holy Creator of the universe, cared about him. Jesus loves me…this I know. It had been true all along. God hadn't abandoned him any more than Todd had.

With new assurance he dared to tell God how afraid he was of losing his father again. Then he asked God to help him find a way to save Ben. God's presence was so real, and there was so much more he needed to say, but it would have to wait.

When he raised his head, David opened his eyes and discovered a new world, one in which God was in control. He got to his feet and looked around, noticing for the first time how blue the sky was, how green the grass. Birds sang, children laughed. A bee buzzed, landed on his hand, and then took to the air again, in search of nectar to turn into honey.

And then, just like that, David knew what he was going to do. He began to walk toward his car, and then he was jogging, and then running.

Five minutes later, he was standing in a telephone booth outside a Texaco station, digging quarters out of his pocket and counting them. Just enough for four calls. He

Bitter Reunion

pulled the phone book up from where it hung on a chain below the telephone and flipped through its yellow pages. It seemed as though half the pages were ripped out, but the section he wanted was still intact. A good omen. He put a quarter in the slot and began to dial, looking at his watch as he did. He hoped he had enough time to do what he was planning. Six o'clock wasn't far enough away.

His first quarter gleaned four names to call, and the fourth and final quarter hit the jackpot. Oliver Melheim was home and willing to make an extra buck. If he was curious as to why David wanted to do what he was asking about, he didn't say so.

"Well, it's mighty short notice," he said, "but ah think ah kin oblige ya. Come on over, and ah'll try to have it ready for ya when ya git here."

It took a second longer to settle on a price for Melheim's services, and then David was back in the car racing toward his destiny.

The first stop along the way was at a variety store, where he could make some necessary purchases before proceeding with his plan.

Saturday shoppers filled the aisles, leisurely inspecting merchandise they had no intention of buying, while effectively managing to block David's progress through the store. Couldn't they see that he was in a hurry? It took far too long to dodge and weave and hunt his way to the departments he needed, and he was all too aware of the steadily progressing minute hand on his watch. What would Hank do if he was late? David didn't want to find out.

At last he managed to round up the things he'd come for, and now it was time to stand in line and wait to purchase them. He only had three items, while everyone in front of him had an entire cart full of stuff. Besides that, there were only two check stands open, and one of the checkers seemed to be stymied over a disputed price and an inability to contact a salesperson to help settle the problem. Naturally, the line that was stalled was his. Murphy's Law.

David changed lines. As if on cue, the other line began to move again, and his new line came to a screeching halt. Impatiently, he shifted his weight from one foot to the other. His palms began to sweat. I haven't got all day! He felt like screaming it out. He wanted to simply dart past all the mindlessly staring zombies with their baskets full of nonessential gadgets, but he didn't. Like everyone else, he waited his turn, and eventually it came.

"That's a nice briefcase," gushed the tall, big-boned brunette behind the counter, as he stepped up. "I really ought to get one like this for my husband's birthday." She turned it over and admired it, as if she were the one interested in buying it instead of him. "It's a little bit bigger than most of them, isn't it?"

David already had the money out of his wallet, but she hadn't even begun to ring up his purchase yet. She looked at him and smiled. Obviously, her idea of good customer service was having a friendly little chit-chat with each person she waited on.

"I'm in a hurry," David said, unable to keep a strong dose of irritation from creeping into his voice. He shoved the green bills toward her, hoping that the sight of them would remind her of the real reason she was standing beside a cash register.

The smile on her face wilted like day-old lettuce left out in the sun. David was sorry he'd been rude. It was just that it was driving him crazy the way everything seemed to be going in slow motion! He still had to get out to Melheim's before he could go back to Hank.

Silently now, but with only a marginal increase in speed, the woman made change and pulled a large plastic bag out from beneath the counter.

"Never mind," David said, grabbing his purchases. "I don't need a sack."

"But don't you want your receipt?" She held it out to him, but he was running for the door and didn't respond.

"The good-looking ones are always jerks," she mumbled under her breath and turned her attention to the next customer in line. By the time she was ringing him up, David had already reached his car.

As impatient as he was to get back on the road, there was one more thing he had to attend to first, and it had to do with the briefcase. It was indeed a nice one, but even so, it wasn't quite what he needed for what he had in mind. Fortunately, he could and would remedy that in a matter of seconds. He lay the case down on the concrete surface of the parking lot beside his car, and then proceeded to make the necessary alterations, using his other two new possessions—a hammer and a small nail.

....

"Please, just don't hurt us. My husband will give you the money, so there's no reason to hurt us."

He bound her hands behind her back, looping the rope through the rails of the cast iron bed frame and then cinched the jute tighter until she cried out in pain.

"You don't get it, do you? Killing the two of you is going to be half the fun."

"Why," Gina asked quietly. "What have we ever done to you?"

Hank gave one last tug on the rope and stepped away from the side of the bed. He stared into her eyes until she looked away, and then he continued to stare. She was attractive. Not a lot of pizzazz, but nice, even with her hair hanging in limp strings. It was almost a shame to have to waste such a prize specimen of femininity.

"I have nothing against you personally," Hank said. "You just happen to have made the mistake of marrying the wrong man."

"But Todd's never hurt you, either. He's never even met you." Gina turned her face toward him again, though her eyes refused to meet his.

"He may not know me, but I know him. He's got it all—fame, fortune and power. Plus the storybook family and the little house with the white picket fence. He's MISTER PERFECT! And he doesn't deserve any of it, because he's nothing but a fraud!"

Hank was breathing hard, practically spitting out the words. He could tell she was frightened by the depths of his passion and it pleased him.

Bitter Reunion

"What do you hope to accomplish by killing us?" she dared to ask.

"It shows who's in control," he hissed. "I'M in control. I took his son and made him mine, and now I'm taking the rest. Don't you see? What's his should have been MINE! And now, in a way, it will be."

Hank ran his finger down the side of her face, and she flinched. He had to hand it to her, though. She wasn't the pathetic, groveling creature that most women were. She didn't cry or plead the way his wives had. There was something different about her. A kind of confidence that was all the more pronounced considering her vulnerability. It confused him.

"Aren't you afraid?" he crooned, taunting her and testing the limits of that confidence.

For the first time, her eyes met his and held. "Yes, I'm afraid, but not as afraid as you should be. We're all going to die, you know. It's just a matter of time. If my time in now, at least I know where I'm going, and it will be the most wonderful place. I will meet my Lord face to face, which will be a joy I can't even comprehend. But you don't know Him, and if you continue on like this, you never will. If you did, you wouldn't feel the need to steal someone else's life. Your own would be enough."

This time Hank turned away. He laughed, dismissing her words as religious mumbo jumbo. It was harder though, to dismiss the conviction in her voice and the soft sympathy he saw in her face. What was the matter with the broad, anyway? He was going to kill her, and she was acting like he was the victim here. It was disconcerting not to see the terror from her that he'd come to expect as his due.

"I hate to disappoint you, darling, but I have to leave this little party early. I've got to watch the window, so I can greet my other guests when they arrive. I'll check in on you later, so don't try to be cute. Any requests before I go?"

He thought she wasn't going to say anything, but then, just before he closed the door on her, she did. "Please, would you bring me a drink? I'm so thirsty."

He left, returning shortly with a tall clear glass of water, filled with ice cubes. Taking a long, exaggerated swallow, he walked to the dresser several feet from the foot of the bed. Slowly and with great deliberation, he set the glass on top of it. Her eyes followed its progress, and he could see the lust in them. This was more like it.

"I'll just leave your water over here," he said. "You can get it for yourself."

The door slammed behind him and Gina heard the click of the latch sliding home.

It was hot…so hot. Maybe this was what hell was like. But no, hell was a place without God. Gina closed her eyes, shutting out the unreachable glass of water, the sweltering confines of the small room and the horrible specter of her own thoughts. In the quiet inner darkness, she could see the Lord and bask in His peace. She felt Ben's body beside her on the bed, and she knew that this is where she was meant to be. It would be O.K.

Five minutes later, Ben began to stir. The lashes that brushed his cheeks fluttered and then he opened his eyes. Startled and disoriented, he jerked and rolled onto his side. And then he saw her.

"Don't be afraid, Beej. I'm here," Gina whispered.

"Mommy?" His tiny voice was filled with reverence, fear and hope. Maybe he was still just dreaming and she would disappear if he woke up.

"Yes, honey, it's really me. Move over closer, baby. I can't reach you. My hands are tied to these bars."

In an instant, his arms were wrapped around her, and his face was nestled against her neck. Gina sniffed and choked back tears of joy. She didn't want to scare him. Despite her efforts, her cheeks were soon wet.

Ben was awake and at least for now, they could take comfort in just being together.

"I'm sleepy, Mommy, and I don't feel good. I want to go home now."

"So do I, honey, but I can't get up. You're going to have to help me. Do you think you can do that?"

"I don't know," Ben said, lifting his head to look at her inquiringly. "What do I hafta do? I don't want the bad man to get mad at me again."

"First of all, we have to be very quiet, so he won't hear us, O.K."

He nodded solemnly.

"O.K. Now, what I want you to do is to try to untie the big knot in the rope around my hands. If we hear anybody coming, or if the door starts to open, you just lay back down real quick and pretend to be asleep."

Ben looked at her as if she'd lost her mind. "I'm good at pretending," he whispered. "I can do that. But you always hafta take out the knots in my shoelaces. How am I gonna get a big hard knot like that one out?" He looked at the knot again and shook his head in consternation. His bottom lip trembled. He was so tired and hot, and his stomach hurt, and now Mom was asking him to do something really hard.

"Just try," Gina coaxed, trying not to let her desperation show. "But first...you see that glass of water over there?"

His face lit up and he scrambled off the bed.

CHAPTER 31

It was almost five-forty when David finally got away from Oliver Melheim. Like the woman at the variety store, Melheim had seemed to want nothing more than to stand around and shoot the breeze. David supposed it was nice that people were so laid-back and friendly in Albion, but right now he would have been happier with fast and curt. New York City would have fit the bill just fine.

With the back of a clammy hand, he wiped perspiration from his forehead and stepped a little harder on the gas pedal. Punctuality was an obsession with Hank, and today was not the day to test his patience. Unfortunately, it was as if the cosmic forces of the universe were conspiring to delay him at every turn. On the way to Melheim's, he'd hit each traffic signal just as the light was turning to red and had then somehow managed to get behind the slowest driver on earth, a gray-haired granny trying to imitate a snail. Hopefully the drive back to Hank's wouldn't be a repeat performance.

As he drove, David thought about his plan. He wasn't fooling himself. He knew it was a long shot, but at least it was better than no plan at all. He glanced at the briefcase on the seat beside him and wondered if the changes he'd made to it would work out. If they didn't, the trap would backfire on him. Hank would know what he'd tried to do, and David's jig would definitely be up. Hank would be furious, making everyone's chances for survival even smaller than they already were.

Melheim lived north of town by several miles, and the route David traveled was densely wooded. A marshy stream meandered off, only to return again to the side of the road, like a faithful dog running with his master. The sun still reigned supreme in a crystal clear sky.

David stared straight ahead, thinking only of one thing—getting back to town as quickly as possible. The Camero, on the other hand, had other ideas. Four miles from Melheim's, it suddenly lost all power, forcing him to coast to a stop. The gas gauge told the story, its needle resting on empty. With all that he'd had on his mind, David hadn't realized that he was almost out of gas.

No, no, no! This was unreal. It couldn't be happening! Now what am I going to do, David wondered desperately. He was still a couple of miles from Albion, with no transportation and a deadline that he was almost surely going to miss. He grabbed the briefcase, and jumped out of the car, locking the doors behind him. There was no sense sitting here lamenting his bad luck while the minutes continued to tick by. There had been a time when abandoning his car, the most prized possession he owned, out in the middle of nowhere would have been out of the question, but now he didn't give it a second thought. The car no longer held the place of importance it once had.

He started jogging, the briefcase bumping against his legs. There was no sign of a house on this stretch of the road, no cars passing by. It was as if he were the only living person on the face of the earth. He ran faster, but knew he couldn't keep up this pace for long. The merciless sun beat down on his back, and already his breathing was labored. If he didn't find another way to get to Hank's, he was going to be too late. Maybe he could hitch a ride. A car was bound to come along sooner or later, hopefully sooner.

In less than thirty seconds, the first one did. It was a light blue Toyota Celica, and it sped right by David without even slowing, as if its driver hadn't seen his outstretched thumb. After that, three other cars went by in rapid succession, but none of them pulled over either, and he began to lose hope that he had any chance of saving Ben. Yet even so, he kept running, knowing that if he stopped, it would make the defeat final and leave him with nothing but his growing panic and despair. He would run until his legs gave out.

Just as he thought his lungs were going to burst, David rounded a bend in the road and saw the house. It was a typical farmhouse, white with a big front porch, something out of Currier and Ives. He hoped it wasn't like a desert oasis and would fade out and disappear as he approached.

He slowed as he neared the house, wondering now what he was going to say to its occupants. He had a feeling they weren't going to be wild about giving him a ride and maybe not even about letting a total stranger in to use their phone. And who would he call anyway? A taxi cab maybe, but it would take too long to get here.

Halfway across the yard to the house, David stopped and stood still. Then, instead of walking straight ahead and to the front door, he veered off toward the driveway and the lone pickup that was parked there. Feeling conspicuous, he tried to open its doors, only to find that they were locked. Looking inside, he discovered that the key wasn't in the ignition, anyway. Not that he'd really expected it to be, but it had been worth checking out. He backed away, trying to decide what to do next, when out of the corner of his eye, he saw the bicycle leaning up against an ivy-covered corner of the porch. It was a red adult sized ten-speed. Maybe it wouldn't be as fast as a car, but it was transportation. Without another thought, except that he had no other choice, David took it.

Straddling the seat and balancing the briefcase across the handlebars, he pedaled out of the yard. There were no shouts of objection and outrage, no barking dogs chasing him as he sped away. I'll return it or buy them a new one, David promised himself, hoping that the bike wasn't going to be missed right away.

It felt weird to be riding a bicycle again. He hadn't been on one in years, but it seemed to be true that once you learned how to ride, you never forgot. The only thing he wasn't quite sure of, was how to change the gears on the thing. David had never owned a bicycle of his own, at least not since that red one his dad had bought him here in Albion. A bike was too big to move from city to city, so Hank had never let him have one.

David fiddled with levers until he managed to pretty well figure out the gear system, which apparently consisted of quite a few more than ten. Either this was a deluxe model, or touring bikes had come a long way in the last several years.

The briefcase was awkward and bulky, making it hard to keep the bike steady. The first few minutes were easy, because the riding was all downhill, but then the road began to gradually ascend until David found himself climbing a steep hill. His leg muscles strained to keep pumping, and his lungs were on fire again.

Bitter Reunion

Each beat of his heart was a hammer pounding against his temples. He panted and pumped, willing himself to keep going despite the pain that consumed him and begged him to stop. Sweat streamed down his body, soaking his t-shirt. In agony, he reached the top of the hill and stopped only long enough to catch his breath and strip the shirt off his back. He let it fall to the side of the road and continued on.

After what seemed like ages, David reached the outskirts of town. Refusing to look at his watch, he pedaled harder. Wait for me, Hank, he said under his breath. I'm coming! Don't do anything until I get there!

He was getting close now. With his luck, he'd probably get stopped by the police for being in violation of the helmet law that Ben had informed him of.

"Every kid's got to wear a helmet when they ride their bike, or they can get a ticket," Ben had said. "My mom would of made me anyway, even before the law thing. It's so my brains won't get scrambled if I fall on my head. And I did once, too!" David could still see the way he'd said it with his eyes big and round and so serious. Oh Lord, he didn't want anything to happen to that little boy. He'd liked him from the first moment he'd laid eyes on him. How could he live with himself if he was responsible for his own brother's death?

The sound of a train whistle penetrated his thoughts and alerted him to the fact that he was approaching the railroad tracks. And there was a train coming. A long train. The brown and yellow cars stretched endlessly behind a giant rumbling engine and then disappeared from view where buildings stood in the way. He had to beat it across those tracks, or he would be stuck here for an eternity!

He frantically called on whatever remaining strength and energy he had left, and surged forward, feeling the burning in his thighs, legs and chest. He prayed to make it, more for Ben's sake than for his own. The crossing arm was coming down, and cars were stopping behind it. David pulled around them. He could feel the vibration of the train and see red lights flashing. Ding, ding, ding…the crossing alarm warned, and then the whistle blasted again, this time so close that it seemed as if it surrounded him. Still, he pedaled. The arm continued to descend as he ducked and swept under it. And then he was hitting the tracks.

The impact of hitting them at the speed he was going jarred him to the bone, and threatened to jerk the handlebars out of his hands, but he held on tight, closed his eyes and let the momentum he had gathered carry him through to the other side.

He'd done it! And it had been close. The train roared by, its engineer probably cursing David's stupidity.

David looked up and ahead and saw too late that though he had inched by the train, he had lost control of the bike and it was now headed straight for the raised curb of a median strip. The front tire hit with a smack. The wheel bent and the bike skidded sideways as David's body flew off. Hitting the pavement hard, his body skidded to a stop and then lay still.

It was the pavement burning into his bare back that he felt first. Slowly, he sat up. Nothing seemed to be broken, but he had left some skin on the road. Painfully, he got to his feet and took inventory of his injuries.

They weren't too bad, mostly abrasions. He'd torn one knee out of his jeans, and blood soaked the fabric below it. Fortunately, he hadn't landed on his head, as Ben had. He would heal. Of more concern to him now was what the accident had done to the briefcase and the bicycle which were lying in the middle of the right lane of traffic, causing motorists to detour around them.

It seemed to be the proverbial case of good news and bad news. The briefcase seemed to be undamaged, but the bike was no longer ridable, its front wheel having been twisted badly by the impact against the curb. It was now nothing more than a useless piece of junk. Furious, David kicked it, and then he kicked it again. He was already late and now this! What was the use in fighting it anymore? He wasn't going to make it to Hank's. It was over.

He picked up the case and walked with it to the side of the road where he sat with his face in his hands.

"Young man! Are you alright?"

David looked up to see that a car had pulled over and stopped beside him, and a woman was speaking to him from behind its steering wheel. Her head barely topped the dashboard, she was so short. She was old, too. Thin and fragile-looking with twinkly pale blue eyes in a wizened face topped by snow-white hair, she must have been at least eighty.

"We have a bicycle helmet law in this state, you know," she said in a firm no-nonsense voice that belied her appearance. "You could have been killed! Next time, at least wear a shirt. If nothing more, you'll get a bad sunburn like that. But never mind now. Why don't you move your bike out of the road and then get in. I'll drive you home."

She waited patiently while he did as she'd suggested. Then, when he'd retrieved his briefcase and gotten into the car beside her, she looked at him quizzically. "Where do you want me to take you?" she asked.

"Just drop me off at the corner of Eleventh and Sherman," David responded, thinking that beneath the wrinkles, he saw the face of an angel.

....

Pete and Nita showed up at the house at six o'clock, worried. The look on Lila's face when she answered the door didn't help.

"What's going on? Why haven't we heard anything yet?" Pete said, barging in without being invited. Nita was right behind him.

"And where the heck is everybody, anyway?"

Lila and Kellie stood huddled together like two lone survivors of a ship wreck. Without warning, the afternoon had veered off its course and gone completely out of control, leaving them confused and at a loss as to what to do about it.

It was Kellie who explained the situation to them, detailing how Gina had taken off for parts unknown, and then how Todd had returned only to leave again with Walt for Belinda Montgomery's house. She told them about David and who he really was, and about Hank and all the events that had transpired earlier in the day. It was a relief to lay it all out before them, even if there wasn't anything Pete or Nita could really do to help.

"This isn't good…this isn't good at all!" Pete exclaimed in his usual straightforward manner. He removed his glasses, wiped them on a handkerchief and popped them back on his nose. The act seemed to have been the outward sign of an inward thinking process, because when he was done, he had arrived at a conclusion.

"We've got to call the police before something terrible happens to Gina and Ben, and maybe the rest of them, too, if they go messing around with this Hank character. Hey, listen, I know about people like him. They got no conscience, and would just as soon kill someone as look at them."

As if to illustrate the point, he made deliberate eye contact with Kellie. "He tried to kill you, right? Why?" He went on to answer his own question. "Who knows? He don't need a reason. Any excuse would do for a guy like that. It's how he gets his jollies."

Pete was right. Kellie remembered all too clearly the feel of the gun in her back and the sound of his voice as Hank had ordered her into her mother's car. The man had taken pleasure in her fear. He had enjoyed the power of life and death that he'd had over her. Even now, just thinking about it sent a cold chill down her spine.

"I agree with Pete, Mom," she said. "We can't just stand by and do nothing. Even if Todd gives Hank the money, I don't think it will be enough for him." The more she thought about it, the more sure she was that her sister had walked straight into a death-trap.

"Please, Mom," she pleaded.

"It's the right thing," Nita insisted, joining in the effort to persuade Lila.

Lila wrung her hands, wishing fervently that Walt and Todd would call and say that they had everything under control. She picked up the phone and dialed Belinda's number. No answer.

"Alright, call the police," she said. "And Pete?"

"Yeah?"

"Before you call them, would you please call Kathy and tell her to contact the prayer chain? Have her just tell them not to quit praying."

CHAPTER 32

David glanced at his watch, noticing with little surprise that its crystal had broken in the fall from the bicycle. It indicated that he was half an hour late, but that was only if it was still keeping accurate time.

The plain white house looked the same as it had the first time he'd seen it, but now the mere sight of it caused his heart to hammer within his chest. Who knew what might have gone on in there while he was gone? It was the second time in one day that he'd kept Hank waiting, and Hank wasn't a patient man.

David looked to heaven and squinted into the sun as if he were trying to make out the face of God in its radiant glow. His heart issued a prayer for one last chance to make everything right. He took a deep breath and let it out, trying to steady his frayed nerves, and then he opened the front door and walked into the lion's den.

As he'd suspected, Hank had been watching his approach from the window and was already aware that David was alone.

"You're late!" he accused, ignoring David's shirtless chest, the blood and the scrapes. "And you didn't bring Hamilton!" His eyes strayed only momentarily to the briefcase. "I told you Hamilton had to come with you!"

"He's on his way…should be here any minute. While we wait for him, why don't we go ahead and count the money? He said it was all here, but I think we ought to check it out, don't you?" David couldn't help it. He was stuttering.

"You're lying, David! I CAN ALWAYS TELL WHEN YOU'RE LYING!" Hank had his gun out again and was waving it in David's face. "Why are you protecting that man? You owe him nothing! I don't care what he told you, he doesn't have any right to claim you! I've had you longer than he did. Besides, you were never really his…you have always belonged to me and you always will!"

He couldn't hold back any longer. David heard the words almost before he was aware of having said them. "You don't have any idea what day this is, do you? It's my birthday. You've never asked me what day my birthday was…never in all these years.

"He knew, though. My father knew that today is my birthday. You know why? Because he loves me. You don't love me, Hank. I don't think you ever even liked me. So why do you want me? Why do you care whose son I am?"

The question took Hank by surprise. There were too many questions today. Gina and now David, asking him why. He wasn't one to analyze his motives. He only knew what he wanted and how to go about getting it. "A man's got to have a son," he said finally as if that explained it all.

"I feel sorry for you," David said, and he meant it. "You don't have any idea how it feels to love and be loved. It's better than all the money in the world! Love is what families are all about, not ownership. My father loves me, and I love him. Nothing can change that. You may be able to force me to stay with you. You may force me to call you Pa, but you can't force me to love you. And you can't make me be your son!"

The quiet that followed was profound, like the calm before a raging storm, and in it David could almost hear the beating of his own heart.

A bloodless death mask, Hank's face contrasted starkly with the venomous black of his eyes, and a throbbing vein at his temple gave warning of the violence to come. His mouth contorted into a grimace and exploded with the sound of rage.

"GO!" he yelled, pushing David roughly down the hall toward the bedroom in the back. David stumbled and recovered himself, his right hand still clutching the briefcase handle. Hank was behind him, prodding and pushing. There was nothing David could do.

He's going to kill us both. David was as certain of it as he had ever been about anything. He wished he could tell his dad how sorry he was for the trouble he'd caused. He'd never meant for any harm to come to Ben. He'd tried his best to protect him. If only he could open the briefcase, they might have a chance, but not with the gun jammed into his back.

The bedroom door was still locked from the outside. As they reached it, David heard a deafening blast at his right ear, and then the knob and door frame splintered, sending shards of wood flying. He felt a sharp pain in his upper right arm. Hank kicked the door, and it slammed back against the wall. Another hard shove from behind propelled David into the room, and then he was falling, his right shoulder crashing against the mahogany headboard as he went down. He heard a sickening crunch at the same time as he felt the searing white-hot pain shoot down his arm. The briefcase slid across the scarred surface of the pine floor and came to rest half under the bed.

"Get Up!" Hank thundered, but his voice seemed to be coming from a great distance.

I can't faint now. I can't. David willed himself not to lose consciousness, to emerge from the murky depths that threatened to engulf him.

"I said, get up!"

The voice was louder, the light brighter. It made David's head hurt. He put his hand to the back of his head and felt a bump and something wet and sticky. He thought he might throw up, but he didn't. He began to slowly struggle to his feet, using only his left hand and arm for leverage. At last, he stood beside the bed, still faint and shaky, but on his feet.

He must be hallucinating because it looked as if someone besides Ben sat on top of the rumpled bedding. It was Gina. Her hands were behind her back, and Ben was leaning against her, his thumb in his mouth again.

"What's she doing here?" David asked Hank, gesturing weakly toward her. "You don't need them. Why don't you just let them go? This should be just between you and me now."

"Shut up!" Hank bellowed.

Ben took the thumb out of his mouth and looked from David to Hank, and then with more courage than a five-year-old should be able to muster, he spoke. "He's my brother. Please don't hurt him, Mister."

Gina met David's gaze and nodded. "I told him about you...Joey. He's glad. We're both glad."

"I said, shut up, and that means all of you!"

Hank was waving the gun maniacally, his finger on the trigger. No one said another word. Hank was poised on the brink of a deep ravine of madness, and they could see that it wouldn't take much to push him over the edge.

Bitter Reunion

Crawling to the side of the bed, Ben tentatively reached out his small hand and curled his fingers around David's.

It was exquisitely wonderful and ferociously painful at the same time. The warmth of the child's hand in his. The touch. It was trust, and love…and life.

"I hate to break up this touching little reunion, but there's unfinished business to attend to."

David instinctively moved closer to Ben and Gina, trying to shield them from the dreadful blank stare of the pointed gun.

"It didn't have to be this way, David," Hank was saying. "You could have had it all, and you threw it away. You always were a fool."

David could feel the briefcase at his feet. So close, and yet so far away.

"So now, I'm going to have to kill you, and then I'm going to have to spend all of that lovely money by myself. That is, if there is really any money in that case at all. Is there, David, or is it full of hot air?"

"Why don't you check for yourself?" David spat the words out. He let go of Ben's hand and reached for the briefcase. He had it in his hand.

"STOP! Set it down on the bed!" Hank barked the command. "What have you got in there? A gun? A hand grenade?" He laughed. "You'd be dead before you could grab it anyway, so I think I'll save you the trouble. I'll just open it up myself, AFTER you're all dead. And if there isn't any money in there, I'll just call up your daddy and make him bring me some. He would do that for his precious family, wouldn't he?

"Oh, and by the way," he continued in a conversational tone of voice, "you'll be happy to know that I've decided to let your beloved husband and father live, after all. He'll have the whole rest of his life to think of all that I've taken from him."

David's left hand inched closer to the briefcase. They were running out of time. The plan wasn't going to work.

"Now, let's get down to business," Hank said, looking almost gleeful. "Which one of you should I shoot fi…"

There was a movement in the hall. Ben looked past Hank and his eyes widened in recognition.

"Daddy!"

With lightning speed, Hank swivelled his body, and for a fraction of a second, he took his eyes off of David. It was all David needed. His left hand, already resting beside the briefcase, quickly released its latch.

"Don't try anything, Hamilton, or I blow them away!"

It was now or never. Ignoring the pain in his right arm, David gathered all the strength he had left and flung the case straight toward the gun.

"Drop!" David yelled, falling on top of Ben and Gina and rolling them off the bed.

Hank aimed wildly at the moving targets and his gun discharged. At the same time, he felt the case hit him. It popped open on impact.

It took him a second to process it, and in that amount of time, the gun discharged again. Hank screamed, a shrill and horrible sound. And then he was shooting wildly, as he screamed again and again.

They were everywhere, an angry, boiling mass of buzzing terror, spewing forth from the briefcase and spreading out into the room.

Bees. Hundreds of them.

Bitter Reunion

Hank turned around and fled, his gun depleted of bullets and rendered useless.

For a brief instant, the room was deathly quiet, and then suddenly Todd was there, and they were all on their feet, hugging, laughing and crying all at the same time.

"Are you O.K., Dad?" David asked, dazed. The bees were beginning to disperse. Only about a dozen still occupied the bedroom.

"I'm fine, son," Todd responded from within his wife's embrace. "He was shooting at the bees, wasn't he?" he asked in amazement. "The closest he came to hurting me was when he nearly ran me down in the hall in his rush to get out of the house."

"But it looks like you're hurt, Joey," Gina said, scooping Ben up and coming to stand beside David.

"No big deal," David's right arm hung at an odd angle at his side, and there was a dried stain of black-red trailing down his arm along with the bloody evidence of the bicycle accident.

"We'll have to see about that," Todd said skeptically. "And how about you, Bud?"

"Daddy, you finally came to get us," Ben said.

"Yes. I'm here, and I won't let anything bad happen to you anymore."

"Your son's a hero, Todd," Gina said. "Tell daddy and Joey what you did, honey."

Ben puffed out his small chest and said proudly, "I found some big sharp scissors in the drawer over there, and I helped mommy get the rope off her hands. But then we didn't have time to get away before the bad man came back."

"Speaking of the bad man, what just happened here?" Todd asked David. "Why did Hank lose it like that when he saw the bees?"

"He's allergic to them," David responded. "I think bees are the only thing in the world he's afraid of. That's why I got the name of a bee-keeper from a health food store. Then I took a nail and poked holes in the briefcase and had him fill it with bees. I'm sure glad the heat and a bad fall didn't kill them all off."

"I'd better go find Hank now," David went on, already halfway across the room. "I've got to see how he is."

Hank was in the front yard, sitting on the ground and leaning against the side of the house. His eyes were glazed, and he was gasping for air.

David came and stood beside him. Curiously, despite everything, he found it impossible to hate the man he'd called Pa for so many years. The sight of Hank as he was now, stripped of the power he'd once held over David and looking vulnerable and defeated, only stirred up feelings of pity and an undefined sense of regret.

David leaned over and spoke gently. "I've got your medicine, and an ambulance is on the way." He didn't know whether or not Hank had understood what he said.

The police showed up before the ambulance did. They had spoken to Belinda in the hospital, and she had given them the same information she had already given Todd and Walt upon waking from the drugged stupor they had found her in. By the time the ambulance got there, Hank was breathing a little easier. Miraculously, he had only been stung twice.

David was glad. His intention hadn't been to cause Hank's death, only to frighten him with the bees, but he had known there was a possibility that Hank would die. He didn't know if he would have been able to live with the knowledge that he had killed the man who, regardless of the reasons, had taken him in at a time when he had been all alone.

The paramedics had wanted to transport David to the hospital along with Hank, but he had declined the ride.

"My wife and I will drive our sons to the hospital," Todd had said.

Ben needed to be checked over, too, for any sign of adverse reaction to the drugs he'd been given over the course of the last few days. Fortunately, he was alert and seemed to be returning to normal, or at least as near normal as possible for what he had been through. He'd even asked one of the paramedics if he had any suckers. "My doctor always gives me one," he'd said in obvious disdain when the poor man had come up empty.

"I wanna go home and see Smokey," Ben said now, watching the ambulance disappear in a cloud of dust.

"Soon, son." Todd took Ben's hand and led him back to the doorstep where David sat. "Ben, I want to introduce you to someone," he said. "This is your brother, Joseph."

"I know, Dad. Mommy already told me." Then, with childlike wonder in his voice, he looked at David and said, "Hey, it's just like in the Bible story, isn't it?"

"Yes, just like that," Todd responded. "Just exactly like that."

"It is, isn't it?" David said, thinking of that first Joseph and all the parallels in their lives. They'd both been separated from the father they loved, and God had united both with their fathers again many years later. Maybe someday he would even be able to see some good that had come from what seemed to have been nothing but a terrible tragedy. He guessed this moment would be the start of that "something good."

"And I'd better get used to being called by my new, or should I say, old, name again."

"Joey Hamilton," Gina said, joining them from the house where she had just gotten off the phone with her mother. "Has a nice ring to it."

"How about 'Joe?'" Joey said, smiling. "I'm not so sure 'Joey' quite fits anymore."

"Did you ask your mom to thank everyone and let them know how their prayers were answered?" Todd asked Gina.

"Of course, and needless to say, everyone is overjoyed that things turned out the way they did, though I'm not sure Dad will ever forgive you for not letting him come here with you, Todd," Gina went on.

And Joe," she said, emphasizing the name, "it may take a couple of dozen roses to make up for all the lies you told Kellie."

"It will be my pleasure." Joe's smile widened. Giving flowers to the most beautiful girl in the world would not be a hardship he couldn't endure. He might have to get a job first, since he was almost out of the money Hank had given him, but that shouldn't be a problem. Probably half of the restaurants he'd eaten at here in Albion had "help wanted" signs posted in the window.

The flowers might have to wait, though. There was the little matter of a bicycle he had to purchase to replace the one he'd borrowed and destroyed. He would buy the latest model, the best he could find, no matter what it cost. He owed a great debt of gratitude to the owner of that mangled bike.

A job, a family, Kellie…a future. As Todd and Gina bantered with Ben, it suddenly hit Joe full force. Hope. It was there again, and now he dared to think it would be with him to stay. No matter what tomorrow might bring, he was up to the challenge because he was free. Really free.

The sound of laughter and easy conversation subsided and Joe looked up to see the three of them standing there together looking at him, the welcome in their eyes saying everything he had always longed to hear.

Todd approached and gingerly put his arm around Joe's waist, helping him to his feet. Then, walking between his two sons, his heart full of gratitude and praise, he said, "Come on, boys, let's go home."

Deborah Barlow

EPILOGUE

Lois Kowolski was dumbfounded. Absolutely, positively, beyond-a-doubt flabbergasted. Three envelopes lay unopened on her kitchen table. They were the usual fare, the electric bill and two pieces of junk mail. It was the envelope that was still in her hand that had her mouth hanging open. When she'd pulled it out of the mailbox with the others, the return address had jumped right out at her. Why, land 'o mercy, it had practically caused her to fall over in a dead faint right there on the sidewalk in front of her house.

She looked at the address again, wondering what on earth could have made Willy write to her. He never had before, not even when he'd gone through that divorce of his years ago. Why, she hadn't even learned of it until almost two years after it happened. It was always Lois who had to do the keeping-in-touch. Conjuring up all kinds of possibilities for William's surprising correspondence, most of them dire, Lois ripped open the flap of the envelope and removed two sheets of neatly folded typing paper. As quickly as possible with her arthritic fingers, she unfolded it and began to read.

Dear Lois,

I hope you didn't faint when you saw this letter in your mailbox. This is probably the first letter I've written to anyone since I was a child.

First of all, I want to apologize for the way I've treated you and Ralph all these years. I've suddenly realized how cold and

Bitter Reunion

distant I've been. I'm trying to change, but it's a slow process. I'll probably never be a people-person like you are, Lois, but I'm gradually learning to at least enjoy being with people. For me, that's a huge step.

You're probably wondering by now what's come over me. Nothing short of a miracle could get your baby brother to write to you, much less to invite you to his house (and I am inviting you), right?

Three weeks ago, I had my nose buried in a computer manual at the library, when this young man who I'd never seen before walked right up to me and tapped me on the shoulder. I looked up, and he said, "You ARE the guy!" Then, without being asked to, he sat down and started thanking me for being instrumental in reuniting him with his family. Well, I had no idea what he was talking about. I thought maybe he was a lunatic of some sort, and I tried to brush him off, but he wouldn't let me. Anyway, he finally started making sense.

You remember that trip out to your house that I made in May? Well, on the way there, I ate dinner at a restaurant in Boise. I left behind a newspaper from Albion, that I had brought with me. This young man worked there, and he cleaned the table where I had eaten. He saw an article in that paper that eventually led to the reunion I mentioned earlier. What an incredible coincidence, right? Well, I've come to believe something the young man told me. He said that there are no coincidences, only subtle miracles. In other words, Lois, just because I forgot to cancel a newspaper subscription, I was directly involved in a miracle! The rest is a long and more than slightly interesting story. I'll tell you all of it when you and Ralph come out.

Deborah Barlow

The young man tells me the whole story, and keeps on thanking me, and before I know it, he's inviting me to dinner at his family's house so they can all meet me. He won't take no for an answer. Believe me, I TRIED to say no. The amazing thing was that part of me actually wanted to go. So in the end, I did go. And Lois, I had a good time. I really did. They were such wonderful people—Joe (that's the young man's name), and his father and stepmother. I also met his little brother, Ben, and his step-mother's family. They treated me just like I was one of them.

They had invited several others to this dinner, too. People who had played a part in the drama of their reunion. There was a couple by the name of Sneed from Portland, whose daughter has AIDS, a private detective, an ex-employee of Joe's father and his wife, and a woman named Belinda Montgomery.

To make a long story short, they invited me back and I went, and then they invited me to church and I went. And then somewhere along the way, I began to want what they had. I started to see how empty my life was.

I don't know how to say it, Lois. It sounds so cliché, and it's the last thing I would have ever thought I'd be saying to you or to anyone. I found something I didn't even know I was missing until I met the Hamiltons. Or I should say, I found someONE. I found Jesus and gave my life to Him. I've discovered a kind of joy I never knew existed.

As I said before, I'm also learning to like people. Believe it or not, I'm even dating for the first time since Arleen left me…how many years ago? Too many to count. Anyway, Belinda (mentioned earlier in this letter) and I have discovered that we enjoy each other's company and have been seeing each other for several weeks now.

I also find myself wanting to get to know you better, Lois. You're the only family I have left, and I've seen how wonderful a family can be.

Write and let me know when you and Ralph would like to come visit, and I'll buy you the plane tickets. It would be nice if you could come for Christmas. Joe's parents will be adopting an infant sometime in November, and you could play grandma to the baby. I hope you can make it. We have a lot of catching up to do.

Love,
William

Lois removed her wire-rimmed glasses and reached for the hanky in her apron pocket. She dabbed at her eyes. "I'll be there, Willy," she whispered, holding the tear-stained letter to her bosom. I'll be there."

Deborah Barlow

ABOUT THE AUTHOR

Deborah Barlow and her husband live in Albany, Oregon and have three grown children. Deborah was raised in Idaho, attended college in Oregon and currently works in the banking industry. Her passions are the Lord, her family and, of course, a really good book.